Kate Hardy has always loved books, and could read before she went to school. She discovered Mills & Boon books when she was twelve, and decided that *this* was what she wanted to do. When she isn't writing Kate enjoys reading, cinema, ballroom dancing and the gym. You can contact her via her website: katehardy.com

Teresa Southwick lives with her husband in Las Vegas, the city that reinvents itself every day. An avid fan of romance novels, she is delighted to be living out her dream of writing for Mills & Boon.

D0766206

Also by Kate Hardy

Finding Mr Right in Florence
A Nurse and a Pup to Heal Him

Also by Teresa Southwick

An Unexpected Partnership
What Makes a Father
A Decent Proposal
The Widow's Bachelor Bargain
How to Land Her Lawman
A Word with the Bachelor
Just a Little Bit Married
The New Guy in Town
His by Christmas
Just What the Cowboy Needed

Discover more at millsandboon.co.uk

SOLDIER PRINCE'S SECRET BABY GIFT

KATE HARDY

MAVERICK HOLIDAY MAGIC

TERESA SOUTHWICK

MILLS & BOON

First Published in Great Britain 2019
by Mills & Boon, an imprint of HarperCollinsPublishers,
1 London Bridge Street, London, SE1 9GF

Soldier Prince's Secret Baby Gift © 2019 Harlequin Books S.A.
Maverick Holiday Magic © 2019 Harlequin Books S.A.

Special thanks and acknowledgement are given to Kate Hardy for her
contribution to the *A Crown by Christmas* series.

ISBN: 978-0-263-27267-3

1119

MIX
Paper from
responsible sources

FSC www.fsc.org   **FSC**™ C007454

This book is produced from independently certified FSC™
paper to ensure responsible forest management.

For more information visit: www.harpercollins.co.uk/green

Printed and bound in Spain
by CPI, Barcelona

SOLDIER PRINCE'S
SECRET BABY GIFT

KATE HARDY

For Cara Colter and Nina Milne—
it was such fun working with you!

PROLOGUE

May

TEN MINUTES UNTIL MIDNIGHT.

Ten minutes until the charity gala was over and the guests were due to leave, and then another three-quarters of an hour to finish clearing up.

And then Tia could go home to bed.

She was exhausted. She'd already done her usual full shift at the café that day, and Saturdays were always a rushed-off-your-feet day. When she'd got home, all she'd wanted to do was to have a long bath and then curl up on the sofa with her mum to watch a movie. But her old school friend Sadie was managing a charity gala tonight and Tia had promised that she'd help out, serving canapés and clearing glasses, and Tia never went back on her promises. Particularly as the cause—supporting children who'd been bereaved—was so close to her heart; she knew first-hand how it felt to lose a member of your family in the armed forces.

Twice.

Their neighbour, Becky, was keeping an eye out for her mum—as she always did on the few occasions that Grace Phillips managed to persuade her daughter to go out somewhere. In less than an hour, Tia could go home.

And tomorrow was late opening, being Sunday, so her shift didn't start until ten. It wasn't so bad. She'd had tougher days.

Though she couldn't shake the feeling that someone was staring at her.

She turned round and caught the eye of a tall, dark-haired man across the room.

There was something very familiar about him. Then again, half the people at the charity gala were house-hold names: everyone from musicians to movie stars to models. All the men were wearing tuxedos, and all the women were wearing the kind of posh frocks and designer shoes Tia would never have been able to afford in a million years. This was another world, one where she was supposed to be invisible—the anonymous waitress who smiled as she served canapés and cleared glasses quickly and efficiently. The guy across the room shouldn't even be noticing her.

As she went out onto the hotel balcony to collect glasses from the abandoned tables, still thinking about him, she realised who he was.

Antonio Valenti.

Prince Antonio of Casavalle, to be precise.

The man who had been her older brother Nathan's best friend, who'd served with him as his team commander in an alliance of international armed forces.

The man who'd broken her heart, and her mum's, four months ago, when he'd brought the news that Nathan had been killed in action. Antonio had delivered the news coldly and calmly: a stoic man in a military uniform who didn't even blink as he told them that Nathan's vehicle had hit a land mine on his last mission and he'd been killed instantly. Tia had been too shocked to say anything, but her mother had collapsed at the news that she'd lost her son the same way as she'd lost her husband, so Tia had had to damp down her own grief to support her mother.

Prince Antonio had clearly cared so little about Nathan that he hadn't even stuck around to comfort Grace Phillips or check that she was all right. He'd left almost as soon as he'd delivered the news. He hadn't even stayed for a cup of tea, let alone turned up at the funeral; and, apart from a formal embossed condolence card which he'd scrawled his name across, he hadn't been in contact with them since.

OK, sure, the man was a prince and he had important official duties as well as being in the army. Tia wasn't stupid. She understood that. But would it have hurt him to spend a few minutes with Grace after delivering the news, just to share some memories of her beloved son with her? Or show his face at Nathan's funeral? Or later, perhaps, he could've sent Grace a photograph or a private note via the Palace press office? It wasn't as if her mother was going to rush to the media and try to get money for it, or sell it online. All Grace had needed was a little gesture to let her know that Nathan had *mattered*.

But there had been nothing from Prince Antonio but silence.

Prince Charming? More like Prince Cold and Uncaring, Tia thought, curling her lip. How on earth had her brother been close friends with someone who was so cold and starchy?

And he was probably only here at the gala because he was attending in an official capacity; a man like him certainly wasn't warm enough to care about the work of the charity, or about the children who'd lost their parents or siblings in war. He certainly wouldn't be there rattling a collecting bucket along with the rest of the volunteer fundraisers or schmoozing people into buying tombola tickets.

She put him resolutely out of her mind and continued stacking glasses on a tray ready to carry through to the kitchens.

Tia Phillips looked absolutely exhausted.

Guilt balled in a hard lump in Antonio's throat.

He'd been there when his second-in-command's vehicle, the one in the convoy in front of his, had been blown up by a land mine. Mercifully, death had been instant, so he knew Nathan hadn't suffered; but Antonio had been shattered by the loss. During his years in the army, his team had become like a family to him. Nathan had been his best friend as well as his second-in-command.

But Antonio had been brought up not to show any emotion in public; as a prince of Casavalle, he was expected to be cool and calm in every situation. He and his elder brother Luca had been brought up knowing their duty always came first. And you never, ever said or did anything that made you look as if you'd lost control of your emotions. That had been reinforced by his military training, so Antonio knew he'd been calm and reserved when he broke the news to Nathan's family.

Too calm and reserved, perhaps, in their eyes.

Antonio knew how much Nathan had loved his family. He knew that Grace Phillips was poorly and that Nathan and his little sister Tia had spent their childhood as her carers rather than having the freedom to be children; and he'd promised Nathan silently by the side of his coffin that he'd keep an eye on Grace and Tia.

But he'd been called away almost immediately on another mission, so he hadn't even been able to attend Nathan's memorial service. He'd written a personal note and asked Miles to post it for him—but he knew that a note wasn't the same as actually being there. It had felt horribly like a weak excuse.

And then the fallout from his own father's death had kept him on special leave from the army. For the last four months, Antonio Valenti had been kept busy supporting Luca as his brother took over the reins of ruling Casavalle. He'd also been helping with the preparations for both the coronation and Luca's upcoming wedding to Princess Meribel, the oldest daughter of King Jorge of the house of Asturias in the neighbouring kingdom of Aguilarez. He'd barely had a minute to himself since returning to Casavalle, so he'd let his unspoken promise to Nathan slide.

Though Antonio knew he should've *made* the time. Especially as he knew how bad Nathan had felt, leaving his sister to care for their mother while he'd joined the army at the age of sixteen so he could send money home to help them financially. He should've done more to help support his best friend's family. Been there for them, because he knew they had nobody else.

Tia had glanced back at him before going out on the balcony with an empty tray, presumably to collect glasses, but he had no idea whether or not she'd recognised him.

Then again, she was clearly working and her boss wouldn't be happy if she stood around chatting to guests at the charity gala when she was supposed to be clearing up. Given her family's circumstances, Antonio knew that Tia needed her job. It wouldn't be fair to risk her losing the job and having that added financial pressure, just to salve his own guilty conscience.

But he couldn't just leave things. Not now he'd seen her again. Surely she could spare him two minutes?

'Please excuse me. I'm expected to mingle,' he said to the guests he was with. As the patron of the charity, he was supposed to talk to every guest and thank them for their support; but he was pretty sure he'd already done that. So his conscience was clear as he headed towards the balcony where Tia had gone.

She was standing on the other side of the door as he opened it, and almost dropped her tray.

'Sorry,' he said. 'Tia. It's good to see you.'

'Thank you, Your Royal Highness,' she said coolly. 'I would curtsey, but I'd rather avoid the risk of dropping my tray.'

He winced, knowing he deserved the rebuke. 'You don't need to curtsey, and it's Antonio to you. Your brother was my friend.'

'Yes, Your Royal Highness.'

Which put him very much in his place. He'd been a stranger and he deserved to be treated like one, despite his current attempt to be friendly with her. Given how he'd behaved, the last time they'd met, maybe it wasn't so surprising that she preferred to keep a barrier of formality against him. OK. He'd stick to formality.

'Ms Phillips,' he said. 'I appreciate that you're working right now, but perhaps we could talk when you've finished?'

'I really shouldn't be taking up guests' time, Your Royal Highness,' she said.

Which was a polite way of telling him he shouldn't be taking up her time, either. Another deserved rebuke, he thought. 'After your shift,' he said, glancing quickly at his watch. 'The gala finishes in five minutes.'

When it looked as if she was going to think up an excuse, he said softly, 'Please. It'd be so good to talk to someone who knew Nathan.'

For a moment, his brown eyes were filled with pain, before his expression returned to its former careful neutrality. So maybe the Prince wasn't quite as cold and uncaring as he'd seemed. That glimpse of pain just now told her that the Prince really *had* cared about her brother. Maybe she should cut the man some slack. Be kind to her brother's friend. Even though part of her still felt he should've made more of an effort, for her mum's sake.

'All right,' she said. 'I'll meet you when I'm done here. But I'm working tomorrow. I can't stay long.'

'Just a few minutes. Thank you.' He paused. 'I'm staying in the penthouse suite. I can of course arrange for a chaperone, if you prefer.'

'That won't be necessary, Your Royal Highness.' Like her brother, Prince Antonio was a man of honour. Tia knew without having to ask that his behaviour towards her would be respectful. 'The penthouse suite,' she echoed.

'My security team will let you in,' he said. 'Forgive me for being rude, but I'd better go back to the guests. I'm the patron of the charity.'

Meaning that he was here on official duties? Though the Prince had been so cold and starchy when he'd come to tell Tia and her mum the news about Nathan, she wasn't convinced he really cared about bereaved children, the way the patron would normally have a personal interest in the cause they supported. Though maybe losing his friend had taught him a little more empathy.

To her surprise, he held the door for her so she didn't have to struggle with her tray of glasses.

This was surreal.

She'd just made an assignation with a prince. In his penthouse suite.

A prince who'd been her brother's best friend, though because Nathan had kept his work and his family separate this was only the second time she'd ever met Prince Antonio. They didn't really know each other. The only thing they had in common was Nathan and the hole his death had left in their lives.

But maybe she should hear what he had to say. Maybe he'd give her some crumb of comfort she could give to her mum. That would be worth her feeling even more tired tomorrow morning.

The next few minutes passed in a blur of clearing tables and attending to the last-minute needs of guests, but finally she was done.

Sadie hugged her. 'Thanks so much for helping tonight, Tia. I owe you.'

'That's what friends are for,' Tia said with a smile. 'And you know it's a cause close to my heart.' She'd been in exactly the same position as the children that the charity helped.

'Get a taxi home. I'll pick up the bill,' Sadie said.

Tia shook her head. 'It's fine. I'll get the night tube. The walk will give me a chance to wind down.' After she'd met Prince Antonio. Not that she planned to tell her friend about *that*.

'Then I'm buying you dinner, some time this week. No arguments,' Sadie said.

'That would be good. Depending on how Mum is,' Tia added swiftly. No way was she going out if her mum was having a tough health day. Family came first.

'Or maybe I could bring dinner round for the three of us,' Sadie suggested.

'That might be nicer, if you don't mind. Mum would really like that.' And the company would help to brighten her mum's day.

'Then we'll do it. Check your diary tomorrow and text me with your free dates,' Sadie said.

I'm free every day, Tia thought, but didn't say it. She was just grateful that one of her old school friends actually understood her situation enough to make the effort to stay in touch. Grace had encouraged her to make a life for herself; even though her grades hadn't been good enough for her to train as a teacher, Grace had suggested other ways into the classroom. Tia could work as a classroom assistant or at a playgroup, perhaps, or maybe she could do a foundation course at university and then do her degree and train as a teacher. But Tia hadn't wanted to leave her mum, knowing that Grace's health really wasn't good. Being away from home would've left her worrying that her mum was struggling, and eventually Tia had convinced her mother that she was much happier staying where she was.

'I will,' she promised.

Instead of leaving the hotel, Tia took the lift up to the penthouse suite. A man in a very ordinary suit leaned casually against the wall opposite the lifts as the doors opened, but Tia wasn't fooled; it was obvious that he was the Prince's security officer.

'Ms Phillips.' It was a statement, not a question. He clearly knew who she was and was expecting her. 'Would you like to come with me?'

It was a polite enough question, but she knew there wasn't a real choice. It was accompany him or go straight back down in the lift.

'Thank you,' she said.

He ushered her over to the door of the penthouse suite, and knocked. 'Your guest has arrived, sir.'

Not 'Your Royal Highness'? Or maybe he was from the Casavallian military.

'Thank you, Giacomo,' Antonio said as he opened the door. 'Please come in, Ms Phillips.'

The carpet was the sort that you sank into when you walked on it. One wall of the sitting room was pure glass, looking out over the Thames; it was late enough that the lights from the bridge and the buildings on the other bank were reflected on the dark water of the river.

'Thank you for coming. May I offer you a drink? Champagne?'

This was her cue to refuse politely and ask him to just get on with it and see what he had to say. But since he had offered refreshment and she'd been on her feet all day and all evening…

'Actually, Your Royal Highness, I could really do with a cup of tea.'

'Of course.' He smiled then. 'You're very like your brother. At the end of the day, most of the team would relax with a cold beer. But Nathan said nothing could refresh you like a cup of tea.'

She could almost hear her brother's voice saying the words, and it put a lump in her throat.

'Strong enough to stand a spoon up in. One sugar. A dash of milk. And in a mug, not a cup,' he added.

That was when she knew for sure that he really had been close to Nathan. Because it was exactly what her brother would've said. And all of a sudden she felt a bit less wary of him.

'I remember,' she said, her breath catching.

'Do you take yours the same way?' he asked.

Normally she was just grateful if her tea was hot. 'Yes. Thank you, Your Royal Highness.'

And he actually made the mug of tea for her himself. No calling room service, no pretensions. Were princes supposed to be like this?

And, she noticed, he joined her in drinking tea. He didn't take sugar in his, though.

'Cheers,' he said, lifting his mug in a toast. 'To Nathan.'

She lifted her own mug. 'To Nathan.'

'You must miss him terribly. As do I.' He looked at her. 'I'm sorry I haven't kept in touch, Miss Phillips. Life is a little bit complicated at the moment.'

'Complicated?'

He shrugged. 'My father died not long after Nathan was killed. Obviously my older brother will be the one to succeed him, but there's a lot of political stuff to sort out.'

She'd had no idea that he'd lost his father, too. 'My condolences on the loss of your father, Your Royal Highness,' she said formally.

'Thank you. I know you've been in that situation.'

'Except I was ten when Dad died,' she said. 'He was killed in action, too.'

'That's tough for you,' he said. 'Losing your father and your brother the same way.'

'It's one of the reasons why I worked here tonight,' she said. 'I wanted to do my bit to help the charity.' To support children who'd been bereaved the way she had, because she knew what it felt like.

'You were a volunteer tonight?' He sounded surprised.

'Yes. Though, actually, my day job's in a café.' A proper Italian café, run by a middle-aged couple from Naples who'd taken her to their hearts and who always sent her home after her shift with treats for her mum.

'It's good of you to help. Thank you.' He paused. 'How is your mother?'

'Fine.' It wasn't strictly true, although thankfully this week Grace was having a good patch where she was fully mobile and not quite as exhausted. Chronic fatigue syndrome was the kind of illness that had peaks and troughs, and Tia knew that a good week like this would be balanced out by one where her mother could barely get out of bed and would need a lot more help with day-to-day things.

'I'm sorry. I should've kept in touch.'

'Or come to his funeral.' The rebuke tumbled out before she could stop it.

He inclined his head. 'My apologies. I intended to be there. But I was called away on a mission, and it wasn't one that I could delegate to someone else.'

That hadn't occurred to her. It was a valid excuse, she supposed, though she still thought he could've sent her mother a personal note.

As if he'd guessed at what she was thinking, he said, 'I did write a letter to apologise for my absence.'

'Mum didn't get any letter from you.'

He frowned. 'I'm sorry it didn't arrive. I promise you, I did write.'

'It must've got lost in the post. That's not your fault.' Though he hadn't followed up on his note after his mission. Surely he could've found the time to at least call her mother?

He took a deep breath. 'What can I do to help?'

'Nothing,' she said immediately. They didn't need to lean on anyone. She and Grace were doing just fine on their own. They had their routines and they had good friends to support them. They didn't need a prince throwing money at them to salve his conscience.

'Nathan said you were proud and independent,' Antonio said gently. 'Which is a good thing. But your brother was part of my team. My friend. And, despite what you must think, my team are like family to me. If I can help to make life easier, Miss Phillips, please let me know. Nathan wouldn't have wanted you to struggle.'

He was offering her a financial handout? She kept her temper with difficulty and said politely, 'Thank you, Your Royal Highness, but we're managing just fine as we are.'

'I didn't intend to offend you,' he said. 'Just...' For a

moment, he looked racked with guilt. 'I couldn't do anything to save your brother.'

'It wasn't your fault that he was killed. And Nathan knew the risks of the job before he signed up for it.' She knew her brother had wanted to follow in their father's footsteps.

'I know. But it doesn't stop me missing him.'

Then he looked shocked, as if he hadn't meant to say that out loud.

And again that bleakness was back in his eyes for a moment before he managed to hide it again.

Prince Antonio, despite his privileged upbringing, seemed lonely, deep inside. Right now she'd been given a glimpse of the man behind the cool, collected mask. And she could almost hear her brother's voice echoing in her head: *He could do with a hug.*

Which would be way outside official protocol. Then again, some things were more important than protocol. So Tia put her mug on the coffee table, walked over to Prince Antonio, put his mug on the coffee table next to hers, and wrapped her arms around him.

For a long, long time, he just stood there, unmoving; but then, just as she was about to apologise and take a step backwards, he wrapped his arms around her and held her back, warm and comforting.

She really, really had intended it as comfort. *Just* comfort. Sharing their grief.

But one of them—she wasn't sure which of them—moved, and his cheek was pressed against hers. Her skin tingled where it touched his. Another tiny movement—hers? His?—and the corners of their mouths were touching.

The tingle spread.

Another infinitesimally small shift, and then his mouth was brushing against hers.

She shouldn't be doing this.

He was a prince and she was a waitress. Their lives were so far apart, it was untrue. Neither of them was in a position to start any kind of relationship. He had official duties and she was busy working and looking after her mother. Nothing could possibly come of this.

But the temptation to take comfort from him and to comfort him in turn was so strong.

Maybe this was something they both needed. Just for one night. No strings.

Because, just as Antonio had shown no emotion when he'd come to tell them the news about Nathan, Tia had locked her own tears away because she'd needed to be strong for her mother.

When he broke the kiss and looked into her eyes, she could see the tears glittering there, the emotion he was trying so hard to repress.

Maybe tonight they could cry together. Find a release together. Comfort each other. *Heal* each other.

Just for tonight.

'Stay with me, Tia?' he whispered.

Common sense said that she should leave. She was due at work tomorrow morning. And there was her mother to think about.

But Becky was only next door if she was needed. Tia could drink coffee tomorrow rather than tea to get her through her shift. Right now, Antonio needed her—and she needed him.

She laid her palm against his cheek. 'Yes.'

He kissed her again, scooped her into his arms and carried her to his bed.

CHAPTER ONE

November

THERE WAS NO other way round it, Tia thought, curving a protective hand around her bump.

Miles Montague, the palace secretary, had been perfectly polite to her just now. But, just as he'd done with every single one of her previous calls, he'd rebuffed her, refusing to put her through to Antonio. She'd begged him to pass on a message, asking Antonio to call her. She'd told Miles that she knew the Prince, and it was really important that she speak to him.

But Miles had left her with the impression that, as an eligible bachelor, Prince Antonio had hundreds of women calling, claiming they 'knew' him because they had shaken his hand once or attended an event where he was on the guest list. The palace secretary clearly thought she was just another in a long line of unwanted callers, and he wasn't going to put her through.

Miles had been kind enough. He'd asked her if he could help. He'd asked her to tell him what the problem was.

But how could she let news like *this* go through a third party, no matter how discreet he seemed or how well he knew Antonio? This was something she needed to tell the Prince herself. That their one night together, the night that was supposed to give them both comfort and never be referred to again, had had consequences.

She'd tried to explain that Antonio knew her brother; but Miles had asked in that kind but immovable way exactly *how* Antonio knew her brother, and she'd ended up in tears of frustration.

How could the palace secretary not even know the names of the people who were on Antonio's team in the international alliance? Surely he'd know information like that?

Frustrated and miserable, she'd ended the call.

She'd tried a dozen times now to talk to Antonio, to tell him about the baby.

And failed a dozen times, too.

She didn't have his email address, and even if she did she suspected that someone else—probably Miles Montague, or one of his team—would check through the messages before they reached Antonio, weeding out the ones they judged unimportant or inappropriate, which would definitely include hers. The same would go for letters. Any message she left would be blocked just as effectively as her phone calls had been blocked.

It left her with no other alternative. She'd have to go to Casavalle herself to tell him about the baby. Face to face.

If she sat on Antonio's doorstep and refused to budge, they'd have to let her talk to him. And she could tell him the news—well, as she was six months pregnant, he'd be able to see that quite well enough for himself, she thought wryly—and then leave.

Originally, she hadn't intended to tell him at all. She hadn't realised for a couple of months that she was pregnant; then, when she'd finally realised her period was a lot later than usual and did a test, she'd seen the centre spread in the celebrity magazine she'd bought for her mum as a treat. A story about Prince Antonio of Casavalle, speculating which of the four women who'd graced his arm that month might be his future bride.

How ironic. Tia had thought she'd had a glimpse of the real Prince, the man her brother had been friends with—but maybe he was exactly what the media said he was. He hadn't really needed her to comfort him, that night, because he had strings of women ready to comfort him. And she'd been so angry at herself for being a fool that it had taken her mum another month to talk her round into telling Antonio about her pregnancy.

Six weeks later, she still hadn't told him—though not for the want of trying.

She grimaced. She didn't expect anything from him, either for herself or for the baby, and she certainly wasn't looking for a cash handout or anything like that. Antonio had been her brother's friend, and she owed it to him to tell him that the baby existed. And that was the limit of their obligations to each other, because their lives were too different for anything else to happen.

She flicked into the Internet. The cheapest flight to Casavalle would get her in at about half-past eight tomorrow evening. She had no idea how far it was from the airport to the palace, but even though she wouldn't have to wait to collect her luggage she would still have to go through airport security and customs. Maybe she'd get to the palace at ten p.m.—which was way too late for anyone to be admitted to the palace offices.

To get there for the early afternoon… She scanned the flight schedules. She'd have to leave London really early in the morning and change planes at Rome, and she'd have a two-hour layover in between. Plus the flight was a lot more expensive. It was money she could really do with elsewhere in her budget; but if she got the cheaper flight and stayed at a hotel overnight, it would cost even more, and she couldn't waste money that she needed to spend on the baby.

She stroked her bump. 'Hopefully we'll find somewhere quiet to sit at the airport, and we'll get a taxi from the airport to the palace.' She'd ask to speak to Miles Montague. And as soon as he saw her he'd realise exactly why it was so important for her to talk to Antonio. Then she could deliver her message—and go home.

Wednesday. 'Hump day', they called it in civilian jobs. The middle of the week.

Except you didn't get a day off from being a prince, Antonio thought.

And you particularly didn't get a day off when you had a long-lost older sister who was very probably going to be the one taking their father's place as the ruler of the kingdom, and an older brother whose fiancée had told him on the eve of their wedding that she was pregnant with her true love's baby, resulting in the royal wedding that the whole country had been looking forward to being cancelled at the last minute. The Asturias family were just as keen as the Valentis to minimise the scandal, so they'd issued a joint statement to the media that the wedding had been cancelled due to 'irreconcilable differences' between the bride and groom.

Luca, wanting to get away from the palace, had gone to meet their long-lost half-sister Gabriella in Canada; which meant that, instead of their original plan of Antonio being the one to go over and meet Gabriella, he was stuck here.

In charge of the country.

Something he'd never really expected to happen, despite being third in line to the throne. He'd thought his father would go on for ever, and then Luca would take over, and then Luca and Princess Meribel would have children who would be next in line.

But, this last year, their lives had been turned upside down. Everything he'd thought he knew turned out not to be true.

Life at the palace was turning out to be much more stressful than taking part in dangerous missions in the army. At least as a soldier Antonio had known what he was doing. He'd had a strategy. He'd had a team he could rely on. They were all working on the same side; his team listened to him, as their leader, and he'd had a brilliant second-in-command in Nathan. In Casavalle, things were nowhere near as clear cut. It was so easy to misinterpret words and put the wrong spin on things; the most innocent comment could swiftly turn into a political nightmare.

Just one day, he thought wistfully. He'd love to have just one single day where he could have the time to gather his thoughts instead of constantly firefighting and dealing with political situations. Had it been like that for their father? Was that why King Vincenzo had always been so remote and distant, even from his sons, because he'd simply been worn out from watching every single word or expression or gesture?

At the rap on his open door, Antonio looked up to see the palace secretary standing there.

'Good afternoon, Miles. What can I do for you?' he asked, forcing a smile and hoping that whatever the secretary wanted from him wasn't going to mean yet more politics and media attention.

'Sir,' Miles began.

The palace secretary was usually unflappable. Right now he looked distinctly nervous and Antonio's heart sank. Was the palace about to be hit with yet another scandal? They said things came in threes, and a long-lost princess and a broken engagement because the bride was pregnant by someone else definitely counted as two…

This felt like living in a television soap opera. And Antonio wasn't enjoying the drama one little bit. Yet again, he wished he was back in the army. Back in the job he was really good at.

'What is it?' he asked.

'I have someone asking to see you.'

Why would Miles be worried about that? 'Who?' he asked, narrowing his eyes.

'A young lady. Tia Phillips. She said she knows you.'

Tia was here?

Antonio shook himself mentally and damped down that little frisson of desire. Their one night together wasn't going to be repeated. They'd both made it clear that it was for comfort, it was for one night only, and neither of them had any expectations of the other. And Miles didn't need to know anything about that. He just needed to know that Tia was telling the truth. 'Yes, she knows me. I served with her brother.'

Guilt flooded through Antonio. In a way, he'd abandoned Tia twice, now—the first time after he'd told her that her brother had been killed, because he hadn't known how to deal with it; then he'd been called back to work, and after that his father had died and he'd been busy with official duties. The second time had been that night in London following the charity gala, when they'd ended up comforting each other in bed. Tia had vanished early the next morning before he'd awoken, leaving him a note explaining that she was due at work.

Which had pretty much let him off the hook.

Part of him had felt relieved, because it meant he didn't have to unpick his feelings and deal with them; but part of him had felt guilty about sleeping with his best friend's little sister. It had been mutual comfort, but he still felt responsible. And he'd planned to call her to see if there was anything he could do to help her mother. He wasn't that much of a cad, no matter that the media liked to call him a playboy who would never settle down. The only true bit about the media's claims was that he didn't want to settle down; he kept his love affairs short and very discreet. And he always made it very clear that he wasn't offering his girlfriends a future. That the relationship was just for now, not for ever.

But, as he'd been about to call Tia, that morning, his mother had called him with the news about Gabriella and her potential claim to the throne. Queen Maria had needed her youngest son to come home to discuss the situation with her and help her to plan what they should do next; and it would all have to be done confidentially because she hadn't wanted to put the extra pressure on Luca, who they both thought had quite enough on his plate ruling the country. All thoughts of Tia had flown out of his head and he'd gone straight back to Casavalle without getting in touch with her.

Antonio and the Queen had been close to working out how to deal with the situation about Gabriella when Princess Meribel dropped her bombshell and Luca's wedding was cancelled. Everything had gone haywire after that, and in the last month Antonio felt as if he'd barely had a moment to breathe.

'She's telephoned the palace a few times,' Miles said, 'but I didn't expect her to turn up here.'

Tia had called a few times? Why? 'Why didn't you put her through?' Antonio asked.

Miles winced. 'I didn't want to repeat the mistake I made with Gabriella's letter to Queen Maria.'

Gabriella's letter. The bombshell that had made it

through to the Queen because it was marked 'Personal and Confidential'. Luca had been quite hard on the palace secretary about it, and Miles had been extremely vigilant about which messages made it through to the family ever since.

But Antonio was the youngest child, and he was pretty sure he was more approachable than his father had been— or even his elder brother. And surely Miles had known him for long enough to realise that Antonio wouldn't go all cold and icy on him if he made a mistake? Things happened unexpectedly; you just had to deal with them efficiently and effectively as they came up.

'And now she's here, wanting to see you,' Miles continued.

Antonio smiled, wanting to reassure the secretary. 'That's fine. As I said, I worked with her brother. He was a good friend. I can spare a few minutes to talk to her. Where is she?'

'In my office,' Miles said. 'But, sir, before you go to meet her, you need to know that she's making some quite outlandish claims. She says she's six months pregnant— and she says the baby is yours.'

'She *what*?' Antonio felt as if someone had just winded him.

'She's pregnant. Very pregnant.' Miles winced. 'You can see the baby moving in her stomach.'

Antonio counted back in his head. May. They'd slept together in May.

And now it was November.

Six months.

Antonio was pretty sure that this wasn't a situation like his brother's, where Princess Meribel had been at the point of possibly passing off another man's baby as Luca's. Nathan had been proud of his little sister, proud of her independence and her loyalty and her resourceful-ness. Antonio believed that Tia wouldn't lie about something like this.

Plus the timing fitted exactly.

'But of course the baby can't be yours,' Miles said.

Oh, yes, it could.

Six months.

Tia must've known she was pregnant for at least three of those months, probably more. Why on earth hadn't she said anything to him before?

Then again, Miles had said she'd called a few times but he hadn't put her through. Clearly Tia *had* tried to talk to him and she'd been gently put aside by the palace secretary.

'How long has she been trying to get in touch with me?' Antonio asked.

'A few weeks,' Miles admitted.

So she must've tried to tell him almost as soon as she knew about the baby, then. If Miles had been stonewalling her for weeks, coming here must've been the last resort for her because she'd had no other way to get in touch with him—apart from going to the media and causing his family maximum embarrassment, and that just didn't fit with what he knew of Nathan's little sister.

'I spoke to Prince Luca about it,' Miles continued, 'and he agreed it was most likely she'd seen your photograph in a magazine, decided she was in love with you and made up a story to—'

'Hang on. *Luca* knew about this?' Antonio cut in.

'That she'd called you. Not about the baby.' Miles squirmed. 'I only found out about that today, when I saw her. The bump is, um, quite noticeable.'

Antonio groaned. 'We'll discuss this later. Luca, too. But I need to see her. Now.'

'You mean she's telling the truth, sir?'

'Yes,' Antonio said grimly, the guilt he felt at sleeping with his friend's little sister intensifying by the second. Not only had he slept with her, he'd made her pregnant. 'The timing matches up, so I'm pretty sure the baby's mine.' And he sprinted out of the room towards Miles's office.

Tia felt sick—and it was nothing to do with her pregnancy and everything to do with the situation. What *had* she been thinking, coming here? Now Miles Montague had left her in his office, her surroundings sank in. She was in a palace—a *palace*, for pity's sake. People like her didn't go to palaces, not unless they were visiting a stately home or museum while on holiday. This was surreal.

And just how was Antonio going to react to the news? With shock? Dismay? Horror? She'd told herself all the way here that his reaction didn't matter, that she'd deliver the news and walk away—but it *did* matter, now she was here. And a tiny, very foolish part of her couldn't help hoping that he'd be thrilled to see her and would sweep her into his arms…

Of course that wasn't going to happen. She was six months pregnant, and he certainly wouldn't try to lift her. And this was his territory. He'd be every inch the cold, snooty Prince who'd told her that her brother had been killed.

Right on cue, Antonio strolled into the room, all cool and calm and unruffled. He didn't even bat an eyelash or look remotely shocked; just as she'd guessed, he was totally cold. And that tiny, daft bit of her that had been hoping for the impossible simply shrivelled and died.

Worst of all, the flare of attraction she'd felt towards him was still there. Stronger, if anything, now she knew what it felt like to spend the night in his arms. Even seeing him made her heart feel as if it was doing a somersault.

How stupid was she? He was a prince and she was a waitress. The stories about Cinderella, Snow White, and Beauty and the Beast were just that: fairy stories to entertain children. This was real life; and her life was about as opposite from Antonio's as it was possible to get. They didn't have a future together.

'Good to see you, Tia,' he said.

Was it? His face was so unreadable, she didn't have a clue.

'I trust Miles has offered you some refreshment?' he asked.

'Yes.' And she'd refused. All she'd wanted was to see Antonio, deliver her message and leave so she could catch her plane home. Now she was here, she *really* wanted to leave.

He looked at the clear desk in front of her and frowned. 'I'll organise some tea. That is, assuming you can drink tea?'

She knew what he was referring to; but she was well past the morning sickness stage. 'Thank you, but no thank you. I'm not staying.'

He said nothing, simply tipped his head slightly to one side to indicate that he was listening to whatever she had to say. He looked every inch a prince, and incredibly remote and forbidding.

She lifted her chin. 'I just came to let you know the situation.'

'That you're six months pregnant, according to Miles. You could have—'

Told him? OK, so she'd waited a month, not wanting to talk to the Playboy Prince. But for the six weeks since her mother had persuaded her to talk to him, she'd been trying, and it stung that he was making her feel as if *she* was the bad guy. 'I tried,' she cut in quietly. 'I rang the palace. More than once, actually. But I didn't want to leave a message about this. I wanted to tell you myself. Mr Montague wouldn't put me through to you when I called. In case you'd lost my number, I left it again. But, as you didn't call me back, I assumed he didn't tell you that I'd called.'

She didn't have a clue about how he was reacting to this. Was he shocked, angry, horrified? This man had inscrutability down to a fine art.

'It meant that coming to tell you in person was my only option. So now you know.'

He hadn't made a single move towards her. That night in London… Well, obviously Antonio had drawn a line under that, a long time ago. They both had. Neither of them had expected consequences. Although she'd left him that note, and a tiny bit of her had hoped that he'd call her, she hadn't really expected him to do anything. That night was what it was. A one-night stand.

Then the reality of it hit her. She'd assumed that Miles Montague hadn't passed on the message. Maybe he *had* given Prince Antonio the message, but the Prince simply hadn't wanted to return her call. How could she have been so stupid?

She clearly wasn't wanted here, and neither was the baby.

Though she'd expected Antonio not to want to know, she'd had time to get used to the idea of being a single mum. She'd cope. Coping was what she'd done every day since Nathan had left to join the army and she'd become her mother's sole carer at the age of thirteen. She'd find a way to juggle motherhood, a job and continuing to care for her mum. Giovanni and Vittoria, her bosses at the café, were kind and sympathetic. It would be fine.

She suppressed the memories that had rushed into her head when Antonio had walked into the room—the surge of desire, the memory of the way his skin had felt against hers, his strength combined with surprising gentleness. Although this man was the father of her baby, she had to remember that first and foremost he was a prince—and her feelings towards him were completely inappropriate, as well as completely unwanted by him.

She didn't even know what to call him.

Your Royal Highness? Prince Antonio?

Considering that they'd spent the night together…

It was all too much for her. She didn't want to stay in this cold, formal palace a minute longer than she had to. She wanted to leave. *Now.* 'Excuse me. I have a flight to catch.' She stood up, gathered her coat under her arm and turned away.

Antonio reached out and touched her shoulder, gently making her turn to face him again. 'Tia. Please stay. We need to talk.'

Even though there was soft cotton between his skin and hers, the contact was enough to stir up old memories, making her skin tingle. Which was completely inappropriate, and it made her feel so out of sorts that she snapped, 'There's nothing to talk about.'

His gaze flicked down to her bump and up to her face again. 'I rather think there is.'

'Look, I'm not expecting anything from you. I haven't come here looking for financial support or anything like that. I'm not planning to sell an exclusive to the gossip columns. I just thought you had a right to know about the baby's existence, that's all.'

'Thank you for telling me. And I'm sorry that the palace made it difficult for you to get in touch with me.'

So was she. But, when she thought about it, she could

kind of understand it. 'You're a prince. For all they knew, I could've been some crazed stalker.'

'You're the sister of my best friend,' Antonio said.

And the mother of his child. Though he hadn't said as much.

'And yet again I owe you an apology. I seem to be making a habit of not contacting you.'

He could say that again.

He'd done it twice now. She wasn't setting herself up for a third mistake, where Antonio Valenti was concerned. How did the saying go? Fool me once, shame on you. Fool me twice, shame on me.

She'd been quite enough of a fool. Though at least he wasn't offering some flimsy excuse. On the other hand, a simple 'sorry' might have been nice. He'd said he owed her an apology, but he hadn't actually given her an apology, had he?

'Tia, please stay. I'm still in the middle of processing the fact that I'm going to be a father,' he said. 'And we have a lot to talk about. But, first, I'm going to organise that cup of tea. And you've come all the way from London, so I'm guessing you haven't had anything to eat.'

'I had a sandwich on the plane.' Half a sandwich. It had made her feel sick. Or maybe that had been nerves at the idea of coming here to tell Antonio about the baby.

'Airline food,' Antonio said, 'isn't the most wonderful.'

'I don't want to bother your kitchen staff.'

He smiled. 'You won't be bothering them. Come to my apartment. I'll make you a mug of tea and a sandwich myself. Or pasta.' He spread his hands. 'Or whatever it is you'd like to eat.'

She blinked at him, trying to take it in. He was offering to make her some food? Seriously? 'But princes don't cook.'

'They do if they're in the army,' he said. 'If they want their team to respect them, they take their turn doing everything. And I mean everything. I've done my share of cleaning duties, too.'

'Oh.' She really hadn't expected that. Even though he'd made her a mug of tea himself, that night in London.

'Come with me,' he said. 'And I'll carry your bags.'

'I don't have any luggage. I have a seat on the late flight back to London via Rome, tonight,' she said. 'I only came to tell you about the baby. I wasn't planning to stay.'

'Don't go. Please.' He blew out a breath. 'We really do have a lot to talk about. I don't know if you've followed the news about Casavalle, but an awful lot has been going on here. It's wall-to-wall scandal sheet stuff. The media is going to take one look at you, rub their hands with glee and start digging for more scandal.'

She hadn't thought of that. 'But they don't know why I'm here.'

'They'll speculate. It doesn't matter whether it's true or not. They'll suggest whatever gives them the most readers. They'll talk to anyone who knows you and dredge up any hint of scandal. Your mother is going to be a sitting target for them. From now until at least when the baby's born, you're all going to need my protection,' he continued. 'Which includes the help of Miles Montague. And, as you know, almost nothing gets through Miles. Even when sometimes it should.'

There was a rap on the office door.

'Yes,' Antonio said.

The palace secretary himself opened the door to his office. 'Sir? Miss Phillips? Is everything all right?' he asked, looking concerned.

'It will be,' Antonio said. 'Miles, I'll brief you properly later. But for now this isn't to be discussed anywhere or with anyone—and that includes my mother, Luca and Gabriella.'

There was a slight note of warning in his tone, and the older man flushed as he walked over to his desk. 'Of course, sir.'

Antonio sighed. 'I'll talk to them when I'm ready,' he said, and this time his voice was a little gentler. 'If anyone needs me urgently in the next hour or so, we'll be in my apartment. But I'd appreciate it if you could stall anyone if possible, Miles. Tia and I really need to talk in private and without interruptions.'

'Of course. If you need anything…'

Antonio patted his shoulder. 'You're there. I know. And I'm grateful for that.'

Miles nodded, then looked at Tia, his expression awkward. 'I apologise, Miss Phillips, for earlier. When you called the office, and when you first came here.'

It had upset her, but she could understand why he'd acted that way. 'You were doing your job,' she said. 'Protecting the Prince.'

'And Tia's going to be under your protection now, too,' Antonio said. 'I'll brief you shortly. Tia, come with me.' He looked at her and added swiftly, 'Please.'

Good. Because she wasn't Antonio's subject or his employee, and she wasn't going to let him order her about.

The palace had seemed daunting enough from the outside: a massive white stone building with towers and turrets and spires and huge windows; a long driveway lined with enormous Norway spruces covered alternately with blue and white lights; and huge entrance doors at the top of the sweeping granite steps. Tia had found the interior even more daunting, with the enormous foyer that felt more like a cathedral space, with a Christmas tree that had to be a good forty feet tall; the angel on top was close to touching the ceiling, and it was beautifully decorated with what looked like priceless one-of-a-kind baubles, one of which seemed to be in a special display. Crowds actually came in to the palace to see the tree, which was how Tia had managed to slip in and ask to see the palace secretary in the first place.

It was magnificent. But it was also very formal, and it didn't leave her with the warmth she felt with their own Christmas tree back in London, with its decorations that had been collected year after year by her mother and every single one of them had meaning and memories. Their rather threadbare artificial Christmas tree didn't go up until the week before Christmas; here, it was early November and already everything was in its place. Then again, she supposed, things were different with the public rooms of a palace; visitors would expect to see decorations on display this early.

Behind the beautiful garlands of fir and pine on the mantels and staircases, the rooms were richly decorated, with cream walls and lots of gold everywhere. There were huge windows, large mirrors that reflected the light back from the windows and the crystal and gold chandeliers and made the rooms seem even more massive, ceilings covered with priceless paintings, Christmas trees in every room whose decorations she suspected had been put in place with a ruler measuring the precise distance between each one, enormous exotic poinsettias gracing side tables, sweeping staircases leading into long corridors, luxurious carpets you literally sank into as you walked on them…

It was another world, one where the likes of Tia could never fit in.

And it was overwhelming.

Tia was aware that Antonio was talking to her as he ushered her up the sweeping staircase to his first-floor apartment, but she couldn't concentrate on what he was saying. All she could see was the regal magnificence of their surroundings, and it left her feeling more and more out of place.

Finally he opened a door and indicated to her to enter.

His sitting room was much more ordinary than the rest of the palace. The furniture here didn't look too antique and too priceless to touch, let alone sit on, and to her relief there was much less gold in evidence. There were photographs on the mantelpiece in what looked like solid gold frames, mainly of what she assumed was Antonio's family; but there were also photographs of Antonio's team in the army, and tears pricked her eyelids when she recognised her brother among them.

'Let me get you that tea,' Antonio said, ushering her into the kitchen—a sizeable room by normal standards, but thankfully smaller than the rooms she'd seen so far in the palace.

'Thank you. That would be nice.'

'What would you like to eat?'

She shook her head. 'Thank you, but I'm not really hungry.'

He gave her a speaking look. 'You're pregnant. You need to eat.'

She didn't reply but, a couple of minutes later, she found herself sitting at his kitchen table with a mug of tea made just how she liked it and a chicken salad sandwich.

'I really didn't expect you to—' she began.

'Eat,' he cut in. 'Then we'll talk.'

It left her with no choice but to follow his instructions. And she had to admit that the sandwich and the mug of tea did make her feel better. He didn't say a word until she'd finished, simply sipped his tea.

And then he looked at her. 'OK. So, first off,' he said gently, 'how are you?'

'I'm fine.'

'*Really* fine? Because I know some women have a tough time in pregnancy.'

She shrugged. 'I had a bit of morning sickness in the early weeks. Nothing out of the usual.' She opened her handbag, took out a photograph and handed it to him. 'I wanted to give you this.'

'Thank you,' he said politely.

'It's our baby. From the twenty-week scan, last month.'

'Our baby,' he echoed.

She still had absolutely no idea what he was thinking, what he was feeling. His voice and his face were completely expressionless as he looked at the photograph. On the surface he was all urbane charm, just as a prince should be. But was he shocked? Horrified? Secretly pleased? She didn't have a clue. Who was the real man behind the royal facade?

'So,' he said. 'I'll ask you the difficult question first. Do you plan to keep the baby?'

'It's way too late for a termination.' Not that she'd wanted that, in any case.

'I didn't mean that. Were you planning to give the baby up for adoption after the birth?'

'No.'

'So you're keeping him. Or her.'

Not 'it'. She was grateful that at least he hadn't said *that*. 'Yes.'

'Then I have financial responsibilities towards you.'

'That isn't why I came. I can manage.' It would be a struggle, but she was used to that. She'd muddle through, the way she always had, working whatever hours she could fit in around the baby and her mum.

'Tia, this is a Valenti baby,' he said. 'There are expectations. If nothing else, this baby...' He sucked in a breath. 'The way things stand, this baby could be fourth in line to the throne.'

She looked at him in shock. 'What? How?'

'It's been a bit complicated around here. Which is why I didn't get in touch with you after...London.'

The night they'd spent together.

The night that clearly hadn't meant anything to him.

The night that had resulted in their baby.

'Uh-huh,' she said, in an attempt to be as cool and calm and collected as he seemed, though inside she wanted to yell at him.

'You left me that note and I fully intended to call you later that day, after your shift,' Antonio said. 'But, that morning, my mother called me to tell me about Gabriella—my father's daughter from his first marriage, except none of us had any idea she even existed until quite recently. My mother needed to talk to me about it and help her decide how to deal with the situation. She wanted to talk to me because Luca already had enough on his plate, ruling the country and preparing to be King. I had to come straight back to Casavalle, because my family needed me.'

Tia could understand that. It was the same for her and for Nathan: they'd been there for their mother because she was their family and she needed them.

'And I'm afraid my mind was so focused on the situation at home, I didn't think to contact you. I'm sorry.'

Tia had been hurt when Antonio hadn't been in touch after the charity gala, even though she knew she was being ridiculous about it: of course a prince wasn't going to fall for a mere waitress. Of course he wanted nothing more from her than their night of passion. It had been a one-off thing. But now she was seeing things from a different perspective. Antonio was part of a much bigger picture.

'At the moment we're waiting for DNA results, but my mother, Luca and I all think it's very probable that Gabriella is indeed the oldest child of our father, which means she's entitled to accede to the throne and rule Casavalle. She has no children, which makes my brother Luca her heir and puts him second in line to the throne. Luca also has no children; although Princess Meribel, his former fiancée, is pregnant, the baby isn't Luca's. So that makes me Luca's heir and third in line to the throne; and that means our baby is my heir and fourth in line to the throne.' He shrugged. 'Though if we're wrong about the DNA test or Gabriella decides not to accede to the throne, then everything shifts up one place and our baby will be third in line.'

It hadn't really hit home until that moment, but Tia realised right then that her baby was of royal blood.

A baby in line for a crown.

'I…' She tailed off, hardly able to take in the enormity of the situation.

'As I said,' Antonio continued quietly, 'it's been a little complicated around here. Luca's wedding to Meribel has been planned for a very long time. But Meribel told Luca on the eve of their wedding that she was in love with someone else and was pregnant with his baby, so she couldn't go through with marrying him. We agreed with her family that we'd say the wedding was cancelled due to irreconcilable differences, though the people of Aguilarez—Meribel's kingdom, on the other side of the mountains—assumed that meant Luca had practically jilted her at the altar, and they blamed him for the wedding not happening.

'It was politically…' He grimaced. 'Let's just say it was

a bit sensitive. If we didn't tell the truth, it could lead to a great deal of discord between our countries. Yet if we told the truth—that Meribel was the one to have the affair—then it would be putting the blame on her, and that would be dishonourable.'

Tia didn't quite understand that. 'How could it be dishonourable when *she* was the one who had the affair?'

'It's still dishonourable,' Antonio insisted.

'So whatever you did, you'd lose,' Tia said slowly.

'Something like that. Except then someone leaked the truth of the matter. Not from our side,' he was quick to clarify. 'Meribel is in hiding right now, and it feels as if the media has put Casavalle under a microscope, scrutinising every move any of us makes and spotting every potential scandal.' He looked at her. 'Someone in the palace will have noticed you, and they will have heard you ask to speak to Miles. They will definitely have noticed your bump. So people will be asking questions about you—who are you, and why did you want to speak to the palace secretary? Whose baby are you carrying? They'll be watching for you to leave the palace.

'And the paparazzi don't play nice, Tia. They'll strike up a conversation at the airport and you'll think you're simply chatting to another passenger to pass the time. They'll ask all kinds of questions and pump you for information without you even knowing what they're doing, and the next thing you know it'll be all over the media. They'll dig on the Internet and they'll know everything about you before you get back to London—where you live, where you work, all about your mother's health. They'll follow you and they'll doorstep you.'

'Doorstep me?' She didn't understand.

'They'll wait outside your front door in a gaggle. The back door, too. There's no escape from them. The second you open any door, the flashbulbs will go off and they'll be yelling your name and asking you questions. If you've ever seen it happen in a film, I can assure you that it's been romanticised. In real life, it's much harsher. You have to push your way through the mob, and all the time there will be microphones shoved in your face and flashbulbs going off and people yelling.

'If you say anything, it'll be spun to suit their agenda. If you say nothing, then they'll speculate, and they'll do it with the nastiest implications—and you won't be able to protest because they'll claim they're asking questions, not making a statement. Your life won't be your own.'

That hadn't occurred to her. She'd simply thought to let Antonio know that their night together had had consequences, then quietly go back to London. 'I... Look, if there's a way you can get me from the palace to the airport without them seeing me, then I promise not to talk to a single person until I'm back home with my mum.'

He shook his head. 'It's already too late for that. As I said, things have been complicated around here lately.'

And she'd just added another complication to his life. An illegitimate baby.

Her misery must've shown in her expression, because he took her hand. 'Tia. I know neither of us planned this. But you have my support now and you definitely need my protection. I think we both need to get our heads round the situation, and the middle of a royal palace isn't the best place to do that. I know somewhere quiet we can go for a few days that will give us a chance to think things through and talk about the future.'

'But I wasn't planning to stay here, not even for a night. I don't have even a toothbrush with me, let alone any clean clothes,' Tia protested. 'And my mum's expecting me back home tonight.'

'Then call her. Tell her that you're staying here for a little while.' He paused. 'Give me three days, Tia.'

'Three *days*?' Tia was horrified. 'What if Mum needs me?'

'Do you have a neighbour or a friend nearby who can keep an eye out for her?' Antonio asked. 'Or I can arrange for a nurse to come in and help her, if you prefer.' He looked at her. 'I apologise. Nathan didn't tell me much about your mother's condition, other than that she'd been poorly since you were small. And I was brought up not to ask personal questions. So I'm afraid I don't know how ill she is.'

'Mum has chronic fatigue syndrome,' Tia said. 'It used to be called ME—myalgic encephalomyelitis.'

When Antonio looked blank, she continued, 'After Dad was killed in action, Mum went down with a virus, and we think that's what triggered the CFS because she never really recovered. It's a bit like having the flu, with joint pains and a headache you simply can't shift, and absolute exhaustion—but it doesn't go away after a couple of weeks, like the flu does. She has it all the time. So she needs to rest a lot.

'It's a variable condition; some days she's fine and to look at her you'd never know she was ill, and other days she can barely get out of bed. And she's *not* lazy or stupid. It's not like when you're feeling just a bit tired after a busy day—she gets absolutely exhausted and physically can't do anything. If she has a day when she's feeling really well and overdoes things, then she'll really pay for it for a few days afterwards. She has to be careful.'

'And you look after her?'

'Yes, and I don't begrudge a second of it. I love her. She's my mum.' Growing up, Tia had had days when she'd wished her life had been more like that of her friends, where she'd had time to do homework and hang out with her friends and meet boys, instead of struggling to keep up with her studies and worrying that her mum's condition was getting worse, and never starting a relationship because she knew it couldn't go anywhere. But she'd done her best to hide it from her mother, because she loved Grace and didn't want her mother to feel as if she was a burden.

Grace had encouraged her to go out with her friends, but Tia didn't like leaving her mum, except when she went to work and she was only just round the corner and could rush back if there was an emergency.

'Tia,' he said gently, 'we're going to need to talk about the best way to support your mother when you have a small baby to look after as well. Because you're not going to be able to do everything.'

Oh, yes, she could. She always had. 'It'll be fine.' She lifted her chin. 'I'll manage. We always do.'

Meaning that she'd struggle and drive herself into the ground.

Antonio was shocked by the sheer protectiveness he felt towards her. And it wasn't just because she was his best friend's little sister. There was something about Tia Phillips. She was brave and strong and independent, not looking for the easy way out—she'd been very explicit that she expected nothing from him. He admired her courage; yet, at the same time, he wanted to take some of those burdens away. What she'd just told him, in addition to the little that Nathan had let slip, made him realise that she must've spent most of her life looking after her mother. She'd never really had a normal childhood.

Well, she didn't have to struggle any more. He could support her. Though he was pretty sure that her pride would get in the way and she'd refuse any help. So he needed to gain her trust, first. And that meant being specific rather than vague.

'Come with me to my house in the mountains for three days,' he said. 'Let's give ourselves a bit of time to adjust to the situation, and then we can talk about the baby.'

She looked torn. 'It depends on how Mum is.'

'Call her,' he said. 'Talk to her. See what she thinks. I'll give you some space. I'll be in the sitting room when you're ready.'

'Thank you,' she said.

He left her to it, and went into his sitting room. Babies. This was the third baby shock in a row for the palace: first Gabriella's mother being pregnant and never telling her ex-husband, King Vincenzo, about the baby and running away without telling him; then Princess Meribel's affair ending in her being pregnant by another man; and now Tia expecting a baby after their one night together.

The media would have a field day. And, although he had the resources to ride out the storm, Tia was vulnerable.

There was only one solution to this.

But he didn't think it was going to be an easy solution. He was going to have to tread very carefully indeed.

Grace Phillips answered on the third ring.

'How are you, Mum?' Tia asked.

'I'm fine,' Grace said, a little too quickly for Tia's liking. 'Did you get to see Prince Antonio?'

'I did.' She sighed. 'Mum, he wants me to stay for a few days—three days, he said. He wants to talk things over.'

'That's a good idea,' Grace said.

'But I don't want to leave you on your own.'

'I'm fine, love. Really. Becky's next door if I need anything.'

'But that was just for today. I can't ask her to keep an eye out for you for three whole days.'

'You don't have to. I'll ask her,' Grace said. 'And I'm not overdoing things, before you start worrying. I can manage.'

Tia wasn't so sure. 'But what if you have a bad day tomorrow?'

'Then Becky will help,' Grace said. 'You need to talk to Prince Antonio, for the baby's sake. And for yours.'

'Mum, I…'

'I know he's from a different world,' Grace said gently, 'but Nathan always said he was a good man. Listen to what he has to say.'

'But I can't stay here. I haven't got any clean clothes with me, or even a toothbrush.' This was ridiculous. Tia was used to being independent, sorting things out. Their financial circumstances had taught her to be resource-ful. So why did she suddenly feel like bursting into tears?

Maybe that fish-out-of-water feeling showed in her voice, because Grace said, 'I'm sure someone at the pal-ace will be able to lend you something to wear, and you can ask them to launder what you're wearing right now. They must have guests all the time. I'm sure they'll have a spare toothbrush and toiletries, at the very least.'

'I don't want to have to ask. I don't want to be de-pend—' Then she remembered who she was talking to. Someone who also didn't want to be dependent on others, but who didn't have a choice because of her health.

'Darling, sometimes you have to lean on others,' Grace said, as if guessing what Tia was thinking. 'Don't worry about me. I'll be absolutely fine.'

'And you'll let me know how you are?'

'I'll text you every day while you're away,' Grace said. 'Or I'll call you. But right now you need to put yourself first.'

Something Tia had never done, and it didn't feel right for her to do that now.

As if Grace guessed, she added, 'And the baby.'

Tia thought about it.

OK. She could do this. But only for the baby's sake. And so her mother wouldn't worry.

'All right,' she said. 'But I want you to promise me you'll let me know if you need me, Mum. I mean *really* promise. Otherwise I'm going to worry myself sick about you.'

'I promise,' Grace said. 'Love you, Tia.'

'Love you, too, Mum.'

After Tia ended the call, she went in search of Antonio. He seemed to be checking something on his phone; he looked up when she walked in. 'How's your mother?'

'She's fine.' It was Tia's stock answer.

'So you'll stay here with me for a while?'

'Three days,' she said, 'until we've talked.' But she needed to make it very clear it wasn't for her own sake. 'For the baby's sake.'

'Good.' He smiled at her, and Tia was unnerved to realise that it was the first genuine smile she'd seen from him since she'd been in Casavalle. A smile that actually reached his eyes.

Antonio Valenti was absolutely gorgeous when he smiled. Tall, with melting brown eyes and dark hair that was just a shade longer than it should be for the military.

Not that she should be noticing how attractive he was, or remembering how good it had felt when he'd kissed her and touched her. They didn't have a future. All they needed to do was to talk about the baby and arrange access—if he wanted it, and she had no idea at all what he was thinking.

'And I need to let my bosses know that I'm staying here for longer than I expected,' she added. 'They'll need to arrange cover for me in my absence.'

'Of course. Call them. Then, when you're ready, we'll go to the mountains,' he said. 'My family has a house in a quiet village there—a bolt-hole, if you like. It's where I go when I need some space.'

Because, as a member of the Casavallian royal family, Antonio must live his life virtually in a goldfish bowl. He was always on public view.

'Is there any way we can stop at a shop on the way?' she asked. 'Just… I don't have anything with me. No toiletries, no pyjamas, no clean clothes.' Even if Antonio happened to have a whole wardrobe of things that his previous girlfriends or guests had left behind, it was pretty unlikely that any of them would fit a six-months-pregnant woman.

'Give me a list of everything you need and your clothing size,' he said, 'and I'll arrange things.'

He was probably used to ordering clothes from high-end designers, whereas she bought hers second-hand from charity shops. And her toiletries were supermarket own-brand basics, not from expensive Parisian perfume houses. She couldn't afford to waste money on luxuries. 'That's very kind of you,' she said carefully, 'but I'm not sure your budget would fit mine.'

He sighed. 'Look, it's my fault that you have to stay here for a few days in the first place. So please, Tia, let me buy you a few basics.'

'As long as they *are* basics,' she said. The idea of having to accept things from him made her feel awkward, even though she understood that a prince couldn't exactly go browsing in a charity shop or a supermarket. 'One change of clothes—and I assume I can have access to a washing machine and a tumble-dryer at this house in the mountains?'

'Yes. Give me a list of what you'd like,' Antonio said. 'And then we'll go to Picco Innevato.'

Snowy Peak, she translated mentally. He was taking her to a place called Snowy Peak. Well, he'd said his house was in the mountains, and it was late November. Winter. The name probably suited the place perfectly.

'OK,' she said. 'I assume we'll drive there?'

'No. We'll fly,' he said. 'I have a private jet.'

She blinked at him. 'Of course you do.' A private jet. Something far, far beyond the reach of normal mortals. She hadn't flown very often, and when she had—like today—it was always economy class. It was yet another reminder of the huge gulf between them.

'Tia, it makes sense to fly. Otherwise we'll be driving on difficult roads in the dark,' he said. 'We'll drive to the airport from here and fly over to the mountains, then drive to Picco Innevato from there. And hopefully that will mean the media won't work out where we are—or at least not until we've worked out how to manage the situation.'

Manage the situation. What a horrible way to describe a baby. OK, so she wasn't the only woman in the world who'd had an unplanned pregnancy, but right at that moment she felt more alone and miserable than she ever had before. Every nerve in her body was telling her to run back to London, where she had family and friends. What was the point of staying here to talk to Antonio? He'd made it pretty clear he wasn't interested. She was pretty sure she knew how this was going to end: with her and the baby living anonymously in London. And her baby would be very much loved; whereas here in the palace the baby would be seen as a 'situation'. If only Antonio would let her go back to London now. She'd sign any bit of paper he wanted her to, releasing him from any obligations towards herself or the baby and promising never to talk to the press. Anything. She just wanted to get out of here, be some place where she didn't feel like something people had to scrape off their shoe.

'As you wish,' she said, only just resisting the urge to add 'Your Royal Highness' and tug at her forelock, and concentrated on jotting down her list. The sooner this was over with, the better.

CHAPTER TWO

WHEN TIA HAD given Antonio her list and called her bosses to arrange an extension of her leave, Antonio's driver took them to the airport. Giacomo, one of Antonio's security officer whom she'd met in London on the evening of the charity gala, accompanied them. And it was nothing like Tia's previous experience of the airport. This time, she didn't have to wait in a queue to show her passport to the border officials, or go through any kind of security—presumably because she was travelling with a member of Casavalle's royal family. And the plane itself...

It was quite a bit smaller than the plane she'd flown on from Rome, but the interior wasn't the crammed-in rows of seats she'd experienced. This felt more like an office or a living room than an aeroplane, with deep carpeting, four massive and very comfortable-looking seats, and masses of leg room. There were tables, too, so there was plenty of room for working.

'This is how you fly all the time?' Tia asked, feeling slightly overawed by it all.

'I would normally pilot the plane myself,' Antonio said, 'but I thought you might prefer some company.'

'You can fly a plane?' She regretted the question instantly. How stupid and naive of her. Of course a man like Antonio Valenti would be able to fly a plane.

Antonio shrugged. 'I learned a few years ago.'

'And this is how you travel with your family?'

'Sort of. We don't tend to go to the same events,' he said. 'And we don't travel together. When we were young, Luca and I would travel with our nanny and our security team, not our parents.'

It hadn't occurred to her before, but now she realised that if a disaster happened in the air or on the road, it would mean the ruler and his immediate successors would all be involved. For their country's sake, of course they would have to travel separately.

'Sorry,' she mumbled.

'I'm used to it,' he said gently. 'It's how things are for me. But I realise it's not how normal families are.'

She could barely remember flying anywhere with her parents and Nathan; since her father's death, either her mother hadn't been well enough to travel, or a holiday abroad had been way out of their budget. The most they'd managed in the last three or four years was the occasional day trip to Brighton, and the effort had exhausted her mother for days afterwards.

'Tell me about Picco Innevato,' she said, wanting to change the subject.

'It means "snowy peak".'

She wondered if she should tell him that she'd learned to speak Italian over the years she'd been working for Giovanni and Vittoria, but decided maybe not just yet.

'It's a very pretty village,' he said. 'In winter it serves the ski resort nearby, and in summer people go there for hiking. My family has a house on the outskirts. The villagers are good to me when I visit; they don't ask questions and they treat me as just another neighbour.'

'I guess it must be like living in a goldfish bowl when you're at the palace,' she said.

'The media are keen to know my every movement,' he admitted. 'But in Picco Innevato I can be myself. I spent quite a few summers there as a child, so I made friends with the local children. We played football and ran around in the park together.'

Things she'd taken very much for granted as a child, going to the park with her mother and Nathan and playing on the swings and slide. It had never occurred to her that other children would have a different kind of upbringing, one where they had to watch everything they did and everything they said. 'That's nice,' she said.

'It was. And I think it kept me in touch with our people better than if I'd grown up only at the palace,' he said.

For a moment, he looked sad, but she didn't want to pry. Because then he might ask her awkward questions, too—things she didn't want to answer.

'May I offer you some refreshment?' he asked. 'The flight will take about twenty minutes.'

She would've liked a cup of tea, but as the flight was so short she could wait. 'I'm fine, thank you,' she said.

They made small talk for the rest of the journey, the kind of thing she was very good at from her job at the café, but both of them skirted round the difficult questions they'd need to discuss later. The baby. What Antonio expected from her. Whether he'd let her just go quietly back to London and disappear—which was her preferred option.

Once they'd landed, they were met by another car; this time, Antonio drove them himself, with Tia in the passenger seat next to him and Giacomo in the back of the car.

It wasn't long before they'd gone from the smooth wide roads around the airport to a narrow pass going through the mountains; the scenery was incredibly pretty, with pine trees and a dusting of snow, but the road was full of hairpin bends and there was a sharp drop straight down the mountain on one side of the car. Not wanting to distract Antonio from driving, Tia remained silent and just tried to enjoy the scenery, even though she felt as if she'd stepped into a completely different world. A magical world, like the ones her mother had read stories about when she was small—where the girl was by the side of the handsome prince and there was a happy-ever-after.

She knew it was unrealistic to expect a happy-ever-after. Her world was so different from Antonio's that she would never be able to fit in. Plus she was six months pregnant—something else you never saw in fairy tales. Of course they didn't have a future together.

Yet, out here, with the mountains and snow and fir trees all around, a tiny bit of her began to hope. Maybe they could find a way to work something out. Maybe he could be part of the baby's life. Maybe he could even be part of *her* life, too. Perhaps it was a fantasy and she'd come crashing back down to earth with a bump: but she'd definitely felt a connection with Antonio, the night they'd spent together. Something more than just sex. Something more than physical attraction. Something that made her understand the glances she'd seen between her parents as a child, that sparkle in her mother's eyes and the special smile her father had reserved for her mother. And when Antonio had kissed her, when he'd carried her to his bed, there had been something special and cherishing about his touch…

She shook herself and concentrated on her surroundings. The village of Picco Innevato was incredibly pretty. Honey-coloured stone houses with terracotta tiled roofs nestled together in the main street, and there was a church with a spire. There was a pretty square in the middle of the village with a fountain and, given that she could see people on ladders hanging Christmas lights, a space for what Tia guessed would be an amazing Christmas tree. It was a picture-postcard village—the sort she'd dreamed about when she was growing up, longing for the space of the countryside rather than being stuck in a cramped flat in a dingy part of London.

Antonio stopped at some gates at the far end of the village and tapped in a code. When the gates swung open, he drove down the long driveway and then parked in front of a large honey-coloured stone house. 'Welcome to my bolt-hole,' he said. 'Let me show you around.'

A bolt-hole to Tia meant somewhere small. This house was huge, especially in comparison with the tiny two-bedroomed flat she shared with her mother.

Feeling slightly intimidated, she followed him up the steps to the house.

Downstairs, there was a massive kitchen that was as big as their entire flat. The counter tops were all polished granite, the cupboards and drawers were solid wood and the sort she recognised from magazines as soft-closing, and the floor was terracotta tiles.

Antonio looked in the large American-style fridge and smiled. 'Excellent. Gina's stocked up for us.'

'Gina?'

'Our housekeeper,' he said. 'She lives in the village, rather than here, but I asked her to do some shopping for me.'

It made sense for Antonio's family to have someone looking after the house, as they didn't live here all the time, but Tia was finding it hard to get her head round the idea of having staff. In her world, people *were* staff. Her previous job before the café had been as a cleaner.

'I'll cook for us tonight,' he said.

Clearly he was trying to make her feel more comfortable, and make her feel as if he was an ordinary man rather than a prince.

Except he wasn't.

He was the father of her baby.

He'd asked her to come here with him so they could talk.

And she didn't have a clue about his feelings. Or her own. The whole thing was a muddle. She couldn't afford to fall in love with someone so out of reach, even if he was the father of her baby. But, if she ignored her practical side… Being in the same room as him made her pulse skitter. It was nothing like the way she'd felt when she'd been on dates in the past. This was something that made her catch her breath, made her feel as if fireworks were going off all around her and lighting up the sky.

And she didn't know what to do about it.

Was it possible that he felt the same? This whole mixed-up yearning and wishing and wondering? Or was she just kidding herself and setting herself up for disappointment?

She forced herself to smile. 'Thank you. And I will do the washing up.'

'We'll share the washing up,' he said.

A prince, doing the washing up?

Then again, he'd told her that in the army he'd done exactly the same tasks as everyone else in his team, including cleaning. And he'd told her that this place was his bolt-hole. So maybe being a prince wasn't the lifestyle he would've chosen for himself.

He showed her around the rest of the ground floor. There was an office, a dining room with a table that seated twelve, and two large sitting rooms, both with plenty of room for several comfortable sofas and armchairs. One had a state-of-the-art television, and the other had a piano and a wall full of books. And finally there was an enormous conservatory with a view over a large and very neat garden, with the mountains looming behind.

'We're lucky here. We can see the sun setting behind the mountains in the evening, and then at sunrise, when the mountains are covered in snow, it looks all pink,' he said.

'That's lovely,' she said, but her voice must've shown that this kind of luxury and space made her feel out of place.

'Tia,' he said gently, 'it's all relative. I know this is a bit big for a normal person's bolt-hole, but please remember it isn't just my house. It belongs to my family. And our security team needs a bedroom and a bathroom each, plus sometimes we have guests to stay.'

'Uh-huh,' she said.

Upstairs, there were eight enormous bedrooms, all with their own bathrooms.

'I thought you might like this room, because it has a view over the mountains,' he said, showing her to one bedroom. It was a fairy-tale suite; the king-sized brass bedstead had deep pillows, a thick duvet and pretty floral bedlinen. The beautifully carved dressing table had an ornate mirror; to one side of the room there were doors that she assumed opened to a built-in wardrobe. There was a comfortable armchair by the window; the small coffee table next to it had a vase of beautiful pink and white roses and copies of the latest glossy women's magazines—in English, she noted, so had they been bought with her in mind?

The bathroom was huge, too: a marble floor and marble walls, a deep bathtub, a shower cubicle with an enormous shower head and what looked like jets coming out of the walls, a gilt mirror above the sink, and a shelf that was already stocked with toiletries and a new toothbrush still in its packaging. She recognised the brands as ones that she couldn't even afford as special presents when they were discounted in the post-Christmas sales. This was sheer unadulterated luxury, and a whole world away from her normal life.

'I hope these are OK,' he said, gesturing to the shelf.

'I... Thank you.' She'd work out later how to replace the toiletries for him. It would put quite a hole in her budget, but she'd always been good at juggling.

'Gina bought a couple of changes of clothes for you,' he said, 'and she put them away in the wardrobe and the dressing table. Though if you'd prefer a different room, I can move everything for you.'

He'd managed to arrange clothes for her already? She stared at him in surprise. 'But I only gave you that list an hour ago!'

He shrugged. 'Picco Innevato might look small, but there are a few shops here. As I said, the village is used as a ski resort in winter, and people come for the hiking in the summer.'

If it was a touristy place, then the clothes sold here would be by expensive designer boutiques rather than cheap and cheerful chain stores or supermarkets, she thought.

As if he was guessing what she was thinking, he said gently, 'It's my fault that you're here as my guest, so I'm simply providing you with a couple of changes of clothes, just as any of my family would do for a guest staying here. The same goes for the toiletries. There are no strings, Tia, and I'll be very offended if you offer to pay for them.'

Although Tia wanted to argue and tell him that she could manage to buy her own clothes, thank you very much, she had the baby to think about—and the fact that she'd be on maternity leave in a couple of months, reducing her budget even further. Which meant she'd have to swallow her pride and accept his kindness. 'Thank you,' she said, feeling miserable and selfish and totally mixed up. She had never relied on anyone in her life, and she didn't want to start now. But, for the sake of the baby and her mother, she might have to.

It would help if she had a better idea of what *he* wanted. The man, not the Prince. But how could she ask without sounding ungrateful? She was stuck.

'Take your time settling in,' he said. 'If you want to take a bath or shower to freshen up, or have a nap, that's fine. We're not on palace time. And call your mother to let her know you're here safely. I'll be downstairs when you're ready.'

'Thank you.'

He left her to look over the clothes. And they were utterly gorgeous—a couple of long-sleeved silky maternity tops, a pair of maternity trousers, a soft cashmere cardigan, a smart black skirt and a pretty floral tunic dress. There was underwear, too, and maternity tights. Three pairs of pyjamas, with soft jersey trousers and lace-trimmed matching camisole tops.

Tia's eyes filled with tears. They were so pretty. And this was so kind of his housekeeper, to do this for a complete stranger.

Antonio made himself a coffee, but he didn't feel as relaxed as he usually did here in his bolt-hole.

What was he going to do about Tia Phillips?

He saw her through a haze of guilt: his best friend's little sister. The woman he should've supported after her brother's death, but he'd let her down. The woman he'd let comfort him. The woman he'd made pregnant—albeit unknowingly—and abandoned.

The woman, if he was honest with himself, who made him feel different—as if he was more than just the younger Prince of Casavalle or a team commander. She made him feel as if she saw right through the pomp and the public face to the man behind it. Just like that night they'd spent together, when she'd comforted him and let him comfort her: he had no idea why, but she'd broken through all his barriers. Though he didn't want to examine it too closely and work out why she was the only one who'd made him feel that way. Emotional stuff made him antsy because he'd never really learned how to deal with it—and he didn't want to deal with it now. Duty was much, much easier than emotion.

Just put it down to sexual attraction, he told himself, and move on.

Because his duty to Casavalle had to come first. He had to think about the baby and what it would mean for his country. And then he would do the right thing.

Miles would be discreet, Antonio knew. So he had a breathing space before he had to tell his family the truth about the 'personal matters to attend to' he'd texted them about. And he had absolutely no idea how they would react to the news of the baby. His mother would be furious. His brother—although Luca knew that Tia had tried to contact Antonio, he didn't know why, so he would be shocked. Gabriella... She was an 'unexpected' baby herself, so she might have a different viewpoint.

But he knew they'd all be disappointed in him.

What he'd done had been very far from honourable, even though it was completely unintentional. And he needed to fix the situation. Now.

He'd never thought he'd settle down and have children. When they'd been growing up, it was always assumed that Luca—as the eldest son—would take over from their fa-

ther, and Luca would be the one who had to marry someone suitable and produce the next heir to the throne. The
arrangement with Princess Meribel had happened years
ago, so Antonio had had the freedom to join the army,
travelling the world and taking on dangerous missions.
He'd loved every second of his job and he'd relished his
freedom. He'd been planning to go back to the army once
Luca was settled as the King of Casavalle—or Gabriella
as the new Queen. Either way, his time in Casavalle had
been temporary.

Now… Now it was different. He was going to be a father. Going back to the army and putting himself in danger was less of an option now. He had responsibilities:
emotional as well as financial.

And that was the problem.

Emotional stuff. The thing he found difficult.

Growing up, he remembered both of his parents being
very formal and his father had been distant. Antonio
couldn't remember his father ever hugging him, or saying he loved his younger son, or saying that he was proud
of him. He'd worked hard in the army and he'd earned his
promotions through merit, not through his connections;
but King Vincenzo had never acknowledged that or made
any comment about how hard his son had worked. Queen
Maria was warmer but, like his father, she'd always encouraged him to put his civic duty before his feelings.

And, although Antonio had dated plenty of women,
he'd never felt a real connection with any of them. He'd
enjoyed their company, but had always made it clear right
from the start that the relationship was strictly short term.

Except for Tia, a little voice said in his head.

Tia Phillips, with her soft brown eyes, her tumble of
black curls, and her petite frame that hid amazing inner
strength. When he had seen her again today in the palace,

he'd felt that leap of his pulse, the slow burn of pleasure that was more intense than he'd ever experienced with anyone else. If he was honest with himself, she was the only person he'd ever really felt connected to. That night in London when they'd shared their grief over losing her brother and held each other tightly. That night when she'd broken through all his barriers. The night when they'd made a baby...

The baby.

Antonio took the photograph she'd given him from his wallet. The baby was lying on his back, knees up, and one arm was raised so Antonio could see a tiny hand. Fingers.

Their baby.

He dragged in a breath. It was miraculous and terrifying at the same time.

And Tia had been dealing with this alone.

The more he thought about it, the more he knew he had to do the right thing by her. Marry her, make their child legitimate, support her. And she'd looked so worried when she'd sat in the palace secretary's office, waiting to tell him the news. Guilt squeezed his insides again as he thought about it. Did she really think he'd abandon her for a third time?

Then again, he hadn't given her any reason to think he'd do anything else. He'd abandoned her and her mother after breaking the news of Nathan's death, and he hadn't got in touch again after the charity gala. Where Tia was concerned, he had a really terrible track record.

So when she came downstairs, he'd reassure her. Tell her they would get married.

On the other hand, he knew that Tia was an independent woman. Extremely independent, according to Nathan; she'd spent her life being their mother's carer, putting her own dreams aside. Dreams of travelling the world and becoming a primary school teacher, so Nathan had said.

In that case, would she even agree to marry him, even though it was the right thing for the baby?

But Antonio knew it was the right thing to do. If they got married, he could fulfil his duties as the baby's father, and he could help Tia with her mother. He could bring Grace Phillips over to Casavalle, where the climate might be better for her health and she'd have access to much more support than she had in London. Then Tia would be able to be Grace's daughter rather than her carer; and, although Tia would need to support him in his royal duties so she wouldn't have the time to become a primary school teacher, she would at least be able to travel the world with him.

And maybe Luca—or Gabriella, whichever of them was crowned—would allow him to have some kind of special responsibilities for education, so Tia could fulfil her dreams that way, working with him.

He had the whole thing sorted perfectly in his head by the time Tia came downstairs.

'Is everything all right? Is there anything you need?' he asked.

'Thank you, everything's lovely. I'm fine.'

He noticed there was a slight disconnect between her words and her expression; although she was smiling, it didn't reach her eyes. He wasn't quite sure what was wrong, but she definitely wasn't fine. 'Tea?' he asked.

'No, thank you.'

Or maybe she was worrying about his reaction to the baby. Maybe she needed reassurance. He could sort that out right now.

'Let's go into the conservatory,' he said.

Giacomo had tactfully gone to his own room, giving Antonio and Tia the space they needed to talk.

Tia let the Prince usher her through to the conservatory and settle her on one of the comfortable sofas.

'I've been thinking,' he said. 'There's a very simple solution to this. We'll get married.'

Married?

Just like that?

Tia stared at him in disbelief.

Of course Prince Antonio didn't want to marry her. He didn't love her. He clearly didn't feel anything towards her except a sense of duty and honour. He hadn't hugged her, he hadn't told her he'd missed her—in fact, he'd barely even touched her other than to support her elbow as she'd climbed the steps to the plane, which she was fairly sure he'd do for any female he accompanied because it was a very regal and very polite thing to do. And, even though her skin had tingled when his hand had accidentally brushed against hers, she was pretty sure it hadn't been the same for him.

Prince Antonio of the House of Valenti was an unemotional *machine*.

Yes, he could put people at their ease—because that was what royals were trained to do. It was all about duty, where he was concerned. He hadn't brought her here to his bolt-hole because he wanted to spend time with her, but because he needed to get her away from the media and protect his family's privacy.

His suggestion of marriage was utterly ridiculous. She hadn't come here to demand he do the old-fashioned 'right thing' by her; her sole intention had been to let him know about the baby's existence and then leave. She'd managed the six months of her pregnancy so far perfectly well without him, and she'd manage the birth and their child's life in exactly the same way.

She'd been born to a couple who hadn't been married but who had loved each other deeply and who'd adored their children. OK, so maybe it had turned out that her dad was wrong about marriage being just a bit of paper; but she understood where he was coming from. You should be with someone because you loved them and the world felt like a better place because they were in it, not because you were bound by a contract.

No way was Tia getting married to a man who didn't want her and who saw their baby as a burden and a duty. That was the complete opposite of what her parents had had. It wasn't what she wanted. At all. Yes, it was honourable of him to suggest the marriage, and she appreciated that: but marriage would be completely the wrong thing for both of them.

'No,' she said.

Antonio looked taken aback.

Which wasn't so surprising: she very much doubted he'd ever heard the word 'no' when he was growing up. Everyone around him was more likely to have said, 'Yes, Your Royal Highness,' bowed deeply and done exactly what the little imperious Prince had demanded.

'No?' he asked, clearly expecting her to say she'd made a mistake and of course she would marry him.

'No,' she said.

'Why?'

Because you're an automaton who has no real emotions.

Not that it would be tactful to say so. But she could still tell him the rest of the truth.

'Because,' she said, 'you don't love me. You're asking me to marry you because of the baby. Because you think it's the honourable thing to do.' Hadn't he talked about honour before, about not letting Princess Meribel take the blame for her own actions even though she'd been the one to behave badly? 'That isn't what I want. So I'm not going to marry you.'

He blew out a breath. 'Tia, this baby is fourth in line to the throne.'

'Not if I don't marry you, he isn't.'

Antonio's eyes widened. 'The baby's definitely a boy?'

'I don't know. They can't always tell on a scan, and I chose not to find out. But I don't want to call the baby "it"; he's a person, not a thing.'

'Fair enough.' Antonio looked at her. 'But I don't understand how you can say that my child isn't in line to the throne.'

'Because surely any heir to the throne has to be legitimate?' she asked. 'Which means we have a very obvious solution to the problem. If you don't marry me, then the baby isn't legitimate and therefore won't be your heir—and that means you have no legal obligations to either of us.'

'It's a matter of honour,' he said stiffly.

Just what she'd thought. This was all about honour, not love. 'My parents loved each other deeply,' she said quietly, 'and I'm not settling for anything less than that. My answer's still no. I won't marry you.'

He frowned. 'Tia, I know I've let you down twice now, and I apologise deeply for that. But I won't make that mistake a third time.'

No, he wouldn't—because she wasn't giving him the chance to do that. She spread her hands. 'I'm not making any demands on you whatsoever. I've already explained to you that I told you about the baby purely out of courtesy. Because I thought you ought to know. Not because I expected anything from you. Marriage isn't an option.'

He raked a hand through his hair, and the slight disarray made him look more human. Touchable. Not the cold, emotionless Prince who'd greeted her at the palace, but Antonio the man.

Oh, help. She needed to get a grip.

Touching really wasn't what she should be thinking about right now.

Touching was what had got her into this situation in the first place. Holding him, because she'd felt sorry for him and thought that a hug would comfort both of them. Except hugging had turned to kissing, which had turned to him carrying her to his bed, which had turned out to be the most amazing night of her life...

Antonio Valenti wasn't the only man she'd slept with, but he was the only one she'd felt a real connection to. He'd made her feel different. Special, as if she was really important to him. The differences between their social positions hadn't mattered; it had been just the two of them, and that night she'd felt as if the Prince had seen her for who she really was, not just the cheerful waitress with a complicated home life. She'd responded to him on a deeper level than she had to anyone else before; it was a fact that scared her and thrilled her in equal measure. She didn't want to be emotionally dependent on a man who kept his emotions in check all the time. She definitely didn't want to fall in love with someone who couldn't love her back.

But between them that night they'd managed to make a baby.

Now she was facing the consequences.

What should she do now?

Antonio was gorgeous. A total fairy-tale prince, except he was real. And that weird feeling she got when she looked at him—it wasn't the baby kicking. It felt more as if her heart was doing some kind of weird somersault, something that wasn't even anatomically possible.

But how could he ever be really hers? He had responsibilities towards his country, so if he ever settled down with someone it'd have to be for dynastic reasons. His wife would probably have to be at least the daughter of a duke, if not an actual princess.

Which meant there was no real future in any relationship between Antonio and herself, despite the baby and his offer of marriage just now. He probably shouldn't even have asked her to marry him without checking with the palace first. If she let herself act on the pull she felt towards him, she'd just be making a fool of herself, and it wouldn't help either of them. She needed to be cool-headed and calm. And utterly, utterly sensible. He didn't love her. And her own feelings towards him were so muddled that she couldn't make sense of them.

'I am *not* marrying you,' she repeated.

Antonio really hadn't expected this.

Tia had refused his proposal of marriage because she wanted to get married for love?

But that was something that just didn't happen in his family. King Vincenzo had learned the hard way from his first marriage, to Sophia Ross. He'd married for love, and look how that had turned out. Sophia hadn't been able to cope with a royal lifestyle. She'd left Vincenzo to go back home to Canada; she hadn't told him that she was expecting a baby, and Gabriella had grown up completely unaware of who she really was.

Then it occurred to him that Tia at least hadn't done what Sophia had done. She hadn't kept the baby secret.

He thought about it some more. His parents' own marriage had been arranged and it had been successful; his father had grown to love his mother, even though he hadn't shown any affection outwardly. But the arranged marriage between his older brother and Princess Meribel had gone badly wrong, because Meribel had been rash and chasing after true love instead of being sensible and joining their two countries' dynasties. Arranged marriages meant that you had to make compromises, but that went with the territory of being a royal. You had to put your country's needs before your own desires. Luca and Imogen had fallen in love and got engaged; maybe his elder brother was just lucky, Antonio thought. Because, on the whole, his own family's experience had taught him that relationships based on love tended to end up in a mess.

Why couldn't Tia see that you couldn't rely on love? That honour and duty was a better solution?

His head was spinning.

Right now he didn't know what to think. He was filled with guilt for the way he'd treated Tia; he was still trying to get his head round the changes in his own family; he missed his best friend and he missed his father, at the same time as he wished that things had maybe been different and he'd been able to make Vincenzo as proud of him as of his elder brother Luca.

And now there was the baby to think about. He was still trying to process the fact that he was going to be a father. Duty said the right thing to do would be to marry Tia and give the baby his name. But there was more to being a parent than just creating a baby. Would he be any good at it? Would he be able to give his child more than his parents had given him—the kind of warmth his best friend had exuded when he'd talked about his parents? Was Tia right and she'd be better off as a single mum, without him bumbling around and making a mess of things because he didn't really know how to do emotional stuff?

He couldn't find the right words to say to her.

And clearly she wasn't impressed by his silence, because she added, 'And that's an end to the matter.'

Oh, no, it wasn't.

They needed to talk about this properly and work things through. Together.

Tia was having *his* baby. And he could give her and the baby the security they needed. His best friend would never be able to follow his dreams, thanks to the land mine that had blown up his armoured car; but perhaps Antonio could give Tia the chance to follow her dreams.

He just had to persuade her to give him a chance, too.

'Tia—'

'It's not up for discussion,' she said. 'We are *not* getting married.'

Nathan had been proud of his little sister's independence, but right now Antonio was starting to get a bit annoyed by her stubbornness. He wanted her to help him here. Be reasonable.

But he realised that demanding that she marry him wasn't going to convince her that marriage was the right thing to do. He needed to persuade her. Turn on a charm offensive, maybe. He needed to take the emotion out of it, the way he always did. Make it a military operation and treat it as clear-headedly as he treated his work: Operation Persuade Tia.

So for now he'd make a tactical retreat. 'OK.'

She looked slightly shocked, as if she hadn't expected him to agree so quickly. So what did she want? Had she wanted him to fight for her affections?

Love and affection wasn't something he'd thought to have. He wasn't entirely sure that he wanted them; he'd seen what a mess they could cause. Yet, on the other hand, he knew there was something missing from his life. Something he rather thought might be important. All the short-term relationships with no promises, no future: if he was honest with himself, they'd stopped being fun a long time ago. But he'd never met anyone who'd made him think that there could be something more. Not until Tia.

'But,' he said, 'we do need to talk.'

'About what?'

'Everything we didn't say at the palace. But now we've got the space and time to talk properly. Let me make that cup of tea, first,' he prevaricated. The English solution to everything, he thought wryly.

At least she didn't argue about *that*.

He left her in the conservatory, swiftly busied himself in the kitchen, and made two mugs of tea.

'Thank you,' she said when he returned and handed her a mug.

'So when did you realise that you were pregnant?' he asked.

'A couple of months after—' She stopped, and blushed.

After they'd comforted each other and it had turned into lovemaking. Yeah. He didn't want to say that out loud, either. He didn't want to unpick the feelings he'd ignored since then.

'I was busy, I lost track of the time, and it didn't occur to me that my period was late.' She sipped her tea and looked away. 'When I finally realised that my period was late, I did a test.' She paused. 'I probably should've tried to tell you about it back then.'

Why hadn't she?

Clearly she anticipated his question—that, or it was written all over his face—because she continued, 'It took me a while to come to terms with being pregnant and think about what I wanted. Especially when—' She stopped.

'When what?'

'You're photographed with a *lot* of women. The celeb magazines talk about you and your dates all the time. They say that you're a playboy.'

Which wasn't what she wanted from her baby's father? He could understand that. And it wasn't who he was. He grimaced. 'I don't sleep with every woman I date. And I have to show my face at a lot of events where I'm expected to bring a plus one. The media try to spin stories when there isn't really anything to say. I'm not a playboy.'

He hadn't been in a relationship with Tia; but maybe he hadn't been as honest with her as he had been with his usual dates. And even though he hadn't been dating Tia so technically he hadn't cheated on her, he'd been out with other women while Tia was pregnant with his baby—which felt like cheating. Even though he hadn't known about the baby at the time. And it made him feel really, really guilty.

Uncomfortable with the direction his thoughts were taking, he turned the subject back to the baby. 'And you want to keep the baby.'

She nodded. 'What happened… It's not the baby's fault.'

'No.' And it hadn't even occurred to Antonio that there might be consequences from that night. He hadn't thought of anything at all recently except his family's situation. They were all still getting used to the new order of things, following his father's death. Trying to support their people and their country, not letting their personal feelings show. He'd kept busy, but inside he'd felt lost and empty, missing his father and missing his best friend, unable to talk to anyone about how he felt.

The only person he'd come close to confiding in was Tia, the night of the charity gala, when they'd turned to each other for comfort. Having her here, close to him again, made him antsy. Part of him wanted that closeness back; yet, at the same time, that closeness had led them to this tricky situation.

Right now, he thought grimly, he could do with the equivalent of an armoured car so he could lock his heart safely away in it.

So what were they going to do?

He'd used a condom when he'd made love with Tia, but clearly the protection had failed. Or maybe it had happened the second time they'd made love, when they'd both been half-asleep and seeking comfort from each other. He wasn't entirely sure he'd used a condom then so, actually, this whole thing was his fault. He should've been the one who'd been responsible. He should've kept himself under control.

'I'm sorry,' he said.

'It is as it is,' she said with a shrug. 'Mum and I manage. And my bosses have been great. Vittoria, my boss, fusses over me a bit and makes sure I sit down between the really busy periods.'

Then it occurred to him what her job was. She was a waitress in a coffee shop. Which meant that she'd be on her feet all the time, taking orders, ferrying drinks and snacks to the customers, clearing tables and rushing about—because, from what Antonio had learned from her brother, Tia Phillips wasn't the sort to slack off and expect other people to shoulder her duties. 'Is that good for you and the baby, being on your feet all day?' he asked.

Within seconds he knew he'd asked the wrong question. She had that stubborn, independent set to her jaw he was beginning to realise meant trouble. 'Women have managed to stay on their feet and work while they're pregnant for hundreds of years, Antonio.'

'Yes. Of course. I apologise.'

Though at least she'd used his given name, rather than calling him 'Your Royal Highness' or awkwardly not calling him anything at all. Funny how that made him feel warm inside; and it made him feel wrong-footed at the same time.

He wasn't used to women making him feel in a spin.

What was it about Tia Phillips that was so different? And how could he get everything back under his control, the way it usually was?

'I eat properly and I rest properly, before you ask,' she said.

He didn't quite believe her on the 'resting' bit. He knew that she was still caring for her mother, meaning that she must be doing the majority of looking after the house and preparing meals when her mother wasn't well, plus she was handling the demands of her job.

'And, as soon as I realised I was pregnant, I started taking folic acid. I know it was a bit late, but it was better than nothing. Mum makes sure I take a vitamin tablet for pregnant women every morning,' she said.

'That's good,' he said, not knowing what else to say.

He was good in social situations. He'd been good at leading his team in the army, he'd been diplomatic with Meribel's family, and he'd helped Gabriella to feel more at ease in the palace, knowing from his experiences in the army how overwhelming the life of a royal could seem to someone who hadn't been brought up in it.

But with Tia, right now, he was all at sixes and sevens. She wasn't reacting the way he expected her to react. Plus, if he was honest with himself, she made him feel things he'd never felt before. A kind of yearning, mixed with something he couldn't quite put his finger on. Not nervousness, exactly, and not the adrenalin rush he was used to at work. This was deeper, tangled up with his emotions, so he couldn't compartmentalise it, and it unsettled him.

'You've had regular appointments with the hospital?' he asked, trying to bring things back to facts. Unemotional facts that he could deal with.

'Only the dating scan and the twenty-week scan—the one where they gave me the photograph. The rest of my appointments are with the community midwife. And, yes, I've gone to every single one.'

There was a slight edge to her tone. 'I wasn't accusing you of putting the baby at risk,' he said quietly. 'I'm concerned about *you*.'

Colour flared into her face. 'Sorry. I didn't mean to snap. I guess…' She grimaced. 'Blame it on the hormones?'

The situation couldn't be easy for her, either. He inclined his head. 'Of course. So your plan after telling me the news was to go back home, have the baby, and then someone would look after the baby while you work?'

'I have a friend who's expecting a baby and she's also a waitress,' Tia explained. 'We were going to try to work out some kind of arrangement, so while one of us was working the other would look after both the babies. That way neither of us would have to pay for childcare, and we'd both be able to spend time with our babies. Although I don't know how realistic that would be.'

But doing that would also mean that Tia would be working fewer hours, which in turn meant she'd be earning less than she did now. Money would be really, really tight. Especially as Nathan was no longer able to help out financially.

Antonio had to find a way around her pride.

And the best way to do that was to persuade her to marry him.

If she insisted on marrying for love... Then somehow he had to make her fall in love with him, and make her believe that he'd fallen in love with her. And then finally she'd let him help her.

'I can see you've thought everything through,' he said.

She narrowed her eyes at him. 'Are you being sarcastic with me?'

'No. Actually, I think your ability to work out a strategy to manage any situation is every bit as good as any general I've worked with,' he said.

She went slightly pink. 'Oh. Thank you.'

'And I appreciate you coming here with me. I didn't bring you here because I'm ashamed of you—or of what we did.'

Her blush deepened. 'Uh-huh.'

Interesting. So maybe she wasn't completely immune to him.

He wasn't immune to her, either.

Not that he was going to let his emotions cloud things. Emotions just made things messy. If the idea of love made it easier for her to accept his proposal of marriage, then fair enough. But he was keeping his mind clear. He wasn't letting his heart rule his head.

'I brought you here,' he continued, 'because I wanted us to have the space to talk, without any pressure. Because what *you* want is important.' And hopefully he could persuade her to want what he wanted, too.

'So you're not going to railroad me into anything?'

'No.' He was going to charm her into doing what he felt was best for them all. And there was a difference. He wasn't a bully. He wanted to look after her and the baby properly, and he wanted her to accept his help willingly.

'These three days are all about us getting to know each other a bit better. Understanding each other.'

'That works for me,' she said. 'Thank you.'

'So perhaps you'll agree to have dinner with me this evening,' he said. 'I'll cook.'

She frowned. 'I don't expect you to wait on me.'

'I thought that maybe we could prepare dinner together,' he said. Doing things together might help. Working as a team. It might show her that they could be good together, despite being near-strangers.

And then she might agree to marry him—and all the fuss and confusion could stop.

CHAPTER THREE

TOGETHER, THEY WATCHED the sun set over the mountains, the sky striped in shades of pink and blue and gold against the snow-capped peaks.

'It's beautiful here,' Tia said. 'I can see why you come here when you need a bolt-hole. But you said the media follows you everywhere. Does that mean they follow you here?'

'Not as much as they'd like to,' Antonio said. 'The villagers are fairly protective of me, probably because they remember me coming here as a child and some of them remember playing with Luca and me when we were young. They're fairly good at misdirection when it comes to the media. And I'm very grateful for it.'

'It must be hard, having to be in the public eye so much.'

'It's one of the reasons why I appreciate being in the army,' he said. 'Obviously the media don't cover me at work, because they know that would be putting me and my team at risk. But, yes, one's position as a royal can be tricky. It's the way things are so easily misinterpreted, the way people look for hidden meanings that just aren't there.' He shrugged. 'But it is what it is. Shall we go and find something for dinner?'

'That'd be nice,' she said.

He ushered her into the kitchen.

'So what do you like to eat?' he asked.

'I eat practically anything. I'm not fussy.'

He coughed. 'Even *I* know that there are things women need to avoid eating in pregnancy, and things that they need to eat for the baby's sake.'

'I'm just going into the third trimester,' she said, 'so I need lots of calcium.'

'So that's milk and cheese, right?'

'As long as it's pasteurised. And lots of dark green leafy veg, dried apricots, sardines and that sort of thing.' She grimaced. 'Though not too much spice, please, as I've discovered that garlic and very spicy foods give me heartburn.'

He looked through the vegetable drawers in the fridge. 'We have spinach and kale, and Gina's bought chicken, but I'll get some sardines ordered in for tomorrow, if you like.' He looked in the cupboards. 'We have dried apricots and couscous, so I could make you a sort of chicken tagine, with spinach and kale stirred in, and I'll keep the spices mild.'

She was surprised. 'You can actually cook a tagine?'

'I learned while I was in the army. With a team assembled from many different countries, you get to learn about other people's cultures and ideas. Thanks to that, I've learned quite a bit about food, and making stews over a fire. And in return I taught my team how to make a really good tomato sauce for pasta, and how not to overcook pasta.' He rolled his eyes. 'My team-mates only ever served me soggy spaghetti once. And don't get me started on pasta in a tin with that orange stuff claiming to be *sauce*.'

This was a side of him she hadn't really seen. She could understand now why her brother had been friends with him: there was a slight bite to his humour. This side of Prince Antonio, the more human side that he clearly didn't let show very often, was one she rather liked. A man whose company she could enjoy—much more than the formal, slightly stuffy royal personage who bossed her about and irritated her.

'You miss the army, don't you?' she asked.

'I do,' he admitted. 'Yes, there are days when I see terrible things that no human should ever have to see, but it's a job where my team and I can make a real difference. Where we can help people.'

'Will you go back to it?'

'If my father had still been alive, I would've been back with my team now,' he said. 'But at the moment my brother, my mother and my new sister need me.'

She could understand that—and she liked the fact that family was important to him.

'So can you take a sabbatical until things settle down, or will you have to leave the army?'

'I'm on special leave for now, but I'll do what it takes to support my family and my country.'

She wasn't entirely sure whether that meant he put his duty first or his family first. Or maybe they were one and the same for someone in a royal family. 'So you'd be happy to stay at the palace?'

He looked at her, as if weighing it up. 'This stays between you and me?'

'Of course,' she said. 'I have no intention of running to the media and gossiping.'

'I was thinking less of the media and more of my family,' he said dryly. 'But OK. Thank you. The palace I can handle. But the politics drives me insane.' He rolled his eyes. 'The senseless squabbles and point-scoring between people. I want to bang their heads together and tell them to stop behaving like pompous kindergarteners boasting "My dad's more important than yours" because there are so many more important problems in the world that need solving, and you solve things much more effectively if you work together as a team.'

She grinned. 'I guess you'd get into a lot of trouble if you did that.'

'Yes. I don't know how my brother copes with it.' He wrinkled his nose. 'Well, I do. He was brought up knowing that he'd serve our country. He's trained for the job.'

'What about your half-sister?' The woman who might end up being Queen.

'She didn't even know who she was until this year,' Antonio said. 'Her mother, Sophia, never told her about her heritage—and Sophia died when Gabriella was three, so Gabriella was brought up by her aunt and uncle. She ran a bookshop in Canada. She certainly wasn't brought up the way Luca and I were. And then she found a letter from her mother while she was clearing out. She contacted my mother to find out the truth of it—and obviously as she's older than Luca that would make her my father's heir. The DNA test will prove things beyond doubt.'

'Do you think she's your father's daughter?'

'Yes. I look at her and I can see my father,' Antonio said. 'A softer, warmer version.'

So his childhood hadn't been idyllic? If his father had been formal and cold, it would explain why Antonio suppressed his emotions. Why he didn't seem to believe in love.

'Is she nice?'

'I like her,' Antonio said. 'She's sensible. I think she's a lot like Luca.'

'It must be hard, suddenly discovering you're not who

you think you are,' Tia said. 'And having to do it in the public eye.'

'She's strong. She'll cope. Plus,' Antonio added, 'there is the palace library. Hundreds and hundreds of rare volumes. I think that will be her bolt-hole. A place where she'll be surrounded by books.'

Antonio's bolt-hole meant that he was surrounded by mountains. Was he trying to tell her something? Or was she reading too much into it?

He let her prepare the vegetables and the couscous while he sizzled the chicken and made the sauce for the stew, and soon the kitchen was filled with a delicious scent.

'I'll just go and see if Giacomo wants to eat with us,' Antonio said. 'I'll be back in a minute or two.'

Tia sat down and sipped a glass of water, reflecting on what she'd learned about Antonio. It sounded as if his childhood had been lonely; although his family was wealthy, it didn't seem as if he had the same close bond that she and Nathan had had with their parents before their father died. And because everything was so formal at the palace, it would explain why he'd seemed so reserved and emotionless there.

Maybe he wasn't really like that, inside. And hadn't he said something about the media making up a story when there was nothing to tell? Maybe he'd grown up not trusting himself to show any feelings, in case they were misreported and it made waves for his family.

Poor little rich boy.

If she'd had to choose between her own impoverished childhood filled with love and his wealthy childhood filled with rules and regulations, it would've been an easy choice. She'd pick love, all the way.

Could Antonio learn to love? Could he be a real father

to their baby and a partner to her? Could they actually make this work?

Or would it be kinder to all of them if she just disappeared quietly back to London?

Antonio came back into the kitchen. 'Giacomo says he's going to have something later, in his room.'

'Does that mean he's speaking from experience and he knows your cooking doesn't taste as good as it smells?' she asked.

Instead of looking slightly affronted, he surprised her by laughing. 'No. But he's probably going to taste this, pull a face and add a lot of garlic and chilli.'

And now she felt guilty. She'd been the one to ask him not to use garlic or spices. Antonio, too, would probably find the meal tasteless. She could put up with the indigestion. All she'd have to do was sit upright for most of the night and take frequent sips of water. 'Sorry. Please don't think about what I said. Add the garlic and chi—'

'It's fine, Tia,' he cut in. 'I'm happy to eat the same as you. Shall we eat in the dining room?'

'Could we eat here in the kitchen?' she asked. 'Otherwise the two of us are going to be a bit lost, sitting at a table big enough for twelve.'

'Sure.'

She laid the table while Antonio dished up. And he was surprised by how nice it felt, eating in the kitchen with her: how cosy and domestic. It was a world he'd never really experienced. It had never occurred to him before that this existed: this feeling of being settled, of belonging, of being close to someone.

Home.

He'd never yearned for domesticity before. He'd enjoyed travelling the world and the adrenalin rush of his job, knowing that he was making a difference. But settling down... Now he was beginning to see what it could be like. And he was shocked to discover how much he wanted this.

'This is good,' she said when she tasted the tagine.

'Not too garlicky or spicy?' he checked.

'It's perfect,' she said. 'Thank you for accommodating me.'

'My pleasure.' Though he was uneasy about behaving like polite strangers to each other when they'd been so much more than that. Her very obvious baby bump was proof of what they'd been to each other, for that one night. And, even though it made him antsy thinking about the way she'd made him feel, at the same time he wanted that closeness back. Here, in the one place he could remember having fun as a child and where he felt free of the restrictions of the palace, he wanted to keep her talking to him. Maybe starting with a neutral topic would help. 'So what do you think of Casavalle?'

'The village here and the mountains are beautiful. And your palace is a bit like a fairy-tale castle, all pure white stone and turrets,' she said.

He'd never really thought about it like that before. 'I suppose so.'

'And that Christmas tree in the palace foyer is amazing,' she said. 'It must've taken ages to decorate.'

'We have a team in charge of decorating the palace,' he said.

She smiled. 'I guess you can't have the King of Casavalle climbing up a ladder and reaching across the branches.'

'We use scaffolding for a tree of that height, actually, but you're right.' He looked at her, suddenly curious. She'd focused on the tree. Christmas for him was a time of duty, but had it been different for her? 'What were Christmases like when you were young?'

'We'd put the tree up as soon as Dad came home on leave, the week before Christmas,' she said. 'We'd go and choose one together, as a family—a real one that smelled lovely. And then Dad would put the lights on, and Mum would get out the box of decorations and we'd all take turns in putting an ornament on the tree. Each year Nathan and I would choose a new one in the shop, and we'd have one each that we'd made at nursery or school.' She smiled. 'Yogurt pots we'd painted and covered in glitter and decorated with a tinsel loop so they looked like a bell, or a star we'd cut out and glued pasta on and spray-painted gold, and an angel made out of a cardboard tube, a ping-pong ball, scraps of fabric and wool. Mum kept every single one of the ones we made; even though they're too worn to go on the tree nowadays, she can't bear to throw them away.'

A small family Christmas, with decorations on the tree that had meaning and had been made with love, rather than being bought *en masse* from a retailer, or priceless baubles that had been part of the family for decades but were never allowed to be played with. So very different from his own. What would it have been like to grow up in a warm, close family like that?

'And every year on Christmas Eve we'd hang our stockings at the foot of the bed. Mum made them herself—she's amazing with a needle—and she embroidered our names and stars on them with silver thread so they sparkled. We'd set out a glass of milk and a chocolate biscuit for Father Christmas, and a carrot for his reindeer; and every year we'd come down to find an empty glass, a plate with just crumbs on it, and a half-eaten carrot.'

His family had never had traditions like that. He

couldn't even remember when he'd stopped believing in Father Christmas.

'When we were little, our stockings would be filled with sweets and a couple of tangerines, a colouring book and crayons, maybe a toy car for Nathan and a bottle of bubbles with a wand for me.' She smiled. 'Even after Dad died and money was a bit tight, Mum would still fill a stocking for us. She used to buy a little something every couple of weeks and she'd hide the gifts away in a box at the top of her wardrobe so we wouldn't find them. On Christmas Eve, we'd go to midnight mass with Mum in the church round the corner and sing carols, then come home to have hot chocolate and marshmallows before going to bed.

'Even when we stopped believing in Father Christmas, we still put our stockings out. Nathan and I used to make a stocking for Mum, too. We'd save our pocket money and buy her nice bath stuff from the market and make her photo frames, that sort of thing. She cried the first year we did it, and we were so worried we'd upset her, but she told us how special the stocking was and how much she loved us.'

Love. A word that was never really used in the palace. Their father had always been distant, even here; although their mother was warmer, Queen Maria was very practical and didn't tend to talk about emotional things. And, although Antonio loved his brother and looked up to him, he wasn't sure he'd ever actually told Luca he loved him, and Luca certainly hadn't said it to him. They just didn't do that sort of thing.

And now he was beginning to wonder if he'd missed out. If his childhood had been so structured and full of regulations that there hadn't been room for love. Grace Phillips had clearly done her best to give her children as much of their dreams as she could afford, but the main thing had been that those gifts, however much she'd spent, had been chosen with love.

'What about Christmas with you? Do you have traditions?' Tia asked.

'You've seen the tree in the foyer. That's one of our traditions,' he said. 'Each of the decorations is a special one designed for us by Buschetta—that's a family of jewellers in Casavalle, a bit like Fabergé. The tradition has been going on for more than a century, and there's a secret compartment in each one. Every year, there's a special ceremony to unveil that year's ornament.'

It was about as close as he could get to the special decorations chosen by Tia and her brother each year. Just on a different scale.

'We have Mass in the palace cathedral, and the day after Christmas we open the palace to all the citizens. There's a buffet, with mulled wine and hot chocolate; the palace kitchens bake for days beforehand. Then Luca and I stand at the palace doors with our parents and greet everyone.' Except this year would be different. The first one without his father. The first year with the new King— or Queen. He pushed the thoughts aside. 'There are ice sculptures in the fountain area, and the hedge maze is all lit up for the children to explore. We make sure we give our people a magnificent, beautiful Christmas.'

'I get that you need to do something for your people—like the Queen of England at Sandringham, going to church with her family on Christmas morning and greeting everyone who's queued up outside to see them,' she said. 'But I didn't mean the public stuff. I meant your *private* family Christmas. What about traditions for you? Did you have stockings or anything like that?'

No, they hadn't. Not in the way she meant. 'As royal

children,' he said, 'Luca and I had masses of gifts from other royal families and from around the world. To the point where we needed people to help us open them and we didn't always know what people had bought us.'

She frowned. 'You didn't have special things just for you, Luca, your mum and your dad? Not a special story they always read to you, or a film you always watched together?'

'No.'

'That,' she said softly, 'is a shame. Because Christmas isn't about the gifts. It's about love. It's about spending time with your family. Playing games—we'd play everything from snap to charades to snakes and ladders, and I think the best year ever was the year Nathan bought me this game with kazoos where we had to play whatever song was on the card we picked up. We were all terrible at it, Mum and Dad and Nathan and me, and we laughed so much our sides hurt.'

That was something he'd definitely never done with his family. It was more like the sort of thing he'd done with his army friends. 'That sounds like fun,' he said carefully.

'It was. And I'm sorry you didn't get to share something like that with your family.'

'We had our duties to perform,' he said. Though, now she'd said it, he was sorry, too. He wished he'd been able to share that sort of fun with his parents and his brother.

Would it be different for his baby? If he could persuade Tia to marry him, would she change things at the palace? Would she institute new, more personal, traditions? Would *he* change, too?

The ground felt as if it was shifting under him.

'So did you always want to be in the army?' she asked.

'I'm the younger son, so there weren't quite the same expectations for me as there were for Luca. I had a lot more freedom. And I liked the idea of travelling the world, of being able to make a positive difference for people.'

'Like Nathan,' she said. 'Like our dad.'

'What about you?' he asked.

'I'm fine as I am.'

'No, I mean, what were your dreams when you were young?' He already knew the answer, but he wanted to hear it from her.

'I didn't want to join the army, but I did want to travel,' she said. 'I would've liked to be a primary school teacher, but my grades at school weren't good enough.'

Nathan had always talked about his sister being bright, and Antonio had seen that for himself when he talked to her. He guessed that, as her mother's carer, she'd been too busy to concentrate on her studies at school. 'You could,' he said carefully, 'train as a teacher now. Be a mature student.'

She shook her head. 'Mum suggested that, but I don't want to leave her. And I'm happy as I am. I like my job. My bosses are lovely, and we have regular customers who tell us all kinds of stories of London in the past.'

He had the strongest feeling that Tia was the sort who'd manage to find happiness in any situation: she was one of those incredibly positive people. And she was also incredibly proud and independent. He needed to back off before he upset her. 'OK.'

Once they'd finished dinner, Tia insisted on helping him to wash up, and then they headed back to the conservatory to watch the stars. Rather than switching on the overhead light, guessing that she'd prefer something softer, Antonio lit the scented pillar candles in their wrought iron and glass lanterns.

'This smells like Christmas,' she said. 'Cinnamon and cloves and orange.'

'I'm glad you like it,' he said. 'Would you like some music?'

'That'd be nice.'

'What do you like?' He knew so little about her.

'Anything.'

'You don't have to be polite,' he said. 'What do you really like listening to? Pop? Classical?'

'This time of year,' she said, 'I really like Christmas music—carols as well as all the old pop songs.'

It didn't take him long to find a medley of Christmas music on a streaming service.

'This is lovely,' she said with a smile. 'All that's missing is the Christmas tree.'

He remembered how her face had lit up when she'd talked to him about the Christmases of her childhood, with her family. Maybe this was a way of getting closer to her. Although he could simply buy everything and have it all shipped in while he took her out for the day tomorrow, he had a feeling that she'd find that much too impersonal—hadn't she said that Christmas for her was all about love and spending time with your family? She'd talked about decorating the tree *together*. So maybe that was what they should do.

'We could have a tree, if you'd like one,' he said. 'Perhaps we can choose one together tomorrow.' He looked at her. 'And maybe we can choose a special decoration for our baby. Together.'

'We're not going to be together, though,' she said softly. 'We come from different worlds.'

'But the baby's part of both of us,' he pointed out. 'The baby's where our worlds combine.'

'I guess,' she said, and there was a hint of sadness in her face.

He wanted to make her feel better. And the only way

he could think of was to go and sit beside her on the sofa, and hold both her hands in his. 'It's all going to be OK,' he said.

'I know. I just wish…' She blew out a breath. 'Nathan would've made such a good uncle. Such a good dad. I wish he'd had the chance. But he never talked about anyone special. I'm guessing it was because he felt responsible for Mum and me so he didn't let himself get close to anyone.'

Antonio thought that was a shrewd assessment. But it was only part of the truth. 'He loved you both,' Antonio told her. 'He didn't see either of you as a burden. He was so proud of you.'

'I was proud of him. So was Mum. And I wish Dad could've seen him grow up past the age of thirteen—and me past the age of ten.' She looked at him. 'I'm sorry. This must be hard for you, too, right now. Your first Christmas without your father.'

He nodded. 'It's…a little strange.'

Her fingers tightened around his, giving him comfort. 'The firsts are hard. Your first birthday without him, his birthday, Christmas, the first anniversary of his death. But he's still in your heart. Always. That never changes.'

But Antonio's relationship with his family was very different from hers. Duty came before everything else. And, like the rest of his family, he didn't allow himself to think about feelings.

Right now, here in the cosy warmth of the room, with Christmas music playing in the background, the view of the mountains lit by moonlight, and the soft glow of the candles illuminating her face, he felt different. As if something was unfurling inside him and spreading through him, something that made him feel warm and mushy and very mixed-up, all at the same time. And he didn't know how to tell her how he felt, just in case he was making a fool of himself and she didn't feel the same. After all, this was the woman who'd refused to marry him—even though she was pregnant with his child. Instead, he said, 'Will you dance with me?'

She blinked. 'Dance with you? I…'

Of course she didn't want that. He was expecting way too much from her. 'Sorry. I shouldn't have asked.' He let her hands go.

'It's not that. Just…' She looked wistful. 'Dancing isn't really something I've done very much.'

No, because when she wasn't working she was looking after her mum. She probably wouldn't have gone out to discos at school, or nightclubs, or the kind of glitzy social events he went to. But if her not knowing how to dance was the only barrier between them, he could fix that. Right here, right now. The words spilled out before he could stop them. 'I can teach you.'

'Teach me?'

And suddenly it was as if there was a kind of electricity in the air. Something that made it hard to breathe.

Would she let him closer? Or would she make an excuse and back away?

Waiting for her answer made time seem to slow down; every second felt ten times as long as usual, as if he was watching a film in slow motion.

But then she nodded. 'OK.'

He drew her to her feet. In bare feet, she was more than six inches shorter than he was, and it made him feel even more protective of her.

'OK. Follow my lead.'

Michael Bublé crooned 'Have Yourself a Merry Little Christmas' as Antonio swayed with Tia in the candlelight. And he rested his cheek against her hair, feeling the softness against his skin and breathing in her light floral scent.

* * *

With Antonio's arms wrapped protectively round her, Tia felt safer than she'd felt for a long, long time. It was amazing to be dancing in his arms by candlelight, to the kind of Christmas music she loved most. It felt as if the room was lit by a thousand stars, and she'd always thought herself a bit clumsy, but right now she was dancing effortlessly in his arms, not putting a foot wrong because he was guiding her.

Just for a moment, she could let herself believe this was real. That he was holding her, not because he was being polite and doing his duty but because he really wanted her—her and their baby. That he *cared*.

But then the music changed and a choir began to sing 'Silent Night'.

Her mother's favourite.

Homesickness washed over her. She missed her mum; she worried about Grace constantly. And Antonio had hit the nail very firmly on the head earlier. Just how was she going to cope with working part time, looking after their baby and looking after her mum? Right at that moment the future felt filled with anxiety.

As if Antonio sensed her tension, he pulled back. 'Everything's going to be OK, Tia,' he said softly.

It was, oh, so easy to say; and much less easy to be sure that it was true. 'Uh-huh,' she said, not wanting him to think she was feeble and weak, or that she wanted to give up and let him sort everything out for her. Because that wasn't who she was. She managed. She always had.

'You've had a very long day and you've done a lot of travelling,' he said. 'Let me run you a bath and make you some hot chocolate.'

Tia was perfectly capable of running her own bath.

But, at the same time, she was bone-deep tired. And

he was right: she'd had a long day and a lot of travelling. She'd been on three planes, two cars and a train. And she was six months pregnant. She had more than herself to think about: there was the baby, too. Just this once, maybe it wouldn't hurt to let him look after her. Right now she was his guest, and you looked after your guests, didn't you? 'Thank you. That'd be really kind.' She gave him a grateful smile.

Antonio was almost surprised that she'd given in so easily. Then again, she was six months pregnant and it had been a long day. He wasn't going to make a big deal about this, and then hopefully it would soften her stance and she would let him do more to help.

Though he had no idea what kind of form that help could take. Tia Phillips was independent to a fault.

Again and again, the only thing he could come back to was that they should get married. She was expecting his baby. A baby who was fourth in line to the throne of Casavalle. It was the honourable thing to do. The right solution. He could look after her, look after the baby, and look after her mother.

Though she'd made it clear that she'd only get married for love.

Did he love her?

They hardly knew each other. He wasn't even sure that he believed in love, let alone love at first sight; how did you even know how love felt? How did you know someone was 'the one'? How did you know it would last?

As a prince, he couldn't afford to risk a relationship that might go wrong and make things awkward for his family. Duty always came first.

And yet... There was something about Tia that drew him. He liked her. He enjoyed her company. He was definitely attracted to her. So that was a start. Somehow, over the next three days, he needed to make her happy and show her that this could work out. That they could have a proper partnership. Work as a team. Learn to love each other, if that was what she wanted.

Once she was back downstairs, clad in pyjamas and with her hair wrapped in a towel, he settled her on the sofa in the living room with a mug of hot milk and a fleecy blanket. 'It must've been hard for you growing up, losing your dad and with your mum ill.'

'We managed,' Tia said. 'Mum took in sewing and mending and she worked from home, so she could rest when she needed to.'

And he'd just bet that Tia had picked up the slack. Now he thought about it, Nathan had been good with a needle, too. No doubt he'd also helped with their mother's work.

'Nathan got a job at the corner shop working weekends, and I had a paper round,' Tia explained. 'I took over at the shop when he joined the army. The manager was brilliant—she knew the situation with Mum, so she'd let me nip home to check on Mum if she was having a bad day. Between us, Nathan and I sorted the housework when Mum couldn't do it.'

Meaning that Tia had had to do it all on her own after her brother joined the army. It was so far away from Antonio's own life of privilege, and he really admired Tia's strength. And Nathan's, too; although his friend had never confided much about his past, he'd had amazing strength of character.

'It must've been tough, though. What about school?'

She shrugged. 'I got by.'

But not, he thought, with the kind of grades her brother thought she was capable of. Even if you were bright, if you were caring for someone else you simply wouldn't have time to keep up with your schoolwork and your grades would suffer. He could see how Tia's dreams of travelling and becoming a primary school teacher just hadn't been possible.

'Don't judge my mum,' she said softly. 'If the authorities had known how ill Mum was and how much help we needed to give her, they might've taken us away from her and put us in care—and they probably would have made Nathan and me live with different families. That happened to someone in my class and I was terrified that it would happen to me. I didn't want to be taken away from Mum and Nathan, and he didn't want to leave Mum and me, either. So we just got on with things and made sure the teachers and everyone didn't really know how ill Mum was. It was fine, because we had each other and we were together.'

This was so much worse than Antonio had realised, and his heart ached for Nathan and his equally brave little sister. 'You didn't have any family who could help? Any grandparents?'

'Mum was an only child, and her parents died before I was born,' Tia said. 'And Dad's family didn't like my mum. There was a big row when they first got together, and they never made it up. Nathan wrote to them after Dad died, but they never replied. But it's OK.' She spread her hands and smiled. 'You don't miss what you've never had. And my mum's brilliant. Even when she's having a really bad day, she never complains. She's the kindest, most loving mum anyone could ask for and I'm really grateful I have her.'

Guilt flooded through him. 'I'm sorry I haven't been there to support you both since Nathan died.'

'*Support* us? Mum and I don't need your money, Your Royal Highness,' she said crisply. 'We're not a charity case.'

He looked at her, horrified to realise she thought that

he'd meant money. 'Of course you're not, and I wouldn't insult you by treating you that way.' He knew she was proud. Offering her money would be the quickest way to put a barrier up between them.

'I'm sorry,' she said, and bit her lip. 'I shouldn't have snapped at you. Just… I guess I've learned that rich people tend to think about everything in terms of money.'

'And, as a prince, I'm from a very wealthy background, so it figures you'd think I'd be even more that way,' he said grimly. 'Though I didn't mean money. I meant I should've come back and given you some emotional support—you *and* your mother. And instead I disappeared and just left you to it.'

'You told me you weren't at Nathan's funeral because you had to go on another mission, and then your dad died so you had responsibilities in your own family. Of course you didn't have time to come and support us. And I apologise. I didn't mean to insult you just now by implying…' She grimaced. 'I suppose it sounded as if I thought that you were trying to buy my silence.'

'But you must've felt that I'd abandoned you when I didn't come back and see you.'

'Not so much me—I was angry with you for my mum's sake,' Tia admitted. 'I thought it wouldn't have been that much of a sacrifice for you just to spend a few minutes with her, sharing your memories of my brother. Or send her a photograph or a personal note or something. Just so she knew he mattered.'

'He did matter. He mattered a lot.' Antonio raked a hand through his hair. 'And you're right, I should have made the time to do that. I handled it badly when I came to see you. I'm sorry I got it so wrong.'

'And I'm sorry for going off at the deep end,' she said, and the sweetness in her smile ripped his heart in two.

'I think,' he said, 'we could both do with an early night. In separate rooms,' he added hastily. 'There are no strings to you staying here.'

'I'm a bit tired,' she admitted.

'We'll talk again in the morning,' he said. And, just so she'd know he didn't make promises lightly, he added, 'And then we can go and get that tree.'

'OK,' she said.

He took her empty mug from her and washed up before heading to bed, but he lay awake for a long time before he finally fell asleep.

Would Tia trust him enough to let her support him?

And, if not, how could he teach her to trust him?

He really needed to think things through properly before tomorrow. He couldn't afford to get this wrong.

CHAPTER FOUR

THE NEXT MORNING, when Tia woke, she felt slightly disoriented. It was strange not to hear the low hum of traffic that she was used to, and even stranger to be lying in a wide bed instead of her narrow single bed. She glanced at her watch, and realised it was a quarter past seven; normally she'd have been up for nearly an hour, getting ready to help her mum and then go to work.

Then again, London was an hour behind Casavalle, so this was pretty much the normal time for her to wake and she wasn't late. Though maybe, given the time zone difference, it was a little too early to ring her mother in London and see how she was.

Tia climbed out of bed and looked out of the window. The sky was streaked with pink and gold. As she watched, the snow on the mountains gradually turned pink. So pretty, and such a lovely way to start the day.

But this wasn't how her life was going to be, so she wasn't going to let herself get used to it.

She showered swiftly and dressed in one of the silky long-sleeved tops and the maternity trousers Antonio's housekeeper had bought for her. The fabric was so soft against her skin and felt so nice.

Tears pricked at her eyelids, and she grew cross with

herself. It was utterly ridiculous, starting to cry over a complete stranger being so kind to her.

'Get a grip,' she told herself. 'You're here for three days and you need to sort out a compromise with the Prince.'

There was no sound in the house, so she crept quietly down the stairs and into the kitchen to make herself a mug of tea. She thought about making a mug of tea for Antonio, but that would mean taking the mug into his room and she felt too shy to do that. How ridiculous that was, given that she was carrying his baby; but he was almost a complete stranger. They were worlds apart. She was a waitress, living in a tiny flat in a very ordinary part of London, and he was a prince who lived in an enormous fairy-tale palace in the middle of the Mediterranean. He wouldn't fit into her life and she wouldn't fit into his.

The problem was she'd felt so close to him last night, when she'd told him about Christmases in the past with her family. It was her favourite time of year—not because of the gifts but because it was a chance to spend time with those you loved, enjoying their company and having fun together.

It sounded as if fun hadn't been part of Antonio's Christmases, growing up. Everything had been so formal and stuffy. All the priceless and historic ornaments on the tree that couldn't be played with in case they were accidentally broken: things that had to be admired from afar. Receiving gifts from people he might never even have met, and gifts he probably didn't get a chance to play with. Standing to greet the citizens and doing his royal duties instead of playing games with his family.

His family.

How could they ever accept someone like her? Someone who didn't have blue blood; someone who didn't have the first clue about protocol and royal etiquette.

So she needed to keep a lid on the attraction she felt towards Antonio Valenti. She needed to ignore the impulse to wrap her arms round him and hold him close when she thought about how lonely his childhood must have been, because this really wasn't her place.

She'd promised him a couple of days to talk things over. She'd keep her promise. And then she'd depart quietly for London and leave all this behind her.

With her hands wrapped round the mug of tea, she walked into the conservatory and curled up in one of the big armchairs, enjoying the beautiful view. At least this was a memory she could share with her baby in years to come.

If only she could share it with Antonio, too.

But he didn't love her, and she wasn't prepared to commit to a life with him without love—for her or for her baby.

She'd promised him three days. Antonio really hoped that would be enough to talk her round to his point of view.

He decided to start by bringing Tia a cup of tea in bed, and then possibly bring her a breakfast tray. Then they'd go into the village and find a Christmas tree together, and choose some ornaments. They'd spend the afternoon decorating the tree. And he could drop hints that this was something they could do with their baby. They could follow her family traditions and there would be a new one from a shop every year, and a home-made one.

It was almost the total opposite of the Buschetta ornament tradition that he was used to. But if Tia wanted things handmade and personal, that was exactly what he'd give her. And, even though he couldn't ever remember sitting down with glitter and glue, he was quite prepared to do that. He'd do whatever it took to make her happy and believe in him. Because maybe, just maybe, Tia and the baby were going to change his life. Fill in the gaps. Just as he could fill in the gaps of her life. He'd thought that these three days were to persuade her, but his feelings towards her had already started to change. She wasn't just the unexpected mother of his baby, the woman he had a duty towards; he was starting to really enjoy the time he spent with her.

He showered and changed into a pair of black jeans and a cashmere sweater, then headed down to the kitchen.

Except, when he went to fill the kettle, he realised that it was still hot.

So did that mean Tia was already up and about? She'd liked the view from the conservatory yesterday, he remembered, so he went in search of her. And there she was, curled up in a chair, sipping tea and looking out at the mountains.

'Good morning,' he said.

And how weird it was that his pulse had leaped at the sight of her. She looked so cute sitting there in a half-dream, with her dark curls caught back at the nape of her neck. She didn't need make-up to emphasise those beautiful brown eyes, either.

This was more than attraction. Antonio kept circling round to the L-word in his head, but love wasn't something that he believed in or could even define. In royal circles, you didn't marry for love; you married for duty and for dynastic reasons. His father had made that mistake in his first marriage, falling in love with someone who couldn't cope with the Royal life that came with him.

Being with Tia, marrying her, was really going to put the cat among the pigeons, politically.

Or maybe this would take his life in a new direction. A better direction. Because being with her made him feel that there could be something more than duty and work in his life. Something he hadn't expected or looked for, but now he'd had a glimpse of it he wanted more. And he definitely wanted that for their baby.

'Good morning,' she said, smiling back at him. 'I hope it was OK for me to make myself some tea.'

'Of course. Please treat the house as your home,' he said.

'I was going to make you a mug, too, but I wasn't sure if you'd be awake yet.'

There was a shyness in her smile that really drew him.

And then he noticed the bump moving; he could see her silky top shimmering in the light. 'Is that…?' he asked.

'The baby kicking? Yes.' She looked at him, then held her hand out. 'Here. Feel it for yourself.'

He let her take his hand and rest it on the bump.

This felt oddly intimate. Strange. He could hardly breathe.

'Say hello to the baby,' she said.

'Hello, baby,' he whispered.

Immediately, there was a strong kick against his hand, as if the baby was saying hello back, and it blew him away. He really hadn't expected to feel that sudden rush of wonder.

'Our baby just kicked me!' He dragged in a breath. Now it felt real.

Of course it was real.

For pity's sake, anyone who looked at Tia could see that she was six months pregnant.

But for the first time Antonio felt as if he'd actually connected with the baby. A baby he hadn't expected, hadn't ever dreamed about—and now he discovered that he really, really wanted this baby. It was a sudden, unexpected, visceral longing, stronger than anything he'd known before.

And it made him look at Tia differently, too. She was the mother of his child. And although he'd been telling himself that they barely knew each other so they couldn't possibly feel anything for each other, now he realised that he'd been totally in denial. Because he did feel things for her. More than just physical attraction. This went deeper. He didn't have the words for it and it scared the hell out of him because he'd never felt anything like this before. All he knew was that he wanted her. Her and the baby.

That kick just now made him even more determined that this would work out.

'Can the baby hear me talking?' he asked.

She nodded. 'He likes being talked to. He really likes it when Mum sings to him.'

Singing to an unborn baby. He'd never thought of doing something like that. 'What, like a lullaby or something?'

She smiled. 'Pop songs. The Beatles, Take That, the Beach Boys. And we watched *Love Actually* again last weekend—Mum and I watch it every Christmas. He kicked like mad to "Catch a Falling Star" and "All I Want for Christmas is You".' She grinned. 'Probably because Mum and I were singing along, too.'

Singing to a baby.

He had so much to learn.

Would she have the patience to teach him?

'Does he—she—our baby,' he amended, 'kick at certain times?'

'He's usually quite lively first thing in the morning,' she said. 'And he's taken to doing somersaults at two in the morning. Mum says that's probably when he's going to wake up, wanting milk.'

'Our baby,' Antonio whispered.

* * *

Antonio's face was full of wonder. And was that a catch in his voice, a shimmer of tears in his eyes as he connected with their child?

For a moment, Tia was filled with hope.

Maybe he'd been right to bring her here. Maybe spending time together would help make the future clearer. Talking about their dreams, their hopes, what they wanted for the baby. Getting to know each other properly—their real selves—would help them find a way forward. Not in the daily grind of London, not in the unreal glamour of the palace, but here in the mountains—the place he'd loved since he was a child and came back to when he needed a breathing space. Here, where Antonio could be himself instead of being what he thought the world expected a prince to be.

'I never expected...' For a moment, his hand curved protectively over the bump. And then he grimaced and pulled his hand away. 'I apologise. That was intrusive of me.'

He was worried about touching her? Considering that they'd made a baby together... On the other hand, he'd been brought up with the strictest of protocols, and his job meant following rules and regulations, too. 'Most people like feeling a baby kick,' she said. 'Perfect strangers come up to me sometimes and ask if they can feel the baby kick.'

He looked surprised, as if it was something that had never occurred to him before.

'And this is your baby,' she added softly. 'It's absolutely fine for you to put your hand on my bump and feel him kick whenever you want to.'

He still didn't look comfortable with the idea. What would it take to make him unbend completely? she wondered.

'Can I get you some breakfast?' he asked.

'Toast would be lovely. Or fruit and yogurt. Whatever you have.'

'I'll call you when breakfast is ready,' he promised.

The toast was perfect, and there was a choice of local honey and jam.

'Would you like to go and choose a tree this morning?' he asked.

She wrinkled her nose at him. 'It seems a little bit extravagant, buying a tree for just a couple of days.'

'I'd like to give you a sort of Christmas in Casavalle,' he said.

Start some memories that they could share with the baby one day? Tia didn't say it out loud, in case she was wrong. But that moment when Antonio had first felt their baby kick, when his eyes had been full of joy and wonder, gave her hope that maybe he could break through the constriction of his upbringing. And if he could unbend, if he really was the man she was beginning to get to know, then maybe they really did have a future together. Maybe they really could be a team and have the kind of relationship her parents had had: the one thing she'd longed for so much but had thought would never happen. And the hope burned, so clear and so bright, in her heart.

'All right,' she said. 'Let's buy a tree. As long as it's a small one.'

Decorating the streets for Christmas seemed to be in full swing when they walked into the village together. There were nativity scenes in every shop window, each slightly different; there was a Christmas tree made out of wine bottles in the wine shop, a nativity scene with a backdrop of beautiful silk scarves in a boutique, another made from spun sugar in a confectionery store, and another made entirely from teddy bears in the toy shop.

'This is all amazing,' she said. 'So creative.'

'The shop windows are incredible,' he agreed. 'Displaying the nativity scene in shop windows has been a tradition here for many years, like it is in mainland Italy.'

Once they'd finished enjoying the displays, he said, 'Let's go and choose our tree. What would you like?'

Thinking of the scarily large tree at the palace, she said, 'Nothing taller than you.'

He grinned and pointed out the massive tree that had just been put up in the central square. 'Not like that, then? Because that might just fit.'

For a moment, remembering the double-height hallway in his house, she wondered if he was serious; then the glint in his eyes made her realise that he was teasing her. Something she hadn't expected, and which reinforced her hope for the future.

Not to mention how cute he was. That little quirk at the corner of his mouth. It made her want to stand on tiptoe, wrap her arms round his neck and steal a kiss.

What would he do if she did that?

Would it be too much, too soon? Would he push her away? Or would he wrap his arms tightly round her and kiss her all the way back?

She didn't dare take the risk. Not until she had a better idea of what he was thinking.

Instead, she kept the conversation light. Decorating was a safe subject. And she wasn't going to mention mistletoe.

'I'd prefer a little tree,' she said with a smile. 'Do you normally decorate the house here?'

'No,' he admitted. 'We're expected to be at the palace from the middle of November. It seems a bit pointless to decorate the house without anyone being here to enjoy it.'

'So do you actually have any decorations for the tree?'

'No. I thought maybe we could choose them together.'

Start a new tradition together, perhaps? But she suppressed the hope before it could take hold.

They headed for the pop-up Christmas stalls in the market place, and finally found the tree with the perfect shape and the perfect height. Antonio paid for it and arranged to have it delivered to the house later that morning.

The baby seemed to be kicking more at the sound of Antonio's voice. Recognising his father, perhaps?

At another of the stalls, Tia was really taken with a fir wreath that had seed pods of honesty sprayed with copper paint threaded through it. 'That's so pretty,' she said. 'I must remember to suggest that to Mum. She always makes the wreath for our front door. Maybe I can ask if they'd mind me taking a photograph.'

'I have a better solution. Would you like this one for the house?' he asked.

'I...' She looked at him. 'Would that be all right?'

'If it makes you happy, it makes me happy,' he said softly. 'And by buying here in the Christmas market I'm supporting the local economy, which is a good thing.'

So everybody won. 'Thank you. That would be really lovely,' she said.

Once they'd finished strolling around the stalls, Antonio steered her into a café. 'Until you've tried the hot chocolate here,' he said, 'you haven't tasted perfection.'

The hot chocolate was thick and rich, yet less sweet than the sort she'd drink back in England, and it was teamed perfectly with a slice of white chocolate and lemon *panettone*.

'Sorry, I'm afraid I need the ladies',' she said when she'd finished her hot chocolate.

'I've been reading up,' Antonio said. 'I gather it's a pregnant woman thing, especially in the third trimester.'

She nodded ruefully. 'I'm afraid so.'

On her way to the toilets, she saw a notice about the village children's Christmas party in the town hall. She didn't think anything of it until she was washing her hands and two women came in, both looking anxious and speaking in rapid Italian.

'I can't believe Mario went skiing yesterday and managed to break his leg. Whatever was my brother thinking? He was supposed to dress up as Father Christmas tomorrow afternoon for the children's party. He can't possibly do it now, not with his leg in plaster,' one of them said.

'Of course not. Poor man.'

'Oh, I don't pity him too much. He knew we were relying on him, but he had to go and show off on the slopes.' The first woman rolled her eyes. 'But now we have to find another Father Christmas, and everyone I've asked has a prior commitment they can't break.'

'We can't let the children down,' the second woman said.

'I'll keep going through my phone book, but I'm beginning to think we need some kind of Christmas miracle to find a new *Babbo Natale*,' the first woman said.

Or maybe they just needed an incognito prince, Tia thought. Antonio didn't have any prior commitments tomorrow at the palace; he'd arranged to spend a couple of days here with her, and she was perfectly happy for him to spend some of that time playing Father Christmas for the children. She almost opened her mouth and suggested it, but a kick from the baby stayed her.

Perhaps she really ought to check with Antonio first before she offered his services as *Babbo Natale*. Would he even be allowed to do something like that? And, if he was allowed to, would he want to, or was she expecting too much of him?

She looked at the poster again on her way back to the table, and took a photograph of it on her phone. If she could persuade Antonio into the Christmas spirit this afternoon, when they decorated his Christmas tree, then maybe he would agree to help save the children's Christmas party and arrange it with his security team.

Antonio had just had the perfect idea for the next stage of persuading Tia to give them a chance. What went with a Christmas tree better than a Christmas dinner?

A full-blown traditional Italian Christmas Eve dinner might be a little rich for a pregnant woman, he thought. But maybe he could cook her a traditional English dinner, the sort she'd shared with her family when she was young. The sort Nathan had told him about, with crispy roast potatoes, Brussels sprouts, sausages wrapped in bacon and, most of all, a huge roasted turkey.

And, with a little help, he could make this a nice surprise for her. He knew he could look up what he needed to know, but there was a quicker way to deal with this—and he needed to get this organised right now, before Tia came back to their table.

He grabbed his phone from his pocket and called Gina, the housekeeper who looked after the place when they weren't there.

'Good morning, Prince Antonio,' she answered. 'How are you?'

'I'm fine, thank you, Gina. And how are you?' he said politely.

'*Bene, grazie,*' she said, and he could hear the smile in her voice. 'Is there something you need me to do for you?'

'I was wondering… How long does it take to cook a traditional English roast turkey?'

'A turkey? It depends on the size.'

'For Christmas dinner, I was thinking a big one.'

'A six-kilogram turkey would take just under four hours to cook, plus half an hour to rest,' Gina mused.

He glanced at his watch. 'That would be perfect. Would you be able to source one for me and get it delivered to the house, please?'

'Of course, Prince Antonio.'

'And I need a few other things, too, please.' He rattled off the things he remembered Nathan talking about. 'And finally a Christmas pudding.'

'An English one?'

'An English one,' he confirmed.

'Now, that,' Gina said, 'will be a problem. A home-made one has to be made at least a month in advance so it can mature. And none of the shops in Picco Innevato is likely to stock an English Christmas pudding. Your best option for that, perhaps, is to have one flown in—either from Rome or from London.'

Which would be expensive. Money wasn't a problem for him but he knew it was a problem for Tia. Antonio was pretty sure she would react badly if he spent so much money on something as frivolous and extravagant as having a Christmas pudding flown in from London. And what if she didn't actually like Christmas pudding? 'What could I make as an alternative?'

'Perhaps a jelly, something that you can serve with fresh fruit and biscuits,' Gina said. 'Or perhaps some traditional Italian Christmas doughnuts.' She paused. 'Prince Antonio, I know I'm stepping outside the boundaries, but may I ask *why* you want to cook an English Christmas dinner?'

'I want to do something nice for my best friend's sister,' Antonio said. 'And I'd like to surprise her with it this evening.'

'Then why not make the meal a mixture of English and Casavallian traditions?' Gina suggested. 'So then you can have ravioli or gnocchi for a starter, the turkey and all the traditional English trimmings for the main, and then an Italian pudding and cheeses to finish?'

'That's a really good idea,' Antonio said. 'Thank you.'

'Your best friend's sister. Hmm. Would this be the same lady I bought the maternity clothes for?' Gina asked.

'Yes, and she loved them. Thank you again for your help,' Antonio said.

'It was my pleasure. And I will organise your turkey,' Gina said. 'Since you want to surprise her, you need to keep away from the house for long enough for me to get everything bought and delivered. Give me, say, two hours. Shall I prepare and cook everything for you?'

That would be the easy way out. He rather thought he needed to make the effort himself, if he was to impress Tia. 'Thank you, but I want to cook it myself. I'd appreciate a note about the turkey, though. I can handle everything else.' Or he could look it up online.

'*Bene.* I will arrange everything, and I will text you when I'm done,' Gina said.

'Thank you, Gina. I really appreciate your help,' he said.

He could see Tia walking back to their table, so he ended the call swiftly and pretended he'd simply been looking at something on his phone.

'Is everything all right?' he asked.

'Yes, thank you.'

Now all he had to do was to keep her away from the house for a couple of hours.

'Shall we go and look for decorations?' he asked.

'Of course. Do you want a particular colour scheme?'

Like the ones in the palace? He had a feeling that she'd

like something a lot more informal. 'This will be my first Christmas tree all of my own,' he said. 'So I'm happy to hear your suggestions.'

'Let's see what they have in the shops and what you like,' she suggested.

'What do you need for a tree?' he asked.

'Lights, maybe tinsel, something for the top of the tree and some ornaments,' she said promptly.

Lights turned out to be incredibly complicated.

'First of all, do you want white lights or coloured ones?' she asked when they were in the middle of one of the shops.

'Do you have a preference?' he asked.

'I like white ones,' she admitted. 'So they look like the stars.'

'Then we'll have white ones.'

But then it was about choosing string lights or LED lights; warm white or ice white; and did they want lights that twinkled, or glowed, or flashed, or moved in a pattern, or came with sound effects?

He didn't actually care, but he did need Tia out of the house so Gina could organise the ingredients for his surprise Christmas dinner, so he pretended to be much more interested in all the different functions than he really was. Ordering Tia about simply wouldn't work. He knew from his army days that if your team felt they had a stake in things and you were listening to them, they'd go above and beyond the call of duty for you.

They'd do this together. The personal way. So Tia would be sure he'd listened to her and wanted to work with her instead of imposing his Royal will. He'd prove to her that they were a good team. And then perhaps she would agree to marry him and the baby would have his protection.

Once they'd chosen the lights, they wandered into the

decorations department. Antonio paid close attention to the things she passed over and the things she seemed to like. In the end she chose silver and blue baubles, fili-gree silver stars, blue tinsel and a large silver star for the top of the tree.

She paused by the stand of glass baubles; there was a special one etched with a picture of the mountain and the words '*Picco Innevato 2019*'.

Hadn't she said that she, her parents and Nathan had chosen a new, special decoration together each year?

He was fairly sure from her expression that she really liked the glass bauble. He was also fairly sure that she thought it was way too much money for one little deco-ration.

'May I buy this for…?' He paused, getting the strongest feeling that she'd say no if he asked to buy it for her. But for the baby, perhaps… 'For our baby?' he said.

She nodded, and he thought he could see the sudden sparkle of tears in her eyes. Oh, no. He hadn't meant to upset her. 'Are you all right?' he asked.

'Yes. It's just…'

Part of her family tradition that would never be the same again, because her brother was no longer with them. He knew how that felt.

'It's a new beginning,' he said softly. 'We can't share this Christmas with Nathan or my father. But we can still share it with others. My new sister. Our baby.'

'Yes,' she said, and this time a single tear really did slide down her cheek.

He brushed it away with the pad of his thumb. Funny how such a light contact sent a shard of desire through him.

He needed to be more careful. This wasn't about his feelings. It was about doing the right thing. The honour-able thing. His duty. He was beginning to think that they might just be in the same direction. Tia Phillips made him feel all kinds of things he'd never felt before. It was unsettling, yet at the same time it made him want to explore further, discover what it was about her that roused all his instincts: protectiveness, desire and...

He didn't quite have a name for the emotion, or at least he wasn't ready to admit it, even to himself. But he did know he wanted Tia around. And this wasn't like his past relationships, strictly for fun and only for now. He wanted more. He wanted all the warmth and the sweetness she could bring to his life.

When they'd finished in the decoration shop, he managed to stall her by insisting on having lunch out at one of the cafés in the village. Even though he'd made it very clear that this was his treat, he noticed that she picked the cheapest thing on the menu, and his heart bled for her.

If only she'd let him cherish her, the way she deserved.

But he was pretty sure she'd see it as an attack on her independence.

Finally, his phone buzzed to signal a message; he glanced at it surreptitiously, relieved to see that it was from Gina.

All done. Turkey in fridge, in roasting tin and foil, ready to go in oven.

She'd added cooking times and temperatures, too.

So Operation Persuade Tia could go full steam ahead.

As soon as Tia headed for the toilets, he texted Gina back.

Thank you.

He'd make very sure to arrange for a delivery of flowers this afternoon to show his gratitude properly. Even though it was Gina's job to look after the house and the family's needs when they were in residence, she was going the extra mile because he'd asked her to, and he wanted her to know he appreciated it.

Back at his house, he asked Tia, 'Where do you want to put the tree?'

'It's your family house, so it's your decision,' she reminded him.

'It's our Christmas,' he countered. 'So tell me what you want.'

'Could we put it in the conservatory?' she asked.

He'd half expected her to say that. He knew how much she loved the view from there. 'Of course,' he said.

While she set out the decorations, he put the Christmas tree up in the conservatory.

And maybe letting her be in charge of the decorating was the way forward, he thought. It would show her that he wouldn't insist on everything being done *his* way.

'So how do you want to do this?' he asked when she came to stand beside him.

'Start with the lights. Check they work, first.'

That was blatantly obvious—before you drove a car or flew a plane, you checked the lights worked—but he wasn't going to snap at her. She seemed to be enjoying the fact that he was deferring to her experience in Christmas-tree decorating. And he rather liked this confident side of her, so he just smiled and plugged them in. 'All present and correct.'

'So then we start at the top, weaving them in and out of the branches as we work our way down. It's probably easiest if we stand either side of the tree and feed the lights round to each other,' she said.

Antonio enjoyed that. Particularly when his fingers

brushed against hers when they transferred the lights to each other, and she blushed.

So she wasn't that indifferent to him, then…

Maybe, like him, she wasn't quite ready to put a name to what she was feeling. And maybe they'd find the courage to admit it—together.

Deliberately he let his fingers brush against hers again. And he held her gaze when she looked up at him. Her mouth was very slightly parted. Soft. Sweet. Tempting.

He remembered what it felt like to kiss her.

He wanted to kiss her again.

Yet, at the same time, he didn't want to push her too fast. These three days were supposed to be all about getting to know each other, spending time together, and talking. Kissing her meant that they wouldn't be talking. Not talking meant that they wouldn't be able to sort things out. So he resisted the urge. Though he noticed that she was staring at his mouth, too. Was she, too, remembering what it had felt like to kiss? To touch?

He nearly dropped a bauble at the thought, but he kept himself under control, the way he always did—both as a prince and as a soldier. Because he was going to do this the right way. Slowly. Well, as slowly as you could get in the three days she'd promised him.

When they'd finished, she turned on the lights and walked round the tree. 'That's great. No dark patches or gaps. Now we can put the star on the top.'

'Don't you do that last?' he asked.

She shook her head. 'Mum always said to work top down.' Her smile was wistful. 'Nathan and I used to take turns in putting the star on the top. Dad would lift us up, even when Nathan was twelve and getting really tall. But we were too big for Mum to lift us after Dad died, so then we used to stand on a chair.'

What would she do if he lifted her up? Would she back away? Or would she melt into his arms? Both options made him nervous. And, although he wanted to show her that they had a future, he didn't want her to feel that he was railroading her into things. He wanted her to want this, too.

He looked at her. 'Your choice. Chair or...?'

Was she going to choose him, or would she pick the safe option?

'Chair,' she said.

The safe option, then. He needed to back off. 'Chair,' he repeated, and fetched one. 'Though I'd prefer you to hold my shoulder for balance.'

She smiled, then. 'From the kick I just got, I think someone agrees with you.'

'Good. Our baby's sensible, then,' he said lightly.

Even though he knew she was only holding on to him for balance as she climbed up and he was careful not to breach any boundaries, his skin still tingled through his sweater where her hand rested on his shoulder. What he really wanted to do was to wrap his arms round her, kiss the bump, and then lift her down from the chair so he could kiss her... But still he kept himself in check. Just.

Once she'd climbed down again, he helped her add the tinsel garland, the baubles and the snowflakes, and then finally the special glass bauble for the baby. Again, his hands brushed against hers, and this time when he turned to her he noticed that her lips were slightly parted and her pupils were enormous.

All he had to do was lean forward and brush his mouth against hers.

She held his gaze for a moment, glanced at his mouth and then up again.

His heart skipped a beat as she closed her eyes.

Now...

He'd closed half the gap between them when the alarm on his phone shrilled.

Her eyes opened again and she stared at him in shock.

Talk about *timing*. 'Sorry,' he said. 'That's my schedule.'

'Schedule?'

'Uh-huh. I need to do something in the kitchen.'

So much for thinking that he was going to get away with this, because she followed him into the kitchen. 'You've got an alarm on your phone to tell you to do something in here?'

'Yes.' He sighed. 'Since you're clearly not going to budge until I tell you, I need to put the turkey in the oven.'

'What turkey?'

'The turkey we're eating tonight. I'm cooking you Christmas dinner.'

'You're cooking me Christmas dinner?' she echoed, blinking at him with surprise.

Oh, honestly. Just because he was a prince, it didn't mean he was incapable of doing anything. He could dress himself, too. The years of royals needing valets and lady's maids had gone long, long ago. And he'd made her dinner last night. 'I *can* cook, you know,' he said, slightly exasperated. 'Putting alarms on my phone means I know when to put things in the oven and when to check them or take them out.'

'You're cooking me Christmas dinner,' she repeated. And this time she smiled. 'I really didn't expect that.'

'It's not a completely traditional English Christmas dinner. It's a fusion,' he said. 'In Casavalle, traditionally we have fish on Christmas Eve. The meal can be eight or nine courses.'

She rubbed her bump. 'I'm not sure I'd be able to manage that much.'

'And some of it's spicy. So that's why I'm cooking a fusion meal,' he said. 'I remember Nathan talking about turkey and the trimmings, so I'm cooking that. I don't have time to soak the salt cod to make *baccalà* for a first course, so I'm doing traditional gnocchi with sage and butter sauce instead—well, I admit it's not home-made and comes from the deli—and an Italian pudding, because the only way I'd get a traditional English Christmas pudding here is to fly one in.'

She frowned. 'Fly one in? That's crazy—it's a total waste of money. You could use that to do something better.' She spread her hands. 'Say, something nice for the villagers here in Picco Innevato.'

'I thought you might react like that,' he said, 'so I'm not flying a pudding in. I'm making *frittelle*—fried Christmas doughnuts. But you're putting me off my schedule. Can you just—well—not talk for five minutes?' he asked plaintively.

She gave him a speaking look, but nodded.

He took the turkey out of the fridge.

'That's enormous!' Tia protested.

So much for her not speaking for five minutes. 'Isn't that the point of a Christmas turkey, to be enormous?' he asked, putting the bird into the oven.

'We'll never eat all that, even if you can talk Giacomo into eating with us this evening,' she said. 'And how did you get this anyway? It wasn't in the fridge when I got the milk out this morning.'

'I called Gina while we were in the café,' he admitted, 'and she organised this for us.'

'Then perhaps you can invite Gina to share Christmas dinner with us,' Tia suggested. 'Does she have a family?'

'Yes. She lives with her husband. Her children are grown up now, and they live in the capital rather than here.'

'That would make five of us for dinner, then,' she mused. 'Though that turkey's easily big enough for twelve people.'

'Isn't it also traditional to have turkey as leftovers?' he asked.

'Well, yes,' she admitted.

'Then it will be fine for five. I'll invite Giacomo, Gina and her husband.'

'So it'll be like a family Christmas.'

She looked wistful, and Antonio realised what was missing. Family. He wasn't asking his family to meet her, not until she'd agreed to marry him; but he could invite hers to join them. 'Yes. I can fly your mother over. Give me ten minutes to arrange it. I'll sort out a private plane so she won't have to wait for a flight, and a car to take her to the airport in London and another one this end.'

Tia bit her lip. 'That's kind of you, but I think the journey might take it out of her too much.'

'Help me here, Tia,' he said softly. 'What do you want?'

'What you planned. That was a really nice thought.'

'But with more people, so it's like a real family Christmas?'

She nodded. 'And I want to help you prepare dinner. Even if you have got a gazillion alarms on your phone telling you what to do.' Her lips quirked. 'Mind you, I should've expected that. Nathan did stuff with military precision, too.'

'It works,' he said.

She grinned. 'So what now—you're going to cut every vegetable exactly the same length, and to make sure of it there's a tape measure next to your knife rack?'

There was a slight twinkle in her eye and Antonio

couldn't help responding to it. 'Are you saying I need a tape measure?'

'Do you?' She lifted her chin.

Right then, she was near enough to kiss, and he almost, *almost* dipped his head to brush his mouth against hers. But then he could see the sudden panic in her eyes, as if the teasing had gone too far and had tipped into something else entirely, something she wasn't quite ready for.

This wasn't about putting pressure on her. It was about getting her to relax. About getting to know her. About letting her get to know him. So he pulled back. 'If we spend all this time talking about doing the veg instead of actually doing them,' he said, much more lightly than he felt, 'then our dinner guests are going to have to wait until tomorrow before we can feed them.'

'Good point,' she said.

'Let me call Gina and talk to Giacomo. And then we'll make dinner together.'

She really hadn't expected this. And she was seeing a completely different side to Antonio Valenti. He was trying to give her the family Christmas she missed so badly and longed for so much. And he wasn't standing on ceremony, insisting on asking the village's mayor and important personages to join them; he was perfectly happy to eat with her and his housekeeper and his security officer. He'd taken on board what she'd said about Christmas not being about money but about spending time together.

So, if she agreed to marry him and give the baby his name, maybe she wasn't going to be trapped in a completely loveless marriage. Maybe he was trying to show her that he could give her what she needed. That he could learn to love her and she could learn to love him.

Maybe, just maybe, this was going to work out.

Once Antonio had arranged for their dinner guests to join them, he brought out the vegetables, pans and sharp knives. 'OK. Crispy roast potatoes and parsnips, carrots, Brussels sprouts and red cabbage. I have chipolata sausages ready to be wrapped with bacon, and I have stuffing— which Gina says I should cook separately. What else?'

'That,' she said, 'is pretty comprehensive. Cranberry sauce?'

'Yes.' He grimaced. 'Though it's not home-made. It's in a jar.'

'A jar is fine. Gravy?'

'I think,' he said carefully, 'I might put you in charge of gravy.'

She smiled. 'So you're learning to delegate?'

He coughed. 'I believe your brother had a saying about pots and kettles.'

She laughed. 'OK. You have a point. I'm not very good at delegating, either.' But his mention of Nathan made her eyes prickle. 'I miss him. Nathan.'

'Me, too,' Antonio admitted.

'I was thinking. If our baby really is a boy, I'd like to call him Nathan—after my brother and my dad.' Though Nathan wasn't the only one Antonio had lost. 'And maybe his middle name could be Vincenzo, after your dad?'

'That,' Antonio said, 'would be perfect.'

Would the baby's last name be Valenti or Phillips? They still hadn't agreed on that bit. But this was a step in the right direction, she thought. They were starting to meet in the middle.

But Tia found herself enjoying the afternoon, preparing dinner together with Christmas music playing softly in the background. It really felt like the Christmases of her childhood, memories that pierced her heart with their sweetness.

Before their guests arrived, she showered and changed into the pretty dress Gina had bought for her.

'You look lovely,' Antonio said.

'Thank you.' So did he, in a formal white shirt, beautifully cut dark suit and understated silk tie. And his shoes were polished the same way as she remembered Nathan and her father polishing theirs, to a military mirror finish.

But could the Soldier Prince allow himself to be ruffled just enough at the edges to deal with a baby?

She pushed the thought aside. Not now. He'd gone to a lot of effort for her, and she wasn't going to start complaining.

Their guests arrived, and Antonio introduced Tia to Gina and her husband Enrico.

'It's lovely to meet you,' Tia said, hugging Gina. 'And thank you so much for finding me such beautiful clothes. It was so kind of you.'

'My pleasure, *piccola*,' Gina said, hugging her back.

Once their guests were seated, Tia helped Antonio bring in the first course, and then the dishes for the main. He carved the turkey at the table, just as she remembered her father doing when she was small, and they all helped themselves to the sides.

Tia was surprised to find how much she was enjoying herself—and how relaxed Prince Antonio was.

Perhaps now was the right time to ask him…

'Do you have plans for tomorrow?' she asked.

'We can go exploring, if you like, take a drive deeper into the mountains,' he suggested.

'I have a better idea,' she said. 'When we were in the café this morning, I overheard someone talking about the village Christmas party for the children tomorrow afternoon.'

'They hold the party every year in the town hall,' Gina explained, 'for all the children in the villages who attend the *scuola elementary* and *asilo*—primary school and kindergarten. I used to help out, in the years when my Chiara and Matteo were young enough to go to the party.' Gina smiled. 'Basically the party's for children under the age of eleven, so there's dancing and games and party food and, of course, *Babbo Natale* to give each child a small gift.'

'Father Christmas,' Tia said. 'But the man who's supposed to be doing it this year can't do it now because he's just broken his leg skiing.'

Antonio looked puzzled. 'How do you know all this?'

'I overheard two of the organisers talking in the ladies' yesterday. They said they couldn't find a replacement Father Christmas.' And this was the thing. Would the Prince think of his own child-to-be and unbend enough to do something kind for the children in the village—something that wouldn't cost him at all financially, but would mean giving up his time and doing something in person? 'And I was wondering,' she continued, 'if maybe you might offer to step in and help?'

'Me?' He looked as shocked as if she'd just suggested that he should take off all his clothes in public to raise money for charity.

He might put his life at risk, the way her brother had, for his job; but putting his dignity at risk was clearly a very different thing. A step too far, perhaps?

But she pressed on. 'All you'd have to do is put on a costume and a beard, maybe tie a pillow round your middle so you look plump enough to be Father Christmas, say, "Ho, ho, ho," a lot, and give each child a present.'

Dress up as *Babbo Natale*.

Antonio tried to get his head round it. This just wasn't the sort of thing his family did. And he hadn't had much to do with children, despite being the patron of a charity for children from an armed forces background who'd been bereaved; he had no idea how they would respond to him.

Then again, in three months' time he would have a baby of his own. He probably ought to take every opportunity he could to have some practice at being around babies and children.

Tia, he thought, would be a natural at being a mother. He could easily imagine her calming a fractious toddler in the coffee shop with a story or crayons, or soothing a baby while its tired mum sat down for two minutes with a cup of tea. And he could understand the attraction of the children's party for her, given that she'd had to put her dreams of being a primary school teacher to one side.

She wanted him to do this.

And it would be another step forward in his campaign to prove to her that they'd be good together and he would learn to be a good husband and father.

He took a deep breath. 'All right. I'll do it. Gina, given that you know about the party, do you know who's organising it?'

'Actually, I have the answer to that one,' Tia said. 'Excuse me for being rude and using tech at the table.' She grabbed her phone and pulled up a photograph. 'There was a poster in the café. The organiser's number is here.'

'Signora Capelli.' Although most of the villagers would speak English for the tourists, the children's Christmas party was for the locals, so the conversation had probably been in Italian. 'Do you speak much Italian, Tia?' he asked, curious.

She nodded. 'Giovanni and Vittoria—my bosses at the café—are originally from Naples. So over the years I've gradually learned from them.'

So even though she hadn't been able to travel, she'd

at least had the pleasure of being able to learn another language.

He looked at her, then switched to Italian. 'If I play Father Christmas, will it make you happy?'

She paused for a bit, as if working out the correct phrases. '*Sì. Molto felice*,' she said.

He grinned. 'Then for you,' he said, switching back to English, 'I will do it. Giacomo, if I call and arrange it, would you…?'

'Sort out the security aspect? Of course,' his security officer said with a smile. 'Actually, sir, I think you would make a very good *Babbo Natale*.'

Antonio wasn't so sure, but he'd do it. 'Excuse me. As you said, Tia, tech at the table is rude, but let me make that call.'

A few minutes later, it was all arranged.

'They're delighted that I can help,' Antonio said. 'But I told them that you were the one who persuaded me to do it, so they'd like to invite you to come to the party as well.'

'I'd love to,' she said, and the sheer pleasure in her eyes made Antonio feel something odd in the region of his heart—as if something inside was cracking.

Once they'd eaten the fresh fruit and little Christmas fritters Antonio had prepared during the afternoon, he ushered everyone through to the sitting room.

'But surely we need to clear up first?' Tia asked.

'No. I'll sort it out later. Tonight is for having fun,' he said. 'Let's go through to the sitting room.'

They played a few rounds of charades, half in English and half in Italian. And then Antonio brought out a box that he'd had delivered earlier that day, containing a copy of the musical game with kazoos that Tia had told him about enjoying so much.

Tears glittered in her eyes as he placed the box on the table.

He went to stand next to her. 'I ordered it online for delivery today. Did I do the wrong thing?' he asked softly, taking her hand. 'Because we don't have to play the game if you'd rather not. I apologise for upsetting you. That wasn't my intention.'

'No, it's a really kind thought.' She swallowed hard. 'I have such lovely memories of playing this with Mum and Dad and Nathan. And now I'm going to have lovely memories of playing with you.'

He didn't want this to be just a memory. He wanted it to be the start of a whole new tradition. But he didn't know how to tell her. Instead, awkwardly, he squeezed her hand.

Several times during the game, Tia caught his eye and his heart felt as if it had done a backflip. And several times he could see the baby kicking. It blew him away. He'd never expected to feel anything like this, and he really wasn't sure how to deal with it. All he could do was be the polite, perfect host, the way he'd been brought up to be. And he wished he could let himself go as easily as Tia, Gina, Giacomo and Enrico seemed to be able to do. But nobody in his family ever let go like that. He'd just have to try harder.

Or maybe that was the point: this should be effortless, and he was trying too hard. And the crack he'd felt inside him earlier seemed to freeze up again.

'Time to make some tea,' Tia said, holding her sides. 'I need a break from laughing.'

'I'll help you,' Gina said. She followed Tia into the kitchen and stacked the dishwasher while Tia filled the kettle and put cups and a teapot on a tray. She winked at the younger woman. 'I know the Prince said he'd clear up tomorrow, but men never stack the dishwasher properly.'

'That's what Vittoria says about Giovanni at work,' Tia said with a smile. Gina reminded her very much of her boss, making her feel completely relaxed and at home.

'I've known Prince Antonio for many years, since he was tiny and his family first came here to this house,' Gina said. 'But this is the first time I've seen him look this relaxed, as an adult. It's not my place to ask questions, but…?' She looked pointedly at Tia's bump.

Tia knew the older woman had Antonio's best interests at heart. 'Yes, the baby is his.' She wrinkled her nose. 'But it's complicated.'

'Antonio needs love in his life,' Gina said softly. 'King Vincenzo was always very formal with both the boys. Queen Maria was a bit less so, but there was still always a little reserve and they never really had a proper childhood, even here. I think you and the baby might be good for Prince Antonio.' She flapped a hand. 'But I'm speaking out of turn.'

'Not at all,' Tia reassured her. 'And I won't say a word of what you said to the Prince.'

It hadn't occurred to her before that maybe the Prince didn't have everything in his life—that maybe her love and the baby would be a gift to him. But, the more she thought about it, the more she realised that he really was the 'poor little rich boy' and their positions were completely reversed. Although she was financially and socially much poorer than him, when it came to love and family she was so much richer.

But would she and the baby be enough for him?

Because, even though she felt she'd grown so much closer to Antonio today—that she was more than halfway to falling in love with the man behind the royal mask—she didn't think he felt the same about her. Antonio was all about duty, and she wasn't sure that she could live a life without love. If he married her purely because he thought it was the right thing to do, could he grow to love her and the baby? And did she really want to live in a world where everything they did or said was put under the microscope of public opinion?

She forced the thought away and took the tray of tea through, smiling at Antonio, Giacomo and Enrico. But her busy day started to catch up with her, and she found herself yawning.

'I'm so sorry,' she said. 'I don't mean to be rude.'

'Being pregnant is tiring, child,' Gina said. 'Go to bed. We understand.'

'Thank you. And thank you all for such a lovely evening. It really felt like a proper Christmas,' she said.

But by the time she climbed into bed, she was wide awake and worrying again.

Antonio had been very quiet after dinner. Was he having second thoughts about this? Could he grow to love her? Should she marry him, give the baby his protection? Or would she be better off going back to London and bringing up their baby in love and relative obscurity?

CHAPTER FIVE

ANTONIO HAD ALMOST finished clearing up in the kitchen when his phone pinged.

Who would message him this late at night? It must be something important, he thought, and picked up his phone to see a message from Luca.

I thought you should know about this before it hits the media tomorrow.

There was an attachment to the message: a PDF of a press release.

Antonio read it and blew out a breath. According to the press release, the DNA test proved beyond all doubt that Gabriella was the oldest child of King Vincenzo, and the palace would like to announce that she would accede to the throne rather than Luca. Luca would remain in his role as the Crown Prince and would support his older sister through the beginning of her reign.

As soon as this news reached the media, Antonio realised, it would be splashed over the front pages of the newspapers. And he would be expected back at the palace as soon as possible. Which meant time was running out for his impromptu getaway with Tia.

His duty meant that he ought to fly back first thing in the morning. Or even tonight.

But he'd promised to play *Babbo Natale* at the village children's Christmas party.

Although he knew the organisers would understand him having to duck out at the last minute, given the news, it would mean leaving them in a mess. And Antonio Valenti was a man who kept his promises. He didn't want to disappoint the children or the villagers—and he really didn't want to disappoint Tia.

But if he didn't go back to the palace first thing tomorrow, he would disappoint his family.

Whatever he did, he was going to let someone down.

Thinking about it logically, he knew that his brother, his mother and Gabriella had each other and all the resources of the palace to support them. Tia had nobody; although she would have emotional support from her mother, Grace Phillips wasn't well enough to deal with the inevitable media intrusion. The stress might even bring on a relapse of her medical condition.

Well, he wasn't going to abandon Tia for a third time.

He typed a message into his phone.

Thanks for update. Will be back in a couple of days. Things I need to do here first.

He was surprised when a message came back almost immediately.

Miles told me who Tia was, but he refused to tell me anything else. Though someone in the office told me she looks very pregnant. Assume congratulations are in order?

Oh. With Tia being so petite, her bump really showed. Of course people would gossip in the palace, even if Miles told them not to, about the pregnant woman who'd come to see the Prince, and Antonio's subsequent disappearance. He'd be naive to think otherwise.

Does Mamma know?

I haven't said anything. I think this needs to come from you.

Of course it did. He already knew that.

Hopefully the media will concentrate on events here. Wrap things up and come back as soon as you can.

Thanks. I will.

Antonio was pretty sure that Luca would leave it at that, but then his phone pinged again.

So do you have a view of snow?

Of course his brother would guess where he'd gone. Antonio had been fooling himself to think otherwise. Picco Innevato was where Antonio always went when he needed some space after a difficult mission.

Yes.

Christmassy. That's nice.

Antonio nearly typed back, *Who are you and what have you done with my older brother?* But, actually, it was nice to feel that for once his older brother wasn't as unbending as their father.

Yes, it is. I put a tree up in the house.

Though he wasn't entirely sure that Luca would understand about him playing *Babbo Natale* at the children's Christmas party. Not when a major announcement was being made and he really ought to be back at the palace, supporting his family.

I'll message you when I'm on my way back.

Good luck. I hope it works out with Tia. Finding someone who loves you—that's special.

And then the penny finally dropped.

Luca had changed. When he'd come back from meeting Gabriella at Crystal Lake, he'd been different. And Antonio was pretty sure that it had a lot to do with Imogen Albright, the woman he'd met out there and become engaged to.

His brother was in love; and that love had melted his habitual reserve.

Antonio couldn't quite get his head round the fact that his elder brother was actually wishing him luck in love.

Then again, he knew he needed luck. If he couldn't persuade Tia to love him, he needed at the very least a good working relationship with the mother of his baby—a child who was definitely going to be fourth in line to the throne.

Me, too, he typed, though this time he didn't send the message.

The next morning, Antonio checked the main news sites on his phone. They were full of the shock announcement about Gabriella, the long-lost Princess of Casavalle who was about to become the new Queen. And quite a few of them seemed to have noticed that Prince Antonio wasn't at the palace and were asking exactly where he was.

Thankfully the villagers at Picco Innevato had always been protective of his family, and he knew that none of them would sell him out to the media. Until he'd persuaded Tia to marry him and let him give her and the baby his protection, he wanted to stay well out of the limelight.

Today was their last full day in the village in any case, but he knew that time was running out. He needed to wrap things up here and go back to the palace.

He sent a holding message to his mother, Gabriella and Miles—all of whom had texted him that morning—saying that he'd be back tomorrow but had some things he needed to do first. He knew the message was vague, and it would no doubt infuriate them all, but he'd learned in the army that you needed to do the right things in the right order. Tia had to come first.

When she came downstairs, he made her breakfast. Now wasn't the time to worry her about palace politics. He wanted to concentrate on *her*. 'I was going to ask your advice.'

'My advice?' She looked surprised. 'About what?'

'The children's party. It's a little outside my usual sphere.' Which was an understatement. 'I've rarely had contact with children with my family duties, even as patron of the charity—I tend to work with the fundraisers rather than the children.'

'And you don't know what to do?'

'No,' he admitted. 'I'm guessing that your customers at the café include families with children.' Plus he knew she'd dreamed of being a primary school teacher. So she must have some idea of how to work with children.

'Just be yourself,' she said. 'After you've finished being *Babbo Natale*—and obviously make sure that none of them see you change out of the costume—I think just join in with the games.'

Could it really be that simple? 'OK.' But then there was the party. 'Maybe I ought to do more for the party. Perhaps I could pay for the presents?'

'Christmas really isn't about money and heaps of expensive presents,' she said softly, 'it's about spending time with people and making them feel good. When you were a child—I know things were a bit different for you, but wasn't the best part of Christmas playing games with your brother?'

He thought about it.

Just as last night hadn't been about presents—it had been about having fun, and that one game he'd bought had meant more to Tia than if he'd bought her the richest and most exclusive of jewels.

'Yes.'

'Well, then,' she said. 'And I'm sure the organisers have already sorted everything out. If you go in and say you're going to buy extra presents for the children, it's kind of like you telling them that whatever they've already done isn't good enough.'

'I hadn't really thought about it in that way.' He looked awkwardly at her. 'Just that with my family's background, I feel I ought to do more.'

'Time's so much more important than money. Anyone can buy gifts; it's the easy way out,' she said. 'And not just anyone's prepared to dress up as Santa and be patient with children who are shy or nervous. The people in the village will appreciate what you're doing so much more than if you call a shop and pay for a huge sackful of presents to be wrapped. You're giving something of *yourself*.

What the children want at the Christmas party is Father Christmas. And today that's going to be you.'

Tia Phillips looked like an ordinary woman. But Antonio was beginning to learn just how extraordinary she was.

'You're right,' he said. 'They want Father Christmas.'

He knew he really ought to tell her about what was going on in the palace, especially as it meant that they'd have to leave Picco Innevato tomorrow, but he knew she was looking forward to the party and he didn't want to spoil today for her. There was time enough for them to have to deal with the politics. He'd tell her tomorrow.

Half an hour before the party was due to start, he and Tia went into the village hall to meet the organisers.

'We're so grateful, Your Royal Highness,' Signora Capelli said.

'It's nice to be able to do something for the village,' Antonio said. 'So what exactly do I do?'

'Once in costume, *Babbo Natale* sits on the chair in the grotto,' Signora Capelli said, indicating the chair festooned with tinsel underneath an arch decorated with more tinsel and cut-out Christmas trees that had clearly been painted by the children. 'He greets each child, wishes them a merry Christmas and gives them a present.'

He could do that.

'We've put the presents into sacks, split by age group, and your helper will tell you the name and the age of each child just before they come to see you,' Signora Capelli continued.

'Thank you,' Antonio said. 'That's very clear. Who's my helper?' He looked at Tia. Given that he was dressing up as Father Christmas, would she be prepared to dress up as an elf?

Signora Capelli smiled. 'I would suggest Tia, but her condition is a little…distinctive.'

Her baby bump. Of course the children would notice that the guest at their party had the same bump as *Babbo Natale*'s helper.

'But perhaps you'd like to help us with the table, Tia?' Signora Capelli asked.

'Of course,' Tia said with a smile. She indicated the other helpers, who were wearing Santa hats or reindeer antlers. 'And I'm perfectly happy to wear a hat or reindeer antlers if you want me to.'

'Antlers. Of course.' Signora Capelli looked anxious. 'Sir, forgive me for being rude, but I assume you know the names of all the reindeer?'

'Rudolph,' he said. Then he stopped. He didn't actually know any others. It wasn't something they'd ever talked about at the palace or in the army.

Tia laughed. 'Don't worry—I do. Dasher and Dancer, Prancer and Vixen, Comet and Cupid, Donner and Blitzen.' She made him repeat the names until he was word-perfect, and it made him realise what a fabulous teacher she'd make.

He changed into the costume and beard. 'You're right. I need padding,' he said.

Signora Capelli found some cushions and Tia, wearing antlers and looking incredibly cute with her huge brown eyes and curly black hair, helped him put the final touches to his outfit.

Tia stood back with her hands on her hips and looked at him. 'Perfect.'

Never in a million years would he have expected to do something like this. Or that she'd have tears in her eyes.

'Are you all right?' he asked.

'Yes. It's just… Thank you for doing this, Antonio.

For making things right for the children.' Impulsively, she hugged him; and the feeling of something cracking in the middle of his chest intensified.

As soon as he was sitting on the tinsel 'throne' in his grotto—a million miles away from the real throne in their palace—the children streamed into the hall and a queue formed to meet him. He didn't have time to watch out for Tia, because he was too busy playing his role, and he found himself improvising when a child asked him about the North Pole and what the elves did there.

'They help me make gifts and wrap them up for the children who would like them,' he said, crossing his fingers mentally.

Another child asked him about the reindeer, and he was grateful that Tia had drilled him on the right names.

Every single child seemed thrilled with their gift from *Babbo Natale*, but it didn't take long for Antonio to realise that Tia had been right when she'd said that Christmas wasn't about the presents: today was all about the gifts of time and love and kindness.

The smiles on their faces warmed his heart. Then one little boy gave him a carrot. 'It's a present for Rudolph,' he said.

'Thank you very much,' Antonio said. 'Carrots are his favourite. He'll be delighted to share that with his friends for dinner.'

Another little girl who must've been about seven shyly handed him a Cellophane wrapper tied with a bow. 'You always bring us presents every year, *Babbo Natale*,' she said, 'but nobody brings you one and I think they should. My *mamma* helped me make this for you this morning and I put special sprinkles on it and I wrapped it just for you.'

There was a huge lump in his throat. A small, thoughtful gift that felt incredibly special. Over the years, as a child, he'd been given incredibly expensive and exclusive gifts; but this one was *personal*. One that taught him the real meaning of Christmas. 'That's so kind of you,' he said. 'It looks so pretty. I'll enjoy that with my glass of milk later today. Thank you so much.'

When he'd given the last child their present, he waved goodbye to everyone and wished everyone a merry Christmas, then headed out of the hall back to the room where he'd changed into the costume. He folded everything up neatly—Tia would no doubt tease him about doing it with military precision, just as she'd teased him about his schedule for cooking Christmas dinner—and then headed back towards the hall.

Tia was waiting for him just outside. 'Are you OK?' she asked.

'Yes. That was amazing—really humbling.' He blew out a breath and nodded through the open doorway. 'See that little girl over there with the curly black hair in the blue dress?'

'Yes.'

'She gave me a cookie, all prettily wrapped. She'd made it especially for me this morning with her mother's help and chose the sprinkles. She said nobody ever brings *Babbo Natale* a present and she...' Suddenly, he just couldn't say anything else.

She hugged him, clearly realising how deeply the gift had affected him. 'That's what Christmas is about,' she said. 'It's the thought behind the gift, how personal it is.'

Right then, he knew exactly what he wanted for Christmas.

Tia.

And their baby.

But he didn't know how to tell her. He couldn't get the

words out. They stuck in his throat. But he wanted her so much. Needed her. Needed both of them.

Why was it so hard to say it? Why couldn't he just open his mouth and say, 'Tia, the way I feel about you puts my head in a spin and I can't find the right words, but please stay with me'?

This wasn't the place, either. And it was too important for him to mess up by simply blurting out the jumble in his head.

'We'd better get back to the party,' she said.

The children insisted that the Prince and Tia should share their party tea—bruschetta, cherry tomatoes, carrot sticks, little cubes of cheese and ham and the traditional Italian *tronchetti di Natale.*

'I love chocolate Yule log,' Tia said with a smile, accepting a slice.

Both he and Tia danced with the children and joined in the games—sticking a carrot 'nose' on the outline of a snowman while their eyes were covered with a scarf, guessing the items in a stocking just by feeling them, using a paper straw to blow a cotton wool 'snowball' in a race to the finish line, and 'Christmas ornament' musical chairs, where the children danced round the cut-out ornaments as the music played and had to stand on an ornament when the music stopped.

It was way, way outside anything Antonio had ever done before, though he suspected from the way that Tia joined in that she'd maybe been involved with something similar at the café where she worked. And he was surprised by how much fun it was, everything from the games to the dancing. It made him feel different—part of the village, more so than he did even as a child, and he really felt connected with his people.

He realised then that the weird feeling in his chest was

happiness. Here in Picco Innevato at the children's party, he felt accepted for who he was, instead of being seen as a remote prince. He'd never even had that feeling in the army, where he had previously been at his happiest.

So much for persuading Tia; what he'd actually done was persuade himself. Because Tia had shown him how good life could be, how it felt to be part of a family—and that was what he wanted. To see her eyes sparkle and her face glow with happiness as she danced with the children, to see her glance over at him and smile with a warmth that made his own heart sing. He wanted to see her look like that while she danced with their own child in the middle of their kitchen. A private moment far from the formality of his day-to-day life.

Once the party was over, he and Tia helped to clear up, hugged all the organisers goodbye, and walked back through the village to his house.

'I believe you now about doing your fair share of the cleaning,' she said with a smile. 'Seeing you wielding that broom with military pr—'

'Tia,' he cut in, 'that particular joke is wearing just a little bit thin.'

'But it was,' she said, her smile broadening into a grin. 'Watching you sweep a floor was like watching a man with a mower making a stripy lawn.'

He thought about kissing her to stop her talking.

But that was too tempting—and too dangerous to his peace of mind. If he let himself give in to his feelings, if he said the wrong thing and scared her away... Plus they were in a public place. He'd wait until they were back at the house. And maybe the walk home would give him enough time to put his thoughts and his feelings back in order. Instead, he said, 'The Christmas market in the square looks really pretty, all lit up for night-time.'

Thankfully it distracted her, and she smiled at him. 'That'd be nice.'

And when she allowed him to take her arm—which was ostensibly for safety in case she slipped, but was really because he just wanted to be close to her—he was shocked to discover that it made him feel as if he'd just conquered the world.

'We have a Christmas market a bit like this on the South Bank in London,' she said. 'You can buy mulled wine, hot chocolate, various foods and gifts. And then you can cross the river over to Somerset House and go to the skating rink. But here it's different—the hot chocolate is much thicker, and there are those gorgeous nativity scenes everywhere.'

When they got to the stalls, she stopped by the little wooden shack offering snow globes for sale, and her eye seemed to be caught by one in particular—a crystalline star suspended inside the globe and set on a crystal base. She picked it up, and her dark eyes gleamed with pleasure. But then she examined the base, looked regretful and replaced it carefully.

Antonio had the strongest feeling that she loved the globe, but she'd just seen the price and it was outside her budget. He knew that Tia would be too proud to admit that she couldn't afford it, and if he insisted on buying it for her right now she'd be embarrassed and awkward. But there was a way around it: he'd buy it without her knowing and give it to her later, in private. A surprise gift. And he'd make it clear there were no strings. He stood behind her so she couldn't see his face, caught the stall-holder's eye and mimed to him to save the snow globe for him. The stall-holder glanced at Tia, clearly checking to make sure she couldn't see his reaction and guess what was going on, then winked at Antonio.

At the next stall, when Tia bought a scented candle decorated with pressed flowers for her mother, Antonio excused himself and went back to get the snow globe she'd liked. The stall-holder wrapped it in a box tied with a bright scarlet ribbon; Antonio slipped the box into his pocket so it wasn't visible. He'd give it to Tia later, when the time was right.

Antonio insisted on carrying Tia's purchase from the candle stall but, when he went to tuck her hand into his arm for balance, somehow they ended up holding hands.

At the party, Tia had seen a whole new side to the Prince.

Sure, he'd been a bit formal and over the top when he'd helped clear up, marching up and down with the broom as if he was on a military parade: but he *had* helped, as if he was just another one of the villagers and not the man who was third in line to the throne of Casavalle. And the way he'd been with the children… Even though she knew he'd had such a formal upbringing and he'd actually asked her advice about what to do at the party, he'd then done his best to fit in and make the afternoon fun for the children. She'd taken a sneaky snap of him on her phone while he'd been playing the snowball-blowing game, surrounded by children and laughing, and he'd really looked as if he belonged.

It gave her so much hope for the future. From what she'd seen, she really believed that Antonio could learn to be a warm, loving father. That maybe he could escape his upbringing and learn to be *himself*. And that maybe she was the one who could help him do that. To think that she might be the one to finally unlock his heart was amazing: it would be a real privilege, even though it scared her because she might not be up to the task. Though, for the sake of their baby—and for themselves—she'd make sure she was good enough.

As they walked up the steps to the porch leading to his front door, he paused.

'What?' she asked.

'What do you see?' he asked.

'Your front door. A Christmas wreath.' The one with copper-painted honesty seed pods that they'd bought together. 'Gorgeous sparkly lights on the trees on either side of the door.' Immaculately clipped cones of yew that were no doubt measured to get them that precise shape.

'And?' He glanced upwards, indicating where she should look.

'Mistletoe.' She caught her breath. Was he suggesting they should…? 'Do you have a tradition about mistletoe in Italy?' she asked, her voice hoarse.

He inclined his head. 'Here it tends to be New Year's Eve when you kiss under the mistletoe. But you're English, so I think perhaps we should use the English tradition.'

Which meant kissing under the mistletoe at Christmas…

Then again, they'd decorated the house for Christmas and he'd cooked them a proper Christmas dinner. This was a sort of early Christmas. It counted.

So she made no protest when he dipped his head and kissed her, his mouth warm and sweet and coaxing. She leaned into the kiss and slid her hands into his hair, drawing him closer. He wrapped his arms round her, holding her tightly, and kissed her until she was dizzy.

There was suddenly a volley of kicks in her stomach, and he broke the kiss, laughing. 'I think someone wants to tell us something.'

'That might be the baby equivalent of saying "Get a room",' she said ruefully.

He rested his hand on her bump. 'This blows my mind. Our baby.'

The expression on his face was a mixture of pride and tenderness and... No, Tia didn't dare let herself hope for anything else. But if he bonded with their baby, that would be a good thing—both for Antonio and for their baby.

She shivered, and he brushed his mouth against hers again. 'Sorry. I shouldn't keep you on the doorstep in the cold.' He unlocked the front door and ushered her inside.

Right at that moment it felt as if they were a proper couple. As if they were just coming home from an event in the village—leaving their coats on the bentwood stand in the hallway and ending up in the kitchen, where he put the kettle on while she got the mugs out.

'So did you enjoy the party?' she asked.

'More than I expected to,' he said.

She showed him the picture she'd taken on the phone. 'You looked as if you were having fun.'

'Something so simple. I never did things like that as a child,' he said. 'But our baby definitely will.'

And Tia felt as if her world had just exploded into colour.

'So, we have leftovers for dinner.' He smiled at her. 'What sort of thing did you do as a child?'

'Cold turkey, home-made chips or French bread, and salad,' she said promptly. 'And Mum used to make vegetable and turkey soup. We used to wrap up warm and go to the beach, the day after Boxing Day, and we'd take a flask of Mum's soup and have a picnic.'

He wrapped his arms round her. 'I know it won't be the same, but we have beaches here. I'd be happy to take you.'

Which sounded as if he saw a future for them.

Even though part of her wanted to be sensible and acknowledge that their lives were too far apart for them to be together, part of her was thrilled by the idea. Warmed by hope that maybe he wanted a future for them—and Antonio Valenti was the kind of man who'd make things happen. If he wanted her, really wanted her in his life, then he'd find a way through the traditions that bound him.

And she'd meet him halfway.

In the end, they made turkey salad sandwiches and ate them in the kitchen, then went into the conservatory to curl up on a sofa together and watch the stars and talk about anything and everything.

Tia was so easy to be with.

Antonio wished it could always be like this, but he knew they'd have to go back to the palace soon and face real life, the politics and the press. Eventually she fell asleep and he sat there just holding her.

He knew now that this was what he wanted: to be a family with her and their baby, to live out of the limelight of the palace and be part of the community of the village. He wanted her to be his wife, his partner in everything.

But he couldn't work out how to tell her. If he asked her to marry him now, would she believe him that he wanted her for herself, or would she still think he was asking her purely out of a sense of duty and honour?

'I want to be a family with you,' he whispered.

She didn't wake, so he gently eased her out of his arms, then fetched a blanket and tucked it round her. She looked so cute, curled up on the sofa. And so *right*. He resisted the temptation to kiss her awake, because there was something else he needed to do. A letter that he should've written a long time ago.

He fetched notepaper, an envelope and a pen from his

office—an impersonal typed letter was absolutely not good enough for this—and took a photograph from his wallet. And then he began to write.

When he'd finished, Tia was still asleep.

He knelt by her and stroked her cheek. 'Tia? Tia, wake up, *bella*,' he whispered.

She opened her eyes, looking lost and incredibly vulnerable.

'Time to go to bed,' he said, and gently helped her to her feet.

'Sorry. I didn't mean to fall asleep on you.' She bit her lip, looking guilty.

'You're six months pregnant and you've had a busy day. I think you're allowed to fall asleep,' he said, smiling.

He was so tempted to carry her up the stairs, though he knew that wouldn't be fair. But at the door to her room he couldn't resist kissing her goodnight.

Her eyes were huge as she stroked his face. 'Antonio.'

He kissed her again.

'Stay with me tonight?' she asked.

Fall asleep with her in his arms. Wake up with her in his arms.

How could he possibly resist?

And this time he did pick her up and carry her to bed.

Afterwards, it took him a long time to fall asleep, because he knew now that this was what he wanted more than anything else. To be with her. And for her to want to be with him.

Please let her want the same thing.

Please.

Later that night, Tia woke when the baby started somersaulting. Antonio's arms were wrapped round her, and she felt safe and warm and cherished.

Could this work out, or was it just a hopeless fantasy?

She and Antonio had come so far over the last couple of days; but she had no idea whether his family would accept her. She knew that her father's family had rejected her mother, and she knew how much the situation had hurt both her parents. What if this turned out to be the same sort of thing?

Then, whatever she did, she lost. She didn't want to make Antonio choose between his family and her, because that wasn't fair; yet leaving him and quietly taking the baby away to live anonymously in London was no longer an option. Not now she'd seen the joy in his eyes when he'd felt their baby kick inside her.

Please, please let this work out...

CHAPTER SIX

THE NEXT MORNING, Tia was woken by the sound of a phone shrilling. At first she was disoriented but then last night came rushing back to her. How she'd fallen asleep on the sofa in Antonio's arms. How he'd ushered her up to bed, and she'd asked him to stay. How tenderly he'd held her...

The shrilling was from Antonio's phone, and he was sitting up in bed, frowning and speaking rapidly in Italian.

He was speaking too quickly for her to follow what he was saying, but something was clearly wrong, because he ended the call and then appeared to be looking up something on his phone.

She sat up. 'What is it?'

'Ah, Tia. Good morning.'

'What's happened?'

He grimaced. 'That was Gina on the phone. Apparently the media have descended on the village. There's some stuff in the news.'

'What stuff?'

He handed her the phone in silence.

It was a newsfeed showing the front pages of various newspapers and headlines for their stories. Someone had clearly taken photographs last night when Antonio had kissed her on the doorstep.

One of the pages had mocked up a kind of photo love

story: in the first photograph he was kissing her, the second had her sliding her arms round his neck and kissing him back, and the third showed her smiling at him while he rested his hand on her bump, obviously feeling the baby kick.

The first one was captioned *Who's that girl?* The second bore the line *A kiss is just a kiss—or is it?* The third had a heart drawn round them and was captioned *Baby Love?*

She read through the actual article. It was asking who she was, and if this was Prince Antonio's secret baby.

Is this the third baby scandal to rock the kingdom of Casavalle in recent months? The oldest child of King Vincenzo, Gabriella, was kept secret for decades, Prince Luca's fiancée was pregnant with someone else's baby, and now it seems Vincenzo's youngest child isn't to be left out of the scandal...

Horrified, Tia realised that the story was going to cause huge waves in Casavalle and also in London. If the media started digging to find out who she was, then her mother was going to be dragged into this.

She skimmed over the speculation, and then came to the last paragraph.

Prince Luca has confirmed that his older half-sister Gabriella will be acceding to the throne instead of him, with the coronation due at the end of the year.

So Gabriella was definitely becoming Queen? Since when? Antonio hadn't mentioned anything about that to her. He'd said that they were waiting for DNA test results and Gabriella's decision. 'Gabriella's actually becoming Queen?' she asked.

'With the support of our family, yes,' he said.

She frowned. 'Did you know about this?'

'Yes. Luca sent me the press release.'

Her stomach felt tied in knots as she took in the coolness of his expression and his tone. She'd been so sure that he was thawing out. But now he'd gone all aloof on her again. He was reverting to being Antonio the Prince, and she realised that she had just been kidding herself. Antonio was a prince first and foremost. Even if he did thaw out with her again, it would never be for long.

'You didn't say anything to me.' The words came out before she could stop them. How stupid of her. Why would he feel he needed to tell her anything about Palace business?

And then a really nasty thought sneaked into her head. If he'd known about the press release, known that the press would be asking about him… Suddenly his actions of yesterday took on a whole new meaning. 'So you must've known the media would want to know where you were, when it was obvious you weren't at the palace.'

'I didn't think they'd find me here,' he said.

How, when it was his family's house so it was an obvious place to look? 'But they did—and they took that photograph.' She swallowed hard. 'On your doorstep.'

'I didn't notice any flash.'

Neither had she. She didn't *think* he was lying. But she did feel manipulated, and she wasn't sure whether she was more angry with herself for not realising that of course he was a prince and the media would follow him relentlessly, or with him for bringing her here in the first place and not letting her go quietly back to London where nobody would know about her or the baby.

The phone shrilled again, and the palace secretary's name flashed up on the caller ID.

'For you,' she said, handing the phone back to him.

She couldn't hear what Miles was saying, and she could tell nothing at all from Antonio's side of the conversation. His face was completely impassive, and all he seemed to say was 'Yes', 'No' or 'I see'.

He ended the call and looked at her. 'Miles says the media knows who you are, that you live in London and you're a waitress.'

She looked at him in dismay. 'Does that mean they're going to go after my mum now?' And maybe her bosses. Her friends. Anyone who'd known her even vaguely in the last twenty years. The media wouldn't care, as long as they got their story.

'It's a strong possibility,' he admitted. 'I'm sorry you've been dragged into this.'

'Are you?' she asked, with the doubts still nagging at her. 'Or did you engineer it, knowing that you're the only one who could protect my mum so I'd have to agree to all your demands?'

He stared at her, saying nothing, and with a sick feeling she realised she hadn't just been hormonal and paranoid. This really was manipulation. She'd been fooling herself yesterday, thinking that he was getting closer to her and hoping that maybe, after all, this was going to work out. He didn't love her, but she was carrying his heir, the fourth in line to the throne, so he thought it was his duty to give the baby his name. She'd already refused to marry him, so he'd put her in a situation where she'd *have* to agree.

The cold, unemotional soldier was a master strategist.

He knew that Tia would do anything to protect her mother. If her mother was in danger from being hounded by the media, then Tia would agree to anything to stop that.

So he'd got close to her. Made her think that he cared. Put her in the perfect position for a photo opportunity.

And now…

This time her mobile phone was the one to ring.

Seeing their neighbour's name on the screen made her heart freeze for a second.

Was Becky ringing to tell her that her mother was ill—or worse? Please, no. She couldn't lose her last family member. Please. *Please.*

'Hello, Becky,' she said, trying to keep the panic from her voice. 'Is Mum all right?'

'Yes, love, she's fine. Don't worry,' her neighbour reassured her.

Which was when she started shivering, in reaction to the fear that had flooded through her.

Antonio moved to put his arm round her, but she didn't believe it was to warm her or comfort her. This was all about duty and control, and she'd been too stupid to see it.

She angled herself away from him, and thankfully he took the hint and backed off.

'But there's reporters and photographers everywhere,' Becky said. 'I went out to get a pint of milk and everyone kept asking me about you. I just told them you were a lovely girl and to leave you alone.'

'Thank you. I really appreciate that.' With neighbours like Becky on their side, at least Tia knew that her mother was going to be OK. She took a deep breath. 'I'll be home as soon as I can. I'll text you when I know the flight times. And I'll ring Mum in a second.'

'All right, love. Don't you worry. I'll keep an eye on her.' Becky paused. 'Your young man's very handsome.'

He wasn't exactly hers, though like a fool she'd let herself start to believe that he might be. And wasn't the old saying, 'Handsome is as handsome does'? But Becky was waiting for an answer. She didn't need to know what a mess this was. 'Yes,' Tia said. 'I'll see you soon. And thank you again.'

'Is your mother all right?' Antonio asked as soon as she ended the call.

No thanks to him. 'Yes,' she said, her voice cool. 'Don't worry. You win. I'll do what you want and marry you so you get your heir—but only on condition you take care of my mum and make sure the media doesn't hassle her.'

At least he didn't look full of triumph.

Then again, he wasn't showing any emotion at all.

How, just how, had her brother been friends with him? Or was he totally different at work?

Not that it mattered.

Nothing mattered any more.

She'd been very naive to think he was starting to care for her. Antonio the Automaton. He'd just been a very, very shrewd tactician.

Military precision.

How stupid she'd been to tease him about that. It was exactly what it had been. Who he was.

'I'll arrange for someone to handle things for your mother in London,' Antonio said. 'Although I think it would be best to fly her to Casavalle.'

'So she gets no say in it, either? Like the baby, she's going to be another royal pawn in a game?' she asked bitterly.

'Tia, it isn't like that.'

'Isn't it?' She looked levelly at him. 'If you'll excuse me, I'd like to shower and get dressed.' In clothes he'd arranged for her, because she'd been so carried away with the gorgeous Christmas he'd made for her that she hadn't done any laundry. Leaving her with no choice. Just as the rest of her life was going to be now.

Stupid, stupid, stupid.

Right at that second, she felt *bought*.

Tia had already made up her mind, so there was no point in arguing with her, Antonio thought. Right now it would only make matters worse. And if he upset her, it would be bad for the baby. He needed her to be calm. Maybe, if he didn't escalate things, when she'd had time to think logically about it she'd realise that he hadn't been trying to manipulate her. That he'd been caught unawares, too.

Instead, he said neutrally, 'I'll arrange for a flight back to the palace.'

'Thank you.'

'And for you to go back to London. Please call your mother and reassure her that I'll do everything in my power to protect her.'

'Of course, Your Royal Highness.'

That hurt. That she could be so formal with him after what they'd shared. That she could believe he'd engineered this whole thing.

Thankfully his upbringing meant that the hurt didn't show.

And he'd do this logically. Get the media spotlight off them, and then once they were in the palace he could start to sort things out with her.

'I'll leave a suitcase outside your door,' he said.

'Suitcase?' She looked surprised.

'For your clothes.' When it looked as if she was about to argue, he raked a hand through his hair. 'Tia. There were no strings to those clothes.'

'I suppose you can't have your bride-to-be wearing cheap chainstore clothes in public,' she said.

Did she really think he was such a snob, that he gave

a damn about money? The unfairness stung enough for him to say, 'Don't be so ridiculous.'

'Ridiculous?'

'I'm not a snob. It's nothing to do with money. I was trying to do something nice for you without rubbing your nose in the difference between our financial situations or making you feel beholden to me.'

She looked crestfallen then, and he felt guilty—because by saying that out loud he'd done precisely what he'd been trying not to do. He'd rubbed her nose in it. She'd been angry and hurt and snapping at him, but he shouldn't have snapped back and continued the fight. Time to back off. Not because he was in the wrong or afraid of a fight, but because she was out of sorts and he needed to think of the baby. 'I'm going to have a shower and go downstairs. I'll make breakfast when you're ready.'

She nodded, and looked away.

He left her room, showered and dressed swiftly, and sent holding texts to his brother, his mother and Gabriella, saying that he'd explain everything when he was back at the palace later that morning. He took the special glass bauble from the tree and wrapped it up, then added an addendum to the letter he'd written the previous night, and stowed them both in his bag along with the wrapped snow globe.

Tia was silent when she finally came downstairs. For a moment, he thought she was going to refuse breakfast. So he just said quietly, 'You need to eat. For you and the baby.'

There was a movement across her stomach. At least the baby agreed with him, he thought wryly.

She shrugged, still looking hurt and angry, but at least she ate her toast. Drank the mug of tea he'd prepared. Climbed into the back of the car—this time, Giacomo drove, and the windows were blacked out to avoid the press.

Tia stared out of the window all the way to the airport, and Antonio didn't push her to talk. She barely spoke to him on the flight back, either.

How could he even begin to fix this? Tia was going to marry him, which was what he'd wanted since she'd told him the news about the baby: but he could see now that it was only to save her mother from the press. Not because she wanted to be with him.

How ironic that he'd been trying to persuade her to fall for him, and what he'd managed to do instead was let himself fall for her. If he told her how he felt about her—if he could even find the right words—he didn't think she'd believe him. Not now the press were involved.

He'd been honest with her and told her how much he hated palace politics, so why did she believe he'd do something underhand? He really hadn't engineered that kiss. He'd *wanted* to kiss her. Wanted to be with her. He'd been so wrapped up in those unexpected emotions that he hadn't noticed the paparazzi hanging round, and he hadn't seen the flash from the camera.

If only he was good at saying what he really felt. But every time he opened his mouth to tell her, it was as if his throat was filled with sand and the words just wouldn't come out.

When they landed, he said, 'Would you prefer to go to the palace or to go straight back to London?'

'Do I have a choice?'

That really hurt. 'Yes. Of course you have a choice.'

'I want to see my mum,' she said. Before he could offer to go with her, she said, 'And I'll go on my own. I expect you have official duties.'

He needed to speak to his family and the palace secretary, yes, but he wanted to support her. He wanted to be with her; he wanted to make this work. And he rather thought he owed her mother an apology and a personal explanation.

He didn't get the chance to tell her, because she continued, 'And I need to see Giovanni and Vittoria, explain everything to them. They've been so good to me and I feel bad about letting them down. And my friend who was going to share childcare with me. I've let her down, too.'

Guilt flooded through him. She had a whole life without him, and he was ripping her from that support network and expecting her to be in Casavalle with him. She wasn't the only one whose life was changed by this mess. 'Look, I'll sort everything out.'

'That's my life, not yours. *I'll* organise it,' she cut in. Which told him exactly where he stood. She'd see any offer of help as throwing his money around, not a genuine desire to make things better.

'Will you at least let my pilot take you back to London?' he asked.

'Are you worried I might talk to someone in the airport while I'm waiting for my flight and say something I shouldn't?'

He remembered the conversation he'd had with her before, and sighed. 'No, Tia. The media will write what they like.' It hurt that she thought he was so underhand, and he had to draw on every ounce of the training he'd had over the years to remain cool and calm and collected. But he wanted her to know his real motivation, so he said, 'I'm asking if you'll let my pilot take you back because you're six months pregnant and the last thing you need is to wait for hours for connecting flights, perhaps without anywhere to sit if the airport's really busy.'

She turned away so he couldn't see her face, couldn't read her eyes. 'Whatever. I don't care any more.'

And how that hurt, to see her so flat and cold towards him, with all her bubbliness gone. Worse, to know that it was all because of him. That she didn't trust him. 'Let me have a word with the pilot.'

He went into the cockpit and arranged with the crew that they'd take her to London and look after her on the way. 'And can you please make sure that this letter's delivered, and these two parcels go to Tia's mum?'

'Of course, Your Royal Highness.'

'Thank you.' He returned to Tia. Although part of him wanted to take Tia back to the palace before she went to London and at least introduce her to his family, from the set look on her face he didn't think she'd be amenable to the suggestion. 'Please let me know when you're safely back in London.'

She huffed out a breath. 'I'm surprised you don't want to put some kind of tracking device on my phone.'

He winced. 'I'm not trying to trap you, Tia.'

'It feels like it.'

He would've done anything to rewind the last few hours—to go back to the children's Christmas party where he'd felt so happy, where he and Tia had worked as a team and he'd thought they were actually getting closer. And last night, when he'd kissed her under the mistletoe. When she'd fallen asleep on him on the sofa. When she'd shyly asked him to stay with her and he'd woken in the night to feel the baby kicking in her stomach. 'I'm sorry. It's not meant to be…' His throat closed. *A prison.* But hadn't he felt like that at the palace, too? Hemmed in and miserable and trapped by all the politics?

On the other hand, he couldn't just throw Tia to the

wolves. The media would make her life miserable without him.

'Safe journey,' he said, and walked to the door of the plane where the stewardess was waiting.

'Look after her for me, please,' he said.

And his misery must've shown in his eyes, because the stewardess forgot herself enough to pat his arm. 'It'll be all right, Prince Antonio.'

He rather didn't think it would.

And he couldn't bear to look back at Tia and see how much she loathed him.

Antonio strolled off the plane, as cool as a cucumber, and didn't even look back at her. He was clearly so secure in his triumph that he didn't need to make sure his new chattel was sitting exactly where he'd left her.

Tia felt sick.

Right at that moment, she wished she'd never met Antonio Valenti.

There was a volley of kicks, and she rested her hand on her bump. 'I don't regret *you*,' she whispered softly. 'But I thought he was different. That he felt something for me. That he cared. That over the last few days he'd shown her the real man behind the Prince, a man I could really love. But none of it was true. All along it was just to manipulate me into a situation where I'm forced to do what the palace wants.'

She'd let everyone down. Her mum, the memory of her dad and her brother, her bosses, her friends.

And life was never going to be the same again.

Antonio had everything planned in the official car back to the palace. First, he'd talk to his family; then to the palace secretary, to make sure that their plans for protecting Tia and Grace were completely in place; and then he'd organise Tia and her mother coming to the palace.

Back at the palace, he found his mother in her study, doing something on a computer. He knocked at the door and, when she looked up, bowed deeply, 'Good morning, Mamma.'

She inclined her head. 'Good morning, Antonio.'

'I'm sorry I've...' He took a deep breath. 'I'm sorry I've brought scandal to the family.'

This was her cue to tell him he was a disgrace, how disgusted his father would be, and how she expected better from him.

But to his surprise she stood up, walked over to him and took his hands, squeezing them. 'Welcome home. Where is Tia? Is she resting?'

'No. She's on a plane to London,' he said.

'I see.' Maria looked disappointed. 'I would have liked to meet her, talk with her a little.'

'It's not her fault, Mamma,' he said softly. 'I accept the blame fully.'

'For putting her on the plane?'

He nodded. 'And for the baby—' he choked '—for everything.'

She shocked him even more by touching his face. 'Antonio. A baby is something never to be sorry for. I'm going to be a grandmother. That's wonderful news.'

'Even though...?' He blinked. 'This baby wasn't planned, Mamma. And Tia and I are not married.'

Maria shrugged. 'She seems very sweet, very genuine. You don't know how glad I am that you and Luca have found someone to love, and that Luca's engaged. I know how much Imogen loves him—and, from the look of that photograph, Tia clearly loves you.'

Oh, no, she didn't. She might've started to feel something towards him over the last few days, but he'd managed to kill it. Right now, Antonio was pretty sure that she hated him.

'I've been worried about you,' his mother said. 'I know you took your father's death very hard.'

Antonio closed his eyes for a moment. All the regrets for things that might have been. 'I'll never be able to make him proud of me now.'

'He was always proud of you, Antonio. He just didn't know how to tell you.'

Antonio didn't believe her.

'Your father wasn't an easy man,' Maria said. 'He was a good king, a good man—but he found family life hard. Especially after Sophia walked away from him.'

This was a subject that was never, ever discussed in their family. But Luca had actually mentioned their father's past in public, after he'd got engaged, so maybe things were changing.

'He loved Sophia, but she was from a different world.'

So was Tia.

'She found it hard to deal with our way of life.'

Antonio rather thought that Tia, on the other hand, could deal with anything.

'Walk with me, my child,' Maria said. 'We'll talk in the garden.'

He helped his mother put her coat on—he hadn't had time to take his off—and went with her into the formal garden. Even though it was almost December, there were still a few roses in bloom.

'I love this garden,' she said. 'Your father did, too. He was the one who increased the collection of roses here. He used to enjoy talking to the gardener and looking over rose catalogues with him. I rather think, if he'd had the time, he would have liked to breed his own roses.'

Was she talking about the same man he'd grown up with? Antonio was amazed. 'I didn't think my father—' He stopped abruptly, knowing his words were tactless and not wanting to hurt his mother.

'What?' she asked gently.

He didn't think his father had been interested in anything else other than ruling. 'Being the King was his entire life,' he said eventually.

'It was a very big part, but not all,' his mother corrected. 'He was a husband and a father as well as the King.'

Antonio struggled to think of a time when his father had showed open affection to his wife or his children. They hadn't even had a pet dog or cat. Even at Picco Innevato, his father had never really switched off. He had been the King first, and everything else had come way down his list of priorities.

As if his mother guessed what he was thinking, she said, 'Vincenzo found it hard to open up about his feelings.'

Yeah. He knew how that felt. He struggled, too.

'And Sophia couldn't cope with royal life.'

'What about you, Mamma?' The question came out before he could stop it. He winced. 'I apologise. That's much too personal. Forget I asked.'

'No, it's a valid question, and you have a point. I should have done more when you were younger,' Maria said with a sigh. 'Your father could never open up because of the way he was raised. In the view of his parents, children should be seen and not heard. They were very closed off and they never told Vincenzo that they valued him for himself—and with hindsight I think he needed to hear that.'

Antonio had never considered it before, and it made him feel guilty. 'I never told him I valued him, either.'

'But he knew you did,' Maria said gently. 'And he valued you, even though he didn't tell you. *I* value you. And maybe I should've told you that more often.'

The lump in Antonio's throat was so huge, he couldn't answer her. But he wrapped his arms round her and hugged her.

Maria stroked his hair. 'Your father was raised to be a king and a statesman, and he made sure he was the very best King and statesman he could be. But he couldn't open up—even to me, sometimes. I think he wanted to try to be closer to you. It's why he suggested that we should buy the house in Picco Innevato.'

'That was my father's idea?' Antonio pulled back, surprised, and looked his mother straight in the eye.

'Yes. So you and Luca would have somewhere to be children, without being in the public eye all the time.'

'That's where I took Tia,' he admitted. 'Picco Innevato.'

'I guessed that,' Maria said gently.

'I asked Miles not to tell anyone anything about where I was going or who I was with.'

She smiled. 'I'm your mother, Antonio. I know things without having to be told. Picco Innevato is where you always go when you need time to think. Where you go to decompress after a bad mission. Luca said that Tia Phillips had been trying to get in touch with you. He assumed that she was someone trying it on and told Miles to ignore her, whereas if either of them had thought to say something to me I could've told them she was Nathan's sister—and I know you blame yourself for Nathan's death.'

Antonio blew out a breath. 'I should've been in that car along with him.'

'I'm very glad you weren't,' Maria said. 'I feel for his poor mother—of course I do, because it's the fear every soldier's mother has, the worry about getting that phone call. I tried never to stand in your way, but I hated you being in danger all the time, and I worried about you every second you were on a mission. So did your father,' she added wryly, 'but he said you needed to do things your own way.'

'He was right,' Antonio admitted. 'I did.'

'I wish he'd written you a letter or something like that, to tell you how he felt. But your father was your father. A different generation.'

'Does Luca know?'

'That your father loved you both and couldn't say it?' She nodded. 'And I think love has changed Luca, too. What happened with Meribel... That was hard for both of them. I feel guilty about that. I should've stepped in and said no, don't agree to marry the girl unless you really love her, because you shouldn't sacrifice yourself for your country.'

'But I thought you said Meribel was crazy to...' Antonio stopped.

'I think,' Maria said gently, 'she will be OK, and in the end she did Luca a favour.'

How would Tia's mother judge him? Would she see him as the man who seduced her daughter, abandoned her, and was now forcing her into a marriage she didn't want? Or would she judge him more kindly?

'So what will you do now, Antonio? About Tia?'

'I...' He sighed. 'I don't know, Mamma.'

'You look as if you're in love in that photograph. And you didn't know it was being taken.'

'She thinks I set it up, to force her to marry me and make the baby my heir,' Antonio said.

'Then you need to talk to her. Find out what she wants. Find out if you can come to some kind of compromise—

one where you both win rather than both lose,' Maria advised. 'Tell her how you feel.'

'I don't have the words,' Antonio said.

'Tell her that first. Tell her you find it hard,' Maria said. 'Ask her to help you. And be as honest as you can.'

Once he'd finished talking to his mother, Antonio went to find Luca, who clapped him on the shoulder. 'Congratulations, little brother.'

'Not yet,' Antonio said. 'I haven't quite followed in the footsteps of you and Imogen. I might have messed things up.'

'If you love her,' Luca said softly, 'go after her. Tell her you love her.'

'Is that what you did with Imogen?'

Luca nodded. 'And it was the best thing I ever did.'

Antonio looked at his elder brother. He'd never seen Luca so relaxed and happy. Was it because he was free of the burden of their father's expectations? Or was it love? And, if it was love, could that work out for him and Tia, too?

And how was he going to convince Tia that they had a future?

He still had no idea by the time he went to see Gabriella.

'Antonio. It's good to see you.' She smiled at him 'I saw all the stuff in the press,' she said. 'Are you OK?'

He grimaced. 'I think I might have been an idiot.'

'The girl you kissed under the mistletoe on your front doorstep?'

He nodded. 'I've acted like every other Valenti man—I've expected everyone to fall in with my wishes, and kept my feelings shut away.'

'But you can change that,' she said.

'Yes. It's time things changed in Casavalle,' he agreed.

And then it hit him. He didn't need to shut away his emotions, like he'd always done in the past. Not any more. He loved Tia. Although he knew she didn't love him back, he loved her enough to give her what she wanted. She didn't want to be stuck here in the palace; she wanted to be with her mother in London.

So he'd go to see her. He'd release her from her agreement to marry him, and he'd tell her that he would support her, the baby and her mother however they needed him—just as Tia had always supported her family. If she eventually came to love him, then maybe she would come and live with him. But he was going to put her first.

Before he could arrange a flight to London, Miles called up to see him. 'I was hoping to have a meeting with you and your mother,' he said.

'If it's about Tia, I'm not in a position to discuss anything just now,' Antonio warned.

'It's about Gabriella,' Miles said.

Antonio frowned. 'Surely Gabriella needs to be part of any discussions about her?'

'They're preliminary discussions so we don't need to bother her just yet,' Miles said.

'What about Luca?'

'Prince Luca,' Miles said, 'is otherwise engaged at the moment.'

Antonio sighed. 'I really need to be in London. When do you need the meetings?'

'If your mother is free, we could start now,' Miles suggested.

Maria was available, so Antonio joined her in Miles's office.

'We're having a presentation ball for Gabriella before the coronation, to welcome her to the country,' Maria said.

'That's nice,' Antonio said, wondering just why he was needed at this meeting. Surely they didn't need his input into a ball?

'And we need to think about possible marriages for her,' Miles added.

Oh. So *that* was it. Politics. Antonio folded his arms. 'If you want my honest opinion, I think we should call a halt to this discussion right now. Gabriella should choose her own groom. The last arranged marriage for this family didn't work out well for anyone.'

'That's true,' Maria said, 'and we do need to repair relations between our countries.'

Diplomacy and palace politics. The two things Antonio loathed most. 'I still think Gabriella should choose her own groom. It's the twenty-first century.'

'The word is that Prince Cesar has broken up with his girlfriend,' Miles said. 'And he will be attending Gabriella's presentation ball. He's been called home to welcome her.'

Antonio snorted. 'I hope you're not marking him out as a potential match, Miles. Cesar Asturias is a smooth operator, a playboy who doesn't take women seriously—and I'm not sure he's good enough for my sister.'

Maria said gently, 'Things aren't always what they seem. Remember, the media calls you a playboy as well. Your girlfriends don't exactly last a long time.'

'Because I never found the right one,' Antonio said, 'and I hope that's just about to change.' He looked pleadingly at his mother. 'Do you *really* need me in these discussions? I think you should talk to Gabriella, not to me.' He took a deep breath. Time to tell them how he felt. 'Mamma, Miles—right now, I don't want to be here discussing politics. I want to see Tia. I need to tell her...' The words stuck.

'Tell her what's in your heart,' Maria advised, and gave him a hug. 'Good luck.'

'Good luck, sir,' Miles said, shaking his hand.

To get Tia to really listen to him, Antonio thought, he was going to need more than luck.

And if his words froze on him again when he was talking to her, he was really going to be in trouble. Maybe he should write them down. Just to be sure.

CHAPTER SEVEN

LONDON FELT GREY, dull and dingy after the bright, open spaces of Picco Innevato.

But Tia's time in Casavalle had all been a lie. She knew she'd be very stupid to let herself believe otherwise.

She'd been such a fool. Fancy thinking that Prince Antonio might really care for her.

And now she was going to be trapped into marriage with a man who didn't love her. And was marrying her purely for the baby's sake. This was utterly ridiculous in the twenty-first century, but she supposed things were different when you were a Royal. If she said no, that would mean the press would hound her mother, and Tia couldn't let that happen. She'd do anything to protect her family.

She rested her hand on her bump. 'Why couldn't he have just let us disappear back here?' she whispered.

The baby didn't kick.

Yeah. She had no idea, either.

There was a gentle knock on her door. 'Tia?'

She forced herself to look all smiling and happy. No way was she going to let her mother know what an idiot she'd been. She didn't want Grace to worry. 'Hi, Mum.'

'I thought you might like to see these,' Grace said, coming into the room with a box that Tia recognised as being full of Nathan's things.

'I'm not sure I can face that,' she admitted.

'I think you need to see what's in here,' Grace said gently. 'I'll leave you to it.'

Tia sat staring at the box for a long, long time. Then she removed the lid.

Inside were books and papers. On the very top was a photograph of Nathan and Antonio in their fatigues, smiling, their arms round each other.

Her eyes prickled. How much she missed her brother.

And the man with him in the photograph—that was the man she'd let herself fall for. Except he didn't really exist, did he?

She turned the photograph over and recognised the handwriting on the back. Nathan's handwriting.

A—the dream team on a good day   N

Why was a photograph that had a message obviously addressed to Antonio in Nathan's belongings? Had her brother never sent it?

The next thing in the box was a letter. Except it wasn't to Nathan—or from Nathan. It was a letter to her mother.

She was about to fold it up again, rather than pry in her mother's things, when she noticed the address at the top of the page.

Picco Innevato.

Antonio's house.

Why would Antonio be writing to her mother?

Was this her mother's way of trying to tell her something?

Frowning, she read on.

Dear Mrs Phillips
I would like to apologise sincerely to you for the way in which I broke the news of Nathan's death back in January. I should have told you back then

that Nathan was like a brother to me, and I miss him terribly. I should also have been there to support you and Tia in your grief.

My only excuse, such as it is, is that I find it very hard to show my feelings. I grew up knowing that duty should always come first. But I want that to be different for my child, whether the baby is a son or a daughter—I know the baby will be loved because Tia is his or her mother, and she's amazing.

I apologise, too, for the way in which I've behaved towards Tia. I truly didn't intend to abandon her, or you. It feels like a weak excuse, but we've had a lot of unexpected events in our family over the last few months and it's been a struggle to deal with them.

Your daughter is an amazing woman. She deserves more than I can ever give her. I have asked her to marry me, and I know she thinks my sole motivation is that the baby will be fourth in line to the throne of Casavalle. But I think a lot of your daughter and I want to be a full part of our baby's life.

I should have asked your permission before asking her to marry me, and I apologise for my forwardness. With your permission, I should like to ask Tia again if she will marry me. It has nothing to do with convention and everything to do with who she is and how she makes me feel.

I am trying to be more open about my emotions, and I hope that she and our baby will find it in their hearts to help me.

I thought that you might like this photograph, taken on the mission before Nathan's last one. It means a lot to me, but I think you should have it.
With kindest regards
Antonio Valenti

The date was yesterday.

The day of the children's Christmas party.

The day when she'd fallen asleep on the sofa; when he'd woken her later, she'd realised that he'd tucked a fleecy blanket round her.

And this letter, where he said that he thought a lot of her... Antonio wasn't one to talk about his feelings. He was aloof and formal and *royal*. So this was tantamount to saying that he loved her.

She couldn't quite take it in.

Did he love her?

Had she misjudged him?

Frowning, she went out into their kitchen, where her mother was sitting at the table.

'Are you all right, love?' Grace asked.

'Confused,' Tia admitted. 'When did you get that letter?'

'Today, when the car brought you back from the airport,' Grace said. 'And there were two parcels, too, with a note asking me to let you rest for a bit before giving them to you.'

'Parcels?'

Grace indicated the two boxes on the kitchen countertop, both perfectly wrapped.

Tia opened the smaller one first, and caught her breath. It was the etched glass bauble for the tree.

In silence, she handed it to her mother.

'That's beautiful. Is that where you were?' Grace asked.

Tia nodded. 'He said he bought it for the baby. For the tree.'

'Just like your father and I used to buy a new decoration every year for our tree,' Grace said softly.

With shaking hands, Tia undid the scarlet ribbon on the second box. And she had to bite back the tears when she saw the snow globe nestled among the packing peanuts that protected it: the beautiful filigree star suspended in a perfect orb, except she hadn't wanted to spend the money on herself.

When had he bought this?

Perhaps when she'd been browsing at the candle stall yesterday. He must have gone back and bought it especially for her.

Antonio Valenti might not say a lot, but he noticed things. He'd seen how much she'd liked it. He'd guessed that she didn't want to spend money on herself when she had the baby to think of, and he'd bought it because he'd wanted to do something nice for her, give her something that she'd denied herself.

Especially given what he'd written to her mother, that snow globe was a definite declaration of love. It wasn't the cost of the item; it was the thought behind it.

With horror, Tia realised that he really did love her. And he hadn't been able to tell her exactly how he felt because he'd been brought up in a formal, public world where he'd always felt forced to hide his emotions away. She hadn't made it easy for him to talk to her, either.

This year, he'd been emotionally swamped: he'd lost his best friend, actually been there when the land mine had exploded and seen Nathan killed; he'd lost his father; and then his life had been turned upside down with the revelations about his brother's fiancée cheating on him and the existence of his half-sister.

And then she'd come along, six months pregnant, and informed him that their one night together had had consequences and he was going to be a father.

No wonder Antonio had had trouble talking about it. It was an overwhelming amount for anyone to deal with, let alone someone who wasn't used to talking about his feelings.

She'd pushed him away because he couldn't tell her

how he felt. She'd made the assumption that he'd manipulated the situation with the media, so she'd be forced to
marry him and make the baby his heir. Yet had she been
fair to make that assumption? If she looked at what he'd
actually done... He'd taken her away from the public glare
of the palace to his family's private home, the place where
he'd spent the summers during his childhood.

He'd tried to make a proper family Christmas for her,
choosing a tree and decorations with her and then cooking her Christmas dinner. He'd agreed to fill in for the Father Christmas who'd broken his leg—the kind of role she
knew he'd never done before, simply because she'd asked
him to. He'd kissed her under the mistletoe, shown her
with actions rather than words how he really felt about her.

And, because he hadn't had the words to tell her, she'd
assumed the worst.

How could she have been so stupid—and so unfair?

And this was the last straw. For the last year, she'd tried
so hard to be strong, kept all her worries locked inside.
Now tears slid down her face. She cried not just for her
brother, but for the man she loved, for her mum, for her
dad, for her baby and for herself.

Grace wrapped her arms round Tia. 'It's going to be
all right, love.'

'How can it be? I've messed everything up. I've hurt
Antonio; and I just don't know what to do.'

'I do,' Grace said. 'Talk to him. Go back to Casavalle
and tell Antonio how you really feel about him.'

'I can't leave you in London, Mum.'

'Yes, you can. I'll be fine,' Grace said firmly. 'I'm
managing. Yes, I'm still going to have bad days, but I
have support here. And I've always felt terrible about you
putting your own life on hold because of me. I know you
love me and you worry about me—but that's how I feel

about you, too. And it's about time you started living your own life instead of trying to fit everything around me.'

'But, Mum—'

'But nothing,' Grace cut in. 'All I want is to see you happy. Go to Antonio and tell him how you feel about him.'

'What if he's changed his mind? What he said in that letter... I didn't give him a chance to tell me any of that.'

'Give him a chance now. It's not too late.'

'But...how can he be with me? How will his family ever accept me?'

'They'll love you as much as he does,' Grace said. 'I know your father's family didn't accept me, but not everyone is like them.'

'But he's a prince, Mum!'

'Think about how he was with you in Picco Innevato,' Grace counselled. 'That's the private man—the man he really is. One who cares. One who might not be very good at telling you how he feels, but look at that photograph.' She brought the newspaper over to Tia, showing her the front page. 'The look on his face when his hand's on your bump and he's feeling the baby kick. You're looking at him with exactly the same expression. You love each other, Tia. You just need to give him the chance to learn how to tell you.'

Tia hugged her mum and cried even more, letting out all the misery and loneliness she'd hidden away for the last year.

And then, once she'd washed her face, she started packing.

She was halfway through when their doorbell rang.

'I'll get it,' Grace called.

When her mother didn't call her, Tia continued packing, assuming that it was a courier wanting them to take in a parcel for their neighbour.

But then Grace knocked gently on her door. 'I'm just going next door to see Becky. And you have a visitor.'

'A visitor?'

'Remember what I said,' Grace said softly. 'Give him a chance.'

Tia's pulse leaped.

Had Antonio come for her?

'I've made you both a cup of tea. You need to talk,' Grace said.

Tia followed her mother into the kitchen. Antonio was sitting there as if he belonged—but how could a prince belong to her world?

'Good luck,' Grace said, patting his shoulder, then left the flat.

Oh, help.

What did she do now? What should she say?

In the end, she fell back on a simple, 'How was your flight?'

'Fine, thank you.'

His face was as impassive as ever. She didn't have a clue what was going on in his head. Was he here to follow up on the letter he'd written to her mother, to try to tell her how he felt? Or was he here because he'd had time to think about it and had changed his mind?

'Why are you here?' The words slipped out before she could stop them.

'I've come to release you from your agreement to marry me.'

It shocked her so much that she ended up sitting down at the table with him, knowing that her knees simply weren't going to support her.

He wasn't here to follow up on that letter. She was too late. He'd changed his mind.

'What I did was selfish,' Antonio said. 'I railroaded you

into agreeing to marry me. I didn't give you the choice and I was wrong. You're a strong, independent woman and you're amazing.'

Tia couldn't quite get her head round this. Was he breaking up with her, or was he trying to tell her something else?

'I'm not very good at showing my emotions,' he said. 'That's true of all the Valenti men—my father, my brother and me. But when you stayed with me at Picco Innevato, you taught me so much. You taught me how to feel—and that it was OK to admit I love someone.'

She stared at him, still not quite comprehending.

'I'm making a mess of this,' he said with a sigh. 'I'm trying to tell you that I…' He paused.

That he what?

That he loved her?

He pulled a piece of paper out of his pocket and looked at it. '"I love you, Tia. I want to marry you, but only if you want to marry me. I'm not asking you out of a sense of duty or of honour, just because you happen to be pregnant with my baby. I'm asking you because I want to be with you."'

She looked at him. 'Are you *reading* that to me?'

'Yes,' he said. 'Because I can't do the words otherwise. They freeze in my throat. I don't know how to say it. That's why I wrote everything down on the plane, in case I froze. So, yes, I'm reading from a script, because otherwise I can't do it and I don't want you to think…' He blew out a breath. 'I'm off script. I'm stuck.'

He loved her.

So much that he'd written it down to make sure, with his usual military precision, he got it right.

'Go back on script,' she said softly. Because she needed to hear what he had to say.

His face brightened, and he looked at the paper again.

"'I know you're strong enough to cope with just about anything on your own, and I admire your strength, but you don't *have* to be on your own. If you'll let me, I'll be right by your side, supporting you all the way. You might have to yell at me from time to time, and remind me to tell you what's in my head instead of assuming that you already know by some weird kind of osmosis, but I'll be there with you all the way. I'll be the best husband I can possibly be to you, and the most loving dad I can possibly be to our baby—and, if we're lucky, to our future babies.'" He lifted his chin and put the paper down. 'I'm going to do it without the script now. I love you.'

'You love me.' She still couldn't quite take that in he was actually saying it to her.

'If I'm really honest with you, I fell in love with you before I'd even met you,' Antonio said. 'The way Nathan described you, so full of courage and strength, I knew you were the kind of woman I wanted to be with. But when I finally met you everything had just gone horribly wrong. I felt guilty that Nathan died.'

'It wasn't your fault.'

'I still felt guilty,' Antonio said. 'Survivor guilt, maybe, but guilty all the same. Plus you were his little sister. You were off limits. I was all mixed up, wanting you and feeling guilty about that, too. I'd wanted to tell you and your mum how much Nathan was loved, how much everyone thought of him—and instead I just closed off and made a mess of it.' He grimaced. 'When I saw you again at the charity gala, I felt so bad that I hadn't stayed in touch.'

'Don't be so hard on yourself. Your father died, and you were needed at the palace,' she said gently. 'I understand.'

He took her hands. 'I still should've done more, and I'm sorry I let you down.'

'It's OK. You're here now—and you're not the only one

who shut your emotions away,' she told him. 'I couldn't cry for Nathan because I thought I had to be strong for Mum, and I was wrong, too.'

'You've been crying now.' He lifted one hand to stroke her face.

She nodded. 'For everything. For you, for Nathan, for both our dads, for my mum, for the baby...'

Antonio leaned over the table and kissed her lightly. 'You don't have to be strong all the time—just as I don't have to be strong and silent, either. We'll have each other's backs. And we can be ourselves with each other and with our baby.'

'I love you, too.' She swallowed hard. 'And I knew before you told me that you love me, because you bought me the snow globe. You noticed I liked it and guessed that I didn't want to spend the money on myself. It's the thought that counts more than the gift.'

'True. You've taught me that, too.' He looked at her. 'So, what now?'

'I told you about my mum—how my dad's family didn't like her.'

'And you worry that my family will feel that way about you?'

'I don't have a drop of blue blood in my veins. How am I going to fit in?'

'By being yourself,' he said. 'Just so you know, my mother told me to come and see you and tell you how I really felt. She said those photographs on the news made her feel better, made her feel that I'd found someone to love and who loved me all the way back. And she's thrilled about becoming a grandmother.'

'Really?'

'Really,' he confirmed. 'Luca told me to go after you and tell you how I feel about you. So did Gabriella. You'll be more than welcome in Casavalle, and so will your mother. I want to… I want to be a family with you, Tia. You come as a package, and that's fine by me—because I come as a package, too.'

Then, to her surprise, he slid off his chair and got down on one knee. 'I know I'm rushing you and you don't have to answer me now, but will you marry me? I'm not asking you because I think it's my duty or yours, but because I hope we both feel the same way about each other,' he clarified. 'Because we both love each other, and we want to make a family together.'

She knew that speech had been tough for him. Telling her how he really felt. Particularly as he'd done it without working out the words and writing them down first.

But it was how she felt about him, too.

'Because we both love each other, and we want to make a family together,' she repeated. 'Yes.'

He got to his feet in what looked like a nanosecond, and wrapped his arms round her. 'I love you, Tia. It feels weird saying it, but I'm hoping the more I tell you, the easier it'll be, and that you'll come to believe me.'

'I believe you now,' she said. 'I love you, too.'

He kissed her lingeringly, and there was a volley of kicks in her stomach.

He broke the kiss. 'Is that baby-speak for "Get a room"?' he asked wryly.

'No. I think it's baby-speak for "I approve",' she said with a smile.

'Good. Let's go and tell your mother the news. And then I'd like to take you, your mother and the baby home with me to Casavalle. Home to our future.'

'Our future,' she echoed.

EPILOGUE

Valentine's Day

TIA PEERED OVER the edge of the cot at the sleeping week-old baby. 'I can't believe we made someone so perfect,' she whispered.

'Nathan Vincenzo Valenti. The most beautiful baby in the world.' Antonio slid his arm round her shoulders. 'It doesn't get better than this, does it?'

'I didn't think I'd ever be this happy,' Tia said. 'But your family's wonderful and they've all made me feel so welcome—Mum, too.'

'Because you're part of us,' Antonio said simply. 'You have been, since the first moment you walked into the palace and gave my mother a hug. And definitely since you stood in our private chapel and said your wedding vows. You've got the Valenti name now. No escape for you.'

She twisted round and kissed him. 'I don't want to escape. I love you, Antonio.'

'Good. Because I love you, too.'

They were still gazing besottedly at their sleeping son when Grace walked into the room.

'Is he asleep?' she whispered.

'Yes,' Antonio said.

'Then I'll come back for a cuddle later,' Grace said.

They followed her out into the living room. 'Are you having lunch with us today, Mum?' Tia asked.

'It's lovely of you to ask, but I'm afraid I can't—I'm already going out,' Grace said.

'Anywhere nice?' Tia asked.

Grace blushed. 'Miles says it's a mystery tour.'

Tia exchanged a glance with Antonio. They'd both noticed that the palace secretary was spending a lot of time in Grace's company. Miles and Grace seemed to have bonded over organising Tia and Antonio's wedding in a private ceremony in the middle of December, and that blush just now made Tia pretty sure that her mother was going out on a date rather than simply doing a bit of sight-seeing.

'Have a wonderful time, Mum,' she said, hugging her mother. 'And don't overdo it.'

Grace smiled. 'I know better than to do that, love. Besides, Miles won't let me. I'll see you both later and I'll be back to cuddle my grandson.'

Antonio smiled at Tia as his mother-in-law left their apartment. 'I have a feeling there might be a little bit of romance in the air.'

'Me, too, and I'm glad,' Tia said. 'Mum's been on her own for much too long. And I like Miles. He's a nice guy. Kind.' She smiled back at him. 'Even if he did refuse to let me talk to you for weeks.'

'He was doing his job. Being diligent. And he'll look after Grace the same way,' Antonio said. 'And now it's my turn to look after you. Sit on that sofa and put your feet up, because a cheese toastie and a cup of tea are in your very near future.'

She grinned. 'Are you ordering me about, Your Royal Highness?'

'I can try,' Antonio said, laughing. 'But no. We're a

team. And I only made that suggestion because I know it's your favourite. You can have anything you like.' He kissed her lightly. 'If anything, I'm yours to command.'

She scoffed. 'I'm no general.'

'No. You're just gorgeous,' he said. 'I love you, Tia. I never thought I'd ever be this happy in Casavalle. But things have changed in the palace. Everywhere feels lighter and happier and less formal. You, Imogen, Gabi and Grace have kind of taken over the palace, and my mother's just blossomed, having daughters and a new best friend. And with you and our baby here with me... My world's complete.'

'Mine, too. I love you,' Tia said, kissing him. 'We don't have to have lunch, you know. We could just go and snuggle up under the covers.'

'That,' Antonio said, 'is an excellent idea.' He scooped her up and carried her into their bedroom.

But just as he was about to deposit Tia on the bed, they heard a wail.

'We,' he said, 'are going to have to wait. Because it sounds as if someone's hungry.' He settled Tia back against the pillows. 'I'll go and get him. And then I'll make you that cup of tea.'

'And join us, I hope,' Tia said. 'Because there's nothing more perfect than snuggling up with my gorgeous son and even more gorgeous husband.'

Antonio kissed her again. 'I agree. You're the wisest of women, Tia Valenti.'

Tia made herself comfortable, ready to feed the baby. The newest Valenti Prince had stolen everyone's heart, and he'd made a huge difference to life at the palace. Their baby was an unexpected gift who'd brought Antonio's family closer together, cracking the reserve and formality at the palace to let the warmth of love radiate through.

Love and tenderness that weren't kept just for private moments: Antonio was openly affectionate, holding her hand and sliding his arm round her and stealing kisses. He'd lost his cold, remote shell for good, and the real Antonio was definitely the man of her dreams.

'Penny for them?' he asked, walking in while rocking the baby on his shoulder.

'Just thinking how lucky I am,' she said.

'How lucky we are,' he corrected. 'And this is something I'll never take for granted. A happiness I always want to share with the world. Because love is the best gift of all.'

* * * * *

Love and tenderness that wrapped deep inside its private recesses. A dam swayed toward affectionate, holding her hand and guiding his own hand her and bracing his—

Had her the Old remake with for, picked a tiredness Ann look, head and by the heart of her dreams—

"You—" Ambhenur, he asked with sinister, unhappy the bury of his, murmur.

She looked at him in the dark, a little hall—

"Now baby we are, he demanded, and this became thing, I'll never be in the ground. A happiness I enjoy now to spare within the world. Because love is the best act of all."

MAVERICK
HOLIDAY MAGIC

TERESA SOUTHWICK

To all the remarkably creative and talented writers
in the Montana Mavericks series
and our gifted and patient editor, Susan Litman.
All of you made working on this book a joy!

Chapter One

Hunter Crawford knew what his father was up to.

It was common knowledge that Max had hired the local wedding planner to find wives for his six sons. Four of them were now off the marriage market and the target on Hunter's back was getting bigger. That's why he was suspicious of the old man pushing this big destination wedding for their brother Finn in Rustler's Notch, Colorado. Hunter was pushing back. He'd much rather stay here on the Ambling A Ranch, where he was more insulated from his father's meddling.

There were four cabins on this sprawling property—the big house, where his father and his brother Wilder lived, and three smaller places.

Hunter lived in one of them with his six-year-old daughter, Wren, and loved the two-story log house. It had four bedrooms, two baths, a great room and kitchen. The place wasn't huge, but it had enough room for the two of them. The biggest selling point was that it had no bad memories from the past clinging to it. He was doing his best to keep the vibe pure of pain, for Wren's sake. Although that could change.

His instinct was telling him that this wedding was somehow going to threaten his resolve to maintain his bachelor designation. The way he saw it, everyone had one great love in their life and he'd had his. Losing her had nearly destroyed him. He was determined not to put himself in a position where that could happen to him again. But his father and Wilder weren't taking no for an answer and had come to give him a hard sell.

He'd reluctantly opened the door to them and they followed him into the kitchen. Might as well get this over with, he told himself as he took a breath and faced them. "I'm not going to the wedding."

Maximilian Crawford stood beside the circular oak table and stared him down. He was a tall, handsome, distinguished man in his sixties. Tan and rugged looking, his lined face suggested a life spent outdoors—and it had been. Now he left the physically taxing ranch work to Hunter and his brothers. His hair had once been brown like his sons' but now it was gray and earned him the nickname "Silver Fox." He was accustomed to getting what he wanted by any legal means necessary, but Hunter had inherited his father's stubborn streak. So neither of them blinked.

Finally, his father said, "Why?"

"I have my reasons."

"It's important to me that the whole family is there. Your brothers and their new wives are looking forward to a little vacation in Rustler's Notch." The older man looked at his youngest son, a "don't just stand there" expression in his eyes.

"Yeah," Wilder said. "You could use a vacation, bro."

"I'm good," Hunter said.

"It's actually not you I'm worried about." Wilder settled his hands on his lean hips. "The truth is, I could use your help. The two of us are the only single Crawford men left. It's Colorado in November. Can you say 'snow bunnies'? It pains me to say this, but I need a wingman."

Hunter glared at him. "Did someone drop you on your head when you were a baby?"

"Maybe." Wilder glanced at their father, then shrugged. "Why?"

"Just to make sure I've got this right…" He paused for dramatic effect. "At this family outing, your primary goal is to hit on every single woman between the ages of twenty and forty?"

"Yes."

It wasn't easy to get under his brother's skin. Hunter wasn't even sure why he tried. "Even if I was interested in partying, which I'm not, I have a six-year-old daughter. Wren and I would cramp your style."

"I wasn't suggesting we bring Wren." Wilder stopped for a moment, clearly thinking that over. "Although, a single father with a kid could be a chick magnet."

"Don't even go there," Hunter warned. "And no, you can't borrow her."

"That's low," his brother said. "I would never use my niece like that."

"He was just kidding," Max cut in.

"Yeah, lighten up, big brother. It would do you good to let off some steam."

"How would you know?" Hunter asked. "All you think about is your next score. You have absolutely no responsibilities. And no idea what I've gone through."

"That's true," Wilder acknowledged. "But it's been six years since your wife died. Everyone else has been tiptoeing around the subject but I'm already in the doghouse with you so what the heck."

"What are you talking about?"

"Lara wouldn't want you to be like this. There's no

law against moving on. And your daughter should see
you out and having fun."

"He's right, son." Max's expression was sympathetic.

Hunter shifted his glare to Max. "You don't get a vote."

Max's wife, the brothers' mother, had left the family
without a word when Hunter was a little boy and Wilder
was just a baby. Their father was on his own raising six
boys. As a kid, Hunter didn't know that his parents' relationship was bitterly unhappy. All he knew was that
his mother took off and he'd believed if he'd been a better kid, a better son, she would have stayed. Max had it
rough but Sheila didn't die. She'd made a choice. Unlike
Hunter's wife, who'd passed away suddenly. The woman
he'd loved was gone forever and there was no one to blame
but himself.

"It's true," Max said. "I can't tell you what to do. But
that doesn't change the fact that I would really like to
celebrate your brother's marriage with my whole family
in attendance."

"Why is this wedding such a big deal to you, Dad?"

Max sighed and looked the way he always did when
something should be clear as day but he still had to explain. "Sarah and Logan had a nontraditional ceremony
at the local bar."

"Nothing wrong with Ace in the Hole. I've met some
nice women there," Wilder said.

Max shook his head and continued. "Xander and Lily
had their wedding at the Rust Creek Falls Community
Center."

"It was nice. My daughter had a great time there."
It was local and this town was a place where everyone
watched out for neighbors. Hunter didn't have to worry
about keeping an eye on Wren every second.

"Knox and Genevieve were secretly married," Max continued.

"So were Finn and Avery," Hunter interjected. "I say again—what's the big deal?"

"I think it's about time we had a big splashy, formal family affair. We have a lot to celebrate, what with four of you boys settled down." Max was known to be a master manipulator, but no one doubted his love for his sons. "Think about it. Five-star resort. Beautiful country. Love in the air."

Maybe for his brothers, but Hunter wasn't interested in love. Not again. "Look, Dad, how many ways do you want me to say this? I don't want to meet anyone. Stop trying to fix me up and call off Vivienne Dalton."

"Matchmaking is not what this is about." Max didn't look the least bit guilty about paying the local wedding planner a million dollars to find wives for his six sons. "And think of your daughter. Think about Wren."

"She's all I think about." She was his world and everything he did was to keep her happy and safe.

"Why would you deny her the opportunity to be with her family? To make memories. And if you were to have a little fun, too, well…" Max let the words hang in the air between them.

"And Finn asked you to be a groomsman along with the rest of us brothers," Wilder reminded him. "Come on, Hunter. You can't let him down. And as far as watching Wren? You've got Logan, Knox, Xander."

"And me," Max said.

"And me," Wilder chimed in.

"Yeah," Hunter said, deliberately surrounding the single word with sarcasm. "Because nothing could go wrong with that scenario."

"That's low," Wilder said. "If you can't trust your family, then who can you trust?"

"A nanny."

Hunter looked at his brother, then both of them stared at Max, who had made the suggestion. "What?"

"Hire a nanny for the wedding." Max shrugged.

"Wedding? What wedding?" No one had seen Wren standing there. But now the little girl was clearly excited. "Can I be in it? The bride and groom are going to need a flower girl."

"Oh, sugar. I'm in deep trouble now," Hunter muttered to himself.

"Hi, Gramps." The blonde, blue-eyed star of his world walked farther into the room and looked way up at the tall men surrounding her. "Hi, Uncle Wilder. I was upstairs playing with my princess dolls. I didn't know you were here."

Max went down on one knee to be on her level. "Hi, Wrennie. We came to talk to your dad about going to Uncle Finn's wedding. I'm going to use my private plane to fly us all there and we're going to stay in a very fancy hotel."

"Oh, boy!" Her big eyes grew bigger. "For real?"

"Yup. And I'm pretty sure Avery is going to ask you to be her flower girl. But your dad isn't sure he wants to go."

She turned her gaze on him. "But why?"

Hunter hated when she looked at him like this. He lost every argument because stubborn was no match for those big blue eyes. "It's a town that's bigger than Rust Creek Falls. In a hotel like that there are lots of tourists—"

"Who?"

"Strangers visiting from everywhere. It will be harder for me to keep an eye on you all the time."

"But the flower girl gets to wear a pretty dress. Not as

pretty as Avery's because she's the bride and that's like the wedding princess, but..."

"I suppose." Hunter was at a loss when she talked dresses.

"And maybe Avery doesn't know anyone else to be a flower girl," Wren said earnestly. "I have to be there."

"That's a good point." Wilder bent at the waist and rested his hands on his knees, making his gaze almost level with hers. "And there's something else you should know. Your dad is supposed to be Uncle Finn's groomsman."

"Would you have to get all dressed up, too?" the little girl asked.

"That's right, Wren," Max said. "Your daddy is going to need a tuxedo."

This was why his dad and Wilder had followed him here to the house to finish this discussion. Despite their words to the contrary, they knew Wren was home from school. The two of them were counting on her to overhear. With her on their side, he didn't stand a chance. But he'd give it one more shot.

"If I'm in the wedding, honey, it means I can't watch over you the way I want."

Wren nodded thoughtfully, then her face brightened. "I heard Gramps say something about getting someone to take care of me."

"Yeah, but I don't think we can find anyone on such short notice." Hunter was beginning to hope there was a way for him to make this situation work in his favor after all.

"I know someone," his daughter said.

Well, dang it. "Who?"

"Miss Merry. She works at my school. She helps in the classroom and she's a playground supervisor at recess and lunch." She smiled. "She's really nice, especially on my first day of school when I was new. She played with me and got the other kids to play, too. She's my first best friend in Rust Creek Falls."

"She sounds perfect," Max approved. "You're not going to disappoint my granddaughter, are you, Hunter?"

"Please, Daddy."

The eyes, the pleading voice. The guilt that she didn't have a mother. Hunter was toast and he knew it. "I'll talk to Miss Merry and see what she says. But if it doesn't work out, that's it. Will you be okay with that?"

"Yes!" Wren threw herself into his arms. "Thank you, Daddy. You're the best daddy in the whole world."

If only. He wanted to be her hero and keep her safe. So he would meet Miss Merry, who sounded like someone's elderly grandmother. In which case this could work.

"You're younger than I thought you'd be."

And you're even more handsome than you sounded on the phone. For a split second Merry Matthews was afraid she'd said that out loud. When the wariness in his green eyes didn't change to fear of the crazy woman, she figured the thought stayed in her head where it belonged.

She'd heard rumors in town about his exceptional good looks, but she had been woefully unprepared to see Hunter Crawford in the flesh. Then his deep voice had her nerve endings sparking and momentarily shorted out a commonsense answer. Now he was staring at her as if her hair was on fire. It was time to say something.

"I'm Meredith Matthews but everyone calls me Merry." She was standing on the front porch of his log cabin house on the Ambling A Ranch. The man practically filled the doorway and she was looking up at him. "And I'm not sure how to respond to that remark about my age, Mr. Crawford."

"Sorry. It's just that my daughter talked about you and I just expected—" He shook his head and looked sheepish and, actually, pretty adorable. A dashing cowboy dressed in a snap-front shirt, worn jeans and boots. There was probably a Stetson around somewhere but he wasn't wearing it. His short hair was light brown and there was the slightest indentation in his chin. "I apologize. That was rude."

"Not really. If you think about it, there's no way to go wrong when you judge a woman's age on the younger side."

"I suppose that's true enough. But now I've kept you standing outside in the cold. Please come in." He opened the heavy door wider and stepped back to let her enter.

Merry glanced at the interior and liked what she saw. There were wood floors with colorful braided rugs strategically scattered over the surface. A comfortable blue couch and a leather recliner were arranged in front of a flat screen TV housed in an entertainment center. On the opposite wall a fireplace held freshly chopped wood just waiting for a match to light it. The place had a woodsy feel and was very cozy.

When she looked at the man again, any hint of sheepishness had disappeared, and he was all business. Which he should be. After all, this was a job interview.

"Please have a seat." He indicated the sofa and took the chair at a right angle to it. "As I said on the phone, Wren mentioned you for a child-care position that I need to fill."

"I'm looking forward to hearing more about it." She really needed the money and appreciated this chance.

What she made as an aide at Rust Creek Falls Elementary School didn't go far enough now. Since her father's death, she'd had to shut down his electrician business and there went her extra income. This could be the break she so badly needed.

She settled her purse beside her and rested the folder she'd brought on her knees. "How can I help you?"

"My brother is getting married in a couple of weeks. It's a destination wedding, in Colorado. A place called Rustler's Notch. Have you heard of it?"

She shook her head. "Sounds quaint and colorful. And interesting."

Exasperation flashed in his eyes, a clue that there was a story here. "Mostly it's inconvenient."

"How so?"

"My father is sparing no expense and insists the whole family be there."

"That's very generous of him. And I can see how you'd think it's incredibly unreasonable," she teased. "Is there a problem?"

Irritation flashed in his eyes again but this time it was directed at her. "I have five brothers. Four of them are married. One has a baby. They've offered to help keep an eye on Wren and have the best of intentions, but all of them have distractions. The bottom line is that she's my responsibility. My daughter is at that stage where she's curious and likes to explore, and while I like to think I can keep up with her, sometimes one person isn't enough."

Merry had taken his daughter under her wing on her first day of school. Wren had been new to town and frightened and Merry understood how that felt because growing up she'd been the new kid a lot. Her father had moved around for work and she'd changed schools often. So it had become her mission to make Wren Crawford comfortable, introduce her to the other kids and facilitate friendships. The little girl had made passing comments about her life. Her mother was dead and her father was sad sometimes.

She folded her hands and set them on the file folder in her lap. "Wild guess here. You don't want to go to the wedding."

He grinned wryly. "And I thought I was being subtle. To be honest, I'd rather not. But I can't let my daughter miss out on the chance to be a flower girl, which she wants more than another princess doll. Also I'm a groomsman, so…"

"You don't feel you have much choice."

"Yes. And—" His gaze narrowed.

Merry had the fleeting thought that his intensity brought out a dark, brooding and slightly dangerous side that made her insides quiver. And that reaction needed to stay inside if she was going to land this gig. "Is something wrong?"

"You're judging," he accused.

"I'm not," she lied. "Just clarifying. Trying to determine your expectations for the child-care professional you're looking to hire."

He nodded. "Because of the commitments I have at the event, it will be impossible for me to keep an eye on Wren one hundred percent of the time, and while of course I want someone to watch her when I can't, it would be great if that person could really relate to her." His mouth pulled tight for a moment. "I want someone who is nurturing, caring and warm with my daughter." Another slight grin ghosted across his face. "No self-defense training is required."

"Your little girl is an angel. I think I can handle the above qualifications without breaking a sweat."

"Wren really seems to like you. But she's a kid. How do I know you're the best person for this position?"

"I brought references." Based on the few things his daughter had said, she'd had a feeling she might need more than just her sincere and friendly smile to get this job. She handed him the folder.

He opened it and glanced through the papers there. "What's this?"

"My résumé. Also I've included business, personal and educational references." They were all glowing declarations of her interaction with people in general and children in particular.

One by one he examined each testimonial. "You're an aide at the school, taking early childhood education classes. And you work for your father's electrical business."

"Not anymore. He passed away recently."

His gaze met hers and there was sincere sympathy in his eyes. "I'm sorry for your loss."

"Thank you." The words were quiet and polite, completely at odds with the pain and panic of insecurity trickling through her.

He nodded, then continued his inspection of her paperwork. "This all looks to be in order. Do you have anything else?"

Really? Apparently he was looking to hire Mother Teresa. She reached for her purse and pulled out her wallet. "Did you miss the part in the principal's letter of recommendation where she mentioned my wings, halo and uncanny ability to walk on water? Here's my current Montana driver's license. Feel free to run a background check."

Merry had kept her tone courteous and professional, though she wanted to be huffy and annoyed. Still, she prepared herself to be shown out of his house. Her recommendations were glowing. That wasn't blowing her own horn, just a fact. If that wasn't good enough for him, then maybe the extra money wasn't worth the trouble. And good luck to him finding a weekend nanny in this town.

The man stared at her for several moments before the corners of his mouth curved up a little. He was fighting a smile. Hallelujah. The cowboy had a sense of humor.

"That won't be necessary, Miss Matthews. The most important qualification for this job isn't on here."

"And that is?"

"Wren likes you. If you still want it, the position is yours."

She looked at him for a moment, not sure she'd heard right. "You're sure? As you probably guessed from what I said, I can sometimes be headstrong and a little outspoken."

"I noticed. And you may have guessed that I am protective of my daughter. Maybe too much, but with her I'd rather be safe than sorry."

"You love her," Merry said simply. And it was quite possibly his most attractive quality.

"I do. Very much. Her mother died so she only has me."

"She told me." Merry remembered the conversation. She'd told Wren her own mom was gone, too, and that made them members of a club that no little girl wanted to join.

"Okay. That means you understand the situation." He handed back her folder. "So, will you take the job?"

"Yes. I'd love to," she said. "And I really wanted it. A chance to earn some extra money *and* the chance to get away for a couple of days at the same time. It's been a rough year for me. So, yes. Thank you for the opportunity, Mr. Crawford."

"If you call me that, I'll be looking around for my father. It's Hunter."

"Okay."

"May I call you Merry?" he asked.

"Wren already does so that works for me."

"All right, then. I'll give you the details."

Hunter explained that his father's private jet would take them to Rustler's Notch, where they'd stay in a three-bedroom suite at the hotel. He told her the salary and the amount was exceptionally generous. Now it was her turn to fight a smile. She would be expected to keep Wren in sight at all times, which meant attending the rehearsal dinner and wedding festivities the next day.

"Oh, this is probably relevant information for you since my daughter is over the moon about the fancy flower girl dress she will wear. The ceremony is formal."

The scenario he described was like a fantasy, until he dropped that bombshell. She didn't have anything to wear to a formal wedding and there was no money in her extremely limited budget for a new dress.

"Is something wrong?" He was frowning at her.

"No. Why do you ask?"

"I don't know. Just a funny expression on your face. Are you okay?"

"Fine." She gave him a bright smile. And without missing a beat said, "That won't be a problem at all."

Nowhere in her personal references had anyone said she was a habitual liar but that was the second whopper she'd told him. The first being that she wasn't judging him. How she wished this was a fairy tale. Then she could count on her fairy godmother spinning her a gorgeous dress out of unicorn sighs.

How in the world was she going to pull this off?

Chapter Two

Merry left the Ambling A just as the sun was dropping behind the mountains. She was in a panic and did what she always did at a time like this. She called her best friend, Zoey Kubiak, who was the other educational aide at the school. Zoey was a semester away from a degree in elementary education and lived with her divorced mother in a little house that had been restored after the Great Flood of 2013. In fact, they'd met when her dad did electrical work for Zoey's mom, Dora. She and her friend had sort of hoped their parents might click romantically, but that had never happened.

She pulled her dad's beat-up old truck to a stop at the curb in front of the gray house. Envy, worry and pain twisted inside her and she missed her father so much. If only he was here so she could talk to him. But, as he'd always said, if wishes were horses beggars would ride.

Merry slid out of the truck and walked up the sidewalk to the front door. It was opened before she could even knock.

"I hate it when you declare an emergency over the phone then say I'll tell you all about it when I get there." Zoey had long straight blond hair and cornflower blue eyes. She was beautiful, loyal, supportive—like the sister Merry had always wanted.

She hugged her friend. "I have a big problem."

"So you said. Together we will find a big solution. My

mom is out for the evening so we have the house to ourselves. I put a casserole in the oven and a bottle of white
wine is chilling. You'll spend the night and whatever is
wrong can be fixed. I promise."

"I didn't bring my pajamas," Merry said.

Zoey shook her head. "Out of everything I said that
was your takeaway?"

"I'm overwhelmed."

"You came to the right place. We're about the same
size so you can wear a pair of my jammies."

"You don't happen to have a cocktail dress lying
around, do you?" It was a joke, a throwaway remark, a
sign of desperation.

"As a matter of fact, I do have a couple." Zoey studied
her face. "What's wrong, Mer?"

"I think we're going to need that wine for this."

"Okay. Follow me."

They went into the small but cute kitchen with white
cabinets and wood floors. Zoey opened the bottle, then
poured the golden liquid into two stemless glasses before
they sat down at the dinette.

"Now, tell me everything."

Merry sucked in a breath, then let it out. "I just left a
job interview with Hunter Crawford. He needs a nanny
for the weekend. His brother is getting married at a fancy
resort in Colorado—"

"Rustler's Notch?"

"Yes." Merry stared. "How did you know?"

"It's the new 'in' place for weddings. I read an article
about it in a bridal magazine. Looks like a gorgeous spot.
Romantic." The excitement level in Zoey's voice rose as
she talked. "And Hunter Crawford is going to pay you to
go there with him?"

"His whole family is going and he's paying me to take care of his daughter for the weekend."

"Isn't she the little cutie who gives you a hug every morning at school?"

"Yes. She's a sweetheart, so smart and loving." Merry smiled. "Watching her will be a pleasure. Besides, I really need the extra money. It's an all-expenses-paid trip combined with a paycheck, which makes it kind of a dream job."

Zoey looked puzzled. "I'm still not seeing the problem."

"It's a formal wedding, Zo. I don't have anything to wear to something like that. And I don't have the money to buy anything. So it's a catch-22. What am I going to do? I have to go to the ceremony. Hunter really needs me there to keep an eye on Wren because he'll be busy with groomsman stuff and family."

Zoey tapped her lip. "Well, as I said, you've come to the right place. I've been in friends' weddings—always a bridesmaid, never a bride, as the saying goes. You and I are pretty close to the same size. Come on. Let's go play dress up."

Merry basically had nothing to lose. She followed her friend down the hall to the bedroom. It was a very girlie space with pink bedspread, flowered throw pillows and lace curtains crisscrossed over the window. From the walk-in closet Zoey pulled out four heavy-duty hangers holding long dresses.

While Merry stripped out of her slacks and sweater the other woman removed the plastic protecting the first dress, a black number with long sleeves. It fit, but neither of them was crazy about it. The next was yellow, but an unflattering shade that washed out her skin. Number three was orange.

Zoey took one look and grimaced. "It was a Halloween wedding. I don't even know why I keep it. Take that off and we will never speak of it again."

"Thank God." Merry did as ordered while her friend took the plastic off dress number four—also known as her last hope. "Well, the black one will work although neither of us thought it was a wow. Still it's... Wow." She got a look at the pale lavender dress Zoey was holding up. "That color is fabulous."

"It will bring out your hazel eyes. And, I confess, this one is my favorite. I've been saving it for last. And I have shoes to match. I'll find them." She disappeared back into the closet.

Merry slid the chiffon over her head and loved the silky feel of the fabric flowing over her body. It was a one-shoulder dress with a floaty skirt, a satin sash and it fit like a dream.

Zoey reappeared with a shoe box in hand and stopped dead in her tracks to stare. "Oh, Mer, that looks fantastic."

"Really?" She thought so but desperation could skew a girl's fashion sense. But in her opinion it was definitely fairy-godmother worthy.

"It looks better on you than me and it looked pretty awesome on me."

Merry moved around the room, then back to the free-standing full-length mirror. "Do you think the slit is too revealing? After all, Hunter hired me as the nanny. I'm not sure if there's a dress code."

"It hits you mid-thigh," Zoey said, studying her critically. "It's not immodest and your legs are great. I think it's fine. Is another brother getting married? The last I heard Finn and Avery had eloped."

"They did. But their father wants a big family celebration for them since the other three weddings were casual."

"He's number four out of six to find true love here in Rust Creek Falls. It would seem that the Crawford bachelors are dropping like flies since coming to town. So, tell me about Hunter." There was a gleam in her friend's eyes.

Merry should have expected this and had an answer ready, but she'd been preoccupied with her wardrobe crisis. Her reaction to him had been instant and visceral—sweaty palms, weak knees, pounding heart. For some reason she was reluctant to share that. Maybe because he'd been very businesslike and serious, but when he smiled... That was a moment with a capital *M*. "What do you want to know?"

"Everything. He's elusive. According to the rumor mill he's never in town by himself, always with his daughter."

"Well, I like him," Merry said. "And don't start. It's not in a crush sort of way. He's a concerned father or I wouldn't have this job."

"I talked to Vivienne Dalton who knows all of the Crawfords. Hunter is a widower and she said he's just as good-looking as the other brothers. Did you get a sense that he's looking to settle down like the others?" Zoey asked.

"No." Merry got exactly the opposite feeling. The man didn't even want to go to the wedding. And her instincts told her that wasn't just about logistics with child care for Wren. "I think his daughter is the only female he's interested in."

"Too bad. Shame for all that hunk factor to go to waste." Zoey sighed. "But I guess dating is hard when you have a child."

"Dating is hard when you don't." Even Merry heard the bitterness in her voice.

"Oh, shoot. I didn't mean to remind you of him." Zoey handed her the shoes to try on.

"You mean Ken? The guy who dumped me when my dad was going through cancer treatment? The one who couldn't say goodbye fast enough because he didn't come first?"

"Yeah. Him."

"You know my dad had very strong opinions on every guy I dated. Not like he hated them all, but he knew the good ones from the bad. And he didn't like Ken Michaelson from the moment they met."

"And he was right on the money. That jerk deserted you when you needed him most," Zoey commented.

"Yet another example that men aren't especially loyal. Even my brother, Jack."

"He's in the military," Zoey reminded her.

"I know. The thing is he joined right after my mom died when I was just a little girl. Dad and I hardly ever saw him and he barely made it home for my father's funeral. So he's pretty much disappeared and that doesn't meet my definition of loyal." She stepped into the pale lavender shoes. "They're a little big."

"Stuff tissues in the toes. They'll be fine," Zoey said. "And I've got a strapless bra, so don't worry about that. I think you're good to go."

"You are a life saver. Dependable and true blue." Merry hugged her. "Unlike most men. Although Hunter's devotion to his daughter is refreshing. I like that."

"Oh, really?"

"Please. Don't start. For crying out loud it's just a weekend."

And now that she had a wedding outfit, it was a weekend she was looking forward to.

Hunter slowed the SUV until he found the address Merry had given him and came to a stop in front of her small yellow house with white trim. There was an old truck in the driveway with Matthews Electrical written on the side of it. He'd promised to pick her up for the flight to Colorado that would take them to his brother's wedding.

"Well," he said to Wren, "this is the place."

"Daddy, I'm going to get Miss Merry." Wren was out of the car before he could stop her.

Hunter turned off the engine, jumped out of the vehicle and followed his daughter up the sidewalk to the porch. He noticed a for sale sign on a sturdy white post prominently displayed in the neatly trimmed front grass. That bothered him a little and it shouldn't because he barely knew the woman. But Wren liked her and he wasn't in favor of any changes that could potentially affect her happiness.

The door opened before he could knock and Merry was there, a smile on her face as bright as the cheery yellow paint on her house. Hunter felt a thump in his chest, one hard whack that seemed to jump-start his heart.

"Good morning, Wren. Hunter."

"Hi, Miss Merry. We're goin' on Gramps's jet. He's taking the whole family on it. Have you ever been on a jet?"

"Yes. Once. But it was a commercial flight, not private. This is very exciting."

"I can't wait." His daughter was practically quivering with anticipation.

"We're running late," Hunter said. "But if you need a little more time, I guarantee they'll hold the plane for the flower girl. Maximilian Crawford will make sure of that."

Merry smiled up at him. "I'm ready to go. My suitcase is right here by the door. My dress is in a garment bag. Is that okay?"

Before he could say it was fine, Wren jumped in.

"Daddy and me have that, too. My dress is so pretty. I'm gonna look like a princess. Right, Daddy?"

"Honey, you look like a princess to me no matter what you wear."

Love expanded inside him when she smiled up at him like that, as if he was her hero. Then he looked at Merry and felt that whack in his chest again. Her blond hair was a mass of curls, and enthusiasm sparkled in her hazel eyes. There was a flush of pink on her cheeks that could be about the chill in the air or the beginning of an adventure. Whatever the cause, he was oddly reluctant to stop looking at her.

"Should we get going?" Merry asked.

That snapped him out of it. They were late. "I'll get your suitcase."

"Thanks." She backed up and let him reach inside to grab the handle of the bag that had seen better days. "I'll get my dress."

"What can I carry?" Wren asked.

Merry thought for a moment. "Why don't you hold my purse while I lock the door?"

"Okay." The little girl took the big bag. "This is heavy."

"It is. Set it on the porch, sweetie." She locked up, then took her purse for the walk to the car.

Hunter hit a button on his key fob and the SUV hatch slowly lifted. He put her bag in the back with the other two, then took her dress and settled it on the rear passenger hook. "Okay, ladies. Let's roll."

"I have to sit in the back in my car seat, Miss Merry. Daddy says so."

"It's safer for you, sweetie."

"That's what he says, too."

"Do you want me to sit back there with you?"

Wren thought for a moment then said, "No. It's nice

for him to have someone to talk to until I'm big enough to sit in the front with him."

That settled that. They all got in and buckled up. It wasn't often there was a woman—a beautiful woman—riding in his front passenger seat. This was different—not bad different, just enough for him to feel a little tongue-tied. Fortunately his daughter picked up the conversation slack.

"We're goin' to Billings. That's where the airport is. I brought my princess bride doll with me."

"That seems very appropriate for this occasion," Merry said.

"My dress is prettier than hers. But she has a tiara. I asked Aunt Avery if I could wear one and she said she didn't think it would go with my dress."

"It was a diplomatic no," Hunter said so only Merry could hear. She laughed, then covered it with a cough.

"I wish I could wear one." Wren sighed and it was loud enough to be heard over the road noise. "Daddy says I'm his princess and everyone knows princesses wear tiaras."

"That makes sense," Merry said thoughtfully. "But a princess is always sensitive to the feelings of people around her. And this is going to be your aunt Avery's special day when she marries your uncle Finn. A princess would never do anything to spoil a bride's wedding day. Don't you think so, Wren?"

That got a grudging "I guess so" and Hunter was impressed by the way Merry handled that situation. When they arrived at the airport he parked at the terminal where they would board his father's Gulfstream jet. The crew met them and took their luggage before Hunter, Merry and Wren walked up the steps and into the aircraft.

Hunter waved to everyone on board and a quick head count indicated they were the last ones to arrive. He started to make introductions but was interrupted by an announcement to take their seats and fasten seat belts in preparation for takeoff. The plush leather and teak-trimmed cabin was configured with individual seats of four with a table in between to form a conversation area. There were also a couple of couches that would accommodate three and only one was left. His daughter plopped herself down on one end. That meant he and Merry would be sitting side by side. Unlike the front seat of his SUV, there would be no console between them.

"Sit next to me, Miss Merry."

"Okay."

Hunter took the empty space beside her and their shoulders brushed, their legs touched. He was grateful the stretchy pants she wore tucked into shin-high black boots meant her skin was not bare. When he fastened his seat belt, his fingers brushed her thigh, or more accurately the cream-colored sweater that covered her hips and butt. She smelled disarmingly female and sweet, a thought that sent a tsunami of testosterone crashing over him.

When everyone was secured, they received permission from the control tower to taxi down the runway and in seconds they were off. As soon as the seat belt sign was turned off, Wren bounced up and said she was going to talk to Aunt Avery and tell her she didn't mind not wearing a tiara.

More than almost anything Hunter wanted to move away from Merry but he didn't feel right about leaving her alone. They all knew he'd hired a nanny for the weekend but the noisy jet made introductions awkward. So, for the duration of the flight, he felt obligated to stay put and introduce her when they were on the ground.

Merry was looking around the interior, eyes wide. "I wonder where they keep the barf bags."

"You don't feel well?"

"I'm fine actually." She laughed but there was a little uncertainty on her face. "It's just nerves. When I get this way, I say weird things. Helps break the tension."

"Okay."

"In fact they probably don't even have barf bags. Most likely there's a rule against getting sick on the expensive leather seats."

"Let them try to enforce that one," Hunter said.

"I know, right?" She glanced a little anxiously at the rest of his family, chatting together in groups. "There are a lot of Crawfords on this plane."

"Yeah. I'm sorry about not introducing you to all of them. I'll take care of that when we land."

"No problem. I'm just the hired help, after all." She was still looking around the luxurious interior with an expression of awe that made her eyes look more green than brown.

"If we weren't in such a rush, I'd have made sure they all met you. It's my fault we were running late."

She looked skeptical. "Something tells me your daughter was responsible for that. I know her from school, remember?"

"Yeah." It was one of the reasons he'd hired her.

"I feel like I need to pinch myself. Maybe I should be paying *you*. I can't believe I'm flying in a private jet. If anyone had told me I'd be doing this, I'd have said they were crazy. People with money really do live differently."

"I suppose."

His gaze drifted to his daughter, the child he'd raised alone almost from the day she was born. Money didn't guarantee you wouldn't lose the mother of your baby girl. He would give up everything he had in a heartbeat if it could bring Lara back.

"I'm sorry."

"Hmm?" He looked at Merry.

"That was unprofessional of me. It was tactless to say that."

He thought her comments were honest and charming. "Why would you think so?"

"It seems as if I've heard you should never discuss money and politics." She tucked her hair behind her ear. "Again, I plead nerves. Apparently getting up at the crack of dawn has disengaged the filter between my brain and my mouth. That's my story and I'm sticking to it."

He smiled, but the movement felt rusty when directed at a woman. It seemed wrong somehow, but he couldn't seem to stop. "Your unfiltered frankness is refreshing."

It seemed her condition was contagious because things were popping out of his mouth, too. Was that crossing a line between employer and employee? If Merry was a ranch hand, he would know where the line was. And it wasn't as if he hadn't had child care before. When Wren was a baby, he'd hired help from time to time. He had to work the ranch, after all. But with Merry he felt strongly about keeping boundaries firmly in place.

"Calling what I said frankness is generous of you," she said. "I always thought of the word *decadent* in terms of dessert. But this experience has broadened the definition for me. However, I will, at some point, get over how special it feels to fly in a private jet."

"You can thank my dad."

"I will, of course."

He laughed. "I didn't mean that literally. Just that it was important to him that this be a fun family event from start to finish."

"You can count on me. I'll take good care of Wren so you can enjoy yourself this weekend."

He already was. With her. And that realization surprised and bothered him. It was almost a relief when the captain announced they were starting their descent into the airport in Rustler's Notch, Colorado. The flight time had, no pun intended, flown. Talking to Merry was pleasant. And distracting. More than he'd expected. Definitely more than he wanted.

It was disconcerting and uncomfortable when he realized he was caught between not wanting the flight to end and being grateful that it had been so short. That was the classic definition of conflict. He didn't like conflict, especially when a woman was involved.

Chapter Three

Merry was a little nervous when the plane landed, then taxied closer to the terminal. Her responsibilities were going to kick in and part of that would be interacting with the Crawfords. Time to put on her big girl panties and a friendly smile. The seat belt sign dinged off and everyone in the cabin stood to gather their belongings. They filed down the stairs and stood in a group not far from the plane.

"Listen up, everyone," Hunter said. "Before we all split up, I want to introduce you to Meredith Matthews—"

"She's Miss Merry," Wren interjected.

Merry lifted her hand to wave everyone a friendly greeting, at the same time hating all the focus on her. "Hi."

Hunter introduced his brothers and their wives one by one. She had already guessed who Avery and Finn were because Wren had spent a good portion of the flight talking princess with the bride. Max, the tall, handsome, silver-haired patriarch, was impossible to forget. But everyone else sort of blurred together.

"There are a lot of you," she said ruefully. "I think you need to wear name tags."

Everyone laughed and assured her there would be no hard feelings for a name mix-up. Then Hunter's father directed the group to the three limousines waiting to take them to Rustler's Notch Resort.

"Don't we need to get our luggage?" Merry asked when they all started to move.

"It will be delivered to our rooms," Hunter assured her. The doubt must have shown on her face because he added, "I promise it will be fine. And yes, rich people do live differently."

"You took the words right out of my mouth. But if I don't have my pajamas—"

"I will buy you whatever you need if I'm wrong."

"Fair enough."

Following Max's instructions, the process was smooth and efficient. He and his youngest son, Wilder, climbed into the car with Hunter, Wren and Merry.

"Mr. Crawford," she said to the family patriarch, "I would like to thank you for this weekend. I will take excellent care of your granddaughter."

The man winked at the little girl, who'd insisted on sitting beside him. "Wrennie is very special to me."

"I can see that, sir."

"It will go to his head if you call him that," Wilder teased her. He looked like a charming rogue, handsome with longish brown hair and piercing dark eyes.

Merry could picture him breaking hearts everywhere he went. He was one of those men most women would be attracted to. Although she wasn't. Glancing sideways at Hunter, she felt a little flutter in her chest that indicated she couldn't say the same about his older brother.

The scenery on the short drive to the hotel was breathtaking. Trees, rugged mountains and blue sky added up to a spectacularly beautiful day. They passed ski slopes but it was early November and there wasn't enough snow yet for them to open. Before long the resort buildings came into view and the car stopped in front. The hotel tower was tall, all wood and beams with a peaked roof that looked chalet-like and just right for this environment.

Merry had never been anywhere like this. Not ever. She was speechless, but Wren did enough chattering for both of them. Following behind the Crawford clan she was able to observe Hunter with his daughter. The trusting way the little girl slipped her small hand into his bigger one. He teased her before effortlessly lifting her onto his broad shoulders as they walked into the spectacular lobby with its wood floors and huge fireplace, where logs cheerfully burned and crackled.

Apparently having money also made check-in a breeze because room keys were waiting and bags had indeed been delivered to the suites. Max instructed everyone to go have fun and they would meet later in the afternoon for the wedding rehearsal followed by dinner. Hunter had already assured Merry she would have her own room, but she wasn't clear on how that would logistically work with a suite. After an elevator ride to the top floor, he unlocked the door and they walked in.

There was a beautifully decorated living room that separated the master and auxiliary bedrooms from the one on the opposite side of the suite. She would have her privacy and still be available to Wren if needed. And, as Hunter had promised, her suitcase was there on the bench at the end of the king bed. Her borrowed dress was hanging in the closet. Quite possibly this hotel suite was bigger than her entire house back in Rust Creek Falls.

Wren ran into Merry's room and grabbed her hand. "Come and see where I'm going to sleep."

Merry let herself be tugged into the room. The puffy mattress was high and the white bedding looked pristine. "This is beautiful. Fit for a princess."

"Come and see Daddy's room. It's way bigger."

That seemed too intimate, too much an invasion of his privacy. Too tempting to think about him and what he wore, or didn't wear, to bed. And her heart was beating just a little too fast, a sure sign doing this would be a bad idea.

"Why don't we unpack your suitcase? And I want to see your dress. It's probably hanging in the closet." Merry saw Hunter in the doorway and wondered what he was thinking with that brooding look on his face.

Wren folded her arms over her thin chest. "You can't see my dress until the wedding. Like the bride."

Merry laughed. "Fair enough. But we should still get your things unpacked. Make sure you have your shoes, tights and everything you need. There are good surprises and bad ones."

The child thought that over then nodded. "Okay."

They made short work of unpacking the small princess suitcase. Once the wedding day accessories were present and accounted for, the little girl started jumping on the bed.

"Wren, stop. You'll fall and hurt yourself," Hunter said sharply.

Merry knew this was pent-up energy and excitement, not bad behavior. It just needed to be channeled in a more positive way. She believed her job wasn't just about babysitting when Hunter wasn't around, but to help out whenever she could. This was one of those times.

"I have an idea," she said.

The child stopped jumping. "What?"

"We should go exploring."

"For what?" the little girl asked.

"Adventures. There are beautiful grounds here at the hotel. Just look out the window."

Wren plopped her bottom on the bed then slid off and

raced over to the window. "I see a lake with water coming up out of the middle. And a sidewalk. And maybe a play area. Daddy, come and look. We should go."

"Sounds like a good start for an adventure. I'll take you," Merry said.

"No. I want Daddy to come, too."

"Maybe your dad wants to rest. After all, he was up pretty early this morning."

The little girl looked up at him. "Do you want to take a nap instead of exploring with me and Miss Merry?"

"Absolutely not." Although he didn't look quite that certain. "I wouldn't miss it."

"Yay!" Wren clapped her hands and headed for the door. "Let's go."

"Put on your jacket," Merry and Hunter said at the same time.

All of them grabbed coats and left the suite. After taking the elevator to the first floor they found the exit leading to the rear of the property and a path lined with shrubs. In her pink quilted jacket Wren took off running as her ponytail swung from side to side.

"Stay where I can see you," Hunter shouted.

"I will," she called back.

Merry walked beside her employer as they moved more slowly down the path. To fill a silence that bordered on awkward she asked, "How do you like Montana? And why did your family leave Texas?"

She glanced up at him and saw his mouth pull tight as a muscle in his cheek tensed. The question had stirred up something not good and she began to wonder if he was going to answer at all.

Finally he said, "When my dad gets an idea into his head it's pretty hard to change his mind."

"Did you want to?"

"I like ranch work, taking care of the animals. I don't much care what state I do it in. As long as my daughter is happy, I'm good." He looked down. "Thanks to you, her school transition was smooth."

"I'm glad I could help. I know how it feels to be the new kid in the class." As they walked, Merry was keeping that pink jacket in sight and she figured Hunter was, too.

"You made the difference. Please tell me you're not leaving town."

"Why would you think I was?"

"I noticed the for sale sign in front of your house."

"Oh. No. I'm not leaving Rust Creek Falls," she said.

"Then why sell?"

Because she couldn't afford the monthly payments and that was humiliating to admit. Merry had faced a lot of speed bumps on the road to establishing her career, which meant that her bank account had suffered, too. She was torn about telling him the truth, then decided keeping it to herself might have him thinking it was something worse.

"My mother died when I was about Wren's age. My brother is ten years older than me and he joined the military." She was the one dealing with memories now and they were sad. It had been a lonely time for her. There'd been no motherly hugs after school, no homemade cookies with a glass of cold milk. Her father had withdrawn into his own grief and she'd felt all alone. "Dad didn't quite know what to do with me so he took me to work with him a lot."

"What kind of work?"

"Electrician. Ed Matthews knew his way around wires and light switches. Not so much about what to do with a motherless little girl."

"I can relate to that."

"And we moved around a lot, going where the work was. Following the jobs. Changing schools all the time."

"That's why you knew how Wren felt, why you looked out for her when she was new to the school."

"Yes." She smiled up at him, then zeroed in on the pink jacket again. For some reason she wanted him to know she was working on her life even though that wasn't what he'd asked. "You're wondering what all this has to do with selling the house. I promise I'll get there."

"Okay."

"My education was choppy, which put me behind. Plus, I helped my dad with the business. Answering phones and making appointments. Keeping the books." It had helped bring them closer and she treasured that time more than ever now that he was gone. "I could only manage college classes part-time. And then in 2013, after the flood in Rust Creek Falls, Dad decided to move there. The damage was widespread and there was a real need for construction workers, plumbers and electricians. It's a friendly, close-knit community and we decided to stay. We bought a house and fixed it up."

"But?"

"How do you know there's a 'but'?" she asked.

"Because your house is for sale."

"Right. I mentioned when we met that my dad died recently. Cancer." She took a deep breath and met his gaze. "On top of missing him very much, without him there is no business or income. I don't make enough at my school job to keep up with the mortgage payments."

"I see." He was frowning. "What will you do when the house is sold?"

"Right now I'm more nervous about the selling process. I have a real estate agent but never handled a real estate transaction on my own, without my dad."

"The agent should explain everything but if you still have questions, my brother Logan has sold all kinds of property. He could probably help you out."

"Thanks. That's good to know."

"And you're still in school." Obviously he'd read and retained the information she'd given him during the employment interview.

"Not at the moment. I had to care for my dad and was barely able to finish the spring semester online. I didn't register for fall because he wasn't doing well. But I'm going back to it right after the holidays."

"And your major is early childhood education. Seems like a good fit." He stuck his hands into the pockets of his sheepskin jacket. "You're really tuned in to my daughter. She doesn't even seem to notice she's being handled."

"Diversion. Distraction. Let them think the idea is theirs. A hard no isn't easy to reverse."

"Tell me about it." The tone in his voice and the look on his face indicated he'd had some experience with that and it didn't go well.

And then she felt bad. "I'm sorry, Hunter. For dumping on you like that. For bending your ear and making it all about me. That was unprofessional."

"Well, I asked," he said gently. "And maybe you needed to talk about it. The grief, I mean."

Hmm. This "getting to know you" felt something like a first date. It wasn't, but that didn't stop her curiosity about him. When had Wren lost her mother? And how? The thing was, it didn't feel right to just come out and ask.

"Do you miss Texas?" she said instead.

"No." That was emphatic and he must have sensed it because he continued. "Rust Creek Falls is small and things move slower than they do in Dallas. This environment is better for my daughter."

And speaking of Wren… The little girl reversed direction and came running back to them.

"Daddy, I'm hungry."

And just like that the spell was broken. Getting to know her employer wasn't part of her job but she'd enjoyed it anyway. Hunter was so much nicer and friendlier than he'd been at first. And easy to talk to, she thought wryly. It was a little embarrassing how much she'd bared her soul, but this was a job, not a weekend getaway, and she better not forget that.

"Daddy, doesn't Merry look pretty?"

So pretty Hunter nearly swallowed his tongue. Wren and her nanny had just come out of the bedroom where they'd dressed for the wedding. Merry's dress was light purple—no, Wren would tell him that was wrong. It was lavender and left one shoulder bare, a very soft and sexy shoulder. There was an equally sexy slit in the long skirt, simple and seductive at the same time. Silky material caressed her body and made his fingers ache to touch her bare skin. He was pretty sure it made her the sexiest nanny in Rustler's Notch.

"Daddy, you look weird. Are you sick?"

"No, honey. I'm fine." He glanced at Merry with her thick wild blond hair semi-tamed, pulled back into a messy side bun. "You do look really nice."

"Thank you." Her cheeks flushed pink.

"How do I look, Daddy?" Wren spun in a circle and the full skirt of her cream-colored dress flared out.

"Like a princess."

"Do you like my dress? Merry says the style makes me look very grown-up."

"I did say that." She smiled at the little girl. "I just hope I did justice to tying that bow in the back."

"It looks good to me," he said.

"The crown of flowers in your hair is so natural and pretty, better than a tiara," Merry said.

He listened as they debated the merits of tiara versus flowers then chattered about dresses, veils, princesses and fairy tales. He loved his daughter more than anything in the world but girly stuff was way out of his comfort zone. Right up there with someday having to explain to Wren about the birds and bees.

That was a long way off, but for some reason he'd been thinking a lot about sex recently. Mostly that he hadn't had it for a long time. That was the safest reason he could come up with for last night's dreams about holding Merry in his arms. Naked.

"You look really handsome in your tuxedo, Daddy. Don't you think so, Merry?"

"Yes, he does." A becoming blush crept into her cheeks.

"Thank you, ladies. I'm glad I passed inspection. But you're the star, Wren. If you're ready, we really need to get a move on or the wedding is going to be missing a flower girl."

Fortunately they had only to go downstairs. Hunter escorted them to the bride's room, where the wedding planner was calling the shots. Merry was going to stay with Wren until just before this shindig got rolling. He proceeded to the event venue, where chairs were set up in two sections to create an aisle and there were so many flowers it looked and smelled like a garden.

Hunter had received his instructions—family and friends of the bride on the left. Groom's on the right. Logistics like this he could handle. It kept him too busy to think about Wren and whether or not she was okay. Before long most of the seats were filled, except those reserved for family in the first two rows.

Then he saw Merry walk in and his heart skipped a beat. She looked so beautiful that for a moment it was difficult to get air into his lungs. When he could breathe again, he moved toward her before any of the other ushers could.

"Hi. How's everything going?"

"Don't worry, your daughter is fine."

"Am I that transparent?" he asked.

"Yes, and good for you being a concerned father. She is so excited. And safe," she added.

"Okay." He held out his arm. "Then I will show you to your seat."

She smiled and put her hand into the bend of his elbow. "Thanks."

He led her up the aisle on the right and indicated she should sit in the front row. "Here you go."

There was surprise in her eyes. "But this is for your family."

"Wren needs to see you. In case she's nervous."

"Right. She might be a little shy with so many people watching her. Okay, then, if you think it's all right."

When she sat and demurely rearranged that silky skirt to cover her legs, Hunter sighed with disappointment. That's when he knew for sure he was going to hell for having inappropriate, sexy thoughts about the nanny.

He made one more trip to the rear of the room and received instructions to take his seat. His brothers and their wives were in place and it didn't bum him out that the chair beside Merry was empty. When he claimed it, things started to happen. Finn walked in accompanied by Max, who was his best man. He'd chosen his father for the job in the spirit of a new understanding between them.

And because he didn't want to choose one of his brothers over another. The minister took his place and then the music started. Everyone stood and looked at the back of the room to get the first glimpse of the bride.

Wren was the first one down the aisle and expertly sprinkled rose petals from the basket she carried onto the white runner. She was followed by a bridesmaid in a dress the same color as the coral bow on his daughter's dress. Then he saw the bride, beautiful in a full-skirted satin dress with lacy sleeves. A veil covered her face and she was accompanied by her father, Oscar Ellington.

Hunter looked at his father and brother and saw tension on their faces. He didn't have to guess what they were thinking. His brothers looked the same way and he figured they were all wondering the same thing he was. Would there be fireworks between the bride's father and the groom's? At the rehearsal dinner last night the two men had avoided each other but they were face to face now.

"What's wrong?" Merry asked. "Your father suddenly looks like his shoes are too tight."

So she'd noticed, too. He leaned over and whispered, "Years ago he was working on a business deal with Avery's father. It went bad and Oscar is still holding a grudge."

Her eyes widened. "Surely he wouldn't do anything to spoil his daughter's wedding."

"We're about to find out."

Father and daughter stopped in front of the minister, who said, "If anyone knows why this man and this woman should not be joined in matrimony, speak now or forever hold your peace."

Hunter didn't miss the warning look Avery gave her father and without a word he lifted her veil and kissed her cheek, then gave his daughter's hand to her groom. It seemed as if there was a collective release of tension in the room and the vows went off without a hitch. Beside him Merry pulled a tissue from her small beaded purse and dabbed at her eyes.

When the ceremony was over, there were family pictures while guests moved into the room next door for the reception. Hunter was at the head table with the rest of his family for dinner and wedding toasts. Again Oscar stood and was the center of attention as well as a source of apprehension. The older man hesitated before speaking, long enough to make the Crawfords wonder if the revenge tirade was coming now.

It didn't. The man was simply gathering his emotions, and he held up a glass of champagne as he wished his daughter every happiness. Hunter couldn't imagine giving away his little girl to the son of a sworn enemy, but to his credit, Ellington did just that. Merry had been right about him not spoiling Avery's special day.

His gaze kept straying to Merry and he was impressed by her ability to chat with people at her table even as she continuously watched Wren. After dinner, when music and dancing started, keeping his daughter under surveillance became even more of a challenge. He was relieved that another pair of eyes was dedicated to that mission. Still, he picked out a discreet place to stand and watch over her.

As if living up to her name, she was flitting and flying all over the room. Right now she was dancing with the bride and groom. The three were laughing one minute and talking seriously the next. Even from this far away he could see his daughter's interest in the conversation and wondered what it was about.

A wave of melancholy washed over him as he thought

how much his daughter looked like her mother. Wren was so wonderful and it made him sad that Lara wasn't here to see. And he blamed himself for that.

The dance floor was crowded but he spotted his family—Logan with Sarah, Xander and Lily, Knox holding his Genevieve. They all looked really happy. He was glad for them, but envy brought back the melancholy and with it some anger.

"Daddy?"

"Hey, kiddo." He'd been so lost in thought she'd sneaked up on him. "Are you having fun?"

"Yes." She clapped her hands together. "This is the best wedding ever."

That was a matter of opinion. He couldn't wait for it to be over. "I'm glad you're having a good time."

"I really am." She looked up at him, concern on her little face. "Are you?"

"Sure," he lied. A falsehood was okay when it was about not spoiling your child's experience, right? "This is fun."

"You don't like it," she accused.

"No?" Since when did she get so observant. "I really do. Like you said, best wedding ever."

"Then why do you look so mad and sad at the same time?" she asked.

Damn. He'd been so sure his feelings didn't show. "Do I?"

"Yes. And you're all by yourself. It's dark over here."

He glanced around the room, at the tables with their flameless candles and the flowers everywhere. There was a three-tiered cake garnished with roses on a separate table. Hanging over the dance area was a crystal chandelier that bathed the guests in a magical glow. The venue was bright and festive but he had instinctively gravitated to the darkest shadows in the room. It didn't take a shrink to tell him he was instinctively hiding from this celebration of love because it was a reminder of everything he'd lost.

"I like watching everyone dance and this is the best place to do that." He hoped that would satisfy her.

"Then why do you still look sad?"

So much for her letting this go. "I'm fine, honey. I haven't seen you dance with Gramps yet."

"I know. He's asking all the ladies to dance."

Hunter easily spotted his silver-haired father waltzing with an attractive brunette. "Yeah. He does that."

"So does Uncle Wilder."

"Yeah." His brother was living up to his name, as usual.

"I have an idea." Wren met his gaze and hers was full of earnestness.

"I know what you're going to say." He grinned at her. "And I should have thought of it myself. You and I should have a dance."

"No."

"What?"

"You should ask Merry to dance. That would cheer you up."

While trying to figure out how to explain that Merry was an employee, Hunter looked over at her. Just then a good-looking man approached the table where she was sitting and held out his hand. Obviously an invitation to dance. Just like that he wasn't sad anymore. The new feeling was a little unfamiliar, something he hadn't experienced for a long time. It was also inconvenient and seemed to put a crack in the wall of isolation he'd spent the last six years building.

He was jealous.

Chapter Four

Since Hunter's daughter fulfilled her flower girl duties a few hours ago, Merry had barely taken her eyes off the little girl. So it didn't escape her notice when father and daughter were talking so seriously about something. Then suddenly he was looking at *her*.

"Excuse me, would you like to dance?"

Merry blinked up at the nice-looking stranger who was holding out his hand. Wren was with her dad right now so there was no reason to decline the invitation. And every reason to accept and distract herself from the way her boss's intense scrutiny was making every nerve ending in her body tingle with awareness.

"Yes. Thank you." She smiled at the patiently waiting man, then stood up and let him lead her to the dance floor, reminding herself that the toes of her too-big shoes were stuffed with tissues. "I'm Merry."

"Really?" He slid his arm around her waist and took her hand. "I've been watching and you don't look like you're having much fun."

"Oh—" She laughed. "That's my name. Meredith, but everyone calls me Merry."

"Right." His smile was self-deprecating. "My name is Don."

"Nice to meet you. And I should confess that I'm actually not a guest—"

"May I cut in?" Wilder Crawford tapped Don on

the shoulder and the man shrugged before giving way. Hunter's brother took her in his arms with a grin that was a little wicked, a lot charming. "Hello, Nanny Merry."

"Good Lord, that makes me sound like I'm a hundred years old."

"You sure don't look it. Not in that dress."

His appraisal was flirty and full of male appreciation, both of which she took as a compliment and nothing more. "Well, I am being paid to supervise your niece, who's with her father at the moment. And that's the only reason I accepted an offer to dance with that man. And you, by the way."

"Why do I feel as if I've just been rapped on the knuckles with a ruler?" His dark eyes glowed with mischief.

"That could have something to do with my working in elementary education. It's my job to keep children under control."

His eyebrows rose. "I'm sensing some disapproval."

"No. Not judging, just observing," she protested. "And it didn't escape my notice that you have danced with many women here at the reception."

"I didn't want anyone to feel left out." His roguish expression intensified.

"So you were being unselfish? It wasn't a screening process to find someone for the evening?"

That surprised him. "I'm sorry, what?"

"It's a well-known fact that at weddings there's that one groomsman who is looking for a hookup—"

"I'm cutting in." Hunter tapped his brother on the shoulder with a little more enthusiasm than seemed necessary.

Wilder looked the tiniest bit relieved when he let her go to his brother. "I hope you can handle her better than me, big brother."

Hunter stared at his brother's back as he weaved his way through the dancers on the way to the bar. "What does that mean?"

"I don't think he's used to being challenged. My guess is that women line up around the block or pick a number if there's a chance to get his attention."

Hunter's eyes glittered with intensity as he took her hand in his and slid his arm around her waist, leading her into a waltz. "Did he come on to you?"

"No. He was flirty, that's all. I think the behavior is hardwired into him." The youngest Crawford was very handsome, and clearly he liked women. But she wasn't the least bit tempted by him. On the other hand, the man holding her was temptation with a capital *T*. "I accused him of being that guy trolling for a woman."

He stopped moving for a moment and met her gaze. "So you called him on his crap."

"I just made an observation. And explained that every wedding has at least one groomsman who makes it his mission to sleep with a bridesmaid or one of the guests."

"You don't pull any punches. No wonder he headed for the bar." Hunter's mouth curved up at the corners. "So, he wasn't too forward?"

"I was the forward one and probably shouldn't have said anything. I think I shocked him. He was a perfect gentleman." She glanced around and spotted Wren dancing with her grandfather. Then she stumbled and stepped on Hunter's foot, the unfortunate consequence of wearing shoes that were too big. "Sorry."

"No problem. And I'm glad he behaved himself."

"I've noticed that between Wilder and your father, single women of all ages are receiving a lot of attention tonight." She smiled up at him. "You're going to have to step up your game big-time to keep pace with the Crawford bachelors."

That remark could go either way but her responsibilities were nearly over. So she didn't really have much to lose.

Unexpectedly, Hunter smiled and his somber seriousness fell away as if a magic spell had transformed the beast back into a handsome prince. And handsome was the operative word. She'd seen him in jeans, boots, Stetson—and the cowboy look made her female parts tingle. But there was something indescribable and luscious about a man in a tuxedo.

Especially a man like this one. The black jacket, pants and bow tie made him look dashing, but the way the starched white shirt contrasted with his tanned skin took her breath away. He was absolutely irresistible and the realization made her trip again and nearly lose a shoe.

"Sorry," she muttered.

"I hardly noticed what with my curiosity about being designated an endangered species. One of the last three Crawford bachelors." Then his smile faded. "Although it's hard to think of my dad like that since he was married. And divorced."

"Everyone in town is talking about him paying Vivienne Dalton to find wives for his sons. Is that rumor true?" Merry asked.

"Yes."

When he settled their joined hands on his chest, she forgot to clench her toes to keep her shoes on and walked right out of one. She would have toppled over without his arms around her.

She sighed. "I have a confession."

"Those are not words any man wants to hear."

"Well, it's not something I'm particularly thrilled to

tell you, but it's better than leaving you with the impression that I'm a hopeless klutz." She held on to his arm while sliding her shoe back on. "I borrowed this outfit from a friend. The shoes match but her feet are bigger than mine. I have to admit when I came to interview for this job I wasn't expecting to dance."

He looked relieved. "Is that all."

Speaking of which, she gazed past him and found his daughter hanging with her uncle Logan, aunt Sarah and their baby daughter, Sophia. Wren seemed in awe of the baby.

Merry was about to go back to her table but another slow song started and Hunter put his strong arms around her again. He was barely moving his feet, allowing her to barely move hers. That kept her shoes firmly in place.

"Problem solved," he said against her hair.

Merry's mouth went dry. Their bodies were touching now from chest to knee because he was holding her more securely. But that was about shoe integrity, not because he was enjoying the closeness as much as she was.

"So," she said, feeling an overwhelming need to break the charged silence. "About your father. Max doesn't look a lot like Cupid, but what he's doing, I mean trying to fix you all up, is actually very sweet."

"You wouldn't say that if the pressure was on you," he said. "Women might throw themselves at Wilder, but my dad is throwing them at both of us."

"Since we're dancing at the wedding of his fourth successful match, it would seem something he's doing is working," she pointed out. "Is it possible he just wants you to be happy?"

"That's a hard maybe. He's into control, when not wrapped up in himself."

"Parents aren't perfect, Hunter."

His look was wry. "That doesn't bode well for me."

"I'm simply stating a fact. By definition, human beings are flawed. That doesn't mean you don't try. All anyone can do is their best." She looked up at him. "When my mom died, my dad became distant and withdrawn. As an adult I understand that he was grieving, but back then... I just felt alone."

"It can't have been easy for him."

The shadows in Hunter's eyes reminded her of how her father had looked when remembering her mom. Merry would bet almost anything that Hunter was thinking about losing his wife.

"No, it wasn't easy. It took time, but eventually we became close. He never said anything, but I always had the feeling he was doing his best to make up for shutting me out."

Hunter shook his head. "You don't know my dad. He makes no apologies, and fixing us up is nothing more than a power trip."

"Daddy!" Wren ran over to them and looked up, grinning from ear to ear. "You and Merry are dancing, just like the prince and Cinderella did in my favorite movie. Are you going to kiss Merry like the prince kissed her at the end when they got married?"

There must be some kind of weird cosmic rule about having almost total silence in a crowded room when something completely embarrassing was said. Merry was pretty sure the child's words could be heard all the way to Rust Creek Falls. Around them dancers stopped and stared and her cheeks grew hot with humiliation.

Hunter went down on one knee in front of his daughter. "Honey, that's not something you should ask."

"Why?"

"It's personal and Merry works for me."

"But you stopped dancin'."

"Because of my shoes," Merry said.

Hunter held his daughter's hand and led her to the side of the dance floor. "Merry is my employee and that would be inappropriate. Do you know what that means?"

"I'm six, Daddy." Her voice was tinged with irritation.

"I know. It means that doing anything personal—"

"Like kissin' her?"

"Yes, like that." Hunter blew out a long breath. "It would make her feel awkward and I would never do that to her."

"But you looked like you were going to. I don't get why—" Tears glistened in her eyes and then she started to cry.

He gathered her into his arms then looked helplessly up at Merry.

"Maybe it's time to go upstairs and chill," she suggested. "This little girl has been going a mile a minute all day and I think she's just exhausted. What do you say, sweetie?"

Wren wiped tears from her face. "Yes."

"Okay."

She held out her hand and the little girl put hers into Merry's palm. "I'll get my purse. My room key is in there."

As the two of them moved toward the table, Merry walked right out of her shoe. And, embarrassing cosmic rule number two, everyone was still staring at them.

Wren stopped and looked up at her. "You lost your shoe at the ball. Just like Cinderella."

"Yeah." But not exactly. The handsome prince wasn't coming after her.

She slid her foot back into the shoe and hurried them both out of the ballroom, leaving Hunter behind. She'd been hired so that he could have a good time at the wedding. And, as Wilder Crawford had pointed out, there was no shortage of ladies for him to have a good time with.

It wasn't in her job description to hate that, but she did anyway.

"Seems as if everyone's having a good time."

Hunter was forced to look at his father and away from the door where Merry had disappeared with his daughter. He'd moved from the dance floor to the bar, where he was watching the other guests milling around, dancing and sitting at tables. It was impossible to miss the bride all in white and her groom holding tightly to her hand. They looked really happy and for some reason that made him unreasonably angry because he realized Merry had taken all the fun with her.

"Yeah."

"Great party, if I do say so myself." Max's tone was full of self-congratulation, but that was nothing new.

"This is Finn and Avery's doing since it was their idea to get remarried in front of their families."

"It was my doing to fly everyone in and make sure there was high-end champagne for the toasts. And people are having fun. I even saw you out there dancing."

That was a mistake, Hunter thought. Merry Matthews had felt way too good in his arms. Her sweet curves fit perfectly against him and she smelled like flowers, just the way a woman should. He could have gone the rest of his life and been just fine without knowing that and now he had to find a way to forget how good she smelled.

"Did you hear me, son?"

Crap. He looked up at Max. "Hmm?"

"I said, my little granddaughter sure picked herself a fetching nanny."

Hunter wondered if that was a criticism or a warning, a reminder that starting something with the hired help was a slippery slope. Twenty-four hours from now she wouldn't be his employee. He wasn't sure whether that was good or bad and took his annoyance out on the handiest target.

"Seriously, Dad? Fetching? What is this? The Middle Ages?"

"What can I say?" Max grinned, looking every inch the silver fox. "I'm a Renaissance man."

"Right."

A romantic ballad started playing and Finn led his bride to the center of the dance floor then tucked her against him. She slid her arms around his neck and they seemed to be in their own world. Hunter had dipped a toe into that world just a little while ago. And then Wren said what she said and he went into damage control mode.

The thing was, he'd been thinking about kissing Merry. He was holding her and she looked so damn cute confessing about her borrowed shoes being too big. Touching his mouth to hers felt like the next step, the most natural thing in the world. He was almost glad Wren interrupted. Although it would have been better if she'd used her indoor voice and not the one astronauts on the space station could hear.

"Where's your brother?" Max asked.

"Which one? I have five."

"Smart-ass." His dad laughed. "I was talking about Wilder. Haven't seen him since you cut in on his dance with Merry. Where do you suppose he is?"

Probably somewhere private hooking up with a woman. Remembering Merry explaining the concept made Hunter smile. "Maybe he just went to get some air."

"Doubtful." Max shook his head.

"And isn't he the one who promised to help keep an eye on Wren so that I could loosen up?" he asked wryly.

"One and the same," his father agreed. "It would appear that my suggestion to hire a nanny has worked out well. In more ways than one."

Hunter refused to get sucked in and ask what he meant by that. "My daughter picked her own nanny."

"My granddaughter is an excellent judge of people. Just like her gramps." Max clapped a hand on his son's shoulder as he scanned the guests. His gaze settled on one in particular. "And I judge that right over there is a very fetching woman sitting all by herself who might like to dance."

"Go for it, Dad."

Turning serious, his father met his gaze. "I could say the same thing to you. There are more than a few women here who could use a healthy dose of Crawford charm. Since Wilder is missing in action, that leaves you and me to uphold the family honor and reputation."

"I'm right behind you." Not.

After his father moved away, Hunter ordered a whiskey neat from the bar and watched all the guests still celebrating. His four brothers and their wives were in a group, talking, laughing, carefree and happy in a way he never would be again. Not for the first time he felt as if he was on the outside looking in. Until moving to Rust Creek Falls, the bond of brotherhood had remained strong, the circle tight. But that was changing, and he truly wished them every happiness, at the same time feeling sorry for himself that they were leaving him behind.

Man, was this pathetic, he thought. His daughter was upstairs in her room and she was his whole world. That's where he should be. So he tossed back the rest of his drink and took his pity party on the road, quietly slipping out of the ballroom. The elevators were like a ghost town and he made it to his floor quickly, then quietly let himself into the suite.

The lights were on and he noticed that Merry's door was wide open but the room was dark. He crossed to where Wren was supposed to be sleeping and found her still awake.

"Hi, Daddy. I'm glad you're here."

"Why aren't you asleep?" He turned on her light, then sat at the foot of her bed. "I thought you were tired."

"I am," she said. "I closed my eyes while Merry read me a story and tucked me in. But my eyes wouldn't stay shut."

"Do you want me to read you another story?"

"No." She sat up. "I'm hungry."

"Didn't you eat at the reception?"

"Cake. I didn't like any of the other stuff. Gross," she said making a face.

If it wasn't chicken nuggets and fries she turned up her nose. Come to think of it, nothing on the wedding menu was kid friendly. So a sugar buzz explained the meltdown and insomnia.

"Okay, kid, let's see if that mini-bar in the other room has something that meets with your approval." Her smile and enthusiastic nod made him grin. "And we have a plan."

She put on her fuzzy pink robe and matching slippers and they raided the snacks that would cost Max an arm and a leg. Served him right, Hunter thought with a smile of satisfaction.

He brought the basket containing nuts, crackers and trail mix over to the sofa, then opened a bottle of bubbly water and poured some into a tumbler and put it on a coffee table coaster.

"Can I have soda?" she asked hopefully.

"No. I'm giving you a moratorium on sugar."

"What's that?" There was a puzzled look on her little face.

"It's like a time-out." He sat beside her and opened the can of nuts.

"Oh." She looked up at him. "Maybe Merry is hungry, too."

There hadn't been a sound from her room since he'd come in. She'd probably left her door open in order to hear if Wren needed anything. "She's asleep. Let's not disturb her."

If only he could say she hadn't disturbed him. She'd been one big disturbance since he'd seen her in that lavender dress and he needed some space to get back his perspective. Talking with his daughter should do it.

"Did you have fun tonight?" he asked her.

"It was the best wedding ever."

"How many have you been to?" He knew the answer was zero. Four of his brothers were married now but this had been the only big event. Thanks in part to their father, it had been a good one.

"Only one," she admitted, "but it was the best. I love my dress."

"There will be lots of pictures for you to remember everything, including how special you looked in that dress." He knew rehashing the event would settle her down so she could get some rest. "What else did you like?"

Thoughtful, she chewed a peanut. "I'm glad Merry was here. Didn't she look pretty, Daddy?"

A vision of slender curves and that sexy slit in the lavender material flashed through his mind, stunning his body as surely as if he'd been sucker punched. "She did look pretty."

"I don't know if there are any pictures of her." Wren frowned.

"The photographer was all over the place. I bet there are a lot of shots with Merry in them."

"Maybe they're of you and Merry dancing." She looked up at him, her face impossibly young, her expression achingly hopeful. "Didn't you like dancing with her? You didn't look sad when you were."

Between controlling the urge to kiss Merry and enjoying the feel of her in his arms, there hadn't been time to be sad. But his emotional quotient was not what was on Wren's mind. And he would have to be an idiot not to see that his daughter was trying to hook him up with her nanny. He slid his arm along the back of the sofa as an overwhelming need to hold and protect his little girl knotted inside him.

"Look, honey, I get that you want Merry and me to—"

"She could be your girlfriend," Wren supplied.

"No, honey—"

"But, Daddy, she was like Cinderella when you were dancing. She lost her shoe. And you helped her. Like Prince Charming. In the story they were in love," she said hopefully.

"But that's a fairy tale. She can't be my girlfriend."

"But why?"

"There are a lot of reasons," he said.

"I hate that you always have reasons." Her look challenged him to make a list.

"It's just not as easy as that." In spite of what his father thought about setting his sons up. "Just because someone wants you to like someone as a girlfriend doesn't mean they will."

"Why not?"

"Well, when a man and woman meet, there needs to be an attraction."

"Like you think someone is pretty."

"Right."

"You said Merry looked pretty tonight. Are you 'tracted?"

Try another way to explain this, he thought. "It's more than just how someone looks. It's about talking to them."

"I saw you talkin' to Merry. You laughed," his observant daughter pointed out.

He couldn't say she was wrong about that. The fact that Merry had called Wilder on his crap seemed so at odds with her innocence that it had surprised a chuckle out of him.

"It's more complicated than that, honey. Merry works for me and it's not right to make her feel uncomfortable."

"After tomorrow she won't be my nanny anymore." There was a wistful tone in her voice.

He'd thought the same thing a little while ago and was conflicted about it. Time for a change of subject. "So, what was your favorite thing about the wedding? Other than your dress."

"Dancing with Uncle Finn and Aunt Avery."

"Okay. Why?" he asked.

"They told me about a diary."

Hunter didn't have to ask what she meant. After buying the Ambling A and moving in, they'd found a leather-bound, jewel-encrusted book underneath a loose floorboard at the main house. Nate Crawford made the connection to the Abernathys, who'd previously owned the ranch, and they'd been doing research on the family. So far no information had turned up. As each of his brothers got married, the brothers had slipped the diary into their wedding-night luggage, claiming what was written inside was passionate and romantic. He was skeptical. And he hoped that his brother and sister-in-law had enough sense not to fill Wren's head with weird, woo-woo stuff.

"What did they say about the diary?"

"That whoever wrote in it didn't get a happy ending," she said.

"That's too bad, honey. But not everyone does."

"Well, they should," she said stubbornly. "Especially you, Daddy. Because Mommy died. But I don't think she would want you always to be sad. You looked happy with Merry. If you were together, you wouldn't be sad anymore."

Out of the mouths of babes... Wren was everything to him, but there'd been an emptiness inside him for the last six years after losing her mom. "Life isn't a fairy tale, sweetie."

"I know." Her tone was sulky and her look could fry eggs. "If it was, the whole family could live together in a castle. I wouldn't have to miss having my aunts around."

"Your aunt Gen and uncle Knox live in one of the other cabins. She's around."

"But she's always working with the horses. And Aunt Avery and Uncle Finn are moving up to that old hunting cabin so they can be alone. No one is there for me." She glared up at him as if this was somehow his fault. "And especially Merry. I like her here. She makes everything more fun, just like she does at school."

"I didn't know you felt that way."

"I'm the only girl around, Daddy." She crawled into his lap and rested her head on his shoulder. "It's always only Gramps and Uncle Wilder and you."

"Thanks for telling me this." And throwing a monkey wrench into everything.

It was sobering to realize that he couldn't be everything to her. By sheer numbers he'd thought he, his dad and brothers had all the bases covered in raising this little girl. He couldn't have been more wrong. And she was getting older. Maybe it would be a good thing to have more of a female presence in her life.

To keep this child happy, he would walk on hot coals. And what he was considering definitely fell under the heading of "into the fire."

Chapter Five

Merry never had hotel room service before. And coffee, orange juice, waffles and eggs brought on a cart and served by a waiter should have lifted her mood after the conversation she'd overheard last night. It didn't. The door to her room had been wide open so she could hear if Wren needed her. The bedside lamp had been off, but she'd been awake, looking at the stars from her window. There had probably still been some in her eyes after dancing with the handsome rancher.

She'd thought there was a connection and had felt a little like the Cinderella Wren talked about. But it seemed Prince Charming had no interest in love. He'd fallen back on the employer/employee dynamic even though in a few hours the work relationship would be over. There could be something if he wanted there to be. Obviously she was the only one with a crush.

Everything Hunter had said was the truth, and it shouldn't hurt, but for some reason it did. Maybe because now she was going back to her regularly scheduled life. With all its problems. So now she was packing her bags. This trip had been magical in some ways, not so much in others, and it was all but over.

She zipped up her suitcase and wheeled it into the suite's living room. Then she walked to Wren's room and poked her head in. The little girl was wadding up her clothes and throwing them into her pink princess bag.

"Would you like some help?"

Wren turned and there were tears in her eyes. "Oh, Merry, it's—"

"What is it, sweetie?" She moved closer, sat on the bed and gathered the child into her lap, holding her tight. "What's wrong, love?"

"We're going home." The words were hard to understand between sobs.

"I know. It's hard going back after having so much fun. But you can't be on vacation forever."

"It's not that." She burrowed in.

"Then what?" Merry pressed a hand to the child's forehead. "Do you feel all right?"

"Yes. I'm just sad."

"Do you want to talk about it? Maybe I can help."

"You can't. I'm cryin' because now I'll only be able to see you at school. You won't be there when I wake up in the morning or at night when I go to sleep."

She snuggled the child closer, trying to offer comfort. Wren had pushed Merry at her father last night and he wasn't having it. He was closed off and not even the daughter he loved more than anything could convince him to change his mind. Her heart hurt for both father and daughter.

From the corner of her eye she saw movement and noticed Hunter standing in the doorway. She wasn't sure how long he'd been there or what he'd heard.

"You okay, Wren?" he asked.

"Fine." The tearful tone was dripping with drama and emotion. It didn't take a mental giant to see that she was telling him what he wanted to hear.

"Do you want to talk about it?"

"No." She sat up and glared at him.

He looked as if he might push back, then didn't. "Okay.

Finish packing, then I'll get a bellman for the luggage. The cars will be here soon to take us to the airport."

"I don't want to go. Cuz I'll have to say goodbye to Aunt Sarah, Aunt Lily, Aunt Genevieve and Aunt Avery."

"I know things are changing. Aunt Lily and Uncle Xander have moved to their own ranch house. Aunt Sarah and Uncle Logan live in town. You can visit them. They fixed up her parents' house and you can visit baby Sophia."

"It's not the same," she said stubbornly.

"You'll see them all again soon. The whole family will be together for Thanksgiving in a couple of weeks."

"It will never be the same again. But I know we have to go." She sniffled then gave Merry a hug. Without another word she slid to the floor and put her nightgown in the suitcase.

"I've got this," Merry told him.

"Okay."

He looked relieved and possibly eager to be off the hook. Poor guy. She felt sorry for him. His daughter was growing up and girls were kind of a mystery to men. Her own father had told her that more than once.

Merry looked at Wren. "I'll check the drawers and make sure you have everything."

"Okay."

Forty-five minutes later those cars Hunter had mentioned unloaded the Crawford family and Merry not far from the jet waiting to take them home to Rust Creek Falls. As the group assembled, Merry looked around and frowned. In the last couple of days she'd sort of gotten used to counting Crawford heads. When your job involved keeping track of five- and six-year-olds, ticking off a list in your mind became second nature. So she noticed that three members were not present and accounted for.

"Wait. Finn and Avery aren't here."

Max happened to be next to her. "They're staying here for a few days."

"Right." Merry shaded her eyes with her hand as she looked up at him and was blinded by the sun. "Their honeymoon."

"Yeah."

He was grinning from ear to ear, but Merry didn't think it was "that's my boy" or "chip off the old block" stuff. The man seemed genuinely pleased that his son was married, happy and the family celebration had gone off without a hitch. However, there might be a hitch in the ride home since one more of them was missing.

"Wilder's not here either. Is he staying for the honeymoon, too?" she asked wryly.

Max's smile slipped. "Finn would have something to say about that. No. He texted and said he would meet us here. And before you ask, he didn't stay in his room at the resort."

Merry wasn't sure why he was confiding this information to her and was reluctant to comment the way she had to Hunter. "I wasn't prying. It's just habit. At the school one of the things they pay me for is to make sure everyone is where they should be."

His glance settled on Wren who was soaking up attention from her three aunts while she still could. Then Max looked at Merry. "I want to thank you for taking care of my granddaughter this weekend. She seems to like you very much and that goes a long way with me."

"She's a very special little girl. It's impossible not to fall in love with her."

"I couldn't agree more." A car pulled up behind the SUVs and Wilder got out. "Seems the prodigal son has arrived."

"That completes the head count."

"Thank you again, Merry." He gave her a quick bear hug. "Excuse me. I have to herd everyone on board."

Merry wasn't the last one to get on the plane, but the seating area in the front section was pretty full. Wren was there with her aunts and uncles so she picked a bench seat in the rear by herself. After all, she was only the hired help.

Moments after she was settled, the stragglers boarded. Hunter was the last and he looked around, then hesitated only a moment before sitting beside her. He didn't say anything so she didn't either. *Let it be awkward,* she thought.

The announcement was made to buckle up and the flight attendant secured the cabin for takeoff. It wasn't long before they were airborne.

Hunter cleared his throat. "I have a check for you."

"It doesn't seem right to take money. Looking after Wren isn't work, and a stay at that fabulous resort was wonderful. A lovely break from my routine."

"Still, I hired you to make sure she was well looked after and she was. So, here."

She looked at the piece of paper he held out. "My employment is officially complete."

"Yeah."

She took it and tucked the check into her wallet. "Thank you."

"You're welcome."

Merry studied his expression and guessed that he was uneasy. "Was there something else?"

"Yeah."

"I thought so."

"Why?" He sounded surprised.

"Because there are other seats open and you sat next to me. I figured it was to talk." Because she knew he wasn't attracted to her. "I hope you were satisfied with the supervision I provided Wren."

"I was. But more important, she was happy." Hunter glanced away for a moment and took a deep breath. "I heard what she said to you earlier. When she was packing."

Merry didn't know what to say to that except, "I didn't put her up to that."

"The thought never crossed my mind."

She nodded. "I wouldn't worry. She's probably just tired. It was a busy weekend."

"And she was up late last night."

Merry was aware of that fact but didn't confirm she knew. It was best he didn't know she'd overheard that particular conversation. "She'll be fine once she's home."

"Will she?"

Merry's gaze snapped to his. "Why wouldn't she be?"

"For one thing, she's become very attached to you."

"And, like I told her, she will see me at school. This weekend hasn't changed anything." That was a lie. After dancing with Hunter, aka Prince Charming, she'd changed. But real life would get her over it. "Going back to her routine will fix whatever is bothering her."

"Maybe that's not enough." He looked lost. "It's possible she needs more female influence in her life. Last night she said some things—"

"Oh?" she said innocently.

His expression was intense. "The words don't matter. I just don't want her to ever think I didn't listen to her. So—"

"What?"

"I'd like to hire you to be Wren's nanny. It will be a full-time, live-in job."

She hadn't seen that coming and was on the verge of

turning him down until he told her the salary he had in mind. Still, she said, "I already have a job at the school."

"The way I see it, there's no reason to quit since you both have the same schedule. You could take her and bring her home. That frees me up for ranch work because you'll be with her."

"Wow, I—" Her mind was racing. She'd literally just been thinking how meeting him had changed her but going home would get her over it. The intense attraction was a very good reason for her to say no.

But she couldn't ignore the fact that accepting the offer would solve two of her most pressing problems—money and a place to live when the house sold. She would be a fool to pass up this opportunity.

"In that case, thank you. I would love to be Wren's nanny."

And if there was a God in heaven, Hunter would never suspect how she felt about him.

The first day back from the wedding was Hunter's first day to wonder what he'd been thinking to hire Merry Matthews to be the live-in nanny. She'd brought Wren home from school then unpacked her own things in one of the cabin's two extra upstairs bedrooms.

Merry had the table set when he came in from working and she greeted him with a sunny smile, a beer and the best meatloaf and mashed potatoes he'd ever tasted. Somehow she'd even flimflammed his daughter into eating her green beans without an argument. So, his problem with Merry had nothing to do with her work and everything to do with his attraction to her.

Now he was alone downstairs while happy noises and laughter drifted to him from the second floor. At the wedding he'd seen how content his married brothers were and he felt like he was on the outside looking in. He'd never expected to feel that way in his own home. It was always him and Wren against the world, but now Merry was here making meatloaf and supervising his child's bath.

He was too restless to watch TV and decided to make sure Merry knew where the soap and towels were kept. At the top of the stairs the master bedroom was on his left. He turned the other way and passed his daughter's room, then stopped. The bathroom door was open and the little girl was standing in front of the oak-framed oval mirror and wearing her favorite pink nightgown. Merry was behind her, combing her hair.

"Hi, Daddy."

"Hey, kiddo. I can't believe you're clean already."

"Merry said if I was fast there would be time before bed to show me how to French braid my hair."

"Did she now?"

"She did," Merry confirmed. "I'm a solid believer in the carrot-and-stick method of negotiation. Better known as rewarding positive behavior."

"And you have the positive results to back you up." He leaned a shoulder against the doorjamb.

"I do. She lived up to her end of the bargain so now I have to pay up." She smiled into the mirror. "So what'll it be, sweetie? Braids? Pigtails?" She gathered the wet strands that lightened to golden blond when dry and pulled them up to the crown of Wren's head. "Top knot?"

"French braids. I already told you."

"Just making sure you haven't changed your mind."

It hadn't taken Merry long to figure out that this child often altered the plan when he thought she'd set her heart on something. Sometimes Wren made his head spin but this woman seemed to take it in stride. Points to her.

"Daddy doesn't know how to French braid," Wren teased. "He can only do a ponytail."

"I'm sure he has other very important skills."

He thought for a moment. "As a matter of fact, I fixed the door on your dollhouse. Remember?"

"Is that true?" Merry's hands stilled as she met the child's gaze in the mirror.

"Yes, ma'am." She nodded enthusiastically and nearly pulled her hair from the nanny's loose grip. "He made it for me, too."

"That big beautiful wooden Victorian dollhouse with the lovely details? The one taking up a large portion of her room. You built that?" Her eyes were wide and full of amazement.

"With my bare hands." He swore he could almost feel his chest puffing out because he'd impressed her.

"Where were you when I was a little girl?"

"Probably a little boy dipping a little girl's French braid in the inkwell."

She laughed. "Actually that was a rhetorical question. But seriously, it's a beautiful job. I would have loved something like that when I was a child." She looked at Wren. "Your dad can't do hair but you're very fortunate that he has some serious dollhouse skills."

"Thank you, Daddy."

"You're welcome."

"That reminds me," Wren said. "In school today we made a turkey out of construction paper. My teacher was tellin' us about the very first Thanksgiving."

"Yeah?" Merry secured the braid she just finished.

"Yes. And she said the holiday will be here before we know it."

"That's true." He was only half listening because the

concentration on Merry's face as she worked was so darn cute.

"We're having a first Thanksgiving, too. Just like the pilgrims."

"You are?" Merry said.

"Uh-huh." Again Wren nodded and this time did pull her hair out of the nanny's hands. She had to start over. "Sorry."

"No problem. Please continue."

"This will be Daddy's and my first Thanksgiving here on the ranch."

"Wow. That's exciting." Her tone was bright and shiny, but her expression didn't match. There was sadness in her eyes. "Sometimes firsts are fun and sometimes they're not."

"You'll be missing your dad this year," Hunter guessed.

She glanced at him and nodded. "This is my first one without him. Ever."

"I'm sorry, Merry," the little girl said. "I never had Thanksgiving with my mom because she died when I was a baby."

Hunter noticed that his daughter had dropped the "Miss" when she talked to Merry. The little girl was clearly comfortable with her new nanny. He remembered that first Thanksgiving without Lara and whatever the definition of fun was, that holiday didn't even come close. He'd been knee-deep in diapers, formula and sleepless nights. But if it hadn't been for Wren and his family, he didn't think he'd have gotten through that dark time at all.

"You know, sweetie, you're very lucky to have all your family close by. And not just for the holiday. Not everyone is so fortunate."

It occurred to Hunter that he didn't know a lot about her family except the little she'd shared. That she and her father had moved to Rust Creek Falls right after the flood. And she had a brother who joined the military. Was she completely alone now? He wanted to know but couldn't phrase the question like that.

"But you have a brother," Hunter said.

"Yes."

He expected her to elaborate, but she pressed her lips tightly together. No one would ever accuse him of being fluent in body language but hers clearly said she wouldn't tell him more. Of course that just made him more curious about her story. Including, now that he thought about it, was there a special man in her life? Fortunately his daughter was oblivious to the signals and didn't let the subject go.

"What's your brother's name?"

"Jack."

"Where does he live?" Wren asked.

"He's in the military. Right now he lives overseas."

"Is that far?" The little girl's eyes grew wider.

"Very far. We don't see each other much."

Hunter wasn't sure why he recognized that this separation pained her, but he did. Maybe because of his own loss, kindred spirits and all that. Still the why of it didn't matter. All he knew was that Merry wasn't living up to her name. And something told him there was more to this than just geographical distance. If eyes were the window to the soul, hers were revealing a painful bruise. Jack had somehow hurt her.

Merry secured the second braid and forced a smile. "Ta-da. You are gorgeous. Do you like it?"

Turning her head from side to side Wren said, "Yes. Can you do it like this for Thanksgiving?"

"Of course. You'll be the prettiest six-year-old at the table."

"I'll be the only one there," the little girl said.

"Really?" Merry tapped her lip thoughtfully. "That's right. Baby Sophia isn't big enough to walk yet."

"She can't talk either."

"True. Not a lot of company in your demographic," Merry sympathized.

"Does that mean I have no one to talk to?" Wren asked.

"Yes." Merry glanced at Hunter and the corners of her mouth curved up in amusement.

"Your aunts will all be there," Hunter reminded her.

"Cool."

"You're going to have a wonderful holiday," Merry said. "And you can tell me all about it."

"But you're going to be there, too," the little girl said.

"I don't know." She shrugged.

"You have to be here. With me. And my family. We can have our firsts together."

"Your first one in Montana and my first without my dad." Merry met his gaze though she spoke to Wren. "It's not up to me, sweetie."

Hunter wasn't sure how his daughter had grown into the thoughtful, caring person she was. He couldn't believe he hadn't extended the invitation already. His only excuse was being preoccupied with Merry's mouth. More specifically how her lips would feel against his own. Would they be as soft as he expected? Maybe she would taste like sunshine and fresh air.

Both of the females in the room were staring at him and for a second he was afraid he'd said that out loud.

"What?" he asked them.

"Da-ad." Wren rolled her eyes. "Is it okay for Merry to have Thanksgiving with us?"

"We can talk about this later," Merry interjected. "I

don't want you to feel like you're on the spot. It's really fine. I'll have dinner with my friend Zoey—"

"It's okay. Wren wants you here and you're more than welcome. So, dinner with the Crawfords on Thanksgiving is a go. The more the Merry-er."

"Like I've never heard that one before." The nanny grinned at him then giggled with Wren.

"So will you? Come with us to Gramps's house for Thanksgiving?" There was a note of coaxing in Wren's tone.

"I wouldn't miss it."

Wren turned and pressed herself against Merry, wrapping her small arms around her waist. "It's a good thing you're here. You have us to spend the holiday with."

"And I am so very lucky." She bent and kissed the top of the little girl's head. "And on that note, it has to be said that it's time—"

"For bed," Wren finished. Then she laughed.

Hunter couldn't believe it. No drama. Zero argument. Just good-natured surrender to the inevitable. Had he been doing something wrong? Was the nanny sprinkling rainbows and fairy dust on his child?

More important—what was he? Chopped liver?

That sounded a little bit ungrateful. It was probably just about the newness of the situation. The little girl he knew and loved couldn't keep this up for long. But contemplating that philosophical question was better than thinking about the one uppermost in his mind. Had it been a mistake to hire Merry? He had decidedly mixed feelings about her living here.

On the one hand, Wren seemed happy to have a woman here. Hence the bedtime capitulation. On the other hand, the moment Hunter came home and saw dinner ready followed by Merry offering him a beer, he'd begun to ache in places he'd been sure had died a long time ago.

He didn't want to feel again but he did, and having her here was the only difference between yesterday and today. This wasn't anything he'd anticipated and he acknowledged it might have been a major miscalculation to offer her the job. But that horse had already left the barn.

Chapter Six

Normally Hunter liked riding fences to check that the posts and wire didn't need repair or make sure a cow wasn't stuck in the fence. But this morning his father was with him. Max had insisted he wanted to come along, but surely he had an agenda. The man always did.

He glanced over and admired the way his father sat a horse, the way he'd taught Hunter and his brothers to ride. Straight, tall and proud. Maximilian Crawford was an imposing figure, but Hunter wished he was an imposing figure in his ranch office instead.

"I think you should start dating again," his father said.

"And there it is."

"What?" There was a little too much innocence in Max's gravelly voice.

"The reason you got up before God to keep me company."

"It does make you kind of a captive audience." Max grinned, completely unashamed. "I just want to talk to you about getting back in the saddle, no pun intended."

"Dating."

"Right."

"Then this will be a short conversation, Dad. I dated a little back in Dallas. I don't want to get serious. Good talk."

Max nodded, his black Stetson casting a shadow that hid his eyes. "I was also thinking about how much I like

Montana. The land. The mountains. Coming here and making a change is going to be good for this family. Hell, it already is. Look how happy your brothers are."

"I agree."

Hunter had noticed, and he envied them but that was his problem. On the other hand, his daughter had never been happier since Merry had come to live with them. He still wasn't convinced hiring her was the right move because every time she walked into a room need knotted deep in his gut. She was messing with his head, had him picturing himself running his hands through all that silky blond hair and kissing her full lips. And it wasn't just his head she was messing with. The rest of his body wanted in on the action. There were so many reasons why that was a bad idea.

Hunter became aware that his father was staring at him as they clip-clopped along. "What?"

"I can't recall the last time you agreed with me about anything."

"Well, I do, about moving to Montana. Wren is settling in really well." Thanks to Merry.

And as if Max could read his mind, he said, "Hiring Merry to be her nanny has made a difference then?"

"Seems so." It had been only a few days since she moved into the house, but they'd fallen seamlessly into a routine. And the woman was making herself indispensable to him, as well. Her being there took pressure and stress off him as far as ranch chores late at night or early in the morning. Like today.

"It doesn't hurt that we left a lot of bad memories behind in Texas," Max said.

"You're not wrong, Dad."

The ranch and city of Dallas itself had reminders everywhere Hunter went. It was where he and Lara had started their life together and where hers had ended. He'd been a grieving husband and single dad who had no clue how to care for an infant daughter.

"How did you manage it all?" he asked his father. "After Mom left, I mean."

"Badly."

Hunter rested his gloved hands on the saddle horn and glanced sideways. He'd never heard that particular tone of regret in Max's voice before. "What do you mean?"

"Your mom wanted out of the marriage, and I didn't want to let her go. Consequently I made a lot of mistakes, as a husband and a father."

"Such as?"

Max's mouth pulled tight and his body slumped a little in the saddle. The image of dejection and sadness. "She wasn't happy but I tried to force her to stay anyway. I tried to control the situation and used my own sons as leverage. That just made everything worse."

"How?" Hunter and his brothers had lived the nightmare of their mom being there one day then gone the next, and never seeing her again. But his father had never talked about this before and he needed to hear it.

"You boys didn't have a mom. I kept you from her to try and get her to come back. It backfired. And now I see the true meaning of that saying—you reap what you sow. The chickens have come home to roost."

"What do you mean? Just spit it out, Dad."

"All of you boys are reluctant to commit to love. And that's my fault."

Hunter sighed. "Correct me if I'm wrong. Four of my brothers are married. That seems an awful lot like commitment to me."

"It is," Max agreed. "But they wouldn't have found love if I hadn't helped them along."

"You call it help, I call it interference."

His father threw up his hands in frustration and startled his horse into dancing sideways. He patted the animal's neck and made a shushing sound. "Easy there."

"The thing is, Dad, you can check me off your conscience. It's all good. I don't need your help because I already did commit and I don't want to do it again. I lost the woman I love just when I thought I had everything. Wren turned us into a family but I lost Lara. Suddenly my perfect family was gone. So, committing cost me everything."

"That's the way I felt about your mother," Max said sadly. "But I was only thinking of myself when I kept her away from you boys. I thought she'd come around but instead I hurt my children. I'm really sorry, son."

"I believe you."

Oddly enough, Hunter understood. As a kid he'd been confused and hurt when his mom disappeared. Always in the back of his mind was the thought that maybe if he'd been a better kid she might not have gone away. If he'd never fallen in love with Lara, he wouldn't get it that a man could do stupid things because of love. He should be mad, but in a weird way he was bonding with his father, maybe for the first time.

"And it's okay, Dad."

"No, it's not. I started to realize it when Wren was born and Lara died. A man's perspective changes when he becomes a grandfather. I watched you hurting and raising her without a mother. That had me soul-searching. You didn't have a choice about losing your daughter's mother, but I did and chose wrong."

"Let me see if I understand this right. You're blaming this recent matchmaking insanity of yours on my daughter?"

"No. Maybe." Max shrugged. "Lara's been gone six years, son. She wouldn't want her daughter growing up without a mother or you to be stuck in the past."

That struck a chord. When Lara's due date had been fast approaching, she'd started to get nervous about giving birth. But she'd taken it a step further and told him if anything happened to her she wanted him to fall in love and be happy again. It was as if she'd had a premonition that something was going to happen to her. But Hunter had blown her off. He'd told her childbirth was the most natural thing in the world and nothing would go wrong. But it had and losing her at what should have been the happiest time of their lives was the worst moment of his. He never wanted to feel like that again.

"Look—" He spotted a problem in the fencing and pointed. A post was tilting and nearly halfway to the ground, pulling the wire down on either side of it. "Need to prop that up."

Finally, something to do and get Max off his case.

They stopped and dismounted, dropping the reins to ground tie the horses. The well-trained animals would stand still and not run off while he and Max handled the repair. His dad held the post upright while Hunter dug the hole deeper with the small hand shovel he'd brought along with the other tools. Then he packed the dirt in tighter.

"There. That ought to do it. This will hold now. We caught it just in time." And the interruption had the added benefit of distraction.

"Looks good, son," his dad agreed.

They swung back into their saddles and continued the ride and fence inspection. Hunter was enjoying the sun, solitude and silence, until Max started in again, right where he'd left off.

"So, I got a call from Vivienne Dalton."

"Who?" Hunter knew exactly who she was but there was no reason he had to make this easy on his dad.

"Come on, son. You know darn well she's the wedding planner working to find—"

"Women for your sons."

"You make it sound unsavory," Max accused. "I'm paying her to find suitable women for marriage. All you have to do is meet them. Believe it or not I'm doing this for your happiness."

"I'm already happy," Hunter insisted.

"Let me try this another way. My granddaughter needs a mother."

"She has Merry."

On the trip back from Avery and Finn's wedding, Hunter had received his daughter's message loud and clear. She was growing up and needed a female's guiding hand. He'd fixed the problem.

"I'm talking about a mother," Max emphasized. "Not someone who is paid to take care of her."

Right. Hunter signed her paycheck and Merry had taken the job because she needed the money. She was an employee. But he had a bad habit of forgetting that when he came in the door after a long workday and she greeted him with a heart-stopping smile and a hot meal on the table. Or when she spontaneously hugged Wren and kissed her cheek. That natural impulsive affection wasn't because of an hourly wage. It came from the heart.

He should probably thank his father for the reminder because forgetting he was her boss could be dangerous. The last thing he wanted was to fall in love again. Been there, done that. He was fine now and would pass on a repeat.

"Look, son, I've made questionable decisions in the past, but I'm trying to make up for it. Vivienne Dalton is a very nice woman and she isn't going to recommend someone unsuitable. And there's someone she would like you to meet."

"Okay."

Max looked at him funny. "Okay what?"

"I will think about meeting the woman Vivienne has vetted."

"Excellent. That's all I ask." His father beamed with approval.

He would agree to almost anything so they could talk about something else. But Hunter found himself wishing Merry was the woman the matchmaker had in mind. Which only proved he'd lost his.

Merry felt as if she'd been thrown into the deep end of the pool—the Crawford family pool, that is. On Thanksgiving. Sure, she'd attended the wedding with all of them, but she'd stayed in the background as Wren's nanny. It hadn't been quite two weeks since she'd started her full-time job for Hunter along with doing her darnedest to control this pesky attraction to him.

Now it was a traditional family holiday and all of them were gathered at the ranch's main house. Most of them were in the other room watching football while she was essentially hiding in the kitchen. It was big and functional although it could definitely use some renovation. But there was a huge sink and a big, if old-fashioned, island with lots of work space. She was helping to prepare dinner for thirteen. Fourteen if you counted little Sophia.

Lily Crawford was doing the cooking. She was a chef and recently married to Xander, third eldest of the brothers. She worked part time at Maverick Manor and not long ago started Lily's Home Cookin', preparing individual meals for customers. Word was spreading and she was steadily building her business.

Today Merry had volunteered to do the grunt work, slicing, dicing, cutting and chopping—anything that would make fixing this meal easier. She would have been nearly immobilized by the pressure of preparing a perfect holiday dinner but the other woman looked serene and confident, as if she was enjoying it. As if she was completely in her element. Which, of course, she was.

Merry was now peeling potatoes, letting the skins fall on newspaper spread over the counter. There was a giant pot in front of her filled with water and she dropped the naked spuds into it. Lily was putting together snacks for the football crowd. She slid a cookie sheet of mini-quiches into the oven, then began to artfully arrange a cheese, raw vegetables and fruit platter.

"You are truly amazing," Merry said in awe.

"It's all about loving what I do. I suppose that's true of any profession. From what I saw at the wedding, you are pretty amazing with Wren." Lily looked up and smiled warmly. "She adores you."

"The feeling is mutual." *And I hope I'm good at it,* she thought. "But you're right. I do love kids."

"It shows." Lily arranged cucumber slices in a circle with berries in the center. "I can't thank you enough for your help. It saved me so much time."

"It's the least I could do. And a bonus for me that we've gotten better acquainted."

"Yes," she agreed. "That was a hectic weekend and I felt as if we were ships passing in the night."

"Plus, there are a lot of Crawfords." Merry put a peeled potato into the pot and picked up another one. "I wanted to put name tags on everyone to keep them straight."

"I can see how it might be confusing." Lily laughed.

"But I have three older brothers so being around this family seems pretty natural to me."

"You're lucky to have siblings. No sisters?"

"No." She sighed. "But I wished for one."

"Me, too," Merry said.

"So you're an only child?"

"No." Although it felt that way to her. "I have a brother. Jack. He's ten years older."

"That's a big age difference. When you were five he was fifteen and in high school and might not have wanted a little sister tagging along. It must have been hard to be close."

"What makes you say that?"

"Your face." The other woman's expression was sympathetic. "You've probably been told this before, but never play poker. Everything you feel is right there."

Yikes! Merry thought. She hoped that wasn't entirely true or she was going to have to work on that. This job with Hunter could get awkward otherwise, and she really needed it.

"It's more than age with Jack and me. There's actual geographical distance. When our mom died, he was eighteen and joined the military right out of high school. He's made it a career and has been gone a lot. I barely see him. He came to our dad's funeral but left right after." It had been nothing more than a duty to him. Being a career soldier taught him about that but nothing about family, or the fact that Merry had needed him to stay for just a little while.

"I'm sorry for your loss. I know it was recent," Lily said. "And it sounds like you didn't have a lot of support."

"From my friends here in Rust Creek Falls, but not family." The rejection still hurt. "It was hard being alone.

And I think about that with Wren. I don't want that for her. A sibling would be—"

Merry stopped. She felt as if she'd known Lily far longer than she had and the woman was way too easy to talk to. That was her only excuse for bringing up something as personal as Hunter giving his daughter a brother or sister. That wasn't a topic the hired help should be discussing with his sister-in-law.

Heat crept into her cheeks as she met Lily's gaze. "Sorry. I think I said too much."

"Even if I agree with you?" Lily asked. "Did you see Wren with Sarah and Logan's baby? That child would be such a wonderful big sister."

"I know, right?"

"And, I may be spreading gossip, but this is Rust Creek Falls after all." The other woman smiled mischievously. "I think Avery's got a little baby bump going on."

Merry was busy with her job at school and Wren. Other than the wedding, she hadn't seen much of the newly married couple. "Really?"

"Yup. She's at that stage where a first thought might be that she's put on a couple pounds, but if you look closely, it's all tummy. In the cutest possible way. And the move to the hunting cabin. Fixing it up. If that's not nesting, I don't know what is."

"Wren will be so thrilled," Merry said. "She'd love to have a sister or brother, but a new cousin is the next best thing."

"Something sure smells good in here."

Merry didn't expect to hear a man's voice and this one belonged to Hunter. She dropped the potato she was holding and peeled a small chunk from her index finger. "Ouch."

"Are you okay?" Hunter quickly moved beside her

and took her hand to assess the damage. "Doesn't look too bad."

"It's fine." Although the scrape stung like crazy. Even though she tried to pull away, he didn't let go and looked concerned. That was like chocolate and chips to her needy hormones. Suddenly she felt no pain and figured this attraction was good for something. "I'm just clumsy."

"I doubt that. Let's wash this off." He turned on the spigot beside them and gently held her wounded finger under the cold water to wash the blood away.

"Here's a bandage and some antibiotic cream." Lily set the things on the counter next to him. "These are staples in my kitchen, as important as the right ingredients. When you're using sharp instruments there are always accidents."

"Thanks," he said.

Merry was shaking but not from her mishap. It was a reaction to the nearness of this man and having him touch her. She'd done the same thing when they'd danced at the wedding. It seemed like forever since that night and her body was quivering with excitement. She really hoped he didn't notice.

He dried off her finger with a paper towel, dabbed on some ointment, then snugly wrapped the sticky adhesive strip around the wound. "It's tight to stop the bleeding. How does it feel?"

So good she didn't want him to stop touching her. But that's not what he meant. And when he continued to look at her, she hoped Lily was wrong about everything she felt being right there on her face.

"It's good," Merry finally said.

"Not too tight?"

"Nope. Everything is fine." She glanced at Lily, who was watching the exchange with great interest, until a timer sounded and she took the little quiches out of the oven. "So, I'm sure you didn't come in here to provide first aid."

Actually, Merry wouldn't have needed it if he hadn't come in here. Her arms and legs seemed to go limp and malfunction every time she saw him.

"What can we do for you, Hunter?" Lily asked. "I'm just putting the finishing touches on snack platters."

With his attention off her now, Merry's brain functioned normally again. "Wren hasn't eaten since breakfast and it's after lunch now. She must be starving."

"She hasn't said anything. Too busy playing princess with Genevieve."

"Our Genevieve?" Lily looked surprised. "The tomboy who does horse pedicures?"

"The same one." Hunter grinned but it quickly disappeared. "Knox said she's practicing for having kids."

"Wren would love more cousins," Merry commented but the look on his face made her want those words back.

"I was just saying how much Wren loves baby Sophia. I think she'd be excited about having more kids around." Lily's expression was innocent, but her green eyes glittered with mischief.

Hunter held up his hands to form a T, the signal for time-out. "I just came in for snacks, not a Crawford family population increase debate."

Merry was feeling a little sorry for him. He was looking cornered and uncomfortable. "And it's two against one."

"Okay. We'll let you off the hook." The other woman finished putting the little quiches on a tray. "I'll help you carry these into the family room."

"Great." He slid Merry a look that said "thank you"

and took the fruit and cheese platter before making a speedy getaway.

Lily wasn't gone long and entered the room laughing. "Wow, that's a ravenous group in there. That food lost any artistic presentation almost before I put the tray down. And my Xander was leading the pack."

The woman's face turned loving and tender when she mentioned her husband. That made Merry curious.

"How did you and Xander meet?"

"Funny story." Lily smiled softly. "As everyone knows, Max is trying to get his sons to settle down and made a deal with Viv Dalton to set them up. I was supposed to go out with Knox—reluctantly, I should add. He canceled at the last minute."

"So you went out with Xander instead?"

"He came to apologize for his bonehead brother and ended up taking me to dinner. I'm pretty sure he felt sorry for me because I'd been dumped. I'd even changed back into my jeans and T-shirt and was all ready to go."

"That was very sweet of him," Merry said.

"Yeah. He'd gotten my attention once before when I met all the guys at the same time. But he pretty much had me at that adorable gesture." She looked up. "Don't get me wrong. We had our ups and downs. Complications to maneuver. Compromises to make. But none of it was any match for love. We both fell hard." She sighed dreamily.

"So, you're happy?"

"Very."

"And I guess in a convoluted way Max was responsible for you two meeting," Merry commented. "But why would he feel he has to help his sons?"

"Apparently he had a rocky relationship with their mother and she abandoned the family when Wilder was a baby. It seems all the brothers have trouble committing. It's just a guess, but I think Max feels responsible somehow and is trying to help. To make it up to them."

Merry knew how it felt to lose her mom to illness but couldn't understand a woman voluntarily walking away from six children. That would surely leave a mark. Except… "But Hunter was married. Obviously he was able to get past the childhood trauma and take a chance."

"True. And his wife died." There was sympathy and sadness in Lily's expression.

"So he won't give it another try?"

"According to Xander he did eventually start to date again back in Texas, but his heart wasn't in it."

"Doesn't surprise me. From what I can see, he only has room in his heart for his daughter."

"I'm not so sure about that."

The teasing tone and mischievous twinkle in the other woman's eyes made Merry wonder. Did her face give something away when Hunter was in the kitchen? Good Lord, she hoped not. It was more likely that Max was trying to set up his son with someone appropriate, someone Viv Dalton had personally selected.

She didn't like the idea of that one bit, but no one asked for her opinion. She'd been hired to take care of Wren, not get involved with the child's father. Their business association took her out of the dating pool, which made her equal parts mad and sad.

And she had no right to either emotion.

Chapter Seven

Hunter was having the best first Thanksgiving in Rust Creek Falls. His family was together and even bigger now that four of his brothers were married. And then there was Merry. She was a breath of fresh air. Even her name was happy and she lived up to it every day. Case in point: when she took a chunk out of her finger peeling potatoes. She'd smiled through the first aid that had given him an excuse to get close to her. He wasn't proud of it, but that didn't stop him from remembering it.

Crawfords were milling around the big dining room, figuring out where to sit. Max claimed the armchair at the head of the table. The perfectly browned turkey and carving knife were placed in front of him. Merry had taken Wren to supervise handwashing and the two of them returned to stand beside Hunter.

"Daddy, I want to sit in the chair next to Sophia's high chair."

Hunter looked at Logan and Sarah, who were close enough to hear.

"That sounds perfect," the baby's mother said. "And I'll sit on the other side."

Wren clapped her hands. "This is the best Thanksgiving ever!"

"Be sure to duck when she starts throwing her food instead of eating it," Logan teased. "And watch out when she puts cranberry sauce in her hair."

"Gross." Wren wrinkled her nose.

"Don't be so quick to judge." Hunter put his hand on her slight shoulder. "You did the same thing when you were her age."

"I don't believe you." His little girl put on her stubborn pouty face.

"That sounds so adorable," Merry said. "I wish I could have seen it. Do you have pictures?"

"Probably not."

There weren't many photos of his little girl's first year. Between ranch work and caring for an infant, he'd been pretty overwhelmed. His focus was on the day-to-day needs of their child. Memorializing that dark time with photos hadn't been high on his priority list.

"I'm going to move this along." Max took charge and told everyone where to sit.

"You're putting me at the foot?" Wilder asked.

"Consider it a metaphor. Maybe that will give you a kick in the—" Max winked at Wren "—backside and knock some sense into you."

The youngest Crawford took his place and grinned across the expanse of the big table at his father. "I'm perfectly happy with the amount of sense I have."

"Well, I'm not." Max watched everyone take the places he'd assigned.

Hunter pulled out Merry's chair and whispered, "My little brother doesn't have enough sense to know he has no sense."

"I heard that," Wilder said.

"Okay." Max picked up the carving utensils. "I'm going to cut this bird and we'll start passing the food around."

Everyone started to talk and the noise level rose. Hunter sneaked a look at Merry and thought she seemed a little tense and sad. Maybe she was intimidated by so many Crawfords in one place. Or maybe she felt out of place because she was his employee. He had a hard time remembering that because she seemed to fit so seamlessly into Wren's life. But this was also her first holiday without her dad, and her brother was also missing.

He wished there was a way to fix this as easily as he had patched up her finger earlier.

"How's your wound?" he asked.

"My what?"

"The finger."

She looked at him and her cheeks flushed. "I think I'll live. But it has to be said, I don't think I've ever peeled so many potatoes at one time."

"Feeding this family is kind of like cooking for an army." It was supposed to be a lighthearted comment to make her smile. It didn't. "Did I say something wrong?"

"What? No." She shook her head. "It just made me think about my brother for a second. I haven't spent a holiday with him since I was a little girl."

Hunter could have kicked himself for making her look so lost. Somehow he needed to snap her out of it because he wanted her to live up to her name again. And she was here to get through the first holiday without her dad.

He looked around the table at his brothers, remembering the testosterone-fueled squabbles they'd had over the years. There were a few black eyes and fat lips in all of their pasts. "We could have used a referee when I was growing up."

Her look was sympathetic, as if she knew their family scandal. "But now I bet you're glad to have every one of your brothers."

She was right. He loved them and wished each one a life filled with love and not loss like the one he'd experienced.

Finally Max, with pointers from Lily, had finished with the turkey and everyone started passing bowls and platters of food. When plates were full, their father announced that the annual what-I'm-thankful-for rounds would commence. Of course, as head of the family, he would start, then it would proceed from eldest to youngest.

"I'm thankful for all of my sons and their new brides. I'm grateful for this wonderful meal, prepared by all of you, especially our resident chef, Lily." She blushed as everyone applauded. Then he looked at Sophia and Wren with raw tenderness on his rugged face. "And I'm more grateful than I can say for these beautiful children, the next generation of Crawfords."

Everyone voiced their approval and there was some not very subtle sniffling from Avery. Wilder jumped in before his brothers could take their turns.

"I'd just like to say that I love all my new sisters-in-law, but, man, I'm glad to be single."

A chorus of boos drowned out the rest of his words but he only grinned. Hunter had mixed feelings.

The sound of a utensil tapping on a glass got his attention and he looked up. Finn was standing at the table, gazing down at Avery with an expression that revealed he was nuts about her.

"My wife and I have something special to be thankful for this Thanksgiving. We're going to have a baby." Spontaneous cheers, applause and hugs followed the reveal. "We wanted to keep the news just for us but we've known for a while."

"So have we," Logan and Sarah said together.

"Us, too," Genevieve said. "The glow. The baby bump."

"Am I showing?" Avery put a hand to her tummy.

"Just a little," everyone chimed in.

The mother-to-be sighed. "At least you didn't think I was just getting fat."

"You look beautiful," Finn assured her. "And I'm going to be a father."

"Better you than me, big brother," Wilder said. "I'm not a dirty diaper–changing kind of guy."

"So I'm gonna have another baby cousin?" Wren asked. When assured that she was right, she said, "Cool. I can't wait. This is the best holiday ever."

Hunter had to disagree. Except for Logan and their dad, he was the only other father in the room. The rest of them were gushing about wanting to expand their families, have babies. They couldn't wait. Even Wren couldn't wait.

Everyone was so happy and he couldn't say anything. All he had to offer was a warning about what could happen and he didn't want to bring everyone down. But it would terrify him if Merry was pregnant.

Whoa. Where the hell did that thought come from? Except he knew. He'd seen her bleed a little while ago and wanted to fix it. Because in spite of all his own warnings, he wasn't just starting to feel. He was starting to care. And that had to stop.

Hunter had been very quiet during dinner. Merry noticed because he'd been uncharacteristically chatty when they'd first sat down. She'd gotten the feeling he was trying to cheer her up. Go figure. Then Finn and Avery had made what should have been a happy announcement and his brothers and their wives had talked eagerly about starting families, too. Wilder had been outspoken in his aversion, but Hunter had clammed up.

They were home now and Merry was in the upstairs bathroom overseeing Wren's quick shower. The little girl was tired and needed to be in bed ASAP. When the water shut off, Merry was ready with a towel. After Wren dried off, she put on her favorite princess nightgown.

"I'll give your hair a quick brush, sweetie."

"Okay." The one word was followed by a big yawn. A few minutes later Wren climbed into her bed.

Merry pulled the covers up over her. "I'll go get your dad to read."

"But I want you to do it," the little girl said.

"Sweetie, your dad always reads to you. It's your thing." Merry felt a tingling at the base of her neck and somehow knew that Hunter was in the doorway hearing this. A moment later Wren confirmed her feeling.

"Daddy, I want Merry to read to me tonight and give me a good-night kiss."

He walked over to the bed and looked down at his daughter. There was no way you could miss the troubled expression on his face before he forced a smile. "Whatever you want, honey. Is it okay if I kiss you, too?"

"Yes, Daddy." She reached out her little arms and he bent down, then swallowed her slight frame in a big hug.

"I love you." His voice was gruff with emotion and some hurt feelings he was trying to hide. As always, he kissed her forehead. "See you in the morning."

"Love you," she said before yawning again.

Merry wanted to say something to Hunter but didn't know what. Even if she came up with the right words, it wasn't appropriate to discuss this in front of Wren. There was a slump to his broad shoulders when he left the room.

"I want the princess story," Wren said sleepily.

It was in a book of fairy tales, her favorite, and was on the nightstand beside the bed. Merry picked it up and started reading. "Once upon a time…"

A few paragraphs later she saw that the child was

sound asleep. Merry set the book down and kissed the girl's sweet little cheek before tiptoeing out. Normally she would go to her bedroom and read, avoiding her employer and her crush on him. But not tonight. She needed to talk to him and make sure he understood that kids were changeable, temperamental and moody. Especially after a long, busy day.

She found him sitting on the sofa in the front room with a tumbler of liquor in his hand while staring at a blank TV screen. His back was to her.

"Hunter? Are you okay?"

He took a sip from his glass but didn't look in her direction. "I'm fine. Kids are unpredictable. Don't worry about it."

"Okay. Good. I wanted to make sure you were aware of that and didn't take offense to her asking for me. Because you are the most important person to her."

"I know." His voice was flat, empty of emotion, and then he drained the liquor in one swallow. When she didn't leave, he looked up and said, "Is there something else?"

"Yes." Stiffly, she sat on the end of the sofa, carefully leaving enough room between them for at least two people. "You got very quiet tonight at dinner. Why?"

"I had nothing to add to the conversation."

"Oh, please. You were talking my ear off until your brother announced Avery was expecting. Then you looked as if someone cut the stirrups off your favorite saddle. Why?"

"You're my daughter's nanny. It's not information you need to do your job."

His tone wasn't angry, abrupt or condescending, which, oddly enough, concerned her more. This felt too controlled. "I disagree. Something's bothering you. Wren is going to notice. Maybe instinctively she already did and that's why she asked me to step in for the bedtime story. I need something so I know how to respond when she asks why her daddy got quiet and stopped smiling."

He set his empty glass on the table beside him and seemed as if he was going to walk away without a word. But then he released a long sigh and looked at her. "Her mother died."

"I know. When she was a baby." But Merry was extremely curious about what happened. She wasn't proud of that but she was only human. "But I don't understand—"

"It's my fault."

"What?" She couldn't believe she'd heard right.

Dark intensity glittered in his eyes. "Wren was a couple days old and Lara complained of headaches, blurred vision and upper abdominal pain. I found out later all are classic symptoms of eclampsia. A complication of pregnancy."

She was quiet for a moment, then hesitantly asked, "But what is it?"

"High blood pressure that caused seizures and compromised her kidneys and other organs. Mostly it's diagnosed during prenatal visits and treated. It's rare to show up after birth but we drew the short straw on that." Bitterness squeezed every single word.

"That's so awful I don't even know what to say." Merry didn't want to look at the misery on his face but couldn't seem to look anywhere else. "But I also don't understand why you blame yourself."

He dragged his fingers through his hair. "I fell for her and wanted to marry her when I was a college senior and she was a freshman. But I didn't want to marry too young like my dad, didn't want to make the same mistakes he did."

In the interest of full disclosure she said, "Lily told me that your mother abandoned her children when you were all really young."

"I was about Wren's age. More than once I thought that if I'd been a better kid she wouldn't have left." He shrugged. "So Lara and I waited and got married right out of college. Both of us wanted kids, but she got a job with a Dallas TV station and was working hard, hoping to be promoted to on-air anchor."

"But?" There had to be one.

"After a year I wanted to start the family we'd talked about. She finally gave in because she wanted me to be happy." He looked anything but. "A classic example of be careful what you wish for."

She didn't know what to say and asked, "What's the second reason?"

"Wren was two days old when Lara's symptoms started. I wanted to take her to the emergency room but she insisted it would pass. She refused to leave her baby—" He stopped for a moment and pressed his lips together. "I should have insisted. Should have picked her up bodily and made her go."

"You're not a doctor, Hunter. You couldn't know what would happen."

"No. But if I'd been a better husband she would still be alive."

So, there was still some of that little boy in him, the one who felt if he'd been better his mother wouldn't have left. Merry sighed. "So you were remembering all of this when Avery revealed that she was pregnant."

He nodded, and when he looked at her, the worry was more focused. "Everyone forgets about the bad things that can happen, but I lived it. At dinner all they talked about was the warm, fuzzy part of having babies. Everyone was

over the moon. But I just can't get excited. Something—"
he touched his chest "—something is stopping me."

"Oh, Hunter." She couldn't stand to be so far away
from him and crossed the distance between them until
she could feel the heat from his body. She touched his
arm. "I understand why you feel this way. But you said
the condition is rare. You couldn't know what was going
to happen. Hindsight is twenty-twenty and if you could
do it differently, surely you would."

He nodded but said nothing.

"Someday you're going to have to tell Wren. So she
knows her family medical history."

There was a tortured expression in his eyes when he
met her gaze. "Oh, God—"

She knew exactly where his mind went. That the same
fate awaited Wren one day. "Don't go there. But this is the
reason doctors want medical history." She waited until
the fear on his face receded. "But if you tell her it's your
fault her mother died, that would be a lie. And you don't
strike me as the kind of man who doesn't tell the truth.
To Wren or anyone else."

"I try to stick to the facts."

"And the fact is, Wren's mother made a choice. You
honored her wishes."

He thought about that for a few moments, then nodded
and almost smiled. "How did you get so good at making
someone feel better?"

"I'm no stranger to having a loved one taken away."

"Gosh, Merry, I'm sorry." He put his hand over hers
where she'd left it on his arm. "This is the first holiday
without your dad and I made it all about me."

"It's understandable."

"No. I'm an idiot. Tell me about your dad."

"Are you sure?" she asked.

"Yes."

His spirit seemed lighter after talking about his feelings. Maybe it would work for her. "When Mom died and my brother left home, Dad didn't quite know what to do with me when he was working. There were after-school programs or a neighbor lady sometimes watched me. But when he couldn't find somewhere to leave me, he took me with him on his electrical jobs." She smiled. "People called him Sparky. And I learned a lot about sockets, wires and circuit breakers."

"I'll keep that in mind." Hunter smiled.

Merry was glad she was already sitting down. The grin transformed his face and he was so handsome her knees went weak. She cleared her throat and continued. "Dad was good at what he did and was busy most of the time, but on a rare day when he was home, we hunkered down and hung out together."

"Doing what?"

"Chores. Playing games. But our favorite thing was watching old movies. He always said they don't make 'em like that anymore."

"We can do that now." He half turned to grab the remote control from the table beside him.

Merry's hand slid off his arm. She was both horrified that touching him felt so darn natural and wistful that the contact was over. Then her head cleared and she realized what he was doing.

"That's okay. I don't want to bore you with old movies," she said.

"Hey, who says it will bore me?" He challenged her with a look. "Besides, you cheered me up. I'm returning the favor. Call it a tribute to your dad."

With the remote he turned on the flat screen TV, then pulled up the guide and scrolled through until finding the channel he wanted. Hunter leaned back and relaxed into the sofa. He held up a fist and said, "Here's to Sparky."

Merry bumped his fist with hers and the TV screen blurred as tears gathered in her eyes. She settled in next to Hunter and said, "Dad would have loved this."

She loosened up and the heat from Hunter's body warmed her, made her drowsy after a while. Her eyes drifted closed and she dozed off. She woke with her head on Hunter's shoulder, not sure how long she'd been out. But the movie credits were scrolling by so it had been a while.

Hunter's breathing was soft, even, and she knew the tryptophan had claimed another victim. She was reluctant to move and wake him. Mostly she was reluctant to move and end the closeness of their bodies.

While she hesitated, the decision was taken out of her hands because he was looking at her.

"Hi," he said, smiling drowsily. His gaze was unguarded and open, revealing raw, unconcealed need.

He slowly lowered his head, tilting it the way a man did to kiss a woman. Merry's heart started to hammer and she could hardly breathe. Anticipation and excitement hummed through her as her eyelids drifted closed.

Then she felt him freeze and her eyes popped open. The happy, sleepy smile was gone, replaced by a bitter twist of his lips.

"I'm sorry, Merry."

In her head she was telling him not to be, but the words stayed where they were.

"That was inappropriate," he said. "It's wrong to put you in this position."

Not if she wanted to be there. "Hunter—"

"Good night." He stood and went upstairs.

Merry tried not to be crushed but wasn't very successful. And knowing how he'd lost his wife and why he was so protective of his daughter didn't help much. It made clear only that he was determined to keep her firmly in her nanny role and at a distance. Unfortunately, the "almost" kiss made it clear how much she wanted him. He also made it clear that she was never going to have him.

Chapter Eight

Hunter couldn't believe himself.

He'd come within a whisper of kissing Merry and that was why he was sitting in a booth at Ace in the Hole with a woman Vivienne Dalton had vetted for him. The whole thing came under the heading of "it seemed like a good idea at the time."

So, he'd said something to Max, who put Viv on the case and she'd set up a meet for the Saturday after Thanksgiving. He'd met Everly Swanson, an attractive brown-eyed brunette, at the local low-key establishment. There was a scarred bar on the far wall and booths around the perimeter. A wooden dance floor with scattered tables was in the center. In the window, a large neon sign of an ace of hearts blinked off and on, along with one that advertised beer.

Everly seemed like a perfectly nice woman, but now he had to make conversation.

She beat him to it. "So, tell me about yourself."

"Okay." He thought about where to start. "I went to Texas A&M, where I was a farm and ranching major. I'm originally from Texas and it's my humble opinion that ranching is the best job in the world—" He was relieved when the bar's owner arrived and stood at the end of their booth.

"Hey, Rosey," Everly said.

"Hey there, lady. It's nice to see you." She gave him a

curious look. "Hunter Crawford. Been a while. It's nice to see you. With Everly. Is there romance in the air?"

"I think that's burgers and fries you're smelling," he said.

"Could be."

Rosey Traven was a curvaceous woman in her sixties. Hunter knew she made it her business to find out what was going on in the personal lives of her customers. He'd come into the Ace a couple of times with Wilder, who kept pushing him into being a wingman. Hunter did his best but it never went well.

Kind of how he expected this evening to go.

"What can I get you?" Rosey looked at each of them.

"Are you ready to order?" he asked the woman across from him.

"I am. I'll have the usual, Rosey."

"Burger basket, no cheese and a glass of red wine. Got it." The older woman looked at him. "For you?"

"Burger basket, with cheese. And a beer."

"Coming right up. I'll get those drinks out in a jiffy." She smiled at them then sashayed away.

"She's sure a character," Everly said. "Don't you love those jeans, boots and that belted peasant top?"

"You mean all women of a certain age don't dress like that?"

"Like a pirate queen? No." She laughed. "But don't let the outfit fool you. That woman has a soft heart and a knack for giving love a helping hand if she thinks two people are made for each other."

"Okay." He tried not to squirm on the faux leather bench seat.

"Since you're pretty new to town you probably don't know Rosey's story." When he shook his head, she elaborated. "She and her husband, Sam, own Ace in the Hole.

He's the former navy SEAL who worked to win her heart and become the love of her life. She'd probably never admit it, but she wants everyone to be as happy as she and Sam are."

Well, damn. This "date" was the opposite of romance. The point was to get his father off his back and Merry out of his system, not do the romance dance. Color him a bonehead for not going somewhere less public and prone to gossip. He intended to get through it by walking a fine line—friendly, but not too friendly. He didn't want to give this woman, or anyone else, ideas.

"Tell me about you." He hoped to get her talking about herself, a safer subject than his life.

"I do clerical work in the mayor's office. I actually grew up here in Rust Creek Falls, but lived over in Bozeman when I was married…but I'm not now." Her lips pressed tightly together for a moment, then she relaxed. "Is there anyone special in your life?"

Merry. The thought was suddenly there. She was special because she took great care of his daughter. At least that's what he told himself. Her qualities appealed to him, and not just the ones that had his little girl behaving like an angel. Merry was sexy and made him laugh. It was a dynamite combination. And none of that was what Everly meant. "I have a daughter. Wren. She's six."

"Adorable name." Her smooth forehead puckered a little. "I confess that Viv Dalton told me your wife passed away after your daughter was born. That must have been hard."

"Yes—"

A waitress walked over with a tray. "Here are your drinks, guys. Food is coming up shortly. Let me know if you need refills."

"Thanks," he said, then looked at the woman across

from him and held up his longneck bottle of beer. "To new friends."

"Friends. Right." She lifted her glass and sipped. "So, you've been a single dad? How do you make that work?"

"I've had help from family and friends. My job is on the family ranch, which means that some chores can be scheduled around my daughter's needs. If they can't be, I used to call on one of my brothers or my dad."

"But you don't anymore?"

"No." He drank from his beer then set it on the cocktail napkin in front of him.

"Obviously she's school age, but she still needs supervision in the afternoons and summers. No?"

"Yes." He toyed with the bottle, reluctant to say more.

Everly wasn't letting him off the hook. "Why don't you call on your family for child care anymore?"

"It's not so easy now. Four of my brothers are married."

"So I heard." One of her eyebrows arched.

"Of course you did. This is a small town, not like Dallas."

She laughed. "So I don't have to explain how everyone knows your business."

"No." And that's why he should have taken her somewhere no one knew them. "But their priorities have shifted. Now my dad and brother Wilder are the only ones who could help me out. Little brother's judgment isn't up to my standards where my daughter is concerned. And my father is busy."

"So what are you going to do?"

"Already done. I hired Meredith Matthews to be her nanny."

"I've met Merry. She's beautiful—which I could seriously dislike if she wasn't so darn nice."

The waitress showed up just then with their baskets

and her timing couldn't have been better. They weren't supposed to be talking about him. How did that happen?

"There's ketchup on the table. Can I get you anything else?" the server asked. When they shook their heads, she said, "Enjoy and if you need anything, let me know."

Hunter dug into his burger as if he hadn't eaten in a month. You weren't supposed to talk with your mouth full, right? But way too soon his basket was empty.

Everly had more than half a burger left. She nibbled at her fries a bit, then said, "So, don't take this the wrong way, but this feels like a kind of forced date, rather than one you were dying to go on."

What was it with women? They could effortlessly carry on a conversation while chowing down on a messy hamburger and still look delicate and ladylike.

"I have to admit I'm here to get my father off my back. What gave me away?"

"You keep looking at the door." She didn't seem upset.

"I'm a little out of practice. Okay," he said, grinning slightly, "more than a little. Is that your way of giving me the brush-off?"

She grinned back. "If that was my plan, I'd have a friend call with a fake emergency. Or, better yet, I'd go to the ladies' room, then sneak out without a goodbye."

"But this *is* a brush-off." He wasn't an idiot, after all.

She shrugged. "I prefer to be direct. I think we both know there's no spark here. But it was nice to go out with a decent guy." She smiled—a little wistfully, he thought.

"You're right. And I appreciate your honesty." She *was* a nice woman—funny, smart, pretty. It wasn't her fault that she didn't have striking hazel eyes and thick, curly blond hair. She couldn't help that she wasn't Merry. "I'm sorry."

"Don't apologize. I would rather know the truth. And a dinner is always appreciated. As is meeting new friends."

"I'd like to be friends," he said.

"Me, too." She took the paper napkin off her lap and wadded it up to toss in her half-empty basket. "But would you mind a word of advice?"

"Probably."

"Too bad. You're getting it anyway." She laughed, then turned serious. "You've been hurt in the worst way possible. I can see why you think it's important to control your feelings and protect yourself. But take it from me, that's impossible. Feelings and emotions have a mind of their own. They have a way of sneaking up on you when you least expect it. And that's not a bad thing."

"Sounds like you've had experience. From your divorce, I guess?"

"Yeah. But I won't bore you with the details." She gave him a smile before sliding out of the booth. "Thanks for dinner, Hunter. Really. And remember, feelings can't be controlled."

Hunter watched her walk to the old screen door. There was a loud squeak when she opened it and let herself out.

He knew she was right about not being able to control his feelings, and he didn't like it. If he could, he wouldn't have been counting the minutes until he could politely leave and go home. And this feeling wasn't new. It got stronger every day when he found reasons to put off a chore so he could get back to the cabin and see Merry.

That made it official. He was in hot water. His child care issue was solved but the solution had created an even bigger problem.

"Daddy went out with a lady."

"Yes, he went to meet someone," Merry agreed.

They were sitting at the kitchen table eating grilled cheese sandwiches and chicken noodle soup. It was the little girl's favorite and Merry decided it might be good for the soul. She was wrong. After one bowl her soul was still not happy about Hunter meeting a lady. And although it didn't matter how many times she reminded herself that his social life was none of her business, she couldn't reconcile the fact that he'd nearly kissed her and two days later he was hooking up with some floozy.

Well, that wasn't fair but she didn't think there was enough chicken soup on the planet to change her attitude. Still, she couldn't let Wren know how she felt.

"Sweetie, now that I'm here to take care of you, it's natural that your dad would want to go out with a woman."

"Why does he have to, Merry? He's got me."

This conversation could easily go in an awkward direction if she didn't choose her words carefully. The last thing she wanted was to tell Hunter she'd been forced to explain sex to his six-year-old daughter. She just couldn't say that the man probably went out because he wanted to sleep with her.

Merry had been ready to go there with him on Thanksgiving but he'd put the brakes on that. Since then she'd tried to convince herself he'd been right, but she wasn't quite buying that.

"Believe me, sweetie, there's nothing he loves more than spending time with you. But there are grown-up activities he wants to do." Darn it. That was going to generate follow-up questions. "Like going out to dinner. Or a movie."

"I like movies." Wren's little face was puckered in an adorable pout.

"Sometimes he might like one that's not about princesses or animated animals. There are a lot that he can't take you to see."

"But he doesn't have to take a lady. Uncle Wilder would go."

"Probably." And the handsome devil would hit on every single woman in the theater, dragging Hunter along with him. "Your uncle wants different things than your dad."

"This is all Gramps's fault." The little girl slurped some soup and sucked up a noodle while broth dribbled down her chin.

"Napkin, sweetie." Merry should have ignored that important and revealing information, but just couldn't. "What did your Gramps do?"

"He's paying that lady to get women to go out with my dad. I heard them talking. They didn't know I was there." She bit off the corner of her diagonally cut sandwich. "I like triangles."

"I'm glad. And we need to have a talk about listening to a conversation when the people talking don't know you're there."

Wren finished chewing her sandwich, then said, "But I wanted to hear what they were sayin'. They would've stopped if they knew I was there."

"Still, next time you should let them know you're there." Do as I say, not as I do, Merry thought, remembering the night she'd overheard father and daughter talking.

"Okay."

"So, did Gramps say why he wants your dad to meet women?"

"He said my mommy would want Daddy to be happy. Gramps tells him that all the time."

"Well, Gramps knew your mom," Merry said gently. "So it's probably true."

"But I don't know the lady Daddy is with." There was a stubborn expression on her face and an angry look in her eyes. "And I'm mad at him. Aren't you mad at him?"

Merry could be on board with that, but she had no right to the feelings. Her responsibility was taking care of Wren, not having an opinion on her father's love life. Being conflicted made this a fine line to walk.

Best to sidestep the question entirely. "Well, sweetie, it might be a good idea for you to talk to your dad about this. Because he might go out with her again. If he likes her."

Just saying those words made Merry's chest feel tight and her soul didn't much care for it either.

"I don't like her already." She folded her arms over her thin chest. Talk about closed body language.

Merry was conflicted again, torn between gratitude that Wren approved of her and a duty to point out that she should give people a chance. She decided that conversation could wait until she was less emotionally at odds with herself. Less talk, more action to turn this evening around.

"Are you finished with dinner?" Merry asked.

The little girl put down her mostly eaten triangle and said, "I'm full."

"Okay. Do you want to make cookies?"

Wren's little face lit up and hostility disappeared. "The kind we can decorate?"

"Yes. With icing and sprinkles and red and green sparkles."

"Oh, boy!" She wiped her mouth then slid off her chair. "I'll take my dishes to the sink."

"Good girl. We'll wash these up real quick and make room for baking."

The child insisted on helping so "real quick" took a few minutes longer. Then Merry got out all the ingredients for her mother's sugar cookie recipe. She'd baked them with her mother as a child, and after her mom's passing, when she was old enough, she'd made them for her dad. They'd always shared memories of the woman both of them loved and missed. This year there was no one to remember with her and she was grateful to have Wren, the blessing of a child to take the sting out of this painful transition to her new holiday normal.

Together they measured everything into a big bowl and Merry let the little girl try mixing. Of course, the powdered ingredients floated over the side and her six-year-old attention span didn't last long. So Merry took over just as her mom had always done with her. Before long, the dough was ready to roll out and the oven was preheated with cookie sheets standing by to be filled.

Wren knelt on a kitchen chair in front of the flour-dusted breadboard with a small mound of dough in the center. "Can I roll it out?"

"Yes." Merry watched the child use the rolling pin that had been her mother's and her vision wavered with unshed tears. Then Wren looked up at her and smiled happily, making her smile, too. It made her heart happy that time spent with her own mom could be channeled to bring joy to this motherless little girl.

Rolling went better than mixing, and Merry let her pick the holiday cookie cutters—a tree, star, Santa Claus, snowman, reindeer, wreath. The first pan was ready to go in the oven when the back door opened and Hunter walked in.

"Hi."

Merry blinked at him. "I didn't expect you home so early." Darn, what was it about this man that had her blurting out things she wouldn't ordinarily say?

"Yeah, well..." He didn't quite meet her gaze but gave his daughter a hug. "Hey, you."

"Daddy your face is cold." She giggled when he grabbed her in a bear hug and squealed when he put a cold hand on her neck. "Did you meet the lady?"

"Her name is Everly Swanson. And yes, I met her."

Merry knew the woman. Beautiful, smart, funny, charming. She was pretty much everything a man could want. She truly liked the woman but right this minute she was struggling with that.

Was she nice?" Wren demanded.

"She was." Hunter touched her cheek with his finger. "You've got flour all over your face."

"I know. Me and Merry are bakin'." She lasered him with a look. "Is she pretty?"

"Yes."

A man would have to be crazy not to be attracted to the woman. Merry desperately wanted to take over the interrogation and find out, but that would be inappropriate. She pressed her lips together before more words escaped that would embarrass her.

"Did you go to the movies?" Wren asked him.

"No," he answered. "Why?"

"Merry said you wanted to meet ladies so you could take them to movies I can't see."

"We just had dinner at Ace in the Hole."

Not especially romantic, Merry thought. Although there were booths in dark corners. If sparks flew, you didn't need amped-up atmosphere. You could be sitting on the sofa in front of the TV and fall asleep with your head on his shoulder and—

"Are you gonna take her to the movies?" The hostility returned to that small face with a vengeance. "A movie that's not a cartoon?"

"I don't think so." He took off his sheepskin-lined jacket and hung it on a hook by the door.

Before he turned away, Merry thought he glanced at her and wondered what the funny look on his face was all about.

"Why don't you think you're gonna take her to the movies?" Apparently, Wren wouldn't be put off.

He walked back to the table where the little girl was still kneeling on the chair. Instead of answering, he studied the baking paraphernalia. "I'm pretty sure I don't have a rolling pin."

"That's mine. Or rather my mom's." Merry thought he didn't look much like a man who'd had a sparks-flying kind of dinner with a woman. He looked more like a man who would bring up ownership of a rolling pin to get out of talking about his evening. "I figured Wren and I would do some baking so I packed up some things and brought them over. Is that a problem?"

"No. I just wondered where it came from." He looked at her then. "Any action on the house?"

"I got an offer about a week ago and accepted it. Guess I forgot to tell you. And the couple want a short escrow so they can be in by Christmas."

"Is it a good offer?"

"Full price. My agent says the terms are good and fair." The loan would be paid off with not much left over after escrow costs. But as long as she was working for Hunter, she would have a roof over her head. Now she needed this job more than ever.

"Daddy?"

"Yeah, kiddo?"

"Did you kiss the lady?"

His brief reprieve was over and he looked acutely uncomfortable again. "I'm not sure that's something you need to know about."

"I think it is." Wren stood up on the chair but he was still taller. "Cuz if you did kiss her, we need to talk. And I need to meet her."

"Oh?" He glanced at Merry then back to his daughter. "And why is that?"

"Because Merry said if you like her I have to talk about my feelings. And if you go out with her again, I should give her a chance before I decide I don't like her."

Hunter looked as if he wanted to both laugh and run for the hills. The courageous man stood his ground. "Okay, then. We don't have to talk because I didn't kiss her."

Wren's gaze narrowed and she put her hands on her hips. "Did she kiss you? Girls do that sometimes, kiss boys first."

"I don't want to know how you know that. And no. There was zero kissing. We had burgers and she left."

Merry hoped the huge grin she was rocking on the inside didn't show on the outside. She was unreasonably pleased that there was no chemistry with the woman. At least that was her guess. If there had been he wouldn't be home so early. And thanks to Wren, she knew no one had been kissed. She wanted to do a triumphant arm pump, then it occurred to her how self-centered she was being.

During the season of hope and giving, she was celebrating that her boss hadn't connected with someone. She couldn't have him but didn't want anyone else to have him either. What a horrible person she was.

A horrible person with a crush on her boss that didn't show any signs of going away. Her house was sold and she needed a place to live and extra income. This job was perfect and she couldn't do anything to mess it up.

Hello, rock and a hard place, she thought. Might as well introduce herself because she was stuck firmly between them.

Chapter Nine

Following church services the next day Hunter drove back to the ranch with Wren and Merry. This felt a lot like a family and when he'd walked in the door last night after being at Ace in the Hole with a woman, he'd felt a lot like a cheater. His daughter's questions didn't pull any punches either. *Did you kiss her?*

Heck, he'd never once even wanted to kiss her. But he had to give the woman credit. She was the one who'd told him it wouldn't work. And she didn't know the half of it.

He turned onto the road leading to the Ambling A, then glanced into the rearview mirror at his little girl secured in her car seat. "I have some work to do in the barn, kiddo. What do you and Merry have planned for this afternoon?"

"I want to go to the barn with you."

Words that he heard way too often and made his blood run cold. "Honey, we've talked about this—"

"But, Daddy, I want to see the barn cats and the goats and the horses," she pleaded. "Merry, tell him it's okay."

"Is there a problem?" the nanny asked.

He glanced at her in the passenger seat beside him, so pretty in a royal blue knit dress and knee-high black boots. Wren was looking to get the nanny on her side. But he'd bet she wouldn't bite the hand that signed her paycheck, or something like that.

"The barn can be a dangerous place for a curious little girl," he said.

"I'm not curious," Wren piped up.

Merry smothered a laugh. "*Curious* is her middle name."

"Tell me about it."

"But how is the barn unsafe?" she asked.

"Ranch tools. Pitchfork comes to mind. Also leather tools for tack and saddles' care and repair—knives, cutters, scissors and splitters."

"I won't touch anything," Wren promised. "Except the cats and goats."

"What about the horses?" he asked. To Merry he said in a voice meant for her ears only, "She's so little. The animals are big enough to crush her like a grape."

"I'm not that little." Wren had really good hearing. "And Merry is here. She can watch me if I get curious."

"She has a point." Merry shrugged. "Not taking sides here, but I could channel her natural curiosity in a safe way."

"Please, Daddy."

"It is what you're paying me for," Merry reminded him.

True enough. But he'd forgotten all about the boss/employee dynamic that night they'd fallen asleep watching a movie. He'd wanted so much to kiss her then and now still felt the ache of not doing it.

He glanced in the mirror again and the drama princess had her hands together in a prayerful, pleading way. Spineless, that's what he was where this child was concerned. "I guess that would be all right."

"Thank you, Daddy."

When they got to the cabin, everyone changed out of their church clothes. After a quick lunch, of which Wren ate very little in her excitement, the three of them walked to the barn. His brother Knox was there helping his wife, Genevieve, trim a horse's hooves and shoe them.

"Aunt Gen—" Wren started to run over to the woman but Merry put a hand on her shoulder.

"Careful, sweetie, you don't want to startle the horse."

"Hi, pumpkin. Merry's right. Give me a second."

Genevieve Crawford wasn't much over five feet tall and her wavy blond hair fell to the middle of her back. But she confidently hammered nails into the U-shaped metal shoe on the horse's hoof, then let the leg down into the hay. The woman straightened, then removed her gloves and tucked them into the back pocket of her worn jeans. She moved away from the animal to stand by the stall's open gate.

"Can I hug her now?" Wren asked the nanny.

"Yes." Merry removed her hand.

"Hi, Aunt Genevieve." The little girl threw herself into the other woman's arms. "When I grow up I want to give horses new shoes like you do."

Knox stood beside his wife and tugged playfully on the child's pigtail. "How does your dad feel about that?"

"He doesn't like me to come to the barn at all cuz there's sharp stuff. And he's afraid a horse will step on me."

"You saw the way she was rushing in just now," Hunter said in his defense. "If Merry hadn't stopped her—"

"She's six and that was normal," the nanny assured him. "But if she was here more often and learned appropriate behavior around the animals, that would minimize any risk."

Genevieve looked at her husband and they both nodded. "Merry's right."

Merry's expression was earnest. "She's a ranch kid. She lives here and there are animals. Teach her about them. Has she ever been on a horse?"

"No." Wren shot her dad a hostile look. "He won't let me. I keep asking and he keeps saying no."

The three adults stared at him as if he'd just lit his hair on fire. "It's my job to keep her safe. If anything happened to her—"

Merry put her hand on his arm. "You know better than anyone that life doesn't come with a guarantee. But it also needs to be lived. If you keep Wren from participating, she might be safe, but how happy will she be? What if Max had kept you and your brothers out of the barn and away from the horses?"

"Ouch." Knox made a nervous face. "That's a scary thought."

It was, Hunter admitted, if only to himself. "What if she gets hurt?"

"Teach her," Merry said again. "Make her barn safe and animal smart. Show her the right way to do things. Put her on a horse."

"Please, Daddy?" Wren clasped her hands together and gave him puppy dog eyes.

He hated puppy dog eyes because it worked every time. Along with Merry's common sense advice. Not to mention Knox and Genevieve giving him pitying looks. He was badly outnumbered. "Okay. But, Wren, you have to listen and do as I say."

"I promise, Daddy. Can you show me now?"

He wanted to say no but didn't think he could hold out against the peer pressure. Or maybe it was the reassuring touch of Merry's hand that made the decision feel right. And the encouragement and approval in her pretty hazel eyes. "I guess repairing the tack can wait."

"Yay!" Wren wrapped her arms around his waist in a spontaneous hug. "Thank you, Daddy."

"I know just the horse for her," Gen said to Knox.

He nodded. "That little pony. Charlotte."

Hunter knew which one his brother meant. A sweet, gentle, even-tempered animal. "I agree. Let's get her saddled. I'll show you how, kiddo."

"I'll help," Merry said.

Hunter led them to Charlotte's stall, then showed Wren the pad that went under the saddle.

"Pull it forward over her withers," Merry instructed, "then back where you'll be sitting. That will make sure the horse's hair is flat underneath the pad."

"Then lift the saddle onto the horse." Hunter did that.

"Place it gently like your dad did," Merry said. "You're not big enough yet to do this but when you are, don't slam it down. That could surprise Charlotte and spook her."

"Okay." Wren's eyes were big as saucers in her little face.

Hunter showed her how to take the cinch at one end and pull it through the buckle.

"Do it in stages," Merry added. "Loosely at first, to see what's right for Charlotte. You want the saddle secure but any tighter than that is an unnecessary discomfort for the horse."

Hunter showed her how to hold her hand out, palm up, so the horse could get her scent and become acquainted but not leave her fingers vulnerable. Then he demonstrated how to take the reins and walk slowly outside into the corral. Lifting the little girl, he coached her to put one pink-sneakered foot into the stirrup and swing her other leg over. And not to sit down too hard and startle the animal.

"Look at you on a horse." Merry smiled up at the little girl. "Way to go."

A huge grin lit up her face. "I want to ride now, Daddy."

"Let your dad show you how to hold the reins first."

sweetie. And how to use them to make her stop, go and turn from side to side."

Hunter was impressed. There was more to Merry Matthews than just working in the classroom. She had some experience with horses and riding. Her knowledge showed again when she diplomatically reminded him not to overwhelm Wren with advanced techniques or too much information. He agreed and let her slowly walk the horse around the corral with him on one side and Merry on the other.

"You're doing great," he told her.

The little girl leaned forward and gently patted the horse's neck. "Good job, Charlotte."

After a few minutes he began to relax. He looked across the horse's rump and met Merry's gaze. "Is it just me, or is she a natural?"

"Not just you."

"I appreciate your help. It's hard not to keep giving her pointers."

"There's a readiness component to learning," she said. "You have to be comfortable with basics before moving to the next level."

He nodded. That made sense. And it occurred to him that his daughter might have gotten her curiosity gene from him. He couldn't resist saying, "And you've been holding out."

She looked surprised. "Oh?"

"I know you're good with kids and your dad was an electrician. But you know a lot about horses. How did you learn?"

"Oh. That." Suddenly Merry didn't look so merry.

"What?"

"My boyfriend works at one of the local ranches. He showed me some stuff."

Hunter didn't like the idea of her with another man, but that was none of his business. The only thing that should concern him was keeping her a happy employee who would stay on as the nanny and take good care of his daughter.

"You never mentioned a boyfriend. I'd have made sure you had time off to see him. Just let me know if you have plans." The words nearly choked him and the idea of her with a guy showing her "stuff" about horses or anything else made him want to put his fist through a wall. It was hard to file this intense emotional response under employer responsibility.

"I don't need time." Her mouth twisted with disapproval. "I should have said *ex*-boyfriend. I broke up with him. When caring for my dad took up more and more of my time, the jerk flat out said if he didn't come first he was gone."

"So you beat him to it." He nodded. "Sounds like a good move."

"Yeah. My dad never liked him." She smiled a little sadly. "He had an opinion on every boy I've liked since I started liking boys in the fifth grade. And he was always right."

"I don't want to even think about Wren liking boys. Ever."

"Ew," came the little girl's voice from above them. "Boys are weird. And gross."

"They won't always be, sweetie." Merry grinned at him, then studied the child, who was starting to squirm in the saddle. "Is your tush getting tired yet, Wren?"

"A little."

Hunter took the hint. "You need to go easy the first time on horseback. Should we stop for today?"

"Good idea, Dad. Charlotte might be getting hungry."

"She might not have eaten very much lunch," Merry interjected.

"Yeah. We'll go in now. This probably isn't a good time to show you how to take care of Charlotte after you ride her."

"Can you show me next time?" Wren asked eagerly.

"Sure." He walked them back into the barn and tied the reins inside Charlotte's stall. He lifted Wren down and she hugged him tight.

"Thank you, Daddy. I can't wait to ride again."

"Okay."

That made him feel pretty great, but Merry looked at him as if he'd hung the moon. And he wanted her to look at him like that again. He watched the little girl put her hand into the nanny's and chatter happily as they left the barn.

"Well, well, well…" Knox rested his arms on top of the stall fence. Genevieve was beside him looking like a cat who just caught a bird and dropped it at his feet.

"What?" he demanded.

"There's a spark between you and the nanny." His brother was grinning.

"Genevieve," he said, looking at his sister-in-law and doing his best to work up a teasing tone, "did you let your husband get kicked in the head by a horse?"

"No," she answered. "But even if he did have a head injury, he's not wrong. I saw it, too."

"Then both of you need your eyes examined. And maybe your heads, too. There's nothing between Merry and me except what's best for Wren."

"You do realize that when you bury your head in the sand, you leave your ass exposed, right?" Knox pulled his wife close and kissed her lightly on the lips. "Trust me, I know all about these things."

Knox and Genevieve were seeing romantic sparks where none existed. They were dead wrong.

"But, Daddy, Merry said the whole town goes to see the Christmas tree light up. What if I'm the only kid in my class who isn't there?" Wren gave her father a pathetic look.

They were eating dinner and Merry had casually mentioned the tree lighting tonight. The little girl latched on to the idea like a dog with a bone. Merry watched him squirm and felt a little sorry for him. The poor man had been up in the middle of the night with a pregnant cow, helping her through a difficult birth. He'd said both mother and baby were fine, but he looked like the wrath of God.

"Hunter, I can take her. I'll just finish up these dinner dishes and the two of us can head out. You get some rest."

"Does the whole town really go?" he asked.

"I've never taken a head count so I'm sure there are some people who don't attend. But it's always crowded."

Wren shook her head. "It won't be the same with just Merry and me. You have to come, Daddy."

Merry recognized indecision on his face along with the fatigue. When they were exhausted, most people resembled roadkill. Not Hunter Crawford. He made the wrath of God look good. He hadn't shaved and the dark scruff, along with the weariness, somehow made him look brooding and sexier than ever.

Then it occurred to her that his hesitation might be about her. Maybe he wanted alone time with his daughter and was trying to figure out how to say so and not hurt her feelings.

"Wren, maybe your dad wants to take you by himself. Just the two of you. A father/daughter outing."

"No." The little girl put on her stubborn face like a superhero costume. "Then you would be all alone. And sad."

"Well," he said, "then I guess the three of us are going. It's the most wonderful time of the year. No one is allowed to be sad. Especially my little princess."

"Thank you, Daddy." She hugged him and he kissed the top of her head.

Merry met his gaze. "I'll make you a cup of coffee."

"Thanks." There was a flicker of something in his eyes, probably regret that he wouldn't get some sleep for another couple of hours.

A little while later the three of them pulled into the town hall parking lot. The large pine tree had been set up on the corner of Cedar Street and North Main. They exited the truck and Merry automatically took Wren's hand because there were cars, moving slowly, but she wasn't taking any chances.

On the sidewalk, Wren said, "Daddy, hold my other hand."

"Okay, kiddo."

The little girl turned a happy smile on both of them. "We're all holding hands."

Merry had no idea why but she blushed and her cheeks grew warm. Since it was dark and Hunter couldn't see it, that wasn't necessarily a bad thing, besides a cold wind was blowing. There hadn't been any snow yet, but they still needed to bundle up. She assessed Wren's pink jacket, matching knit hat and fur-lined boots.

"Are you warm enough, sweetie?"

"Yes."

"Are you?" Hunter was looking at Merry.

Could he see the flush on her face? Did he resent her for intruding on this outing? After giving him an out, she wasn't going to dwell on the fact that he hadn't told his daughter no. She had on a cream-colored hat with a pom-pom, matching mittens and a quilted jacket.

"I'm a little chilly but we'll all huddle around the tree for the lighting and the crush of bodies will block the wind."

It would be lovely if the two of them snuggled up and shared body heat. But that would be a Christmas miracle since there was about as much chance of that happening as Santa actually coming down the chimney.

"I see the tree," Wren shouted. She tugged them along and they moved with a lot of other people all heading in the same direction.

The community tree was situated in a grassy area beside the town hall. They found a spot and eased into it next to an older couple.

"Daddy, I can't see very well."

Merry bent down to the little girl's level and pointed to a break in the bodies. "Look right through there, sweetie."

"I'm tryin', but they keep movin' back and forth. I'm gonna miss the lights."

"I promise you won't," Merry assured her. Knowing Rust Creek Falls, she was sure astronauts on the international space station could probably see this tree when it was lit.

"I'll put you on my shoulders," Hunter said.

"Can you?" Merry tried to gauge his fatigue level. "Are you too tired?"

"Coffee and the cold woke me up." He grinned at her then effortlessly lifted his six-year-old onto his broad shoulders. "How's that, kiddo?"

"Awesome! I can see everything from up here."

Problem solved, except for the part where Merry wanted to sigh at the adorable sight of this swoon-worthy man making sure his daughter had a fulfilling experience. After he'd been up half the night.

They weren't far from a raised platform with a microphone for the town officials—mayor, deputy mayor, sheriff. All of them were assembling now so it shouldn't be too long.

The tall silver-haired woman beside her smiled and leaned close. "What a beautiful family you have."

"Oh, they're—"

"I remember when my daughter was that age and still believed in Santa Claus." She whispered that part so Wren couldn't hear. "Then some little twerp at school told her there was no such thing, before she or her father and I were ready to let that go."

"That's too bad. Kids don't have a filter. And when they learn something that rocks their world, they don't keep it to themselves."

"Isn't that the truth." The woman smiled ruefully. "Not unlike the majority of adults in this town who spread gossip like jam on toast."

"There are plusses and minuses to small-town living," Merry agreed. "That's one of the negatives."

"It's not a deal breaker, though. This is a good place to raise children. Take it from me. My daughter moved away when she got married." She looked at Wren on her father's shoulders. "Don't let your little girl do that."

Before Merry could explain that she was Wren's nanny, there was microphone static. Then Mayor Collin Traub did a sound check. A few years ago the man had won the mayoral election over Nate Crawford, who was a distant relation of the Crawfords at the Ambling A. The man was now the owner of Maverick Manor, the town's upscale hotel. The current mayor had skillfully guided the town through recovery after the devastating flood and did such a good job, he'd been reelected by a wide margin.

"Can everyone hear me?" His deep voice traveled well and the crowd murmured that they could. "I'll keep this short because it's cold out here. But you all know that. Let me start off with a public service announcement. Tonight the stores will be open late for you to start, or continue, your holiday shopping.

"Welcome to the Rust Creek Falls annual tree lighting. From now through Christmas there will be lots of holiday events sponsored by the city council. Check the dates and times in the *Rust Creek Falls Gazette* and on the RCF website.

"I want to wish everyone a very merry Christmas and a happy New Year. Now let's get the season going and light up this tree. On the count of five."

The crowd counted along and when they got to one, green, red, gold and blue lights flashed on giving off a brilliant glow. Ornaments covered the branches and gold-trimmed ribbon wound around the tree. There was a dazzling star on top.

Almost as one voice the crowd said, "Ooh! Wow."

"It looks so pretty. A princess tree. Best one ever!" Wren clapped her mitten-covered hands together. "Don't you think so, Daddy? Aren't you glad you came?"

"I am," he said.

Merry grinned. "So you're not mad at me for mentioning it?"

"Only a little." But his grin said otherwise.

"When are we gonna get our tree?" His daughter looked down at him from her perch on his shoulders. "We hafta get one soon."

"We will. Next week we'll cut one down."

"I can't wait."

The crowd was slowly dispersing and Merry looked for the older woman beside her. She planned to set the record straight about Hunter and Wren not being her family, but the lady had moved away. Part of Merry was glad she didn't have to correct the woman's assumption. Belonging to this family was such a lovely idea. But she wasn't a child who could visit Santa and ask for the gift that meant the most to her.

Hunter set his daughter on the ground. "Thanks for making me do this, princess."

"You're welcome." She smiled at him and the look said she had another request. "Would you thank me for making you get me hot chocolate at Daisy's Donuts?"

He laughed and shook his head. "I don't know. It's a school night. What do you think, Merry?"

She quivered and was pathetically happy just being here with them. If the night went on forever it would be okay with her. "Well, I think that you'll be a little tired at school tomorrow, along with all the other kids who are here. But this only happens once a year."

"Is that a yes?" Wren asked.

"Affirmative," her father teased.

"Does that mean yes?" the little girl demanded.

"It does." Merry held out her hand. "I know you're big, but I need you to hold my hand crossing the street."

"Daddy, too?"

Merry figured he could handle it on his own. He was a grown man. She looked at him and was a little surprised at the intensity on his face. It disappeared when he noticed her watching.

"If he wants," she answered.

"He does," Wren said for him. "Let's all hold hands."

Merry defied anyone to tell this child no. And the three of them crossed North Main Street along with a few other spectators who were walking to Daisy's. A lot of people apparently had the same idea and there were only two tables next to each other that were free. The woman in front of them told her husband and son what to order for her and said she was going to grab one of the tables.

"Good idea." Hunter looked at her. "Why don't you stake out the last one. Wren and I will get hot chocolate."

"Sounds good."

She sat at a circular table and put her purse and jacket on two other chairs. The woman at the table beside her did the same.

Merry smiled at her. "Good idea to grab these."

"Yeah." She looked thoughtful. "Aren't you an aide at the school?" She didn't wait for an answer. "My son is in sixth grade and I'm sure I've seen you there."

The woman looked vaguely familiar. "Yeah. I work in the primary grades. There are going to be a lot of tired and crabby little ones tomorrow."

"Your little girl doesn't look like she ever gets cranky. And your husband is wrapped around her little finger, I bet." She smiled. "You have a beautiful family."

The words were like a solid whack to the chest, the second one tonight. It was such a wonderful idea, but that's all it was. Just an idea, a notion without a chance of being real.

She smiled and could feel the sadness around the edges. "He's not my husband and that's not my daughter. I'm just her nanny."

"Oh—" The other woman looked distressed. "I'm sorry. I shouldn't have assumed."

Merry didn't hear the rest. A traditional family was everything she'd ever wanted but the dream was not looking good. Since Thanksgiving night Hunter had been different, distant. Oh, he teased and bantered but when their eyes met, she could almost see his barriers securely in place. There hadn't been a glimmer of the raw need she'd seen when he'd almost kissed her. But she must have been mistaken about that.

There was no way he had feelings for her. Not the way she did for him.

Christmas carols played softly in the background. But for her, the most wonderful time of the year wasn't so wonderful.

Chapter Ten

After school the next day Merry met Wren just outside of her classroom for the walk to the truck. Last night's excitement at the town Christmas tree lighting and a fairly substantial sugar high at Daisy's Donuts immediately after made it way past bedtime when the little girl was finally asleep. Merry had expected to collect a tired, cranky and out-of-sorts child that afternoon, but that's not what happened.

"Merry!" Wren ran over and was practically jumping up and down. Clearly she was excited about something. "You'll never guess what happened."

She made an exaggeration of studying the happy little face. "Well, I'm guessing it's something pretty fantastic judging by that deliriously happy smile."

"It is. I got a big part in the Christmas play." She clapped her hands together. "It's going to be at the community center and my teacher said almost everyone in town comes to watch."

"Oh, sweetie, that's wonderful." She bent down to hug her. "What part did you get?"

"I'm going to play Rudolph's best friend, Dancer."

"Awesome."

"It's the second-biggest part and there are a lot of lines to learn." The smile dimmed just a little.

"I can help you with that, sweetie. And you have a really good memory. That's probably why your teacher picked you. Learning your lines will be a piece of cake. You'll see."

"We better go home so I can start."

"Okay." When the little girl trustingly slipped her hand into Merry's, there was a definite tug on Merry's heart. She hoped she was creating a positive difference in this young life. That would go a long way toward making this hopeless crush on Hunter Crawford mean something.

Hand in hand, they weaved through the crowd of children who'd just been dismissed from class and walked to the lot where Merry's old truck was parked. She took the pink backpack and set it on the back seat, then lifted Wren up. Without a running board it was next to impossible for six-year-old little legs to breach the distance.

"Hop on into your car seat, sweetie."

"You always say that."

"Because I always want you to be safe."

"You always say that, too." Wren spontaneously hugged her.

That gave Merry's heart another delicious tug and she squeezed the small body close for a moment. "I'm very glad to know you listen to what I say."

"I do."

"Good." She pulled away and winked. "Now, make sure you—"

"Buckle yourself in," Wren finished.

They were both laughing as Merry closed the truck door. She walked around and opened the driver's side and climbed behind the wheel. "Okay, let's get you home. Are you hungry?"

"Yes. Can I have peanut butter on crackers and some apple slices? I like the way you cut them up into skinny pieces."

"Of course. That sounds like a very nutritious snack.

And we have everything. I don't have to stop at the store before we leave town."

She put her key in the ignition and started the engine, then backed out of her space and headed slowly for the exit onto South Main Street. She made a right turn to go north out of Rust Creek Falls toward the ranch.

It was awfully quiet in the passenger area. "Everything okay back there?"

"Yes. I can't wait to tell Daddy about the play."

"He's going to be pretty excited and very proud of you." She glanced in the rearview mirror and noted an uneasy look on that sweet face. "Something wrong?"

"My teacher said for the play the whole class gets to help make fake snow out of construction paper because when Santa and the reindeer land the sleigh, it slides on snow."

"Good. Then the whole class will feel like they're part of the play. Everyone makes an important contribution. No one gets left out. That's the meaning of Rudolph the Red-Nosed Reindeer's story."

"That's what my teacher said."

Merry noted that she still sounded a little concerned. "What's really bothering you, honey?"

"In Texas there wasn't any snow where we lived but Daddy said Santa is magic and would come anyway because there isn't snow everywhere he goes."

"Your dad is right."

"But before we moved here to Montana he told me there would be snow by December and there isn't any."

"That's true. It has been unseasonably warm this year," Merry admitted. "But look at that sky. If those aren't snow clouds I don't know what are."

"I hope so. I'm so tired of waitin'." There was a whole lot of emotion in those words.

"If it's not a problem for Santa, why is it so important?"

"Mistlesnow."

"What now?" Merry asked.

"When it starts to snow, you make a wish and it will come true."

"That's sweet. I never heard that before. What a lovely idea."

"It didn't snow for Uncle Finn and Aunt Avery's wedding. And it got cold here, too, but there's nothing. I've been waitin' and waitin'. I never saw it snow before. And I can't hardly wait to make a wish."

"Well, I've lived in Montana for a while now and it's snowed every winter. And I'm pretty sure it's in the weather forecast for today. So, just keep an eye on that sky."

"Okay."

Merry glanced in the rearview mirror again and saw the little girl staring eagerly out the truck window. She smiled and was charmed yet again by this special child. Obviously she had her mother's DNA but she'd been raised solely by her father. That made him a pretty special man. Clearly he had so much to give. It was a darn shame that Hunter was so closed off and that made her sad.

A few minutes later she made the turn onto the road that led to the Ambling A Ranch. She drove about a mile in and the cluster of buildings came into view. Moments later she parked in front of the log cabin. Hunter was standing on the covered porch, which wasn't a surprise, but Merry's heart skipped a beat at the sight of him. That wasn't a surprise either. The same thing happened nearly every day because he was almost always waiting to make sure his daughter got safely home so he could hear about her day. After that he went back to whatever job he'd been doing.

He stepped off the porch and lifted a hand in greeting. She sighed a little at the intensely masculine sight of him with his black Stetson pulled low on his forehead and his sheepskin jacket accentuating broad shoulders. He moved to the truck's rear passenger door to lift out his little girl.

"How was your day, kiddo?"

"Daddy, it was the best day ever." She told him all about the play and her part. "Merry is gonna help me remember my lines."

He met her gaze. "Thank you."

"No need to thank me. I'd be happy to do it even if it wasn't part of my responsibilities."

"Still, I appreciate it." There was gratitude in his expression along with something hot and intense.

The look lasted only a moment before the spark flickered and was firmly extinguished. What a shame. But she understood. Life had kicked him in the teeth. Who could blame him for protecting himself and his daughter?

"You're welcome. Because, it has to be said, your child can be so difficult." Since she was the exact opposite of that, the teasing words made him smile. "Seriously, I should pay you. She is a joy to be around."

"Yeah, she's a pretty great kid. I think I'll keep her—"

"Look!" Wren pointed at a few fluffy white flakes drifting down from the sky, then held her palm up to catch one. "Is it snow?"

"Yes," Merry said.

"You were right. Merry said it would snow today." The little girl hugged her. "Mistlesnow. Quick. Make a wish."

Wren closed her eyes and there was a look of fierce concentration on her face. Merry wished for the first thing that popped into her head. Hunter just looked confused.

"Mistlesnow," Merry said. "It's a new thing for me,

too. When it first starts to snow, you make a wish. I'm told it will come true."

"Then I wish for the snow to stop," he said. "I've got work to do."

"Daddy, you can't say your wish out loud," his daughter scolded. "It won't come true."

"My bad." He shrugged those impossibly broad shoulders. "I'll make another one."

"Too late," Wren told him. "You only get one wish."

Merry's eyebrows lifted. "Apparently she's the mistlesnow police."

Hunter laughed and for the third time that day she felt a tug on her heart. He didn't smile nearly often enough, so the bonus of that cheerful sound was particularly satisfying. On the down side, the brooding man was gone, replaced by this smiling one who could so easily make her weak in the knees. A memory of the kiss that never was went through her mind and she sighed with disappointment. She just knew it would have been the best kiss she'd ever had.

Even a mistlesnow wish wouldn't be powerful enough to confirm her suspicions. It was no match for his defenses. She was grateful for Wren's rules of keeping a wish to yourself. Hers had been about Hunter, an involuntary yearning to be with him that had popped into her mind. Saying it out loud would have been humiliating.

But that was nothing compared to the pain of wanting something she could never have.

"There are a couple more things I need to run by you, Dad." Hunter had been pacing in his father's office up at the big ranch house. Wilder was here for this meeting, too. "I want to increase the herd."

Max leaned back in his cushy leather chair and steepled his fingers. "Are you sure about that, son?"

"Yes, sir, I am. I know we started this operation small because of the move. The plan was to increase slowly. Grazing management is more cost effective with a bigger herd. By that, I mean it's quicker and more efficient to check on, say, five hundred cows in one herd than a hundred cows in five herds."

His father looked at Wilder, who was sprawled in one of the chairs in front of the big desk. "Do you agree with your brother?"

"Yes, sir. He's the one with that fancy college degree in ranching from Texas A&M. But it's just common sense. Increase profits without a big investment in overhead."

Max nodded. "Okay then. Go for it."

"Okay. I'll start the process." Hunter grinned.

It always felt good to have his father's approval. Max Crawford didn't become successful by making stupid decisions. His personal life was less praiseworthy and the six brothers had paid a price for that. But Hunter wasn't going there. He still had to finish this meeting.

"Also," he said, "I'm going to look for a used baler. More cows means more hay to feed them in the winter."

"What about buying new?" Wilder asked.

"A used one is cheaper. That keeps down the cost of expanding the herd."

"What if it needs repairs?" his brother wanted to know.

"You and I have learned to make repairs. But if something happens that we can't handle, there's a local guy. Brendan Tanner. He's an ex-marine who's supposed to be really good at fixing machinery."

"How do you know this?" Wilder gave him a look that said "you've been holding out." "No offense, bro, but you're not very friendly. You make hermits look social."

"I'm social. I just talk to different people than you." And by that he meant women. His brother went out of his way to talk to them. Hunter didn't. He preferred chatting with local ranchers about cattle prices and machinery. "But I do get around."

Like Thanksgiving night when he'd almost kissed Merry. The regret of not doing that got bigger every time he saw her. And the temptation to follow through with what he'd started was becoming nearly impossible to resist. Then he saw his brother studying him with questions in his eyes and forced himself back into the moment.

"I ran into Paddy O'Reilly in town. He's a local rancher and Brendan is his daughter's husband."

"I think all your plans look good." Max nodded. "And I've carefully considered the spreadsheets you gave me and the bottom line is impressive. I think you should allocate some funds to start fixing up your house."

"Do this place first," he said, looking around the office. The house was livable but needed updating, especially the kitchen, according to his sister-in-law, Lily. "My house is fine."

"I know. But Wren is growing up. She'll be wanting to have her friends over before you know it," Max pointed out.

Hunter didn't want to think about her getting older. That meant more freedom, independence, social situations where he couldn't always be there to make sure she was safe. But, if she felt comfortable inviting her friends to the house, Merry would be there to supervise. Or not. She was a beautiful woman and wouldn't necessarily stay on forever.

From experience he knew that men plan and God laughs. He couldn't count on anything being the way he wanted it to be.

Still, he would rather have his daughter socializing here on the ranch. "You have a point, Dad."

"I do?" Max's eyebrows rose.

"Don't look so surprised," Wilder needled.

"Hard not to. I get more pushback than agreement from you boys."

"We have our reasons." Hunter rested a hip on the corner of the desk.

"I know." Max's voice was deep, serious. "There's been some hard knocks in this family. But lately you've got more of a spring in your step."

"Me?" Hunter asked.

"Yeah, I'm looking at you." The twinkle was back in his father's eyes.

"I've noticed that, too," Wilder said. "You've been much easier to work with lately."

"You're both full of it." Hunter glared at his brother. "And I've always been a sweetheart of a guy to work with."

His younger brother laughed, a mocking sound. "Are you serious? You're like a ticked-off grizzly bear, and that's on a good day. But recently you've mellowed."

Max nodded his agreement. "I think this move to Montana has been good for you. A change of scene, not just for you, but Wren, too. It's been just the thing to get you out of the rut you've been in."

"I wasn't in a rut," Hunter protested. "Working and raising a daughter are what I do."

"That's called a rut," his brother said.

"What do you know? Your life is work and women. That's what you call a rut," Hunter countered.

Wilder shifted in the chair and met his father's gaze. "Now that you mention it, Dad, his attitude adjusted pretty recently. Right around the time Finn and Avery got married."

"Ah." Max nodded knowingly. "That's when you hired Merry Matthews full time. By the way, how are things working out with her?"

"Wren loves her. And knowing she's there taking care of my daughter gives me peace of mind." Knowing she was under his roof at night gave him no peace at all. It drove him crazy. She slept just down the hall and he was tied up in knots from the longing to go to her, hold her. And more.

"But is it just about Wren?" Max asked.

Since when could his father read minds? Or figure out what someone else was feeling? Hunter was starting to feel like that ticked-off grizzly his brother had called him. "What do you mean?"

"Merry is obviously wonderful with my granddaughter. But she's also quite a lovely young woman. Smart, sweet and pretty. I can't help wondering if she isn't— well—making you merry."

Hunter narrowed his gaze on his father. "This has to be said. It makes me skittish when I have your approval. Especially about a woman."

"He has a point, Dad." Wilder glanced at him then back to their father. "You have to admit you're not the best judge of character where women are concerned."

Hunter recalled Max admitting that he'd done some things to manipulate their mother, controlling moves to get her to stay. Misguided love could best describe what they'd had. But the woman had given up on her kids.

"My brother is saying you chose a woman who walked out and left six boys motherless. And he has a point."

"You'll never know how much I regret what happened with me and your mother." Max really did look sorry. "I made mistakes. But I can't change the past. My concern is for your futures. Four of my sons have settled down. It's just you two left to take care of."

"It is what it is, Dad. Just leave it alone."

"Seriously, Hunter?" His brother laughed but there was no humor in it. "Have you met our father? When did he not stick his nose in our business thinking he knew best?"

"There is that." Hunter braced for a blistering retort from his father and was surprised when it didn't come.

"I deserve that. You may not believe this, but everything I do is out of love for you boys." Max sighed a little sadly. "But you're men now. All grown up. And I can see how what I've done wrong has affected you. I'm going to fix it, though. I will see all of my sons happily settled down with families of their own, or die trying."

Wilder jumped out of the chair as if a snake had bitten him in the backside. Something about the sheer force of will in their father's expression had obviously spooked him. That and the fact that his four older brothers had fallen like dominoes and were married.

"I'm good, Dad. Really," Wilder said. "Don't waste your time on me. I'm perfectly happy playing the field. Settling down is not my game plan. I mean, can you really see me as a father?" He shook his head and shuddered. "Not gonna happen. So—and I mean this in the best possible way—back off."

Max just smiled.

That made Wilder even more nervous. "I assume this meeting is over. It is for me anyway. The horses must need feeding. Chores are waiting. I'm out of here."

Hunter watched as his brother couldn't get out of the room fast enough. "Good luck with him, Dad."

"I'm not worried. He'll come around."

Then he noticed that his father's determined gaze was

trained on him. Suddenly he understood how cornered his brother had felt. They both said he'd been happier since Merry had come to work for him. Their imaginations were working overtime. He hadn't changed.

"Look, Dad, don't analyze me. Wren and I are good. She loves school. By the way, she's in the Christmas play and excited about that. She's looking forward to Christmas. If my daughter is happy, I'm happy. It's as simple as that."

"If you say so, son." Max looked like the cat that swallowed the canary. He wasn't buying this.

Hunter felt as if every time he opened his mouth to make the case for his recent positive mood change, he actually made his father's case for Merry being at the heart of it. He wouldn't let that be true, even if it killed him. And now he was starting to think like Max Crawford, who'd admitted to manipulating his sons to get them settled down.

It was time to follow his little brother's example and beat a hasty retreat. "Speaking of Christmas, I need to get my little girl a tree to decorate."

"If I know my granddaughter, she's going to want her nanny to come along," Max pointed out with some satisfaction.

The man wasn't wrong, Hunter thought. And if he was being completely honest with himself, he wouldn't mind Merry's company either, and not just to look out for Wren.

Her smiling face seemed to make everything better. But neither wild horses nor his father could drag that admission out of him.

Chapter Eleven

Merry felt awful about asking Hunter for the evening off. He'd just returned to the house after a meeting with his father and said something about taking Wren to chop down a Christmas tree. But her house was closing escrow very soon, and she needed to pack up what was going into storage, then clean out, toss out or give away what was left. Hunter had generously agreed to her request. Since his daughter had said she wanted Merry to go, they'd put off the excursion until the following day. That sweet little girl's words made Merry's eyes well up with tears every time she thought about it.

Now she was in the kitchen along with a stack of boxes she'd gotten from Crawford's General Store, and bubble wrap and a tape dispenser in order to securely seal the box flaps.

Shaking her head, she looked around at the cupboards and knickknacks. Fortunately it was a small kitchen, but still… "This is going to be the worst," she said aloud.

The doorbell rang and she was grateful for the momentary reprieve. She'd asked Zoey to give her a hand, and her friend was standing on the porch with more boxes, flattened for easier transport.

"I am so glad to see you." Merry hugged her friend. "So much to do, so little time. I'm suddenly feeling very overwhelmed."

"Don't worry. We'll get this done." There was a confident, reassuring look in her friend's blue eyes.

Merry really needed that. "It's going to be emotional, too."

"I know." Zoey gave her a hard squeeze then let go. "So, what are we doing first?"

"Kitchen." Merry took half the boxes and led the way to the back of the house. After leaning the stack against one of the dinette chairs, she said, "This is going to be the biggest job. After dad died I cleaned out his room and donated his clothes. Most of his tools sold in the garage sale. That leaves the furniture and my things. And the kitchen."

"Let's get down to business," Zoey said.

Working together, they wrapped dishware, then arranged it snugly in a box to minimize breakage. When it was full, Merry sealed the top and labeled it with a black Sharpie.

"Now we have to box those pots and pans, and that cast iron skillet that was my mother's."

"My mom has one, too. She swears by it." Zoey opened a cupboard next to the stove and studied the contents—a lot of spices. "Are you sure you don't want to bring some of this stuff out to the ranch? You're cooking for Hunter and Wren, right?"

"Yes."

"Might be nice to have some of the cookware you're used to. And these bottles of spices won't do well in storage."

"I hadn't thought about that." She mulled it over and nodded. "It's a good idea. I'll run it by Hunter."

"I'll get some of the flat boxes ready for packing the other stuff," Zoey said. "Speaking of the ranch, how is it going? Living there, I mean."

"The timing of it all couldn't have worked out better," Merry said, ruefully surveying the open cupboard. There were things inside she used only once a year and had forgotten about. She wrapped up a gravy boat and handed it to her friend. "At least I don't have to worry right away about where I'm going to live."

"Do you think this ranch arrangement is permanent?"

"Is anything?" Merry was the poster girl for change. "Right now Wren seems really happy that I'm there."

"And her father?"

"What about him?" Besides the fact that his deep voice sent shivers down her spine and made her tingle in places she'd never tingled before.

Zoey gave her a "duh" look. "Is he happy you're there?"

"He hasn't said he's not." Technically that was true, but she saw looks on his face when he didn't know she was watching. Dark expressions that made her wonder if he was questioning the decision to hire her.

Zoey took a wrapped glass and set it in the box. "I know you're fiercely independent and all that, but you don't ever have to worry about a place to live. My mom considers you another daughter. We will always have room for you."

"Oh, Zo—" She blinked at the moisture suddenly in her eyes. "You're gonna make me cry."

"Don't you dare. Or I'll start." She sniffled. "Now hand me another glass."

"I appreciate the offer more than I can tell you. But—" She shrugged. "It's all good."

"Then why do I keep reading between the lines? It's all good—right now. It's fine—but..."

"I don't mean to imply that," Merry said. "It's just that life has given me more than one lesson about how things can change from one day to the next."

"Yeah. That's something we all need to keep in mind."
Zoey studied her carefully. "It's just that I can't shake the
feeling there's something not the same about you."

The only difference was working for Hunter and fighting the attraction that stubbornly refused to go away. But
she was shocked to find out that it showed and hoped with
every fiber of her being that Hunter wasn't as observant
as her friend. She had to sell the pretense that nothing
about her had changed, starting now.

"Obviously I'm different," she started. "My dad died
and I sold the house." She wrapped up four small custard
dishes. "That would change anyone."

"I understand that, honey." Her friend looked sympathetic. "But what I see didn't start until you began working at the ranch."

"And don't forget that I have another job. That makes
two. So I've got a lot on my plate. No pun intended," she
said, handing over a platter.

Zoey grinned, then her expression faded into a thoughtful look. "You worked two jobs when you filled in as clerical staff for your dad, but I never saw you like this."

"Exhausted?" Merry wished her friend would just
drop the subject. Talking about her feelings was a waste
of breath because it wouldn't make Hunter return them.
"So, what you're really saying is that I look really bad."

"Oh, honey, not at all. In fact, just the opposite. Every
time you mention Hunter your eyes light up. There's a
sort of glow about you."

"Just so you know," she said wryly, "I'm not pregnant."

"That never crossed my mind. But, trust me, I never
saw you look like this before you started working at the
Ambling A." Then Zoey's gaze narrowed. "Come to think
of it, I noticed a difference when you came over to the

house to try on dresses for the wedding. Right after you met Hunter for the first time."

Love at first sight? Not if she could help it. But it was time to come clean. Zoey was her BFF and their relationship was based on honesty and support. The least Merry could do was be honest now.

"He impresses me, Zoey. I respect him a lot. He's such a good father and it can't have been easy. His wife died a few days after Wren was born. Complications from childbirth."

"Oh, my God." Her friend's eyes widened. "That poor man. And sweet little Wren without a mom—"

"Yeah. I can't even imagine what it was like to never know your mother." She pulled the last couple of glasses out of the cupboard. "He had his father and brothers. They're great. I spent time with them at the wedding and Thanksgiving. Four of them—"

"Are married. I know. So do all the single women in Rust Creek Falls. Trust me, we're doing the math. We can subtract. There are only two eligible Crawford bachelors left. Three if you count their father."

"Oh, brother." Merry rolled her eyes. "But Hunter is a package deal, what with having a daughter. The thing is, you can't help falling in love with that little girl."

"Are you in love with Hunter, too?"

"That would be stupid," she protested.

Her friend slid a half-filled box closer to where Merry was working by the stove. "But stupid doesn't make it not true."

"I don't have time for that. And, seriously? You're helping pack up my house. The one I just sold. My life is nothing but one big challenge. I don't need more." She turned away to empty out a cupboard. "I have two jobs and soon

I'm going to be taking online classes again to finish up my teaching credentials."

"Again, Mer, none of that means you're not falling for him."

"Well, I'm not." *Please, God, let that be true.* "I admire him. I like him. But love? Hardly. If anything besides my boss, he's a friend. And I'm grateful to him."

"For?"

"After being dumped by a selfish jerk, he's shown me that there are still good men around."

"So…" Zoey was giving her the "I'm seeing hearts all around you" look. "Love is a possibility?"

"Not a chance."

"Why do you say that?"

Merry hated to crush her friend's romantic notions, but the BFF code of honesty was carved in stone. "In so many ways he's shown he's one of the good guys. With his brothers and his father. But mostly with his devotion to his daughter. He's completely wrapped up in her. Unfortunately, he's so focused on being one of the good guys, there's no time or room in his life for anyone else."

"That's too bad." Zoey nodded a little sadly.

Usually talking to her friend made her feel better. Not this time. Saying the words out loud was like a stone on her heart. But something else bothered her even more. If Zoey could see she felt something, it was possible Hunter could, too. And soon she had to go back to her job at the ranch and hope he didn't notice her eyes light up when she looked at him.

After school the next day Merry was in the truck with Hunter and Wren, driving to Fall Mountain to cut down a fresh pine tree for Christmas. There wasn't a cloud in the sky, and she was wearing dark glasses to protect her eyes from the sun's glare. Or was it to have some protection against giving away her feelings?

She glanced at the man in the driver's seat and actually felt her heart skip a beat. This stretch of road was flat and straight and he was in control of the truck with one hand on the steering wheel. What in the world made that such a sexy look? If she could figure that out, it could be the key to controlling her attraction.

He looked over and met her gaze. "Everything okay?"

"Fine." She cleared her throat. "I just wanted to thank you for putting this off a day so that I can tag along."

"Wren insisted you be here." The subtext was that he was a no vote on her presence, but because he was devoted to his daughter she got what she wanted. "But it turned out to be a good thing because I got a chance to dig through a bunch of moving boxes that are still unpacked and find the stuff for the tree."

"Then it's a win-win."

He nodded. "Speaking of moving boxes... Did you make progress on your packing?"

"Yes. My friend Zoey helped." She could see they were going uphill now and there were more trees.

"Are we there yet, Daddy?" Wren piped up from the back seat.

He looked in the rearview mirror and smiled. "I thought you were asleep."

"Nope. I can hardly wait to pick out my tree. A real tree."

"We usually have an artificial one," he explained. "This year she wore me down. Someone in town told me about a spot up here on the mountain where the sun hits just right to make the pines full and fragrant."

"I sure hope we find it pretty soon." Wren's voice was just south of a whine.

"We're getting there," he said.

Halfway up the mountain they reached an unpaved road and he made a left onto it, then drove slowly until coming to a stop in front of a thick grove of trees. There were stumps scattered among them that looked freshly cut, as if they'd recently been chopped down by others who'd come before them. Patches of snow from the recent storm managed to survive in shady areas beneath thick branches where the sun didn't touch them.

Hunter turned off the engine and announced, "We're here."

"Yay!" Wren quickly freed herself from her seat belt, opened her door and jumped out of the truck.

Before she could race off, Merry called out, "Stay where I can see you, sweetie."

"Oh, man." The little girl was impatient. "You guys are too slow."

"It would be easy to get lost in all these trees," she explained firmly. "I need to watch you."

Hunter chuckled. "And that's another reason why I didn't mind waiting for you to be available. I'm glad you're here to be the enforcer."

"You'd handle it if I wasn't."

"Yeah. But I'm glad you are."

His voice was warm and smooth, two parts gravel, one part velvet. Her breath caught for a moment but she managed to say, "Two pairs of eyes are better than one."

"Daddy, Merry, come on," Wren said impatiently.

"We're coming."

They exited the truck and Hunter grabbed a long-handled ax from the bed. Merry stood beside Wren, wanting to take her hand. She'd seen too many news stories about people lost for days in the wilderness and surviving by eating bugs and drinking water from tree leaves. As far as she could tell, pine needles were not an especially good receptacle for liquid. But the need to give this child a little independence won out over her protective instinct.

"Do you see anything you like, honey?" Hunter asked his daughter.

"This one." The girl pointed to the tree beside her.

He nodded. "Not bad. But don't you want to look around?"

"Can we?"

"Of course," he said.

They walked a short way, assessing the height, fullness and symmetry of different pines that caught their interest. Merry noticed Hunter was subtly guiding them in a pattern that always kept the truck in sight. That told her they were on the same wavelength about getting lost.

"What about this one, Wren?" Merry pointed out a pine tree that was a foot or two taller than Hunter. Using his height as a gauge, she judged that it would be prefect for the cabin's living room.

The little girl walked around the perimeter, giving it a critical once-over. "Does it have holes?"

By "holes" she meant places that were less full than others. Merry walked around it. "I don't see any."

"Daddy, what do you think?"

He did the same circuit and nodded. "This could be the one, kiddo. Just say the word."

She grinned happily. "I like it."

"Okay, then. You stand out of the way with Merry and I'll chop it down." He pointed to a spot and the two of them obediently walked over and stood there. Then he took a whack at the trunk on the opposite side of the tree from them.

Merry just had to ask. "Have you ever done this before?"

The look he gave her was amused. "Nervous?"

"No. Yes. Maybe."

"Here's how it's done." He indicated the mark he'd made on the trunk and started cutting on a forty-five degree angle. "I'll give it a thinner, less angled wedge, a few inches above the first cut. It will fall away from you. Trust me."

Trust was hard for her, but that was emotionally speaking. He would never risk his daughter getting hurt. Watching his powerful swings, she was distracted and way more interested in the masculine display of manliness. He looked so hot in his Stetson and sheepskin jacket. If there was a better word to describe him, she didn't know it. The man appealed to her in a very big way, on every level she could think of.

He came around and did his thing on the other side of the tree and it fell exactly where he'd said it would.

"Timber." He grinned and his grin said, "I told you so."

"Nice job, Daddy." The little girl ran over and hugged him. "Can I carry the ax back to the truck? It's not too heavy, I promise."

There was no way she could know that since Merry was almost positive her father would not ever have let her touch the thing.

"No, honey. It's really sharp," he said, confirming her guess.

"I won't touch that part." She gave him puppy dog eyes.

On top of that look, Merry could see a lot of stubborn sliding into Wren's expression. She decided a diversion would be good. "Is anyone else cold? I sure am. If we hurry home, I can make hot chocolate." She looked at the little girl and asked, "With whipped cream or marshmallows?"

"Can I squirt the whipped cream right out of the can into my mouth?" Wren began the familiar negotiation. "Cuz you don't usually let me."

"Hmm. You drive a hard bargain. But since it's tree cutting day, I think we can make an exception."

"Okay." Wren put her hand into Merry's.

"That sounds like a plan." Hunter gave her a thankful look, then rested the ax handle on his shoulder with one hand. He grabbed the trunk of the fallen tree with the other and dragged it back to the truck.

The sun was low in the sky and getting ready to disappear behind the mountain when they got back to the ranch. Another distraction was needed when the little girl wanted to jump right into decorating and was told the tree needed to be hosed off to get rid of bugs and any other critters lurking in the branches.

Then it had to dry because they couldn't bring a wet tree into the house. Merry knew Wren was hungry and tired, which could easily cause a meltdown and spoil her holiday experience. For their first Christmas in Montana, in this cabin, Merry was determined not to let anything mar the memories.

"I have an idea," she said.

"What?" Wren's expression was part pout, part suspicion.

"While the tree is drying, we'll have something to eat. I made chicken soup and we'll have a little salad. You can have your hot chocolate—"

"With whipped cream?"

"Of course. That will give you energy for decorating and make the waiting go faster."

Wren thought that over and finally nodded. "Okay."

"I'll go wash off the tree." On his way out the kitchen door, Hunter stopped and said so only she could hear, "You're the child whisperer. That was pure genius."

"Thanks."

The compliment made her feel warm and gooey inside, but their faces were inches apart. She could feel his breath on her cheek. With very little effort she could touch her lips to his. And she wanted that so badly, there was an ache inside her the size of Montana itself. Something hot flashed in his eyes, something that looked like regret, just before he moved away and out the door.

After dinner Merry fast-talked the little girl into a quick bath before decorating, while her dad brought in the tree and set it in the stand. The lights were strung by the time they came downstairs.

"Let the decorating begin," Hunter said.

The three of them carefully placed brightly colored ornaments then draped a garland. He easily lifted his daughter up to set the angel on the top.

"Perfect," he said, just before he put her down. "Just one more thing to do. I'm going to plug it in."

When he did, the white lights went on and Wren's look of wonder was priceless. "It's the best Christmas tree ever," she said reverently.

Hunter came over to stand beside them. "Looks pretty good. You picked out a winner, kiddo."

"It smells wonderful," Merry said. "Like a pine forest."

"Best day ever." Wren leaned against her and yawned.

It was the sign Merry had been waiting for. "Wow, look how late it is. We've been so busy I didn't even notice that it's past your bedtime, sweetie."

"Okay." The little girl headed for the stairs without being told.

Hunter met her gaze and his was full of surprise. "Wow. No pushback. That's amazing."

"Not really. Fresh air. Excitement. Activity. I'm surprised she held out this long."

They tucked her into bed and Merry tiptoed downstairs to look at the tree again while Hunter read the nightly story. Five minutes later he joined her.

"How did you get away with skimming that book?" she asked.

"I didn't have to. She fell asleep. Out cold in the first two minutes."

"She's a trooper, but it was obvious that she was worn out."

"By the way," he said. "Thank you for today. You're so good with her. Things could have gone sideways so many times, but because of you they didn't."

"Happy to help." She wanted to add that it was what he was paying her for, but she didn't. This was a moment and she didn't want to go there.

"The tree looks good." He crossed his arms over his chest.

"Beautiful." She was feeling wistful and just a little sorry for herself. When she was busy, it was easy to forget that she was facing a move and a lot of uncertainty about her future. But for now she had a roof over her head. "Thank you."

"For what?" He sounded surprised.

"If I wasn't here, I wouldn't have a tree this year."

"Because of the move," he said.

She nodded. "I have to be out before Christmas. All my things are packed and will go into storage with the furniture. I have to figure out the logistics of making that happen."

"You're going to need help. Let me know when and I'll give you a hand."

"I couldn't ask you—"

"You didn't ask. I volunteered. I won't take no for an answer. And I'll bring Wilder. The two of us should be enough muscle to get the job done."

"Really?" She stared up at him. "You'd do that for me?"

"Of course. It's the least I can do to thank you for going above and beyond the call of duty with Wren."

Merry had worried so much about how she was going to pull off this move. She'd felt so alone since her dad died and even before that. Caring for him by herself when he was so ill had been isolating and scary. To have someone take half the load now was such an incredible relief.

"Oh, Hunter—"

Happiness bubbled up and she couldn't stop herself. She threw her arms around him. "I can't thank you enough."

He went completely still and she instantly realized she'd made a huge mistake. Employees didn't generally hug their boss. She'd just crossed the line and somehow she had to fix this.

She took a step back. "I'm so sorry—"

"Merry, I—"

His eyes went hot and dark just before he pulled her back into his arms and kissed her.

Chapter Twelve

Merry was completely swept away. She'd never expected to feel this way. Not ever. But wrapped in Hunter's arms, the warmth of his body, the feel of his mouth on hers was more powerful than she'd imagined. And so was his kiss. It was real, solid and it was truly happening. She slid her arms around his neck, loving the sensation of his big hand moving gently up and down her back.

Heat poured through her and she ran her fingers through his hair at the nape of his neck. His breathing was uneven and she could feel his heart pounding as hard as her own. When he stopped kissing her she thought he was just coming up for air. But that wasn't it.

He stepped away, then took her hands in his and squeezed them gently before letting go. "Merry, I'm—"

"Don't you dare say you're sorry."

The strong fragrant pine scent surrounded them and the glow from the Christmas tree highlighted his surprise. "Okay. Then I'll just say this is all my fault."

"Fault?" She blinked at him. "You kissed me. I kissed you back. Fault implies there's something wrong with that."

He rubbed a shaking hand over his face. "I shouldn't have done that."

"If someone has to take responsibility for something, an argument could be made that it should be me. Because

I hugged you first." She glared at him. "And, for the record, I'm not sorry. At all."

"I'm not asking you to be. Your caring nature is one of the qualities I like most. It's why you're so good with my daughter. And you shouldn't have to change that." He let out a long breath. "But I need to maintain a higher standard."

"So you're ashamed of this?"

"I'm disappointed in myself for not being stronger."

She stared at him for several moments. "Should I be flattered or insulted?"

"For God's sake, Merry. You work for me. I don't want to put you in a compromising position."

So he was being noble. "That's really sweet."

"No." He shook his head. "It's the right thing to do."

"So this compromising position…" She couldn't believe she was going to do this. But some instinct warned that if she turned her back now she would regret it for the rest of her life. Instead, she closed the space between them and looked up, needing him to see in her eyes everything she was feeling. There was no trying to hide it now. "It's not a compromising position if that's where I want to be."

He resisted for a second or two and then his face softened. "So, that's a yes?"

She laughed and took his hand in hers, intertwining their fingers. "Affirmative."

Without another word they walked upstairs to his bedroom and closed the door behind them. Hunter flipped a switch on the wall and a nightstand lamp went on.

Merry had no doubts about this but that didn't mean she wasn't nervous. Gripping his hand a little tighter she said, "I feel it might be a good idea to manage your expectations—"

"Have you changed your mind? It's okay—"

"No. I'm very sure. It's just—" She couldn't quite meet his gaze. "I haven't had a lot of experience."

He nudged her chin up until she met his gaze. There was a gentle smile curving the corners of his mouth. "I'm the one who should be warning you about expectations. But I do have protection even though it's been a long time for me."

That hadn't occurred to her and she was grateful he had thought about it. "Okay."

Something must have shown on her face because any trace of teasing disappeared from his. "That's not why I want you. This is not something I take lightly."

She smiled. "I wouldn't be here if I thought you did. So, let's turn down the bed."

She walked to the far side and they dragged the top of the comforter to the foot of the bed, then folded it over one more time. Hunter opened the nightstand drawer and took out a square packet, setting it aside. Never letting her gaze stray from his, she knelt on the mattress. He did the same on the other side and they came together in the center of the king-size bed.

He reached for the hem of her sweater and she lifted her arms, letting him drag it up and over her head. She tugged his shirt from the waistband of his worn jeans and unsnapped the closures, one by one. Before she was halfway done he pulled on the sides of the shirt, opening all the snaps before quickly shrugging it off.

With trembling hands, Merry unhooked her bra and he brushed the straps off her shoulders, then tossed the scrap of white somewhere. With the light behind him, she couldn't see the expression on his face, but his breathing was ragged and his hands shook a little when he touched her.

He cupped her breasts in his palms and caressed them with his thumbs. "You're beautiful—"

"You make me feel beautiful."

"Merry—"

He sucked in a breath when she put her hands over his to hold them in place on her bare skin. He kissed her then, and pulled her against him, tunneling his fingers into her hair. His chest was wide and muscular and the dusting of hair scraped her skin in the best possible way. She opened her mouth to him and their tongues dueled as he explored while she did the same to him.

The room was filled with the sounds of their harsh breathing. Then she reached for the buckle on his belt as he undid the button on her jeans. The rest of their clothes came off and were tossed carelessly aside. He settled on the mattress and pulled her down on top of him. Finally she was in his arms, bare skin to bare skin.

Rolling her to the side, he slid his hand down her back, over the curve of her waist, and came to rest on her hip for a moment. He squeezed gently then moved his palm between her legs and slid one finger inside. Her muscles contracted as an ache cracked open and the need to be filled grew unbearable. A yearning that she'd had almost from the moment they met became too much to resist. Her hips arched toward him, telling him without words what she was asking for.

He moved away and grabbed the condom, then put it on. Seconds later he was kissing her again, angling his mouth over hers, trailing kisses over her cheek, jaw and neck. Taking his weight on his forearms, he covered her body with his own and gently nudged her legs apart. When he slowly entered her, she lifted her hips to meet him and take him deeper inside.

She touched his broad shoulders, slid her palms over

his muscular biceps and met him thrust for thrust. Her breathing grew shallow and harsh as he took her higher and higher, right to the edge. After hovering there for a moment an explosion of pleasure ripped through her and she trembled from the force of it.

"I've got you," he whispered against her hair as he held her.

When she came back together again, she smiled up at him and said, "I've got you, too."

She wrapped her legs around his waist, holding him to her as he started to move again. He thrust once, slowly, then increased the pace, finding their rhythm together and igniting her desire once again. And then he groaned and tensed. Reaching her own climax once more, she held him close and they clung to each other until their shudders slowed and finally stopped.

Merry didn't know how long they stayed in each other's arms without moving. She just knew this was a perfect moment in time and moving would mean it was over.

As if suddenly coming to his senses, Hunter rolled to the side. "Oh, God, I'm crushing you."

"No—"

But he slid away and off the bed. Seconds later a light in the bathroom went on. She missed the warmth of his body, his arms around her. And as quickly as that thought formed, he was back. He lifted the covers and slid in beside her, drawing her against his chest.

She stretched her arm over his abdomen and snuggled close. "I'm speechless."

"I don't believe that." There was laughter in his voice.

"It's true. I'm sleepy, but most of all very happy."

Silence stretched between them longer than it should have. He didn't move a muscle but his tension was obvious. "Merry, we need to talk."

Those were words no one ever wanted to hear, especially after sex. "Okay. What's on your mind?"

"I'm thinking that we should keep this…change in status to ourselves."

"I see." She tried to keep her tone light in spite of the jab that statement gave to her heart. "Although you should know I wasn't planning to broadcast this on social media."

"I didn't mean that." He brushed his thumb over her shoulder. "It's just that our arrangement is delicate and I don't want any fallout for you."

"I appreciate that." He was being noble again. She tried to read his expression but his face was in shadow. "We're not doing anything wrong, Hunter. We established that downstairs, before—"

"I know. It's just…" He sighed. "If anyone figures out our relationship has changed, there's no way Wren won't find out. I don't know about you, but I wouldn't look forward to *those* questions."

She realized that was a joke. He was trying to ease the tension and she appreciated that. And, of course, he was right. His child was their number one consideration. "I agree that Wren should be protected."

"I knew you'd understand."

She understood what he was saying but sensed there was more he wasn't. He wanted to keep the two of them a secret and she would bet anything that it wasn't all about his daughter. He was holding something back and she couldn't shake the feeling that it had something to do with protecting himself.

A few days after the best night Hunter could remember in a very long time, he kept his promise to help Merry move. At her house, he and Wilder picked up a recliner and carried it to the enclosed rental truck backed into the driveway. They tucked it snugly between a full-size mattress and the small dinette set.

"This is the last thing going in here." Hunter's cell phone pinged and he glanced at the text message. "It's from Wren."

"Is she okay?" Wilder asked.

He looked at it. "Yeah. She and Gramps are decorating his tree."

"I know she wanted to help Merry move. How did you get her to stay at the Ambling A?"

"I didn't." Hunter smiled at the memory. "Somehow Merry convinced her that she was helping with the move more than anyone by keeping Gramps company."

His brother lifted his Stetson and then set it more firmly on his head. "She sure has a way with your daughter."

Not just Wren. Hunter couldn't forget holding Merry in his arms and making love to her. And the questions shadowing her eyes when he'd asked her to keep their secret. The last thing he wanted was for his brother to know.

"There are still some boxes in the kitchen and garage," Hunter said. "Why don't you go on ahead and drive this load to the storage unit. Everything that's left will fit in her truck and mine."

"Here she comes now."

Hunter saw that Merry was carrying a square, clear glass platter. And she looked very close to tears.

"Can we put this in the truck?" she asked. "I found it when you guys moved the hutch in the kitchen."

"What is it?" Hunter asked.

"My mother's serving tray. It has her initials etched in the glass—IMM—Ina May Matthews. Dad gave it to her on her last birthday and she loved it." She was talking a lot, a sure sign that she was trying too hard to be in good spirits. "It's an awkward size, though, and didn't fit in the cupboards so Dad stood it up behind the hutch. I'd forgotten all about it until today."

Hunter could see the emotional strain in the dark circles beneath her eyes and the tightness in her mouth. He took it from her. "Sure, we've got room for that. But I think if you've got some towels handy, or sheets, we should wrap it up. Keep it from getting chipped or scratched."

She nodded and brushed a hand across her cheek. "There are some towels in that box in the garage."

After she walked away Wilder shook his head. "This has to be really tough on her. Moving out so soon after losing her dad. In a couple of months her whole life has changed."

"Yeah."

Hunter knew the changes had started when her father was diagnosed with cancer. There were appointments for treatment and eventually she gave up college classes and a boyfriend to take care of him. And finally planning a funeral and selling the house. He had no idea how she stayed so darn positive and cheerful through it all and admired the hell out of her because she managed to.

She came back with a couple of blue bath towels and a roll of duct tape, then took the tray and wrapped it up securely. After climbing up into the rear of the truck, she wedged the bundle between the mattress and box spring.

Smiling sadly, she said, "Mom and Dad are together again."

"That's a nice way of looking at it," Hunter said.

"I think so." She pressed her full lips together, probably to keep the grief from spilling out.

Hunter wished there was something he could do or say to make her feel better but he came up empty. In the end he reached out and put his hands at her waist, lifting her down. If Wilder hadn't been there, he'd have pulled her into his arms and just held her. But he couldn't, since he was the one who'd insisted they keep the personal turn in their relationship a secret.

Wilder cleared his throat. "So, Merry, Hunter suggested I drive this stuff over to your storage unit while he helps you put everything else in the pickup trucks. Then you can meet me there."

She looked concerned. "But we're going to be a little while. You can't unload this truck by yourself."

He shrugged. "I'm going to grab something to eat and I'll make some SOS calls. Logan. Knox. Xander. Finn. One or all of them will give me a hand."

"I've already inconvenienced one third of the Crawford brothers. I feel bad asking for more help."

"You're not asking. I am," Wilder insisted. "Although I will drop your name because they'll do it for you, not me. They like you."

"If you're sure…" She looked hesitant but he waved a hand in dismissal of her concerns. "I don't know how to thank you. Both of you."

She met Hunter's gaze and he knew he would do anything for her if she kept looking at him that way. The powerful feeling rocked him to the core.

"Don't mention it." Wilder looked at him and held out his hand. "Do you have the keys to the truck?"

"Yeah." Hunter had picked up the rental and driven it here. He fished the keys out of his jeans pocket and handed them over. Then the two of them pulled down and latched the truck's rear sliding door. "When we're finished here, we'll meet you there."

Wilder hesitated a second, then gave Merry a quick hug. "We got this, Mer."

"It's really sweet of you to help. Thanks again."

The smile she gifted his brother with actually made Hunter jealous. He knew Wilder was just being neighborly, supportive, but for reasons he didn't want to explore that didn't seem to matter. Some primal part of him turned green with jealousy at the thought of any man touching her. Even his brother, who he knew was just being a friend. What the hell was wrong with him?

These thoughts scrolled through his mind as he and Merry stood in the driveway and watched the truck slowly rumble away down the street. Almost everything she had in the world was going into storage. It was like stepping into limbo. He had experienced that feeling in Texas when he'd packed up for the move to Rust Creek Falls. But for him it was a fresh start.

Life as Merry knew it was ending. Her second job with him helped make ends meet. That and the roof over her head were dependent on him. He felt the crushing weight of that responsibility, especially because he'd crossed a line and slept with her. Every night since had been a test of his willpower not to have her again. He resisted the temptation because it had been more than physical and he didn't want to get in deeper emotionally. And the thought went through his mind one more time: What the hell was wrong with him?

"I'm going to back my truck into the driveway." Merry was looking up at him.

"Hmm?" He forced his thoughts back to her.

"To load boxes."

"Right. I'll do it for you." He held out his hand for the keys and she dropped them into his palm.

"Thanks. I've got cartons scattered in different rooms. I'll move them all to the garage."

"Okay."

Hunter moved the truck, then began to load up the rear bed while Merry brought out the rest of the things from the house. One by one she carried cartons to the tailgate and let him arrange them, maximizing space. More than once he saw her lift out a book, or a framed picture and stare sadly before replacing it and folding the flaps of the box. Every time, he could swear that it was like a sharp stab in her heart. And every time, he wanted to take her in his arms and tell her it was going to be fine.

She lifted a box up to him. "This is the last one."

He took it and rearranged some cartons, nodding in satisfaction when he finished. "It's all snug in there. Nothing is going to slide around."

"Good. The Realtor is setting up a cleaning before the new owners move in so I guess this is it." She looked up. "I'm going to walk through and make sure I didn't miss anything."

"Okay." He watched her go into the garage and disappear through the door and into the house.

She looked fragile and heartbreakingly alone and his instincts were urging him to comfort her somehow. He understood the heartbreak of losing a loved one. Part of him wanted to keep his distance. He didn't want to care about her, not deeply. But he cared enough and just couldn't stand back and let her face this final goodbye all by herself.

Hunter found her standing in the center of the empty living room staring at the corner. "Merry."

She jumped. "I didn't hear you come in."

"I just wanted to check up on you. Everything okay?"

"Yes." There wasn't much conviction in her voice though. "No. Not really."

"What are you looking at?"

She released a shuddering breath. "That's where we

put the Christmas tree. I was just remembering the holidays we had in this house."

He moved beside her and slid his arm across her shoulders because words alone wouldn't ease her sorrow. "It's a crappy time to have to move."

"Any time would be hard." She leaned into him. "I know it's just a house. But—"

"What?"

"I feel as if I'm losing him again."

"I understand." He was pretty sure he did. "When I left the house in Texas where I lived with Lara, I felt something like you're feeling now. But it wasn't all bad. It was time for a change of scene."

"I know you're trying to help," she said. "And I appreciate it very much. But I just feel so lost."

Hunter studied her face and saw how hard she was trying to be brave and not give in to the profound grief, and his heart squeezed painfully. He would never be sure whether it was for her or himself, but he folded her against him.

"It's okay, Merry. Feel the feelings."

Her shoulders shook with sobs then and he held her, doing his damnedest not to take his own advice and feel his own feelings. He badly wanted to tell her that he would make it okay. But he knew better than anyone that was impossible. And if he gave in to this urge to try and fix her heartache, he would be risking a pain he was all too familiar with. Losing someone a second time would destroy him. And not only him. Wren was already attached to Merry. He didn't want to deepen the bond by crossing a line and hurt his daughter, too.

Everything inside of him was saying, *Don't care for*

this woman. And he was trying his damnedest not to. But somehow Merry was invading his heart in spite of his resolve. And he didn't know how to make it stop.

Chapter Thirteen

'**Y**ou are going to be a fantastic reindeer." The play was going to start soon and Hunter was backstage trying to reassure his anxious child. That was a tall order since he looked a little frantic himself.

"I'm scared, Daddy."

Merry recognized the classic signs of stage fright because she'd experienced it herself.

After countless hours memorizing lines and practicing being Rudolph's best reindeer friend, Wren knew her part backward and forward. In fact, preparation had consumed them in the days after Merry had moved out of her house. She was grateful for the distraction because it had kept her from dwelling on the sadness of saying goodbye. And she was thankful that Hunter had held her when she cried. It was the last time he'd touched her and she'd been waiting for a good time to talk to him about that. But first the play. One crisis at a time.

Spectators and performers were gathering in the Rust Creek Falls Community Center. It was bigger than the school's multipurpose room in order to accommodate the students and their families, along with anyone else in town who wanted to attend. Most people did. Wren's whole family, headed by her beloved Gramps, were all out in the audience somewhere.

The noise level was high, which probably added to the anxiety. Wren was already in her one-piece reindeer costume. Merry had pulled the child's blond hair up onto the crown of her head, then curled the long strands and made ringlets. She'd used brown eyebrow pencil to darken her little nose and there was only one accessory left.

"Let's put this on." Merry was holding a brown headband with antlers attached. After the little girl's tentative nod, she slid it into place then fluffed out the curls. "Oh, my—"

"What? Is it bad?" Wren asked anxiously.

Hunter took a picture with his cell phone. "You look great."

"It's kind of like a tiara," Merry said.

"Can a reindeer be a princess?" she asked.

"Yes," Hunter said instantly. "As far as I'm concerned you are Dancer, the reindeer princess. Reindeer are the only deer species in which the females also grow antlers. So, tap into your inner royalty and you'll do fine."

"I'm afraid I might forget my lines."

If possible, Hunter looked even more nervous than his daughter. "I don't suppose it would help to tell her to picture the audience in their underwear," he whispered to Merry.

She shook her head. "She's probably too young to understand the concept."

"I'm a parent. I feel like I should know just what to say that would help her not freeze up." Frustration darkened his eyes.

Merry had thought a lot about her parents since cleaning out the house. She'd gone through a lot of mementos she kept of her mother and a memory came back to her now, as clearly as if it had happened yesterday.

She went down on one knee in front of the little girl. "When I was about your age I was in a school play, too.

I was so frightened I could hardly talk. But my mother said something to me that really helped."

"What?"

"She said, 'When you come out on stage, just look for me in the audience. And remember that I love you, no matter what.'"

"Okay." The little girl nodded.

Merry gave her a hug, then stood. "So if you're nervous, look for me."

Hunter was standing next to a break in the curtains and peeked out. He moved next to her and whispered in her ear. "It's starting to fill up out there. Why don't you go grab a couple of seats before all the good ones are gone. I'll stay here with Wren."

His breath stirred the hair by her ear and made her shiver with awareness. Part of her wanted to melt into him. The other part that was annoyingly rational knew that was a bad idea.

"Okay." She looked at Wren. "We are going to be right where you can see us. Break a leg. That's a show business expression that means you're going to do great."

Merry gave her one last reassuring smile, then exited stage right and surveyed the audience seating, concentrating on the center seats near the front. She spotted two in the second row and moved quickly to grab the chairs.

There was an older woman sitting next to them and Merry made eye contact. She indicated the two empty chairs. "Are these taken?"

"They are now." The silver-haired woman smiled. She looked to be somewhere in her sixties.

Merry sat beside her and plopped her purse on the empty chair to make sure it was saved for Hunter. "Thanks."

"I've seen you around town but I don't believe we've met. I'm Linda Dempsey."

"Merry Matthews. I'm an educational aide at the elementary school."

"Your father is Ed, right? The electrician? I heard he passed away a few months ago. I'm very sorry for your loss."

"Thank you."

The woman's expression was sincerely sympathetic. "Your dad did good work. And he was a nice man. He'll be missed by folks in this town."

"That's very nice of you to say." It was comforting to know the father she'd loved so much would be fondly remembered. "How long have you lived in Rust Creek Falls?"

"All my life. Born and raised here." She smiled wickedly and her expression was decidedly conspiratorial when she leaned closer. "I know I don't look old enough, but I've seen my share of feuds, clandestine affairs and generally outrageous behavior involving some or most of this town's prominent families. Not much stays secret around here. Rust Creek Falls isn't that big and gossip spreads fast."

"Sounds like some interesting history," Merry commented.

"That's for sure." Linda glanced at the stage where the sound of young voices drifted from behind the curtain. "Do you have a child in the play tonight?"

"Yes. No. Well, kind of." She laughed and shrugged. "In addition to my other job I'm also a nanny for Hunter Crawford's little girl."

"So that's you. I heard he hired someone." The older woman looked thoughtful. "Didn't the Crawfords buy the Ambling A Ranch? The old Abernathy place?"

"Yes." She remembered the diary discovered beneath a rotted floorboard at the main house. She'd heard the book was jewel encrusted and with the letter *A* on the front the theory was that it had belonged to one of the Abernathys. "Did you know the previous owners?"

"I heard stories about them." That didn't really answer the question.

"Stories?" There was a commotion behind her, female laughter as a group of women filled in the row.

"The Abernathys left town in the middle of the night without saying anything to anyone. The rumor was that Josiah Abernathy got a girl pregnant. And that the baby was stillborn. It's said the heartbroken mother had a breakdown and went crazy. From what I hear, it was a huge scandal at the time."

Merry heard the Crawford brothers talk about a girl being pregnant but the diary just mentioned her initial. *W.* "Do you know the pregnant woman's name?"

"No. I never heard," the woman said. "Such a sad story if it's true. I much prefer lovers to have a happy ending."

"Maybe the rumors are wrong," Merry suggested. "Maybe Josiah and his mysterious love lived happily ever after."

Linda smiled. "You're a woman after my own heart. I like you."

"Thanks. I like you, too." Merry smiled.

This woman hadn't given her much but it could be another piece of the Abernathy family puzzle. The way the Crawfords talked about the romantic passages Josiah had written to his beloved W, she had a feeling they would be very interested in this information.

She'd been so focused on what Linda was saying, Merry was surprised when she saw that the community center was nearly full. Finding two seats together was impossible now and couples were having to split up. A man she recognized as the father of a boy in Wren's class stopped at the end of her row.

He pointed to the place holding her purse. "Is that seat taken?"

She nodded. "I'm saving it for Hunter Crawford. His daughter is in the play and she's nervous so he's with her for moral support."

"Okay. Thanks anyway." He moved on.

"So, that's Hunter Crawford's nanny."

Merry heard the comment from a woman in the row behind her.

Another female voice said, "I heard they're an item."

"Well, she lives with him. That makes her awfully handy." The third comment was catty and from yet another woman.

A trio of mean girls. Merry told herself to feel sorry for them but it was hard to pull off when her face was burning with embarrassment.

Linda patted her hand. Obviously she'd overheard. "He's a very good-looking man and women notice that sort of thing. So it hasn't escaped attention that you're dating him."

This woman was right. Not much that happened in this town was missed. They'd come to the tree lighting, then had hot chocolate. People had obviously noticed, but that didn't mean they'd gotten the details right.

"We're not dating," she told Linda.

"That's probably a good thing." There was sadness and sympathy in the woman's eyes. "It's common knowledge that he's a widower. For five years I was with a man who'd lost his wife. He never could care about me the way he did for her. In time I could see that I was never going to get my happy ending with him so I broke it off. I know from experience that competing with a dead woman for a man's heart is not just a losing proposition. It's also painful."

Merry was stunned. It had bothered her when Hunter had suggested they keep their relationship a secret. Did he not want anyone to know because he was still in love with his wife?

What if there was no room in his life for someone else? Merry knew she couldn't settle for that. Obviously he'd been hurt and could be protecting himself. She could deal with that. But there was no way to win if he was still in love with the woman he'd lost.

The day he helped her move, when he'd held her in his arms, he'd said he understood how it felt to leave a place you loved. When he left Texas he'd had to say goodbye to his wife. What if that was about still loving her?

Wren looked like she was going to cry, and walking away from her backstage was one of the hardest things Hunter had ever done. But the teacher basically kicked him out, in the politest possible way. So he gave his little girl a big smile and left.

He spotted Merry right away. Something about her thick blond curls stood out and caught his attention. Sliding past the people filling in the row, he took the seat beside her when she moved her purse.

"Thanks for saving this," he said.

"Sure."

It was only one word but something about her tone was off. He couldn't put his finger on it except that she sounded very un-Merry-like. That was to say not very cheerful.

Hunter looked at her and noticed a paleness to her normally rosy cheeks. She'd been her normal self backstage, giving Wren a pep talk.

"Are you okay?" he asked quietly.

"Fine."

The snap in her voice said otherwise. It was a reminder of how much he hated that word coming from a woman. Or maybe it was just that he knew something was bugging her and they were going to talk later. Come to think of it, he didn't like that either.

It wasn't often that circumstances saved a guy from putting his foot in his mouth, but he got lucky when the curtains parted, the house lights dimmed and a little girl was standing onstage in a red velvet dress. She was the play's narrator and set up the story of Rudolph the Red-Nosed Reindeer. There was enthusiastic applause from the standing room—only audience after her short speech. Then the eight reindeer trotted out followed by a discouraged-looking Rudolph. The big red nose was a clue to his identity.

Hunter zeroed in on Wren, who sidled up to the dejected Rudolph. He would die for his child and wanted to protect her from any conceivable hurt, including public humiliation. This was where her dialogue was supposed to start and she looked terrified, hesitating too long. His chest felt tight.

"Look at me, sweetie," Merry whispered.

Almost as if she'd heard, Wren scanned the audience and grinned. He saw that Merry was holding up her hand with the pinkie, index finger and thumb up while the other two fingers curled into her palm. The "I love you" hand sign.

His little girl turned to Rudolph and said in a loud and confident voice, "Why are you so sad?"

The words were full of emotion. She'd nailed it and he breathed a sigh of relief. The rest of the story was a traditional telling of the red-nosed reindeer dealing with teasing because he was different. After saving Santa's mission on a foggy night, he was, of course, a hero. And the last line of the presentation was Wren's.

"The moral of the story is to be kind to everyone, not just at Christmas, but every day of the year."

The small performers held hands and took a bow while the audience clapped and cheered. Hunter snapped pictures with his cell phone as did a lot of other people watching.

"She did great," he said.

"Perfect." Merry discreetly wiped away a tear. But it didn't escape his notice that she was still giving him one-word responses.

After the first graders were finished, every other elementary school class put on their performance. As each group exited the spotlight, he was aware that Merry chatted with the older woman sitting next to her but said nothing to him. He also noted that her new best friend kept giving him looks, as if sizing him up. And he caught snippets of conversation from the women in the row behind him. Enough to know that they were definitely sizing him up. Sneaking a glance, he saw that they were young and attractive.

He also experienced an odd sensation. It was weird how he felt like he was cheating on Merry by noticing the women. He wasn't married and never planned to be again. Yet she was constantly on his mind, always in his dreams, and he couldn't seem to control it. He liked everything about her. The cheerful disposition, sense of humor, positive outlook and determination to be a teacher.

On top of that, she was so damn beautiful and that hair… The way she handled Wren was nothing short of amazing. Which was why he was determined to keep things uncomplicated and not mess this up and lose her.

The overhead lights went to full brightness as the stage curtains closed, signaling the end of tonight's performances. After that, kids of all ages still wearing their costumes streamed down the aisles looking for family members and friends. Thanks to Merry, his daughter knew right where to find them.

"Hunter?"

"Hmm?" He met Merry's gaze and was surprised to see shadows in her eyes.

She indicated the woman beside her. "This is Linda. She's lived in Rust Creek Falls all her life and knows a lot about the town's history. Including the Abernathy family."

Could be she had information about the diary his brothers were so convinced was some romantic lucky charm. He didn't believe in that sort of thing.

He shook hands with the woman. "It's nice to meet you."

"Likewise. Welcome to Rust Creek Falls. Although I know you've been here a few months. Better late than never."

"Thanks."

"There's a rumor going around that your father has hired someone to introduce all his sons to women and get them married off." Her tone was teasing even as she glanced at Merry. "Heard he's been getting pretty good results with the whole thing. What with four of your brothers now spoken for."

"Dad will take any credit he can get. The truth is that he has no business peddling romance, with or without help. His own marriage was a failure because he rushed into it."

Hunter wasn't sure why he shared that information with a virtual stranger. Although he suspected it had something to do with rebelling against the thoughts he'd been having about Merry.

Linda didn't seem put off by his tone. "It's a shame about your folks. But is it a total failure when they have six strapping sons to show for it?"

And his mother walked out on all of them. That abandonment was and always would be a part of him. And all it meant was that his parents had sex at least six times but that didn't mean they were happy.

"From what I hear, your married brothers are head over heels in love," the woman said.

He wanted to say they were for now, but that made him sound like the Grinch. He couldn't help it. Every time he thought about Avery's pregnancy and the things that could go wrong, it bothered him. And the fact that all of his brothers were talking about starting families meant more worry. From his perspective, it was hard not to look at the dark side.

Maybe a subject change was in order. "How is it you're here for the play? Do you have grandchildren at the school?"

"No. I never married."

"I see." Merry sighed a bit sadly.

"I can see you're feeling sorry for me. Don't. I'm resigned to it now. And the way I see it, all the elementary school kids are mine. I come every year to support them. They're so doggone cute. And that little one of yours is a real sweetheart," she said to Hunter.

"You'll get no argument from me." He grinned. Looking around, he noticed that the place was emptying out pretty fast. "Speaking of Wren, I wonder where she is. Maybe I should go look for her."

Linda stood. "It's time to take my old self home. Nice

to meet you, Merry. And you, too, Hunter. Happy holidays."

"Same to you," they both said.

"Now go find that little angel of yours. Or should I say *reindeer.*" She grinned. "Good night."

Linda left the row and Hunter was alone with Merry. She wouldn't look at him and he was about to ask her what was going on. But just then he spotted his daughter skipping toward them with a happy smile on her face. She headed over to their row, squeezed right past him and threw herself into Merry's arms.

"I saw you and then I remembered my lines. This is the best day ever," she said.

"You were fantastic, kiddo," Hunter told her. "You got all your lines and it was an awesome performance. There's never been a better one in the history of school plays."

"No, Daddy." She climbed into Merry's lap and snuggled close for a moment.

"No, what? I think you did a great job."

"That's not why it's the best day." She smiled tenderly up at her nanny. "It's the best because I finally had a dad and a mom to see me. Just like all the other kids."

He felt as if he'd been sucker punched. When Wren's mom died, he'd always been thankful that she was too young to remember and feel the agonizing pain of losing her. Now he knew she felt it anyway. How could he not have seen how much she missed having a mother? How much she wanted one.

He'd been afraid of her getting too attached to Merry, but here they were. She'd stepped seamlessly into the role of mom, and his daughter had responded to that with love.

He should have realized there was no way to shield her. When he hired Merry he was damned either way.

And what about him? Just a little while ago he'd

been thinking he liked everything about Merry. And he couldn't get her out of his mind. Was he starting to love her, too? After so short a time?

That would be rushing into a relationship just like his father had done. A disaster scenario with history repeating itself. Even if he believed it would be different for him, he'd loved a woman once and losing her nearly destroyed him. Raising Wren had forced him to put one foot in front of the other. But if he let someone in and lost her again, it wasn't just about him. This time he would have to watch his daughter be destroyed, too. He couldn't stand that. He wouldn't do it.

Abruptly he stood. "It's getting late. We need to get home."

Chapter Fourteen

Wren chattered happily on the drive back to the ranch. Merry wished Hunter would say something but he didn't, not much anyway. This awkward silence was about his daughter saying that she was like all the other kids with a dad and a *mom*.

When that child had enthusiastically climbed into her lap, Merry's heart had never felt so full. She loved the little girl so much and apparently Wren returned the feelings. Why would he have a problem with someone loving his little girl? Love was good, right? And Merry had never consciously tried to take her mother's place.

Suddenly she knew what the problem was and felt cold all the way to her soul. It was about love, all right, but not hers for Wren. This had to do with Wren's mother.

To finally meet a man who could love so deeply and completely was nothing short of astonishing. And clearly the universe was having a great laugh at Merry's expense. Why else would she realize that she was in love with him and figure out at the same time that he'd never stopped loving the woman he'd lost?

"Daddy, can I stay up a little later tonight? I don't have school tomorrow."

"You don't have school for the next couple of weeks. The play just kicked off your holiday vacation." Hunter had just turned onto the road leading to the Ambling A. In the distance, lights from the compound of buildings were visible through the darkness. "What do you think about her staying up later?"

The question snapped Merry out of her dark place. She tried to make her response as lighthearted and normal as possible. "Well, since you don't have to get up early, I think the success of your theater debut should be celebrated."

"Can we do that with hot chocolate and cookies?" the little girl asked.

Merry would prefer something a little stronger to take the edge off the ache in her heart, but this was all about Wren. "That sounds like the perfect thing."

She stole a glance at Hunter, who was nailing the role of the strong, silent type. The sharp angles of his profile were outlined by the truck's dashboard lights and the intensity surrounding him was sucking all the oxygen from the air. At least for her. These weeks with him and his daughter had been some of the best in her life but now everything was awful. Wren was a bright little girl and would notice the tension. She noticed everything.

Hunter pulled up to the house and turned off the truck, then they all got out. Just as he was opening the front door of the log cabin, her cell phone rang. She looked at the caller ID and saw that it was her brother, Jack. Things were tense between them, too, but talking to him would be a welcome break from Hunter's exhausting silence.

She answered and said, "Hi, Jack."

"Hey, Merry. How are things?"

A little while ago things took a turn into suckiness, but thank you for asking, she thought.

"Hold on for a second, Jack." She put her hand over the phone and said, "It's my brother."

"Okay. Wren and I will go whip up some hot chocolate and give you privacy."

After he hustled his daughter into the kitchen, she stepped into the living room and stood beside the Christmas tree in the front window. It was the farthest she could get from the kitchen. Not that she was going to say anything personal about Hunter, but… Better safe than sorry. How ironic was that thought? She knew a lot about sorry but had very little experience with safe.

She put the phone to her ear again. "How are you, Jack?"

"Fine."

"Good." But it didn't sound like he was fine. Still, how would she know? They'd barely spent any time together since she was a little girl who'd lost her mother.

"How are you?" he asked.

Shouldn't be a problem pulling off a lie. Once they'd been close, but he couldn't read her like a book anymore. "I'm fine."

"You don't sound fine," he said.

Well, color her surprised. "Okay. You don't sound fine either."

He laughed. "I'm as fine as can be expected what with being halfway around the world at the holidays."

"Can you tell me where you are? Or would you have to kill me?" She smiled at the memory of his very first deployment when he'd started that joke.

"Where I am doesn't matter." No question about it. He wasn't fine either.

"Are you in danger?" Her chest went tight at the thought of something happening to him. The two of them had their problems but the idea of him not being on this earth at all was inconceivable to her. She loved him and he was all the family she had left.

"That's not why I'm calling." The non-answer was

probably a yes on the danger thing. "I'm coming home for Christmas."

"That's great." And it was, but things had changed dramatically since his whirlwind visit for their dad's memorial service.

"But?"

"How do you know there's a but?" she said.

"I know you. I could hear it in your voice."

She let out a long breath. "Jack, I was Dad's executor and he left the house to me because you were gone, and I wasn't."

"Okay."

"I had to sell it. I couldn't pay the mortgage without the income from Dad's business. And without him there was no business."

"Why didn't you tell me?" He sounded shocked and upset.

This was not the time to get into all that. When they were face-to-face, they could discuss why she did what she did. "It was the best option. I'll tell you when I see you."

"Okay. But what about you? Where are you living?" There was a protective note in his voice that brought back flashes of their once-cherished relationship.

"I've taken a live-in nanny job. I'm okay."

Was telling a lie so close to Christmas worse than a lie any other time of the year? Probably. But being on Santa's naughty list would save the big guy a trip, for her anyway.

"Okay, then," he said.

"I'm sorry, Jack. If I'd known you were coming, I'd have put off the sale. But I didn't. And I can't ask my boss to put you up." Unexpected disappointment rocked her. She hadn't realized just how much she needed to see her brother. For so long she'd felt alone, but something about hearing his voice tapped into a deep well of yearning for the bond they'd once shared.

"Don't worry, sis. I'll be there before Christmas and figure something out."

"Okay. I can't wait to see you." That was truer now than ever before.

"Gotta go. Bye, Mer."

"Travel safe and—" The line went dead. Loneliness like she'd never known settled heavily on her heart.

She shook it off as best she could because she had a job to do. For the moment anyway.

She walked into the kitchen and tried to act as if nothing was wrong. Wren was sitting at the table with a mug of hot chocolate in front of her and beside it a small plate with a reindeer cookie on it.

"So, how goes the celebration?"

The little girl shrugged. "Okay. Daddy's hot chocolate isn't as good as yours."

A small victory but Merry would take it. She met Hunter's gaze for the first time since his daughter had said what she had at the community center and changed everything between them. His eyes were dark and guarded.

"Sorry about that," she said, holding up her phone. "I haven't talked to Jack in a while."

"How is he?" The tone was polite but cool.

"Fine." So he'd said. "He's coming for Christmas."

Almost too quickly Hunter said, "I'm sure you're looking forward to spending as much time with him as possible. Why don't you take the week off, with pay, and have a quality visit?"

"But, Daddy, it's our first Christmas in Rust Creek Falls." The little girl's eyes suddenly filled with tears. "It won't be the best one ever if Merry isn't here."

"Oh, hell," Hunter mumbled. Then he went down on

one knee beside her chair. "But, kiddo, her brother has been gone a long time. They have a lot of catching up to do."

Obviously he wanted her anywhere but here and that made Merry's heart hurt more than she'd have thought possible. "Sweetie, don't cry. You'll have a wonderful holiday with your dad and Gramps and your aunts and uncles and cousin."

As big fat tears rolled down her cheeks, Wren turned her tragic gaze on first her father then Merry. "It won't be wonderful. Why can't your brother stay here with us for Christmas? We have room. Right, Daddy?"

"We do." Hunter was crumbling under the weight of her sad expression. "Of course he can stay. But that's up to Merry and her brother."

Now it was her turn to feel the full force of not being able to tell this little girl no. It was also an answer to the problem of where Jack could stay on such short notice. She looked at Hunter. "If you're sure? I promise he won't be any trouble. We'll do our own thing—"

"He's more than welcome. Giving a soldier serving his country a place to spend Christmas is the very least we can do."

The words were right but it felt all wrong. A few hours earlier this would have made everything perfect but not now. "Thank you, Hunter. I'll let Jack know."

Wren hugged her father. "It's going to be the best Christmas ever."

"Whatever you say. But now I think it's time for bed."

"Okay."

Without another word to him Merry took the little girl upstairs for a quick bath and bedtime story before lights out. She remembered all the fun and carefree nights since she'd come to work for Hunter. Especially that night in his bed, in his arms. Now she knew there wouldn't be any more sweet and happy times in this house.

More than anything Merry wanted to go to her room and curl up on her bed, but there was something she had to do first. She went downstairs and found Hunter in the living room staring at the Christmas tree. He was holding a glass with a small amount of Scotch in it.

"Can I talk to you?" she asked.

"Of course." He downed the rest of the liquid in his glass then turned To look at her. "Is Wren okay?"

Merry couldn't help a small smile. "Zonked. It's exhausting being a star."

"Yeah. The meltdown was a clue."

"About that…" She stuffed her hands into her jeans pockets to hide the fact they were shaking. "It's really not necessary for you to put Jack up while he's on leave. We can make other arrangements."

He shook his head. "I meant what I said. He's a soldier and it would be my honor to have him here. Show my gratitude for the sacrifices he's made for his country. And my daughter wants you here."

"Okay. But there's something I have to tell you and that might change your mind."

He frowned and his gaze never left her face. "What?"

"I'm giving my two weeks' notice."

"You're quitting?"

"Yes."

"But I thought you liked it here."

More than she could possibly put into words. But that was before. Now she knew he couldn't return her feelings and it was just too hard. And there was no way she could tell him that.

"Your daughter is—" Emotion closed off her throat so she simply put her hand over her heart to express her deep feelings for his child. "But you and I both know this arrangement was only temporary. So it's best to make a clean break. I won't abandon her at Christmas or leave you in the lurch while she's out of school. But I'm going to start the new year with an aggressive push to finish classes and get my teaching credentials."

"I see."

Merry blinked at him. She wasn't sure what she'd wanted to hear, but that wasn't it. Something along the lines of begging her to stay would have been nice. And that's when she realized hope was hands down the cruelest of all emotions. It set you up just to disappoint you again. And the second time was so much more painful and disheartening.

The chance to get out of this encounter with her dignity intact was slowly slipping away. It took the last reserves of her strength to smile but she managed a shaky one.

"I just wanted to let you know so you could start looking for someone else to be Wren's nanny." That said, she left the room and went up the stairs before hope could blindside her again.

Mostly she had to get away before her facade crumbled and Hunter could see that she was in love with him. Tomorrow she would worry about how she was going to hide that truth and pretend nothing had changed. For the record, this was going to be her worst Christmas ever.

On Christmas Eve, Merry was alone in the cabin, waiting for her brother to arrive. Hunter had taken Wren to the big house for dinner with his father and brother. It would give his little girl a chance to work off some Christmas anticipation energy. Max and Wilder could help with that.

Merry had been invited but declined to go, wanting to be here when Jack showed up. Hunter had seemed relieved but Wren didn't censor her disappointment. It hurt Merry's heart because in a very short time she would not be the child's nanny. But she was trying not to think about that. In a few hours it would be Christmas and Jack had said he would be here. But why should his visit go the way she wanted? The rest of her life certainly wasn't.

That's the Christmas spirit, she told herself. A pity party during the most wonderful time of the year. Bah humbug!

She started pacing and kept checking her phone for messages, but there was nothing. Maybe nothing was all she could ever expect from Jack Matthews. But he'd sounded lonely. And sad. And very sure he'd be here in time for Christmas. How would she even know who to call to find him? What if—

A knock on the door kept her from going to a very dark place and she rushed to answer it. There on the porch was a man dressed in military camouflage and a matching fleece-lined jacket.

"Jack!" Merry threw herself into his arms, forgetting their differences in the sheer joy and relief that her big brother was safe, and more importantly, here. "I was getting worried."

"Traveling with the military is not an exact science." He hugged her tight, then held her at arm's length. "It's so good to see you, Merry. You're beautiful."

"You, too. Not beautiful. Just good to see you." She laughed and opened the door wider. "Come in. How did you get here? I'd have picked you up in—well, wherever you were."

He walked inside and looked around. "I caught a ride from a buddy who lives in Kalispell."

She looked at the duffel in his hand. "I'll show you where your room is so you can stow that."

"Okay." He followed her up the stairs and into the empty room next to hers.

"Hunter managed to find a mattress and box spring in storage up at the big house. I hope it's comfortable. You'll have to share the bathroom with me and Wren—"

"The little girl you take care of?"

"Yes. I can't wait for you to meet her. You're going to love her."

"And the father? Am I going to love him, too?"

Merry hadn't seen that protective look in his eyes for a long time. "Hunter is a good man and a devoted father." And that's all she was going to say about that. "Are you hungry? I'll fix us something to eat."

"It's past dinnertime. You haven't eaten yet?"

"I couldn't. I was worried about you," she said.

"Yeah, I could eat." Dark circles under his eyes were a clue that he was exhausted as well as hungry.

"It's just leftover stew," she warned, "but Hunter said it was the best he'd ever tasted."

She chattered away as they walked downstairs and kept it up while she reheated the food. Before long they were sitting at the table, eating. Jack scarfed his dinner up in record time.

"How about a second helping?" she asked. "Before you answer, you should know there are fresh baked cookies, too. Mom's recipe."

The sparkle in his blue eyes dimmed. "I don't think I could eat another bite. But thanks, Mer."

It didn't escape her notice that his expression changed at the mention of their mother. But before she could call him on it, the front door opened and closed. Moments later Wren ran into the kitchen and came to a screeching halt when she saw the new arrival. Hunter was right behind her.

"Are you Jack?" the little girl asked.

"I am."

"My name is Wren. You're finally here. Merry was waitin' a long time. It took you forever, Jack."

"He's Mr. Matthews," Hunter corrected her.

"Jack is fine with me if that's okay with you." He stood up and held out his hand to Hunter. "Nice to meet you."

"Same here. Hunter Crawford," he said, gripping the other man's hand.

Merry watched them sizing each other up. Both were big men, muscular and solidly built. Jack's hair was lighter, a dirty blond, and would have riotous curls like hers if allowed to grow longer than his short military cut. The two of them reminded her of predators circling each other, waiting for a show of weakness.

Jack broke the standoff. "I want to thank you for your hospitality. I'm sorry it was last minute but I appreciate you letting me stay here for Christmas."

"Happy to have you. Thank you for your service," Hunter said.

Wren looked way up at her brother. "Santa's comin' tonight, Jack."

He hunkered down to her level. "That's right. Have you been naughty or nice this year?"

"Mostly nice," she answered. "And Daddy says that Santa knows no one is perfect."

Jack laughed and Merry realized she hadn't seen that in a very long time. The magic of a child to touch someone's heart in a miraculous way was beyond measure.

"How was your dinner?" Merry asked her.

"Fun. Gramps let me open one of my presents. It's a princess Christmas nightgown."

"I can't wait to see it on you." Technically Merry had seen it. Max had requested her assistance for ideas and she'd bought it. "She loves princesses." That was for Jack's benefit.

"Can I get ready for bed now?" Wren was practically quivering with excitement.

"I think that can be arranged," her father said. "I'll supervise so Merry can visit with her brother."

"Yay!" Wren clapped her hands together then said to Jack, "I'll see you later."

"I look forward to that."

She ran out of the room and Hunter started to follow. He stopped in the doorway then turned and said to Merry, "Mission accomplished."

"You're welcome."

When they were gone Jack asked, "What was that all about?"

"Her grandfather asked me for gift ideas and I suggested the nightgown, knowing she would want to put it on right away. So it checked two boxes—a gift to open Christmas Eve and an incentive to get ready for bed and, if a miracle happens, go to sleep at a reasonable hour." She shrugged. "It worked."

"That's something Mom would have done," Jack said wistfully.

She'd been young when their mom died and wouldn't have recognized this as one of her strategic moves. Not without her brother to point it out. "Really?"

"Yeah. You remind me a lot of her."

"I remember her saying you were her firstborn, the one she spent the most time with. You loved her a lot, didn't you?" She put a plate of cookies on the table, then poured him a glass of cold milk.

"Yes." Sadness welled in his eyes. "I know you did, too."

"I was devastated. And Dad was drowning in grief

when she died. Then you joined the military and went away." She met his gaze and didn't bother to even try and hide the hurt and resentment in her own. "It felt as if I lost my whole family. As if I was alone. The big brother I adored, the one I looked up to, the one who was my hero and always protected me, was just gone. You abandoned me, Jack."

He stared at her for several moments as if he was lining up his argument, then just sighed. "I'm so sorry, Mer."

"Why did you disappear? How could you do that to me? To Dad?"

"Mom was sick for a long time." He took one of the cookies and broke off a piece but didn't eat it. "She got sicker, thinner. She died a little more every day. Pieces of me died along with her. After she was gone I just had to get out of there, away from all the painful memories."

"I guess I was one of them." Merry couldn't hold back anymore. It didn't matter that tomorrow was Christmas. This conversation was long overdue. It would either make things better between them, or he'd never speak to her again. Either way she had to get rid of the bitterness that was eating away at her. "Because you got away from me, too, and Dad."

"Not my finest hour."

"I took care of Dad alone, Jack. There was no one to share the pain and burden. You were his son and you couldn't even get home to see him."

"Yeah." He crushed the cookie into crumbs. "I was on a military mission, but that's not an excuse. I should have tried harder to be there for both of you."

"Damn right. You were in and out of his memorial service so fast it made my head spin."

"I know. You have every right to be angry."

"I don't need your permission. It sucked and I'm still pretty mad at you."

"I deserve that. All I can say is losing Mom just broke me. I was stupid, impulsive. Young."

"Not as young as me," she snapped.

He pushed the plate away. "If it's any consolation, I've been paying a big price for what I did. I loved her so much and it feels as if I've been running from love ever since."

He looked so completely miserable that Merry didn't have the heart to keep this up. The anger she'd carried around for so long seemed to explode inside her and then the fragments just went poof and disappeared. Gone.

She put her hand on his arm. "I understand."

"How can you? You were just a little girl."

"Losing Mom is a part of me, of who I am. A motherless little girl." She met his gaze. "Wren never knew her mother. She died from complications of childbirth."

"Damn." Jack looked shocked.

"The Crawfords moved from Texas and when she started school here, I sensed something, the void in her life, and responded to it. I'm grown up now and I get it. I understand how it feels to grow up without a mom. It's one of the reasons I took the job as her nanny. And it's why I'm still here through the holidays even though all I want is—"

"What?" Jack prompted. "To leave?"

"I didn't say that." But she'd said way more than she meant to. "It's just been hard losing Dad. Selling the house. My life isn't what I planned but I'm making it work. I refuse to settle. I'm—"

"In love with Hunter," Jack finished for her.

"Why in the world would you jump to that conclusion?"

"I saw the way you looked at him."

"Oh, please," she scoffed. "You're a guy."

"I am a guy, but I'm also your brother. I know you. Just because I've been an idiot doesn't mean that the bond we shared is gone. I can read you like a schematic. You're in love with Hunter Crawford."

She winced. "A little louder and they can hear you in downtown Rust Creek Falls."

"You haven't said I'm wrong," he pointed out.

She met his gaze and realized taking responsibility for your actions and feelings worked both ways. He'd been honest about what he'd done and why. The least she could do was be truthful about her own situation.

"Okay. As much as it pains me to say this, you're right. I am in love with him."

"But you're going to walk away?"

"I have no choice. When Wren goes back to school after New Year's, I will no longer be her nanny. I have to go. It's too hard to be around him when he's still in love with the wife he lost."

"So you've talked to him about this?"

"Well, no. I just gave him my notice, but—"

"No. Mer—" Jack put his hand over hers. "Running away because you're afraid isn't the answer. Trust me. I know all about that. I've been doing it for a long time."

"So you're saying I should fight for him?"

"Only you can decide whether or not he's worth fighting for. If he is…" Jack shrugged. "You'll know what to do."

In spite of her doubts and fears, Merry smiled. "It's so good to have you back. You're still my hero, Jack."

"I'm glad." His eyes twinkled for a moment then he turned serious. "But something tells me I might need to make room for someone else on this pedestal."

Chapter Fifteen

Merry was alone after Jack went to bed. It felt so wonderful clearing the air with him, and she filed their repaired relationship under Christmas miracles. But she was restless after their talk and ended up in the front room, sitting on the floor by the lighted Christmas tree with brightly wrapped packages underneath. She couldn't help thinking about what he'd said. Would it be more painful to tell Hunter about her feelings and drive him away? Or to lose him without ever having tried?

Before he went upstairs, she and Jack had reminisced about past Christmas Eves when she was little. Their father had made a big deal out of leaving milk and cookies out for Santa Claus, but there was always a carrot for the reindeer, too. The memory made her smile. Death couldn't steal everything from her, but it also made her miss her dad more than ever.

He had an opinion on every boy she ever liked and she used to roll her eyes at him, especially when the review was negative. But he'd always been right. What would he think of Hunter Crawford? Would he advise her not to give up without a fight? What she wouldn't give to have him here, be able to talk to him one more time.

Lights from the tree reflected in the window but she caught a glimpse of fat white flakes floating past. It was starting to snow. She smiled, remembering Wren telling her about mistlesnow wishes. Heck, what could it hurt?

She rolled to her feet and looked outside. "Daddy, if you can hear me, I wish you would give me a sign. I'm leaning toward fighting for him, but it would sure help to know what you think."

"Merry?" It was Hunter. "Are you okay?"

She thought she was alone and his voice startled her. Taking a deep breath, she turned to face him. "I suppose that depends on whether or not you think it's okay to talk to yourself."

"In my experience you always have something smart to say, so…" He shrugged.

That was something anyway. "You're still up."

"Yeah, it took Wren a while to settle down. I guess your brother called it a night?"

"He did. Traveling for over twenty-four hours is exhausting. I insisted he get some rest. He finally gave in when he kept falling asleep in the chair. Too stubborn for his own good."

"That sounds like my daughter." He looked around. "It was so quiet I thought I was the only one still up."

"No." She folded her arms over her chest. "But why are you?"

"I have to put out the presents from Santa."

"Right. And the big guy is supposed to get milk and cookies." She glanced at the empty coffee table.

"Damn." He dragged his fingers through his hair. "I forgot about that."

"Uh-oh. Your daughter would have something to say. And this isn't your first rodeo. You can't even claim it's a rookie move." She figured he probably had a lot on his mind.

"Yeah." His expression was adorably sheepish. "I'm not sure what happened but I can give you the perfect storm of excuses. The first Christmas in Montana. Big dinner at Dad's. A military guest of honor. And Wren didn't remind me."

"Still, Hunter—" She teased him with a pitying look. "Epic dad fail."

"Yeah, I know."

"Waking her up is not a good move, so plan B. Take before and after pictures. Full plate, then cookies with bites out of them. Drink half the milk. Show her Santa was here. She'll believe."

"Good idea. And you're right about not waking her. It will have to do," he said.

"Trust me. With hours of therapy she'll be fine."

His mouth curved up slightly at the corners. "I feel much better now. No guilt at all."

"Happy to help." For a few moments she'd managed to forget she would be gone soon and then the sadness of that fact was back. But for right now she was still his employee. "Do you want a hand putting out her Santa presents?"

He hesitated a moment, then said, "Yeah. I'd appreciate it."

Together they made several trips up and down the stairs, carrying gifts wrapped in paper and ribbon that Wren hadn't seen. They'd been hidden in his closet. Merry knelt under the tree to arrange them. In spite of her heavy heart she was glad she would still be here to see the happy look on that little girl's face tomorrow morning when she would first see this pile of presents. At least Wren would have a carefree Christmas. The following day it would be time to break the news that Merry was leaving.

She looked at Hunter. "I'll help you put that snack out for Santa."

"Right." He held out his hand to help her up.

She wanted to touch him, partly because it might be the

last time. She put her fingers into his palm and savored the warmth of his big hand around hers. But dwelling on that was going to make her cry.

After he pulled her to her feet, she quickly broke the contact, then walked into the kitchen and got a Christmas-themed paper plate. After opening a tin of homemade cookies, she asked, "How many of these can Santa eat?"

"Two and a half."

"So, three it is." She set them on the plate then poured milk into a glass tumbler. "Okay, I'll set this on the coffee table."

"Wait." He went to the refrigerator and opened it. "Just one more thing."

"Santa, what a big appetite you have."

"It's not for me." He reached into one of the crisper drawers and pulled out a carrot, then held it up. "This is for the reindeer."

"What?" She'd just been remembering the Santa snack from when she was a little girl. Who did this besides her father? Merry felt tingles from head to toe. "Why?"

"I'm a rancher. I feed the livestock. Horses have to eat frequently because they're big animals. So are reindeer." He held up the raw carrot again. "Bon appétit, Rudolph."

"It's a sign," she whispered.

"I'm sorry?"

She would bet everything she owned that her father, wherever he was, approved of this man and was encouraging her to not give up without a fight. "Hunter, we need to talk."

"About?"

"The elephant in the room," she said.

He looked puzzled but said, "We're going to need a lot more carrots."

"I'm serious. Ever since the night of Wren's play you've

been acting weird." Merry could almost see his guard coming up and emotion shutting down. This time she was having none of it. She'd faced the worst-case scenario and could live with the consequences. There was nothing more to lose. It *would* hurt more if she let him go without trying. "I'm not imagining this. You started acting weird right after Wren talked about it being the best night ever because she had a dad and mom, like all the other kids."

"Merry, I don't know—"

"In case you aren't already aware of this, I love Wren very much. She makes that very easy. And I'm so happy to be in her life, hopefully making a positive difference. But I'm not trying to take her mother's place. There's no way I could do that."

"I know." He reached a hand out then lowered it to his side without touching her. "I know you're not."

"Then just answer one question. It doesn't matter what you say as long as you tell me the truth. I can deal with it either way." She took a deep breath then asked, "Are you still in love with your wife?"

The direct question seemed to take him by surprise and he didn't say anything right away. He was thoughtful for several moments, then sighed. "I loved Lara very much and I always will. But I'm not in love with her now."

"You sound very sure of that." There was a flutter in her chest and she was pretty sure that was hope stirring to life. "Are you?"

"Very."

"How can you be?"

"Because I'm in love with you," he said simply.

For a second, happiness exploded inside her, given that the words were everything she wanted to hear. Then the glow faded and pesky reality sneaked in before she could shut it out. She still had questions.

"If you love me, why are you pushing me away?"

He looked lost and his eyes were grim. "The only explanation I have is that I'm messed up." He spread his hands in a helpless gesture.

"I appreciate your honesty." She truly meant that. It was something at least after trying to guess what he was thinking, why his mood changed so suddenly. "And it makes sense. You've been through a lot."

He nodded. "It's just that I'm having a hard time putting myself in a position where I could go through it again. And protecting Wren is the most important thing—"

"She could get hurt, too."

"Yeah," he whispered.

Merry saw the conflict raging in him and longed to offer comfort. She had to touch him and pressed her body to his, putting her arms around him before resting her cheek against his chest. His heart was hammering. *Proof of life*, she thought, *and it should be lived*. After losing her father, she was more convinced of that than ever. And Hunter had so much love to give.

"I can't give you a guarantee that the future will be perfect, but with a great deal of certainty I can say that it won't even be close to that if you don't take a chance."

"Merry—"

"I'm not finished. And you don't have to say anything, but I need you to hear this." She moved away from him, just far enough to see his face, the look in his eyes. "You are one of the best men I've ever known. I'm not going anywhere. And I promise that I will wait for you to figure things out. As long as it takes. Because that's the way I love."

He nodded but there was no peace in his expression. Without a word he moved away from her then grabbed his sheepskin jacket hanging on the hook beside the door. And then he walked out. He was just gone.

Merry desperately wanted another mistlesnow wish. This was a bad time to realize that giving him the okay to say nothing was without a doubt her most boneheaded move. Looking at the plate of cookies with a side of carrot, she smiled sadly.

"I didn't win, but at least I fought for him, Daddy."

If only her father was there to hold her while she cried.

"Wake up! It's Christmas."

Merry opened her eyes and it wasn't easy. The sun was barely up. And wait. Didn't she just fall asleep five minutes ago? Sleep was hard to come by when the man you loved walked out. Come to think of it, she'd been awake for hours after that and didn't hear him come back.

She sat up and looked at Wren standing by the bed. "Is your dad awake, sweetie?"

"He's not in his room. I checked. And I'm not s'posed to go downstairs by myself and see if Santa came yet."

"Maybe your dad is feeding the animals. I'll throw on some clothes and go find him."

"I wanna go with you."

"Okay. Get dressed." She put on a brave face along with jeans, boots and a sweater, but this situation was not good. Everything Hunter did was about being a devoted dad. No way he wouldn't be here when his daughter woke up on Christmas morning. Unless something was wrong.

Merry steered the little girl out the back door to keep the "Santa surprises" a secret until, hopefully, her father could be here to see her reaction. His truck was gone but he might have been hauling hay for the animals or using it for any of a hundred other ranch chores that had to be done even on holidays. It wasn't by the barn either, but they still checked the stalls and tack room without success.

"Where could he be?" Wren asked.

"He must have had an errand." It was the hardest thing she'd ever done, but Merry managed to keep her voice neutral and calm when she felt just the opposite.

"But I wanna open presents. I've been waitin' so long."

"I know, sweetie. It must be an important errand."

Or something bad had happened. Something that needed the sheriff involved. With every step back to the house it was harder to hold off the panic and Merry didn't know what to do.

When they walked back into the kitchen, Jack was there. He was dressed in jeans and a flannel shirt but his hair was sticking up and there was a shadow of stubble on his face. But he'd never looked better to her. She wasn't alone.

"Merry Christmas." There were questions in his eyes. "When I woke up to an empty house, I thought this was a *Twilight Zone* holiday."

"Sorry." She looked down at the little girl pressed tightly against her, then rubbed a hand reassuringly down Wren's arm. "We went to see if Hunter was in the barn."

Jack nodded slightly, letting her know he got her concern and wouldn't say anything alarming. "What does a guy have to do to get a cup of coffee around here?"

"Push a button." The water and grounds were ready to go in the coffee maker. It's one of the things she'd done when sleep wouldn't come last night. "Wren, why don't you show him how it's done?"

"Over here, Uncle Jack."

His eyebrows went up, an indication that he didn't miss his elevation in rank. "I'm right behind you, squirt."

That's what he used to call her, Merry thought.

Although Wren loved to do it, she magnanimously allowed her new uncle to do the button-pushing honors. Moments later the sound of water dripping into the pot filled the kitchen, followed quickly by the rich aroma of brewing coffee. Normally Merry loved it but her stomach was in knots and she was afraid she was going to throw up. Every second that ticked by without a word from Hunter was like a shot of adrenaline to her nerves.

She looked at Jack. If Hunter was at the main house he would have walked so his truck would still be there. And it wasn't. He'd gone somewhere and hadn't returned. "I'm wondering if I should call the *S-H-E-R-I-F-F*."

"Sheriff?" Wren's eyes went wide.

"I forgot how smart you are." Some teacher she was going to be, Merry thought. And a crisis management failure on top of it. She tried to smile at the little girl and hoped somehow it was reassuring. "I'm sure everything is fine and—"

The sound of the front door opening interrupted her. Then a deep voice calling out, "Ho, ho, ho. Merry Christmas!"

"Daddy!"

The little girl raced out of the room and Merry was right behind her. Jack brought up the rear and the three of them came to a dead stop when they saw Hunter. He was wearing his ever-present Stetson but on top of that was a deluxe Santa hat with faux white fur trim and a matching pompom. His arms were full of wrapped presents that he'd just carried inside.

"It's a beautiful day." He put everything under the tree, then said to Jack, "There's more in the truck. Mind giving me a hand?"

"Happy to."

The two men brought everything inside and set the

presents by the tree. It looked like Christmas exploded in the cabin's front room.

Wren hugged her father. "We couldn't find you, Daddy. Merry was gonna call the sheriff. She spelled it but I knew anyway."

Hunter picked her up. "I'm sorry you were worried. I had some last-minute shopping to do."

"All night?" Merry asked.

"In Kalispell a few stores were open all night. But there was this one—" He smiled mysteriously. "It took a little longer than I expected."

Wren's arms were around his neck. "Can we open presents now? Santa came and I don't think I can wait much longer."

"Let's do it." He squeezed her tight for a moment, then set her down.

It was a paper-ripping, gift-opening free-for-all that seemed to go on forever. Wren was giddy with excitement when she saw her new princess doll with its royal wardrobe. Other packages revealed socks, pajamas, mittens, a scarf, a scooter and a sparkly pink helmet.

Hunter handed Jack a box. "You look like a Scotch drinker. It's not imaginative, but next year I'll do better."

Jack's eyes narrowed for a moment, then he nodded his understanding. "Later I'll open it and we'll drink to next year."

Merry heard that exchange and added another question to the list she had for Hunter. Right now she was keeping busy shoving used wrapping paper into a trash bag. Finally all the packages had been opened and the contents neatly stacked under the tree.

"It looks like that's a wrap. Pun intended," she said.

"Merry, look." Wren pointed to a tall present sitting alone by the front door. "There's one more."

Hunter grabbed it before his daughter could. "That's not for you, kiddo."

"Who then?" she asked.

"Merry." There was an expression in his eyes that had never been there before. He set it down in front of her. "Merry Christmas."

"Hunter, I—"

"Just open it, please."

"Okay." It was tall but she had to get on her knees because her legs were shaking. Her hands were shaking, too, as she carefully unwrapped the beautiful gold foil paper to reveal a plain box. She lifted the flaps and found another wrapped box inside. Puzzled, she met his gaze. "What—"

Emotions scrolled across his face too quickly to identify. "Keep going."

She nodded, then lifted out the gift and slid the paper off, only to find yet another box. This happened three more times and her excitement and anticipation grew even as the boxes got smaller. Especially because they got smaller. Finally, there was one left and she found a black velvet jewelry box inside.

"Hunter?"

"There weren't any jewelry stores open twenty-four hours on Christmas Eve. But when you have enough money and determination, doors open for you."

"So this is what took you so long?"

"Yes."

"Merry said you must be doing something important," Wren said.

"I definitely was." He smiled down at her before moving in front of Merry. He took the box from her palm then helped her to her feet.

"What are you doing?"

Without answering, he went down on one knee and

opened the box, revealing a stunning vintage diamond engagement ring. He looked at her expectantly. "Will you marry me?"

Her heart was hammering so hard she wasn't sure she could speak. That was incredibly inconvenient at the most important moment of her life. The love for him that she'd kept bottled up inside was straining to be set free. But she had to know something first.

"Does this mean you figured things out? That you're not afraid anymore?"

"Oh, I'm terrified." But he didn't look it. Hope sparkled in his eyes where once there'd only been emptiness. "The only thing that scared me more than taking this step was not taking it."

"So, you figured things out pretty fast."

"As soon as I walked out the door last night," he agreed. "I'm in love with you and will always be afraid of losing you. But I won't let it be because I gave up on us without trying."

Merry stared at him for several moments, too stunned to speak. Her brother, on the other hand, had no problem at all.

"For crying out loud, sis, will you put the man out of his misery and say yes already?"

Hunter nodded at him. "I'd have asked your permission the old-fashioned way, but due to my own stupidity and the necessity of a big gesture to cancel it out, the timeline had to be altered."

"Understood," Jack said. "Permission granted."

And Wren, who'd been uncharacteristically silent through all this, said, "Are you going to marry Daddy? Can I be a flower girl? And wear a tiara?"

"I'd say she approves." Merry smiled at him.

"So is that a yes?" Hunter asked. "I want it to be. But only if it's what you want, too. I don't want to push—"

"Yes." She held out her left hand for him to slide the ring on. When he did, she sighed at the exquisite diamond and the perfect fit, then tugged him to his feet. "I want this more than I can say. It's what I wished for on that very first mistlesnow."

"See? I told you mistlesnow wishes worked," Wren said happily. "And I told you this was going to be the best Christmas ever."

"You were right," Merry and Hunter said together.

And then he kissed her. No mistletoe required.

Epilogue

Hunter held tightly to Merry's hand as they walked to his father's place. Wren had run ahead with Jack right behind her. Walking beside the woman he loved so much made him happy and he planned to do it for the rest of his life. The darkness he'd carried inside him for so long didn't stand a chance against a woman named Merry.

"I can't wait to tell everyone our good news," he said. "How do you feel about a short engagement?"

She leaned her head against his shoulder. "That works for me. Maybe we should go to Rustler's Notch for a destination wedding. Max would like that."

"I'm more interested in what you want." He looked down at her, golden hair framing her face like a halo. An angel. And she was his.

"As long as the whole family is there, we can get married in the barn for all I care." Smiling, she met his gaze. "We'll talk to Jack and see how long the military can spare him. I feel as if I have my brother back and I want him to walk me down the aisle."

"Sounds like a plan."

They were almost at his father's, and in front of the two-story log cabin it looked like a car lot with all the vehicles lined up. There was a decorated tree in the window with white lights twinkling. On the front porch they smiled at each other, then took a deep breath.

"Here we go," he said. "Are you ready?"

"Are you?" she teased.

"More than you can possibly know."

Hunter didn't bother knocking. Family never did. He opened the door and walked into Crawford central, where everyone was talking excitedly. Wren was with her aunts and Jack was shaking hands with Max. Introductions had apparently been made. Someone, probably Lily, had been cooking because mouthwatering smells were coming from the kitchen.

"Hello, everyone." Hunter let go of Merry's hand long enough to wave a greeting. "Merry Christmas."

The whole crew stopped their conversations and welcomed them.

Wilder said to their father, "Everyone is here. Can we eat now?"

"Don't ask me. That's up to our chef. Lily?"

"It's all ready. But I could use extra hands to put everything out on the table."

"Oh, let me help," Merry said. "I feel like such a slacker for not pitching in."

"No worries." Lily's green eyes sparkled with more than Christmas spirit. "You've had a lot going on today. What with your brother visiting," she added.

Everyone rallied around and brought out mashed potatoes, freshly baked biscuits, various side dishes that were enough to feed an army and a standing rib roast. The seating went pretty much like Thanksgiving with Logan and Sarah on one side of a high chair for Sophia and Hunter's daughter on the other. Seeing Wren with her baby cousin reminded Hunter of their earlier conversation. After his proposal, Wren had asked for a baby sister and Merry had given the child a hard yes on that. She loved children and was going to be a teacher, after all. He would be nervous for nine months but he'd deal with it. And something told him it would turn out all right.

After much juggling and repositioning, everyone was finally settled and Hunter wanted to make his announcement while there was still a shred of sanity in the room. He tapped his fork against the water glass by his plate, demanding their attention.

"Before we start, I have something to say." He smiled at the amazing woman beside him. "I proposed to Merry and she said yes. We're getting married."

Hunter was prepared for everyone to start talking at once. He anticipated hearing congratulations, good-natured teasing and sincere wishes for a lifetime of happiness. And from Max he figured there would be some taking credit for the match because he'd suggested hiring a nanny for that wedding weekend. None of that happened. There was total silence.

Baffled, Hunter looked around the table. "Who are you people and what have you done with my family?"

They all looked at each other then burst out laughing.

"Gotcha," Logan said.

"Do you really think we didn't know?" Genevieve looked at her husband and Knox gave him an I-told-you-so smirk.

"There were so many clues to pick from." Finn took Avery's hand and she smiled at him. "You couldn't stop touching each other."

"Not to mention that ring," Lily chimed in. "That rock is so big and shiny I think it's visible from space."

Merry held up her hand to give them all a better look. "It is beautiful, isn't it? Hunter has very good taste. I'm a lucky woman."

"And he's a lucky man." Max wore an expression of fatherly pride on his face, but there was something else, too. It was the unmistakable satisfaction of a conspiracy. "But if there was any doubt about this engagement, your daughter took care of that when she spilled the beans as soon as she ran into the house."

"I didn't spill anything, Gramps." Taking the remark literally produced an expression of self-righteous indignation that his little girl had perfected. "I just said that Daddy was going to marry Merry. I get to be in the wedding and she's going to be my mom."

Those words didn't produce complete silence. There were some sniffles around the table, and not just from the women.

"Oh, hell," Wilder blurted.

"Language," Hunter reminded him.

"Sorry. But I just thought of something." He glanced around the table at all the couples and got only blank stares. "This means my brothers have all deserted me. I'm the last Crawford bachelor."

Max chuckled. "Don't look now, son, but I'm right there with you."

If anything, Wilder's tragic expression deepened. "Says the man paying to get us all married off. That doesn't make me feel any better, Dad."

"Suck it up, kid," Finn told him. Then he looked at Hunter and Merry. "You two will be the next Crawford couple to take on the mysterious diary."

"Oh—" Merry looked at Hunter. "What with everything going on I forgot to tell you. The night of Wren's play I found out something—"

There was a knock at the door, as loud and startling as a gunshot. Hunter wondered who it could be. The whole family was here and none of them would knock anyway. He and Wilder were closest and both of them stood at the same time.

With Max right behind them, they hurried to find out who was there. Hunter opened the door and heard the sound of a car driving away. Then he looked down and what he saw shocked him to the core. It was an infant car seat with a sleeping baby inside. There was a note pinned to a blue blanket.

Wilder, this is your baby. I've done the best I could for four months and I can't do it anymore. A boy needs a dad and you're Cody's, so it's your turn now. Please take good care of him.
L

Hunter looked at his brother and felt shock and a little bit of satisfaction. Wilder was the one who'd wanted Hunter to be his wingman at their brother's wedding and help him hit on women. The same man who'd advised him to let off some steam even though he had a six-year-old daughter to take care of.

"Well, little brother, looks like you got a baby for Christmas." He didn't know if this was karma or payback but either was a bitch. "Loosen up. You're going to have to be a dirty diaper–changing kind of guy after all."

* * * * *

MILLS & BOON

Coming next month

SNOWBOUND WITH THE HEIR
Sophie Pembroke

'Tori, sweetheart.' Jasper whispered the words against her hair, kissing her head softly as her cries lessened. 'Wake up, love.'

And she did.

Lifting her head, she blinked up at him, tears still glistening in the half-light. 'I was dreaming…' She shuddered at the memory.

'About Tyler?' he asked gently. She nodded. 'Would it help to talk about it?'

This time, she shook her head, her hair whipping around in defiance. 'I just want to forget.' She looked up at him again, and there were no tears this time. Just a new fierceness to replace the armour she'd lost. Her body shifted, and suddenly every inch of her seemed to be pressed up against him, tempting and hot and everything he'd never even dreamed of.

That was a lie. He'd dreamed about it. Often. Especially since the night they'd spent together.

But he'd never imagined it could actually happen again, not here and now.

She raised her mouth, pressing it firmly to his, her tongue sweeping out across his lower lip, and his whole body shuddered with want and desire as he kissed her back. The kiss was deep and desperate and everything he remembered about their other night together. When she pulled back, just far enough to kiss her way along his jawline, Jasper could barely remember his own name.

'Help me forget?' she murmured against his ear.

And suddenly the heat faded.

Not completely, of course. The lust she'd inspired was still coursing through his blood, and certain parts of his anatomy were absolutely on board with her plan—right now, preferably.

But his brain, that frustrating, overthinking part of him—the part that had come up with a dream of a frozen river and this woman's hand in his—had other ideas.

'Tori...' He pulled away, as far as he could without falling out of the narrow single bed. 'Tori, not like this.'

God, he wanted her. But he wanted her to want him too. Not just forgetfulness, not just oblivion. He'd had enough of that sort of relationship himself, when he'd first moved away from Flaxstone. The kind of sex that just blocked out the world for a time, that helped him pass out and sleep without dreaming of the life he'd thought he'd had and the lies that had lurked behind it.

He didn't want that with Tori. Not this time.

Continue reading
SNOWBOUND WITH THE HEIR
Sophie Pembroke

Available next month
www.millsandboon.co.uk

COMING SOON!

We really hope you enjoyed reading this book. If you're looking for more romance, be sure to head to the shops when new books are available on

Thursday 14th November

To see which titles are coming soon, please visit

millsandboon.co.uk/nextmonth

MILLS & BOON
MEDICAL
Pulse-Racing Passion

Set your pulse racing with dedicated, delectable doctors in the high-pressure world of medicine, where emotions run high and passion, comfort and love are the best medicine.

MILLS & BOON

THE HEART OF ROMANCE

A ROMANCE FOR EVERY KIND OF READE

MODERN

Prepare to be swept off your feet by sophisticated, sexy a
seductive heroes, in some of the world's most glamourou
romantic locations, where power and passion collide.
8 stories per month.

HISTORICAL

Escape with historical heroes from time gone by. Wheth
passion is for wicked Regency Rakes, muscled Vikings or
Highlanders, awaken the romance of the past.
6 stories per month.

MEDICAL

Set your pulse racing with dedicated, delectable doctors
high-pressure world of medicine, where emotions run h
passion, comfort and love are the best medicine.
6 stories per month.

True Love

Celebrate true love with tender stories of heartfelt roma
the rush of falling in love to the joy a new baby can brin
focus on the emotional heart of a relationship.
8 stories per month.

Desire

Indulge in secrets and scandal, intense drama and plen
hot action with powerful and passionate heroes who hav
wealth, status, good looks…everything but the right wor
6 stories per month.

HEROES

Experience all the excitement of a gripping thriller, with
romance at its heart. Resourceful, true-to-life women a
fearless men face danger and desire - a killer combinati
8 stories per month.

DARE

Sensual love stories featuring smart, sassy heroines you'
best friend, and compelling intense heroes who are wor
4 stories per month.

To see which titles are coming soon, please visit

millsandboon.co.uk/nextmonth

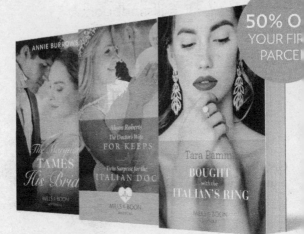

JOIN US ON SOCIAL MEDIA!

Stay up to date with our latest releases, author news and gossip, special offers and discounts, and all the behind-the-scenes action from Mills & Boon...

 millsandboon

 millsandboonuk

millsandboon

...might just be true love...